MW00640303

The WRITER AND THE THRONE

WARFARE OF THE GODS SERIES

BOOK I

This work is fiction. Although names, locations, terms, and ideas are from historical and/ or religious beliefs, the story itself is a complete product of the author's imagination.

First printing: 2021

Published By: Open World Publishing, Seattle, WA

ISBN: 9781736109526

Email inquiry or requests to
OpenWorldPublishing@gmail.com
or CTOrtega.com

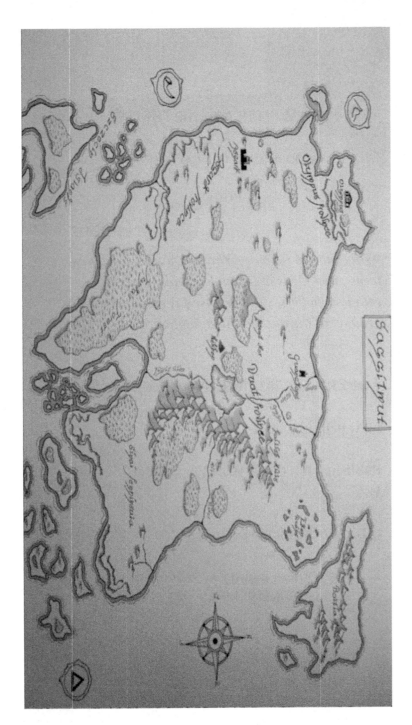

Chapter 0 *Down to Two*

The two goddesses, Asherah and Idunn sat at the small wooden table talking. They had been there in the white room nearly all morning without having made any progress. Frustrated, Asherah grabbed her cup of tea and took her first scalding sip.

"Damn it!" she shouted at the cup. "You bastard." Idunn chuckled to herself, blowing at the rim of hers.

"I just do not get it," Idunn said, taking her first sip. "In the end, who cares? Just let Dagon pick this Aaron kid. It is not like he is going to be fighting on any one side or something. Although, after seeing him I would love to see him try to put on some of the Hoplite armor. Oh, can you imagine him trying to hold an Asgardian axe with those arms?" Laughing, she looked over at Asherah, who was staring into her steaming cup, shaking her head in frustration.

Seeing her friend flustered Idunn continued, "He is just writing whatever happens. It is not like he will be somehow able to sway any of the other gods. You do know that whoever is chosen is going to have no effect on the outcome of their war right? So, I do not think it will matter either way."

"Are you kidding?" Asherah retorted, staring into the cup in disgust. "Of course it matters.

Whoever writes this book has unbelievable power. Whatever they write will be read by literally everyone in Saggilmut, god, and mortal alike. If he is stupid and believes every little thing some of these idiot gods will tell him who knows what he will end up writing?"

"I just cannot understand why the Most High even uses people in the first place," Idunn responded. "It seems disrespectful to have them writing for us."

"I agree, but that is neither here nor there now."

"Listen, I agree with you," Idunn said. "Suri is a better pick in my eyes as well. She is obviously more intelligent, and probably more capable of avoiding being handled by these gods, but Asherah, everyone is biased whether they mean to be or not. You cannot write for either of them, so the truth is we do not know which of the two will be a better writer, Suri or Aaron. And since we only have a little time left for you and Dagon to come to some sort of agreement on which should be chosen I suggest--"

"We will never agree," Asherah said, "I really do hate him."

"Anyway," Idunn said, tired of hearing that old conversation, "Can you imagine being brought here from Earth and just like that, you are being put into an assembly standing next to hundreds of gods?

No matter which is chosen I can say it will be amusing to watch."

"I do not care about that," Asherah answered, shaking her head. "I just want to get the right one and Aaron is not it."

"And why not?" Idunn asked while sipping her tea. "Try not to compare him to Suri, who granted, is a better fit, then ask yourself what makes him so terrible?"

"Do you know what he does for a living? How he uses his free time? He is a waste of life. At least Suri has aspirations and goals. She could have made something of herself."

"He is young. He just needed time to figure himself--"

"He was nineteen and headed nowhere," Asherah blurted. "He cannot stand in a room full of gods and function. He would probably crap himself."

"Oh my," Idunn said, shaking her head. "Please, not while I am having my tea."

"No seriously," Asherah said, frustrated. "Odin and Zeus are headed to war with one another. Do you think he is going to be able to watch and observe these gods? Idunn, what if he writes something terrible about someone I actually do like or care for? I do not want people in Duat province looking bad toward Thor because of something he may write. To Sheol with that."

"Thor still on your mind?" Idunn asked, smiling into her cup.

Asherah glared toward Idunn. "Let me tell you, how he writes could tell the entire world of Saggilmut who they should worship. You want to put that much power in the hands of someone like that, like *an Aaron*?"

"I do not know," she replied. "He did take care of his family. There is something to be said about that. How easy would it have been for him to just have run away and gone to live the single life, letting his mother and sister to fend for themselves?"

"For how little he provides I believe it may be better had he just left."

Idunn shook her head. "That kid woke up early every day, and rode his bicycle to work to provide for them."

"It does not matter anymore. You are right," Asherah said. "We have only a short time before the assembly anyway. I already know Dagon is not going to cave in and pick Suri, so I will just get Aaron so the Most High does not get angry at us."

"I will join you," Idunn said, putting down her empty cup on the table next to the untouched biscuit. "I love watching them panic when they get called here from Earth. They always have that sick-pale face like they could vomit, pass out, or both. I love it."

Chapter 1 *The Writer in the Hall*

"I am sorry to be the one to have to tell you, but we do not have much time," said the abnormally tall, beautiful woman. She towered over Aaron. He had no idea who she was, but he doubted the sincerity of her tone.

"A coma? But that doesn't make sense," he answered, rubbing his forehead and trying to recall where he was before he found himself in this hallway. The hall was completely white with a bright glare. It had no windows or actual light fixtures. It was the walls themselves that were giving light.

"Just listen, all your questions will be answered soon enough. We do not have much time. I am Asherah, a goddess here in Shamayim, and you are going to be the new Writer. We are now headed to the Hall where you will sit in on an assembly. Which are normally conducted every century."

"So, I'm dead?" he asked, examining his hands as if it would help, trying to get some grasp on what was happening.

"We must go now, but I will describe as much as I can on the way," she replied. "Follow me."

She began walking, but Aaron hesitated.

"This is crazy," he said, frantic. "I can't be here. I can't be dead. My family needs my help, please."

"Aaron," she said forcibly. "Now." He

glanced at her and could see she was irritated. As if her time was being wasted. *Just go*, he thought to himself and took to her side down the hallway.

Hurrying down the hallway, she offered details. "Aaron, as I said, you are the new Writer. Your task is to record and write everything you see. Do you understand?"

"No, I don't understand anything that's happening," he said, still trying to gather himself.

She answered, "A writer is someone who details the events of the gods so it may be archived. You are to watch everything that will be unfolding soon and write them down." She answered, taking a breath and looking down at him.

"All right," she said calmingly. "Let me try this a bit slowly for you. From man's earliest years we gods have been with you. Teaching, guiding, and at times even intervening. The Most High dictated that many of these events need to be recorded. So, he instituted the Writer. They recorded whatever they had seen or been told by the gods. From people drawing in caves to many holy books, as you call them. You may recognize a few like Moses, the Buddha, Nostradamus. "

"Who's the Most High? Is that another God?" he asked.

"Again, for now just listen," she insisted, "but to answer your question, the Most High is the Creator. He made all things whether it be here, Saggilmut, or on Earth as you call it. Many gods who live in Saggilmut, you know it as heaven. The best way I can describe it, for now, is that it is where you go when you die."

Following her, Aaron noticed the hallway

8

appeared to have no end. There were no doors, no connecting hall, it just went on.

"So, there are two different heavens then? I don't think I can pronounce either of them. Shamim--" Aaron started.

"Shamayim is where the Most High lives. Only a few of us live here for one reason or another. The rest live in Saggilmut, which can be traveled to using a bridge. We call it a Crossing. Think of heaven as nothing more than another land. The Most High lives on his personal island and the rest share one continent."

"Okay, fine he lives on Shama-, Shayi-."

"Shamayim," she said, looking at him shaking her head.

"And you all live on Sagglmet, or whatever. I'm just confused about what *I'm* doing here?"

"I knew you should not have been the one picked," she said to herself aloud. "I suggest that you wrap your little brain around this quickly. Very soon you will be in a room full of gods. Your job will be to watch and learn so you can later write about everything happening. Here we call them writers, but in your world, they are called prophets."

"Like a reporter?"

"Sure, Aaron, like a reporter," she said slowly, sarcastically.

She continued down the hallway, and said, "There are three different sects of gods; the Duati, Asgardians, and the Immortals. You have heard of many by name, I am sure. Those in good standing with the Most High are allowed to be at this assembly. For now, you will only be asked to record this single meeting, but I suspect you will write for longer."

"So when do I get to go back home then?" he asked.

"It is not that simple," she replied. "You were...nevermind. Just let me help get you through this assembly first."

Aaron was amazed, trying not to stare at her. He thought she was incredibly beautiful even though the top of his head barely reached her shoulders. She had warm bronzed skin and dark brown hair that flowed into three large braids tying off at the small of her back. But her name, he kept thinking, as unique as it was, sounded quite familiar.

"Who are you?" he asked. She stopped and faced him. Raising her left arm straight out from her side, it went into the wall. The wall appeared to remain solid, causing her arm to disappear. As she lowered her arm it became visible again as it withdrew from the wall.

"You see?" she asked, "Follow me." She turned and walked directly into the wall, disappearing completely. Aaron raised his hand trying to touch the wall, but his arm vanished into it. He moved his fingers and everything felt normal, so he decided to follow. He lifted his other arm, took a step, walked through the wall, and entered into another room, a magnificent room.

Chapter 2 *The Gods*

The room was massive. It had the same illuminating white walls as the hall, a raised ceiling, and two large pillars side by side with a beautiful pure white throne in between them. The chair sat against the wall, facing the room on seven large steps. Anyone sitting on it would sit well above even the tallest in the room. In the middle of the room was a white table standing, its longest side facing the throne. The length was astonishing, and it had matching chairs running along each side.

Along the walls, there were similar chairs for extra seating. Unsure of the amount of detail he was supposed to record, he thought he might as well count them, but didn't want to get embarrassed holding up his fingers since the chairs sat so close together.

"How many-" Aaron quickly stopped asking himself after seeing Asherah staring at him. He knew that look. His mom gave him the same one after she had decided she had enough of his crap.

"This is the Hall," she said, finding a chair for herself. "Others will begin to arrive very shortly." He took a chair next to her and waited for her to continue with her instructions. After a pause and noticing she had no interest in speaking, he decided he had better pursue the conversation first.

"So, after this is done I'll just wake up or something?"

"No," she answered. "I did not want to tell you until after the assembly. I do not want anything getting in your way from doing your job. There is no way for me to get you to understand the importance of what you have been called to do Aaron, but..." she paused. Aaron could tell she was actually flustered trying to tell him.

"What?" he pressed.

"You were selected from a group of people that are dying. You are going to die. I do not know how to tell you in a way you would understand, but you are here, while your body is not. Your physical body remains on Earth at a hospital where they have just finished surgery. You suffered severe head trauma from being hit by a driver on your bicycle. Aaron, you are in a coma. We suspect you have a few weeks, maybe one month at most before they will choose to let you die." His mind immediately went numb. He heard her, and it made sense, but it felt surreal, foreign. The realization of death hadn't hit.

"I was headed to work," he said, thinking aloud. "Yeah, it was dark, and I was pulling up near the gas station right before the school, and--"

"And that is where you were found laying on the street," she said, finishing his sentence. "As I said, I am sorry to have to be the one to tell you this, but the Most High deemed he wanted a writer for this meeting, and because of what happened, and the fact that you are going to die, you were selected." He stared at her for a moment, then turned his head looking at his shoes.

"Okay," he said with a shrug.

Unable to process what she had said, he decided to change the subject, "What do I do when they get here? Do I bow? What do I call them? Is

12

everyone's name actually God? I mean, I wasn't really raised religious so--"

"The gods will be arriving shortly, Writer," she replied, ignoring his questions. "Stay here and do not forget that from the moment they arrive you will need to watch carefully. What you write will have a lasting effect on your readers."

"Who are my readers?"

"Listen, nether, stop with the questions, all right? I have explained enough for now, and I'm sure you can figure out the rest. It is not complicated. Remember whatever you see so you can write it when the time comes. They will be here shortly." It was apparent to him that she was disgusted by him for some reason. Watching her he deduced that talking to him was a job of some type she was assigned to and she wasn't at all happy about it.

"Who sits there on the throne?" he asked. No response. "Asherah, if I am to record everything as you asked--"

"The Most High," she said abruptly. "Now wait and you will know everything you need to know in the coming moments."

"The Most High, like *the* God?"

"Yes," she replied. "He sits as the God of gods, the Most High of all, He is our creator as well as yours."

Aaron's mind raced. The lingering thoughts of his demise were crushed with the idea of seeing God. Then a concept he learned from Bubbe, his ultra-religious grandmother, hit him.

"I was always told that if you see God's face that you would die?" he asked. He didn't want to say it was his grandmother and give Asherah more of a reason to look down at him.

"First, you are already going to die, or have you already forgotten? Secondly, no one can see him, but we will all see him with our mind's eye, not the actual self."

Made sense to Aaron.

More questions flooded his mind. Each one seemed more important than the last, but before he could ask, two gods walked through a portion of the wall. Their long flowing beards that reached their stomachs were not only braided fantastically, but had matching ornaments woven into them. One of the men was older than the other, with grey hair and beard. There was a black eye patch over his right eye and by the scars his face carried, appeared as the more tested of the two.

"Who are they?" Aaron asked, staring at the younger. He was amazing in every way. He was tall with a large build. His eyes were intense as if he was hunting for someone. His light brown hair was thick, pulled back, and tied off on the back of his head. His beard was red and full. He had symbols and designs tattooed from his neck flowing around to both mammoth arms. The colors of the tattoos were vibrant and appeared alive, flowed like a stream, and shimmered with gorgeous colors. They reflected like a rainbow off the light and seemed like they were layered as if they were three dimensional.

Asherah leaned in and said, "That is Thor of the sect called the Asgardians and his father, King Odin."

"Yeah, o-of course, he is," Aaron sputtered.

Aaron, being normal height, and thinner than most, could barely grow a mustache, let alone a beard. He felt in no way eligible to stand in the presence of this god. Thor walked by Aaron toward Asherah, not even acknowledging his presence.

"Asherah, *heil ok sæl*! It has been so long," he said, leaning in and kissing her on each cheek. She was much taller than Aaron, yet only reached up to Thor's chest. Odin had seemed to take no interest in greeting Asherah and immediately went for a seat at the table.

Asherah kissed Thor's cheek, and held the sides of his beard. She looked into his ocean blue eyes and smiled, obviously enamored.

"It has been too long," she insisted. "I miss you and think of you often. Please let us spend time together after the assembly."

"Of course, I will come and find you," he replied. He seemed as if the conversation wasn't keeping his interest.

Aaron's attention was drawn away from Thor, as difficult as it was, to the surrounding walls. They each became transparent as more gods began to enter the room. The gods were all much taller than Aaron.

Each dressed distinct from each other. Some had fair skin and blonde hair, others were darker toned with shaved heads. They also appeared to be many other physical types in between. Each god and goddess wore distinct style garments, every one of them glorious.

Few greeted each other, and even Aaron could see the tension between some. No one other than Odin sat, although many stood behind their chairs. Aaron gazed at the room trying to remember his various mythology classes from school in the hope to identify who was there. If Thor, who he knew from folklore, comics, and movies was a god, then he assumed he may be able to recognize others.

He let his eyes wander the room until they settled on two standing together. It appeared as if they were wearing incredibly vivid helmets. One had a black helmet resembling a canine, while the other's was a bird of some type. Aaron stared more intently, realizing that they were not helmets at all.

He could see the dog's mouth moving as he spoke. The other bird-headed god seemed satisfied standing quietly to himself. Aaron couldn't help but stare engrossed at their facial expressions and mannerisms. The canine-headed god was speaking to another god who had a human appearance, like most in the room.

"What are their names? They're Egyptian gods, right?" Aaron asked, pointing with a glance.

Asherah leaned in and whispered, "There is no such thing as Egyptian gods, only gods. They are only known as Egyptians because that is who they chose to spend their time with on Earth before we were all expelled."

"He is Anubis," she said softly, pointing with her hand toward the canine god. "He is speaking to Hades of the Immortal sect. And the other there is Horus," she said, alluding to the god with the falcon's head. "They are of the Duati sect now."

"Wait, I know Hades is a god of the dead in Greek mythology, but isn't Anubis also the god of the dead, just for the Egyptians?"

16

"Neither is the god over death, or anything else for that matter," she answered. "Actually, no god was ever assigned to lord over anything by the Most High. Much of what you know of us are fabricated tales by the gods told to writers to glorify themselves in your eyes. Anubis believed that if he attached his name to something meaningful to people, he in turn would become meaningful to them. Nothing was more meaningful than understanding death to the Egyptians in the era of the Pharaohs."

She continued, "You see Thor there, Seth right there," she said, pointing to another god with a different type of canine head, "and Zeus, they all claim to the nethers that they are the god of thunder. Showing off for nethers, it makes no sense. These gods are *evilim*."

"*Evilim*?"

"Fools, it is Hebrew. Are you not Jewish? Is that not your *holy* language?" she replied in disgust.

"I'm more Jew-*ish*, but wait, how do you know that?" he asked.

"Before you were selected we conducted a basic data pull. You were not my choice," she replied.

Zeus looked exactly how he would have imagined from the stories. Silver grey hair, bold blue eyes, and a curly silver beard that appeared to hide a cleft chin. He wore a white flowing robe tied with a red sash around his waist.

The room was filling quickly. From his estimation, there must have been over two hundred gods present. He looked for clues to know who many were, but there were none aside from the ones that had the animals heads. But even then, he wasn't familiar with them in general. As he sat he tried to listen to conversations taking place. Zeus was speaking to someone who looked like a younger version of him, with bleached curly blonde hair and a pale complexion. Zeus referred to him as his son.

"Who's he?" he asked. Asherah was speaking with another god and was acting as if she didn't hear him.

"Excuse me, Asherah. Who's he?" he repeated. This time she turned toward him rolling her eyes as she did so. He was taken aback that a goddess would turn her eyes like that. Reminded him of his sister when she didn't like what he had to say on a matter.

"He's Apollo, and next to him is Jove," she answered. Apollo closely resembled his father, Zeus. He carried the same heroic cleft chin under a beard. He resembled what every mythology book led him to believe the Roman/Greek gods looked like, perfect.

Watching Jove, the first thing Aaron noticed was that he was tall, even among the gods. He had blonde wavy hair to his shoulders and a matching beard. It was almost difficult to see where one began and the other ended. His blue eyes appeared strong, beaming behind the black eyebrows and tanned complexion.

"Why do some have animal heads?" he asked.

No longer trying to hide her annoyance, she answered, "When the Most High created the gods he made them of both spirit and body. One cannot separate one from the other as they are tied together.

This is no different than how you would all be made much later when for whatever reason he created your kind. In his crafting of the animals, he then decided to make some additional gods with characteristics of what he felt were a combination of all his greatest creations --spiritual, physical, and instinctual. They were called the Sh'losh, which translates to the *Three*. Satisfied?" He nodded and she turned away again. It began to dawn on him that she apparently had to answer his questions though she didn't want to.

Watching the room, he wanted to ask about each god that walked by or made any sort of eye contact. He saw one in the corner with a frog's head and another who was larger and broader than even Thor. He noticed every goddess was uniquely beautiful.

As he continued admiring the gods, a mental cloud fell over his eyes and the looming thought of his sister appeared. She must have known about his accident by now. She was probably at the hospital staring at his lifeless body laying on a bed with tubes everywhere.

Suddenly the thought of being among the gods wasn't as meaningful as just being with his sister, Sarah. *Who was going to pick her up from school today?* He thought. He knew it was a meaningless thought with everything unfolding before him, but it mattered. She mattered.

He sat back down into his chair, mind rushing with thoughts of his sister, when a loud blast from what he thought was a trumpet startled him. He closed his eyes as the shrill sound made everyone pause.

The sound ceased. The gods stopped any conversations and found their way to their chairs. It didn't appear to Aaron that they were assigned any seating, rather everyone just stood behind a chair at the table and those gods that were near a wall stood in front of theirs.

Four angelic beings wearing matching incandescent white garments entered through each corner of the room simultaneously. They were not as tall as the gods, nor as impressive. Their faces matched each other, radiant, but without expression. They directed themselves toward the main chair, the throne of the Most High.

"Holy, holy, holy," they shouted from the corners of the room. With each call, they lifted themselves onto their toes to push their voices just a shred more. The conversations ended abruptly and no one dared move. As the Most High entered Aaron paled, paralyzed by fear.

Chapter 3 *The Rebellious One*

He appeared through the wall. There was absolutely no doubt in Aaron's mind that this was anyone other than the Most High. He towered over all the other gods in the room. His face was translucent. Giving off no color of its own, rather it reflected the light of the room creating blasts of colors streaking off. His eyes were bright, like the sun, but without burning Aaron's eyes. His beard was vivid and tied into seven braids. As he made his way to the throne its colors fluctuated, shifting between the darkest of blacks or flawless white and all in between.

His hands resting by his side were brightened in an aura. He was wearing a modest gray robe that flowed to his ankles, tied off around the waist with a simple grey sash. He wore no crown on his head, and no jewelry as many others were wearing, yet was far more impressive than anyone else. He was the most beautiful thing Aaron had ever seen. Aaron's hand shook, hitting his leg. He forced himself to grab hold of his pants to attempt to settle, but the sheer presence of this being was incredibly frightening. The Most High stood in front of his chair between the two pillars, taking his time to gaze around the room.

"Odin," Dagon, a Sh'losh with a fish's head, called out, standing to the Most High's side near the pillar. Odin remained in his seat, leaning on his armrest.

"Odin," Dagon snarled. Odin sat unwaveringly.

"Odin, stand in the presence of the Almighty," Dagon called out a third time with a threatening tone. Aaron scanned the room and realized that the gods were just as shocked as he was at the blatant disregard Odin was showing. Even Thor, his son, seemed at a loss.

Refusing to rise he proclaimed, "I, Odin the Asgardian, first in all creation of the Most High, heir to become King of the gods, demand an audience with you alone before this council proceeds." The Most High focused on Odin with lowered brows, contemptuous.

"You?" A loud cry came from the other side of the room. The gods on that side stepped away, revealing Zeus.

Zeus continued, "You prove by your actions that you and your sect are nothing more than barbarians. How dare you sit there foolishly boasting like you should be an heir to anything? Now stand up behind your chair and ready yourself like the rest of us."

"By my own name, I curse you, Zeus," Odin shouted, shaking his fist at him.

"Your name means nothing to me!" Zeus yelled.

"You are nothing more than a spoiled child among adults!" Odin barked back at him. "You waste this council's time with your continued boasting of yourself, though you have never accomplished anything. You do nothing but tell lies to the writers in the hope to gain glory. What battle have you weathered? When have you beaten certain death? No, you know nothing of being a king. Wasting your power on eating and hunting for your next woman to lay with." Hera, Zeus' wife, stood behind her husband quietly, unshaken by Odin's remarks. With tensions between the two sects already heightened, she quieted herself.

Zeus lifted his arms at Odin's three sons standing together and mockingly asked, "*This* is your King? Is there no one better in your province to rule? Fools."

"Be careful, Zeus," Tyr, a thinner god, advised standing near his fellow Asgardians. "Maybe it is best if we all calm ourselves. We all want true peace, and although tensions are high between our sects, we do not have to do anything to ignite it. We can still meet some type of agreement if we--"

"Close your mouth, brother." Thor stomped his. "If that fool wants to incite our anger against him then let him."

Even Zeus shook his head at Tyr and said, "You are a fool Tyr if you believe--"

"Enough!" commanded Dagon after a subtle hand gesture from the Most High.

Odin boiled over, his face red behind his beard. He screamed furiously toward the Most High, leaping from his chair so quickly it toppled over, "I did not come here to be judged by this bastard. There will never be peace between us. It is obvious this assembly is a waste of time." The Most High looked at him, jaw clenched.

Odin continued, "I will no longer be a slave to this fictional dream. These foolish gods will never learn to acknowledge me as the rightful god to be selected as the King of the gods. They are unworthy to even stand in my presence. Forget actually sit in a chair near me and have a conversation as equals."

"Why now?" the Most High challenged in a calm voice. "You are in good standing within this assembly, Odin, once even beloved by both gods and men. Why not work back toward that? Why fight?" Odin turned his head, glancing through his one eye at Aaron.

Odin pointed at him, then said, "These nethers need to be ruled, but not by gods that are too busy with their courts, their politics, and scheming. These gods have no more wisdom than the very ones they desire to rule over. I can bring peace, true peace, and you know this. You know I am the only one that can bring Saggilmut to its full glory. I should be chosen by you as your first creation, forget any idea of an election. They will never select me, because of their own ignorance. Especially him," he said, pointing again toward Zeus. "A god so weak he would let his own gods die and watch as a helpless spectator. You have wasted enough time sitting here lording over us with this foolish presumption of bringing us together. You mock me with your games. *You* need to be ruled too."

The room was in absolute silence. There was a shared sense of shock, everyone watching to see what the Most High might do. Even Aaron had felt the gravity of Odin's insults, despite not being privy to anything other than the short backstory Asherah had shared.

Aaron watched, having forgotten anything to do with being a writer. He forgot his impending death. Locked in the moment. The Most High glared at Odin, glanced back at his throne, and sat down. He took a deep breath and looked away from Odin for a moment, scanning the many faces in the room.

"Son, listen--" the Most High gently pleaded.

"Do not call me your son," Odin demanded without hesitation. "Call me what I am, the rightful King of Go--" Odin's words were taken. He was unable to draw a breath. The Most High stared into the eye of Odin and waved his hand, calling the very air from his chest. Odin, suffocating, fell back over his chair, grabbing his chest, choking.

"Holy, holy, holy is the Most High," the four beings declared as Odin lay convulsing. Thor and his brothers watched helplessly.

The Most High, still waving his hand, spoke up, "I remember in man's earliest of days when you learned of the very first murder on Earth, you traveled to where the body was slain, sitting there crying for days. You once embodied love. What happened?" Relaxing his hand, he allowed Odin to breathe again. Odin rubbed his neck, coughing, and gasping to remain conscious.

The Most High stood up from his throne and said, "We will give weight to what has happened today and the council will pause for now." He glared at Odin. "I do hope we can reconvene with mutual respect for all in the room when we continue, my children." Turning back, the Most High walked the same route back toward the wall, but first, stopped and said a few words to Dagon before he disappeared through the wall. The four heralds declared, "Holy, holy, holy is the Most High," turned around and in unison exited the room.

Dagon took a step forward, raised his hands, and announced, "All will be asked to return at sunset this evening and the council will begin again." He turned and followed the Most High in exiting. For a moment no one moved. The tension was still too palpable.

Slowly, the room relaxed, the moment dissipated, and murmurs filled the room. Aaron watched as a number of the Viking gods, Thor first, went to aid Odin, who remained coughing and breathing heavily. He sternly batted their assisting hands, working his way to his knees.

Without notice, Odin then staggered to his feet, and as quickly as he could, he stumbled to the wall flailing his arms at anyone who sought to assist him. He disappeared through the wall. None chased to his aid. Thor and Baldr, a larger god, with a burly chest and thick beard, began to exchange words quietly, standing chest to chest. Tyr remained at a distance, watching them.

Asherah looked at Aaron and said sternly, "You must record what you saw here today, Writer. This will surely lead to catastrophe. In the history of the gods, no one has ever stood up to the Most High in such confrontation." The problem was Aaron felt that he had no real concept of what had transpired. He was still baffled that these gods now standing before him were the same ones he had learned about. That the God of the universe had stood in the same room as him. He was still lost, absolutely lost.

"Wish I was home," he mumbled to himself. "Maybe even at work, I guess."

Chapter 4 *Meet your Maker*

"What happens now? I mean, is there time now for you to catch me up?" Aaron asked. He hadn't noticed Asherah had already taken a few steps away and was speaking to another goddess. He glanced over, thinking maybe he could recognize her, but still had no idea who she was.

She was stunning, with short golden-blonde hair that feathered near her ears, and light-blue eyes. Her freckles seemed to make her appear more appealing than her demeanor. Her leg was shaking and it seemed like Asherah was trying to calm her down by placing her hands around her shoulders.

Listening in, he heard Asherah call her Athena. He remembered the name from Greek mythology in Mr. Wagner's class, but couldn't remember what she was the goddess of. As he tried to recall, a thought hit him: If the gods are not actually lord over anything, then what other things had he been taught that were wrong?

"Excuse me, Asherah," he said, hesitant.

Asherah, animated in conversation, glanced quickly at Aaron and shooed him off with her hand. Aaron scanned the room hoping for help. Someone he could tell, someone to help him. *What am I supposed to do*? He thought. *This is insane.*

"Aaron," called a voice from near the throne. Standing near the chair on the bottom step,

Dagon was staring his way, waving for him. Frantically, he turned toward Asherah like a child asking for guidance, permission, or both. He was lost. Aaron had felt lost from the moment he blinked and found himself seemingly transported in front of this rude goddess and her mythological nightmare.

"Go, nether," she said in an annoyed tone. He didn't understand what she had called him but figured it probably wasn't a term of endearment. He half-heartedly wanted to stay because she was the only one who had spoken to him. But he was hopeful as he headed toward Dagon that he couldn't be any worse and standoffish than she had been.

On his way through the large room, Aaron observed as many gods as he could. He spotted who he believed was Mercury. The god held a silver helmet with a set of grafted wings flaring out.

Aaron next saw a god who resembled a painting on a wall of his favorite hole-in-the-wall local Indian restaurant. The owner had told him his name, but he couldn't recall. *Shiva, or maybe Shaver.*

The god was pale with a wheatish complexion, totally disheveled hair, and bleary eyes. As he passed him, he couldn't help but smell the strong scent of frankincense. The god was swaying, and moving his arms back and forth, almost in a dance.

Aaron then noticed two feline headed goddesses speaking in the corner of the room. They appeared to be pointing and laughing at someone, but he couldn't tell who. One caught him and raised her brow curiously, gazing back at him. He turned away, trying to appear casual, but couldn't help himself and quickly looked again. They were both now openly staring at him and laughing. *Cat gods*, he thought. *Must have missed that class.*

Only a few steps away from Dagon he felt another set of eyes watching him. Trying to be inconspicuous, Aaron reached up to scratch his chin, tilting his head enough to give himself the angle needed to take a glance at who it was.

She was gorgeous. A beautiful goddess even above the others. She had an olive complexion with contrasting black hair that flowed to the small of her back. Her eyebrows were sharp and alluring. She stared unabashedly back at him.

Aaron reached the one calling for him and, while still gazing at her said, "Yes, I-I'm Aaron."

"I am Dagon. Come, the Most High demands your audience." Dagon's fish eyes were black and jumped around quickly. Aaron glanced away, attempting not to make it obvious he was more than a little freaked out.

Dagon led the way to the same wall where the Most High had exited. Aaron raised his hands out in front of him apprehensively as he walked through. He knew he must have appeared like a kid with a new toy to these gods, but shrugged it off, concluding he must look like a kid by his height alone.

"Aaron," Dagon said, now a short distance down the hallway, "You do not keep the Most High waiting."

Crap, Aaron thought and took a few quick large steps to catch up. Although rushing, Aaron couldn't help but notice the hallway. It had beaming colorful shapes overlapping each other and appeared to be more than just a flat wall, it had depth. As they walked together, Dagon said nothing, which didn't bother Aaron. He was consumed with the growing fear of meeting the Most High.

At the end of the hallway were two reddish-green wooden doors. They were incredibly tall, and even from a distance, he could see intricate symbols elaborately designed on both of them. Aaron had seen this symbolic image on the doors a thousand times--it was the tree of life. The tree and its branches appeared to jump off the doors and it appeared as if the leaves were rustling.

"Amazing," Aaron whispered to himself, awed by the wonder of it all.

"Do you know why you are here?" Dagon asked.

"Asherah said I'm the Writer," he answered, posing it more as a question than an answer.

"The Most High is on the other side of these doors," he replied. "He will explain some things that you need to know. I suggest you be open and honest with him." Dagon touched the door, and it automatically opened inwardly just enough for them to walk through. The realization of meeting God created a pit in his stomach. His nerves were racing, and he felt the urge to run to the restroom. *Damn*, he thought. *Too late now.*

Chapter 5 *Face to face*

Entering the room, Aaron felt a breeze from the door's artwork brush along his face.

Breathing in a gentle wind coming from the design on the door, he sensed a sweet-crisp flavor. The images of fruit hanging off the tree shared an aroma of freshly cut watermelon. Any thought of needing a bathroom was swept away by the delicious scent.

"You may enter," Dagon instructed, holding the door open. Aaron rushed by, nodding gratefully in passing.

Entering the room, Aaron stopped immediately after a single step. He stood frozen, legs together, jolted with fear as the Most High sat leaning back in a chair. Aaron couldn't bring himself to look around the room, although it appeared to be a much smaller version of the hall where the gods were. Bright white walls and clean white marble style flooring.

The Most High sat near another, much smaller chair that faced him.

"Aaron," his thunderous voice exclaimed, "Come and sit with me." Aaron wanted to but struggled to get his legs to react. It was one thing to see the other gods and goddesses who, outside of the animal-headed gods, appeared like ordinary persons, albeit taller. This was different; he was different. He made the gods seem ordinary; he was beyond beauty. The more Aaron tried to step the tenser his legs got.

"Aaron," the Most High said softly. "Come, sit. We do not have as much time as I would have hoped to have with you." Aaron took his first step, forcing his leg forward. He couldn't draw his eyes away from this being. All self-consciousness was gone. The only feelings he had room for in his mind were both fear and amazement at his grandeur.

Aaron sat in front of him.

The Most High's face had no defined skin color of its own. The pigment glowed, but the color was changing rapidly, constantly morphing. His eyes were continually altering in size, shape, and even color. It happened so quickly they were blurring together. His nose and lips were doing the same. Within his face was a collection of all peoples, a blending conglomeration of countenances each revealing itself simultaneously.

"What did Asherah tell you your role as the Writer is?" he asked.

"That I just needed to w-watch everyone and remember as much as I can to w-write it down," he stuttered, mesmerized.

"Anything else?" he asked.

"No, not really," Aaron replied. He still hadn't blinked since sitting.

"Relax Aaron," he said gently. "I have a lot to tell you since she has chosen to neglect her task, but I need you fully present to listen."

"Do you know what a writer does?" he asked.

"I understand it to be like a reporter in some way," he answered.

"Fair answer," he said, "but you are more than that. I am sure you have a knowledge of many ancient books based on gods, correct?" Aaron didn't know how to answer.

Nervous, he sputtered, "Yes, yes Sir. I mean God, yes God? Most High? I'm not sure what to call you. Honestly, I know there's a lot of religious books, but I'm not, I mean-- I didn't know it was all real so I can't say I studied it."

Smirking, the Most High said, "You are fine, Aaron, please just relax." Aaron closed his eyes, then bringing his hands to his face, blew a long breath into them.

"Okay, okay, I'm fine," Aaron said, settling his hands back to his lap. He sucked his lower lip into his mouth, a habit he had since as far back as he could remember.

"All right then," the Most High continued, "Many of those books you know to be religious books came about by what we call Writers. In the beginning of your world, I allowed the gods to visit Earth without limitation. They would travel there, teaching them a great many things. It was the writers that would record these things. They shaped the world, Aaron. Unfortunately, many of the gods, seeing how man was so enamored with them, became less interested in teaching and more interested in being worshipped. Desiring to be praised, they fabricated many of the stories you know to build their reputations and followings on Earth. So as people died and went to Saggilmut they arrived under the false belief that their chosen god was--well, whatever they told them."

"Damn," Aaron muttered under his breath.

"Indeed," he agreed. "Many of these gods you saw in that hall began to call themselves the creator of the universe, all-powerful, or whatever else they thought would assist them to become more renowned. They proclaimed themselves as lords and judge, leading people to believe whatever they want to fabricate, calling it truth. The point is, many people in what you understand as heaven have no idea about the gods they serve. I believe you can help." Aaron was struggling to keep up.

"Are you following me, son?" he asked.

"Yes," he answered in a low tone, but he knew he didn't sound convincing. Questions were racing in his mind. *Were the gods evil? Why would he let them lie to people like this? Were any of the religious books right?* He chose to settle for his most hopeful question.

"You're saying everyone goes to heaven?"

"Yes, but there is more to it than that," he replied. "Unfortunately, Aaron, I do not have the time to explain that, but all your questions will be answered in the upcoming days by Dagon when I send you there. For now, I must have you understand how events led us to everything that just happened with Odin."

"Okay," Aaron agreed, despite his mind still reeling.

The Most High leaned forward, rocking in his chair for a moment, then said, "Odin was my first creation. We would talk, laugh, and enjoy each other's company for what must have been centuries. In truth though, I cannot tell you how long it was because it was before the concept of time. Odin became more than just my creation. I thought of him as a son; he was my everything. We began to speak on the concept of creating others to join us, believing it would only be beneficial to our reality. I believed he understood the value of creating life and told him that we should make both gods and mankind together in our image."

He continued, "Odin agreed, and stated it was important that each individual creation have their own unique sense of wonder, creativity, and wisdom, but most of all to live by their own choices. He would say after their inception, watching them learn and grow, that he knew he would become a father to them as I was to him. He called it fate." A sadness swept over the Most

37

High's face. Aaron could see just speaking on it was difficult.

Taking a breath, the Most High continued, "With more gods came more choices, and in turn a more diverse understanding of free will. As time went on and with man's attention becoming the currency of the gods, infighting broke out and sects were formed."

Aaron, finally releasing his lip, said, "Yeah, Asherah mentioned the three sects. Immortals, Asgardians, and..." he hesitated, unable to recall the third.

"Duati," the Most High added. "Now they all live in a divided Saggilmut. Aaron, that is not what I ever intended *heaven* to be. Tensions are worse now than ever before. That is why I called this assembly. I had hoped to open communication between the Asgardians and Immortals, who I am worried could reach a breaking point between each other at any moment. I am worried about the people who may be in danger because they have sided with gods under their false claims. And now, after what happened with Odin, I am even more concerned than ever."

"People die in heaven?" Aaron asked terrified at the notion.

He answered, "Death on Earth is not forever. Death in Saggilmut is. I made it that way so it had more weight for a number of reasons. We have suffered too many deaths already. These sparse attacks have been slowly growing between the two sects and have caused more than we can bear anymore. I need you to understand that war is coming, and there is nothing I can do to stop it anymore."

"But," Aaron paused, thinking about another lesson from his Bubbe, "I was always taught you are all-knowing, all-powerful. Are you?"

"I am. I am as you say, but there is more to it than that. If I use these virtues, then what use are the gods? What use is mankind, and what use are you? The very reason I created life was for them to enjoy the very nature of living. I chose to ignore my omniscience so that I could enjoy speaking to others without knowing the outcome of the conversation or thoughts they possess. I chose to ignore my omnipotence to allow others to rise and give strength and support. I ignore my omnipresence to allow all to act in accordance with their choice without fear I am here to merely judge them. If I neglect my virtues, then others are more liberated to be themselves, good or evil. They are free to live, Aaron. I have no desire for worship in servitude. What I want is for everyone to feel my acceptance and be at peace."

"So, you'll let a war happen and not do anything?" Aaron asked boldly. "I mean, I get free will, but--"

"Yes," he replied without hesitation, leaning back in his chair. "Without free will to choose, then you are not *living*."

Aaron looked down at his feet and considered if he should continue pushing the limits of his questioning.

"I cannot imagine what you must be thinking," the Most High said. "But there is no need to get ahead of ourselves. I need you to simply understand that you must prepare to write all that you see. You will not dictate the outcome of whatever battle is coming, but your story will share how they win or lose, and maybe something about their true personalities. I am sure you can see how writers have been a prominent force in shaping your world?"

"Absolutely," Aaron said.

"Good, then you will understand how big your role will be viewed as Saggilmut's first writer?"

"What?" he asked, dumbfounded. "I don't get it. I'm writing for people in Sagglemet?"

"Saggilmut," he said, correcting Aaron's pronunciation, "Aaron, you have been selected because your time on Earth is now limited, as I am sure you have learned. You have no real knowledge of the gods that you will now be spending time with. You are unbiased, and that is crucial if this first book is to be accurate. You must understand that every god and person in Saggilmut will read your work. You must paint a true picture, because what you write can and will shape how mankind living in eternity may understand the gods. To this point in your life, everything you know about the gods has been told by the gods. Every book on the gods in your world was dictated by their own doing. *Your* writing will be from a source they cannot taint. You will help create a clear portrait of the gods. Do you understand?"

"I think so," Aaron answered, seeking reassurance.

"What you write will shape how they view the gods. You are providing information so the people of Saggilmut cannot be swayed as they had been on Earth."

"Well crap," Aaron said. "I am not sure you picked the right guy."

"Free will is the greatest gift I can give to all my creations," he replied smiling. "I am asking you, not commanding you." Aaron leaned back in his chair, shaking his head. The weight of the situation was beginning to overwhelm him.

"I'll do it," Aaron said, "I'll use my free will to help you, I guess."

"Thank you," he said. "I really must go and prepare for tonight's assembly. We will speak again afterward. I ask that you go and speak to Asherah and ask her to explain how this conflict began."

41

Chapter 6 *A Writer has no heroes*

Heading back down the hallway, Aaron was far less inspired than when he was on his way to meet the Most High. He didn't care to gaze at the colorful designs. He didn't care to be lost in the wonder of how the heavens operated. He was numb, bland. He felt the same as when his dad would sit down and give him *the talk* about how somehow every single choice he made would lead him down a path of either success or ultimate failure.

"May I speak?" Dagon said, following behind him by a step and allowing him to contemplate.

"Of course," Aaron replied, surprised that a god would even ask him. "Please."

"How are you feeling?" he asked.

"I really don't know. I feel perfectly fine, as weird as that might sound. I feel odd just saying I'm fine. I mean, in the last hour or so I learned I'm dying, I'm in heaven, and God just asked me to be Moses on steroids."

"Desensitized?" he asked.

"Yeah, I am. I want to care, I really do," he answered.

"This is because you people have been created by the Most High to process such important information like this exactly how you are now. A person can feel emotions and connections toward one person much easier than the connection of millions. It is far easier to mourn for the death of a single person than the death of a million. Your mind cannot comprehend the pain on that level. This is the case now; the severity of the situation cannot allow you to fully grasp it. May I offer a bit of advice?"

"For sure," Aaron replied, looking at Dagon. "Yeah, anything that you think will help."

"Do not think about the weight of your writing with regard to the fact that literally every soul to ever exist will read it, or how important it is."

"Well crap, you're not making it any--"

"Wait," Dagon said, resting his hand on Aaron's shoulder. "The importance will get lost. Since it cannot be fully processed, it is too big for you to handle. Instead, think of a single person in your life you care for and imagine them reading it. Think of them reading it and how you want them to understand the things you have already seen. Write for a single person to know the truth." Aaron immediately thought of his sister.

"Okay," he said, "I get that."

"Good," he answered. "You have to understand that since the beginning, the gods have controlled the narrative. They told mankind who they were, what they needed to do, and how they had to do it. Every religion ever created was because of some god telling a group what they wanted, and no matter how insane or stupid, people did it. You have the chance to share what the gods are truly like. You will teach everyone in Saggilmut the truth."

Aaron trapped his bottom lip between his teeth. Biting a little harder than normal and crossing from a sensation to slightly painful, he began to worry. If the gods fooled other writers into having them believe they were something they weren't, then he had better be mindful to not become netted in their snares.

Noticing that Aaron was now emotionally upset, Dagon said, "Now you are ready to properly observe and write. Now you are better invested." Aaron silently entered the room again. His stomach in knots and his nerves spiraling out of control, he went back near his chair searching for Asherah, but couldn't find her. The room was still nearly full, as most seemed content just biding their time waiting and conversing.

Aaron's stomach growled, not out of hunger, but because the stress of everything was becoming more real. Placing his hand over his stomach, he bit down on his lip again. *Gotta do my job*, he thought and decided to scan the room. His eyes quickly turned to Thor and Baldr. The two gods were angry, but Aaron could not tell if it was at each other or something else.

"Screw it," he whispered and walked near to them to see if they would entertain the thought of speaking to him. Getting close, he looked toward them, waiting to catch their attention to possibly spark a conversation. He stood no taller than where their beards rested on their stomachs, so unless they happened to randomly glance down, he wasn't going to get their attention.

"I will kill him!" Thor exclaimed to Baldr. "All of this is on him, that *bacrauf!*"

Baldr, not at all trying to quell Thor's anger, replied, "And I am with you, but remember where you are, brother. Now is neither the time nor the place. We have no weapons here. Let us wait until we go back and speak it over with our father."

"I'll do it with my bare hands," Thor said. "Enough is enough." Baldr scanned around the room, patted Thor on the shoulder, then raised his hand holding his two fingers up, pausing their conversation. He left Thor's side, walking toward the lovely goddess who had watched Aaron as he exited the room when he went to speak to the Most High.

Her plain white dress flowed like a liquid over her curves. Her eyes held hues of blue, green, and hazel intermixed. Her full lips offered an enticing promise. Aaron was mesmerized, drawn to her, powerless to resist her appeal. It seemed to him that everyone in the hall shared what he felt, wether they were gods or goddesses.

"You the Writer?" a voice asked from behind him. Startled, Aaron turned with a half leap, feeling as if he had been caught spying.

"Yes, yes, and you're Thor?" Aaron replied, tilting his head upward. "It is great to meet you." Aaron offered his hand out to shake. Thor ignored the gesture.

"Listen," Thor insisted, leaning down to Aaron. "I have had a great history with past writers. A damn good one. There is a reason why I am so well known in your world. People come to Saggilmut when they die excited to come and live in Asgard."

Thor then took a step closer, "Do not mess that up, boy."

Aaron stared up at him bright-eyed, needing to tilt his head to make eye contact. He knew what intimidation was. His dad used to do the same thing, though often delivering on those threats.

"I guess I can throw out the idea of you and me being friends?" Aaron asked, still staring at him. He didn't take it from his dad, and he wouldn't take it from him.

"You can think whatever you want," Thor admonished. "I am no kiss-ass. Just do not try and sabotage me in your writing."

"Well, it was nice talking with you, but I have to go-- somewhere else," Aaron quipped. Walking away, he felt a rush of nerves rushing through his body. *Why would Thor be worried about being sabotaged*? he thought. *What does he think I could write that could possibly mess up his reputation*? No matter the reason, he decided Thor was no longer his favorite superhero.

"Leave him alone," another voice said, half-laughing. Aaron looked and saw another god from Norse mythology. He was not as tall or as broad as Thor was. He had sandy-blond hair with a reddish tint in his much shorter beard that was braided with silver ornaments.

"Do not mind my brother," he said. "He likes to have fun at the expense of others. I am Tyr." Thor glared at his brother, unimpressed, and walked away.

"Good to meet you," Aaron answered with his hand out to shake, risking being denied again.

"I cannot do that," he replied. Aaron, disappointed he was being treated so unfairly, shook his head. Tyr then raised his right arm toward Aaron. His wrist ended at a silver cap where his hand should have been.

"How about like this?" Tyr said, lifting his left.

"I'm sorry, it's- it's just that--nevermind," Aaron said, feeling smaller than he already appeared to these gods. Aaron lifted his left hand, and Tyr grabbed hold of his forearm, wrapping his large hand around it, shaking vigorously.

"This is how we greet each other," he said.

"C-cool, thanks," Aaron replied, still feeling like an ass.

"Really though," Tyr continued. "Thor means well for his people. He just sometimes does not do a good job at conveying it."

"Okay," Aaron said. "I'll keep that in mind." He didn't know what to make of Thor now, but Tyr had seemed cool, he thought. Aaron decided he would see if he could overhear Baldr talking with the goddess. *Why not?* he thought. *If I'm going to die anyway, it might as well be talking to the most beautiful goddess in the universe.*

He walked by most gods completely unnoticed since he was barely waist-high for many of them. He settled himself, standing near a corner of the room behind Baldr.

"Aphrodite, please," Baldr said. He sounded like he had been there begging for awhile. His voice sounded broken.

Refusing to offer a smile back, she replied, "I am not making any promises, but I will mention it when he comes back."

"You have to do it before the assembly begins, or there will not be an opportunity after," he stated, nodding his head toward Thor. Even standing behind Baldr and his worn fur, sprinkled with mud, smelling terrible, Aaron caught a scent of soft jasmine; it was her. He closed his eyes, focusing all his attention on smelling only her while trying to drown out Baldr's lack of hygiene. *She even smells beautiful*, he thought.

"I said I will try," she said, sneering. Even that couldn't make her any less gorgeous. The two continued speaking as Aaron wasn't sure if he should keep watching them or try and talk with other gods.

Chapter 7 *The water begins to boil*

Zeus then entered the hall alone through a wall. Aaron chose to try his luck with him. Hoping not to make the same mistake he had with Thor, he shook off any preconceived notions. Which wasn't hard since all he knew was that Zeus, like Thor, was known as a god of thunder. Maybe the lack of attention he had given in Mr. Thornberg's class would pay off.

"Excuse me," Aaron said, calling out to him.

"Writer," he replied, acknowledging him cheerfully.

"Can I speak with you?" he asked.

"Of course," Zeus replied, and turned to face him. "I am Zeus. I suppose this all must seem surreal for you?"

"You have no idea," Aaron answered, chuckling to himself. "It is. I have so many questions. I feel lost right now. I don't even know what this meeting is really about."

Putting his hand on Aaron's shoulder, Zeus said, "I will see if I can attempt to answer a question or two before we begin again. But first, what is your name?"

"Aaron."

"Well Aaron, we are meeting in hope of keeping what little peace we have left between my sect, the Immortals, and the Asgardians. There has been conflict between our two sects for some time."

"Yes, I've heard there are issues, but I wasn't told what happened. What started your fighting?" Aaron asked.

Zeus smirked. "It is quite complicated. I am sure you know by now that it was Odin of the Asgardians that was causing the scene earlier?" Aaron confirmed this with a nod.

"Good, at least Asherah was not a complete waste of your time. At any rate, he recently went to the king of the Duati sect, Osiris, insisting he side with him in his hope to gain him as an ally to then attack Olympus."

"Osiris?" Aaron asked.

"Yes, that is him there," Zeus said, pointing. Osiris was impressive, even compared to the other gods around them. He was dark in complexion, well built with broad shoulders. His clothing was in the same vein as both Horus and Anubis, although less gaudy in style. He was bald, and wore a long goatee that was braided finely, and held with golden beads. He had a chiseled face and darkened eyes.

"He's king of the Duati?" Aaron asked, still looking at him.

"Yes, Osiris is their king. Anyway, Odin asked him to take up arms against my people, claiming it would finally bring peace to Saggilmut. Thankfully, Osiris is no fool. He saw through Odin and messaged to the Most High for a meeting."

"That's crazy," Aaron said. He sighed, trying to absorb everything.

Zeus then continued, "Listen, Osiris was called by the Most High to come and give his testimony about Odin at the assembly. We Immortals already had little hope of peace with the Asgardians, as this fighting has gone on for so long, but now, after what happened, things may be totally lost. He will more than likely be removed from good standing with Shamayim and this assembly, which means he can no longer attend these meetings. If he cannot be here representing Asgard as king, then he will probably lose his position as their king."

"And that's a bad thing?" Aaron asked.

"Being that the alternative may possibly be Thor, yes for sure. You see, as wild and unpredictable as Odin was, Thor is worse. If Thor is king the question is no longer *if* they will attack, but how long do I have to prepare?"

Aphrodite winked at Aaron before turning her attention toward Zeus. She leaned closer to Zeus and softly said, "He needs a moment of your time before the trumpet sounds."

"About?" Zeus asked.

"Thor," she said, turning her eyes toward Aaron again. "After what happened earlier, I believe it best you give him some of your time, my King." Zeus twirled a curl of his beard while eyeballing Baldr. After a moment he nodded, agreeing.

"When?" he questioned, turning his body and attention toward her.

"If you agree, then he said you should go and approach him now. In this environment, any onlookers will think nothing more than that you only desired to wish him well, since he is next in line to be king if Odin is removed. Maybe an outreach of peace is needed. No one would really suspect anything."

"And you believe he wants peace?" Zeus asked.

"I believe," she paused to ensure she used the right words. "That he is more worried about his own well-being than peace with us."

"All right," he agreed. "Aaron, I wish we could speak more, but please feel free to talk to Aphrodite here about anything. She is as wise as she is beautiful." Zeus placed his hand on Aaron's shoulder, patting gently, and made his way toward Baldr.

"Hello there, love. I am Aphrodite," she said in her soft, breathless voice.

"Hi," he responded, wondering if he sounded like an idiot. "Uhm, what's happening there?" he asked, nudging his chin toward Zeus, who was headed toward Baldr. Something about being near her was intoxicating. *Stay focused*, he thought to himself. She smiled, and he could tell she enjoyed seeing what little masculinity he had crumbling in front of her.

"Quite possibly our only chance for peace," she replied.

"What do you mean?" he asked. She took a step closer to avoid being overheard. Aaron leaned his head forward, squinting at Zeus, trying to pretend that his focus was solely on them and not her dress at eye level.

She said, "Odin will surely lose his good standing with the assembly tonight, which should make Baldr the new king. That means we finally have hope for peace between our two sects."

"Why him?" he asked.

"They are a monarchy, and he is next in line," she answered. "He is not going to be a good king, but with Thor, who is a true danger, behind him in line for the throne, we hope that Baldr will at least try for peace with us. With what just happened with Odin, we are all worried."

"Odin's outburst could end your war then?" Aaron asked, not wanting to tell her that the Most High had said something quite different.

"We can hope," she answered, watching Zeus and Baldr speaking.

"Writer," Jove said, getting Aaron's attention. Aaron's head pulled back, shocked at Jove's bold-blue eyes, which were so much more intense up close that when he noticed them with Asherah.

"I see you have met Aphrodite. My name is Jove and I am from the Immortals sect, like her." Jove offered his arm, and this time Aaron was prepared, reaching out to grab hold of his forearm.

"Already know how we greet each other, I see," Jove said, smiling.

"Yeah, it's--different," he said.

Pulling his arm back, Jove gestured toward another god standing with him. "This is my dear friend Pangu, of the Duati, but we will not hold that against him." Pangu was bronzed with midnight black hair, and his eyes were oval with a gentleness to them. He appeared to be one of the few gods without a beard, although his mustache had grown on both sides of his lips, flowing down to his neckline.

"Hello, and your name is?" Pangu asked, putting his two hands together and presenting himself with a slight bow toward him.

"Aaron," he replied, returning a slight head nod in return. He had never heard of Pangu in any of his classes. *Why not?* he thought to himself, deciding to just ask, he seemed friendly.

"Can you tell me about yourself?"

"Of course, I assume you mean in connection to your world?" he asked. Aaron nodded.

Pangu said, "Well then, the best answer I can give is that my proudest achievement on Earth is that I helped guide China through the period known as the Three Kingdoms. Thankfully, we made it through together, and they have since strived to be a nation united."

Aaron beamed. "Yes, I heard about that. It was around two thousand years ago. Yeah, I remember reading something like forty million died in that war."

"Yes, we lost many," he answered. "But I am grateful I have gotten to meet and get to know many of them, seeing many daily in Saggilmut." Aaron smiled, but wasn't sure what he had meant. *He gets to know them*? he thought. Unsure, he glanced back to Jove.

"Jove, to be honest, everything I know about you I learned listening to the audiobook of *The Odyssey* by Homer. Which was very long and kind of hard to understand, so I missed some parts. I had no idea I'd be meeting you one day, or I would have taken it a tad more seriously. Can you tell me about yourself?" The group laughed. Pangu laughed the hardest at his friend, pushing him.

"Honesty is something I hold more important than intelligence, my good friend," Jove responded, still laughing. "I am glad you have not read it. If you have not been told yet, you need to know that not all the writers were always accurate. Sometimes it was the gods' fault. Other times the writers." Still chuckling, he added, "especially Homer."

Chapter 8 *Between a rock and...*

Zeus had taken Baldr near a wall to talk privately. Baldr was nervous about what had transpired with Odin. His face was redder than normal, and he couldn't stop pulling on his long ruddy beard, unbraiding it with each tug. Many of the Immortals in the room appeared to take notice of them, especially Neptune and Poseidon standing together, who both despised the Asgardians. It wasn't common for the two sects to speak, ever.

Baldr hated them as much as they loathed him. He enjoyed mocking them, referring to them as the *useless twins*. They resembled each other, with their long wavy silver-blonde hair and longer matching beards.

The twins watched in disgust, until Jove nodded toward them to stop. Neptune brazenly shook his head at Jove, looking frustrated, but agreed, and turned around. Baldr couldn't help but lock eyes with Thor, who stood near the table in the middle of the room, arms folded, focused solely on them.

"Listen, we do not have much time," Baldr insisted to Zeus. "What happened earlier was not without provocation, but that is irrelevant. We both know that after tonight's assembly Odin is going to be banished. He is definitely going to lose good standing here in the Hall. My brother earlier tonight already mentioned that *when* he is king he plans to attack you all. He has already decided to ignore me altogether as the rightful heir. I cannot stop him, which means he will be king. My father will more than likely be killed under Asgardian law, and then you will have a serious problem."

"Your brother would take the throne from you?" Zeus asked.

Without pause, he answered, "I know that by the end of the night, if I do not submit the right to the throne as the firstborn, he would either kill me once we arrive back to Saggilmut, or challenge me in a *Hel*, then kill me inside the pit in front of all the gods there, then become king anyway."

"Why not use alchemy against Thor?" Zeus questioned.

"I am one of the few that practice alchemy in Asgard. I would be impaled on a stake at once if he was ever found poisoned," Baldr replied, dismissing the idea. "Everyone would know it was me. We are not governed by elections and voting like Olympus. We do not exactly have a fair court system."

Shaking his head, he continued, "You have to know that Thor is coming to Olympus with everything he has under his arsenal."

"Why are you telling me this?" Zeus probed.

Disregarding his question, Baldr said, "I cannot tell you when," he said, placing his hand over his mustache, and sliding it down taking a hold of his beard. "But if Odin is removed from good standing here in the Hall, then he will also be removed as king over Asgard. Listen, if this all unfolds like I am telling you right now, then I will keep you informed of Thor's plans if, and only if, you swear to me now you guarantee after Thor's death that you will not, in turn, attack us in retaliation."

"Baldr, I swear in my own name that I would not attack." Zeus agreed. "But what do you really demand of me?"

"If I *could* kill him and get away with it, I would. You must believe me," Baldr added.

"You did not answer my question," Zeus said, placing both hands on his hips, and puffing his chest.

"I want what all benevolent gods want. Peace between the sects, and we can do that if I am affirmed as King without my brother's interference. Then, we three kings can rule as a pantheon."

"For now we wait for the outcome of Odin," Zeus replied. Zeus seemed hesitant. Baldr knew Zeus didn't trust him. "If he is indeed ousted, we will need to meet back in Saggilmut soon," Baldr added.

"Meet me in four days at noon. Come alone to the south edge of Mount Hor by the wellspring," Baldr quickly blurted. "If I have any changes, I'll send a hoopoe messenger bird to you." Zeus nodded, and Baldr walked away, headed back toward his brothers, Thor and Tyr, who were now both standing together watching him.

"What could you have possibly had to say to *him*?" Thor said confrontationally, his arms still folded tensely. Tyr, the youngest and least acknowledged of the brothers by the gods, stood to Thor's side, brows raised, waiting for what Baldr could possibly answer.

"He came near to mock us, but I told him he had better prepare for war," Baldr said, putting Thor at ease. Tyr's head tilted, looking at Baldr. He didn't believe him, but Baldr didn't care for Tyr's lack of trust. Baldr hated Tyr nearly as much as the twins.

Chapter 9 *The straw that broke*

Tyr left his brothers and walked past Aaron to a nearby Asgardian goddess. She was radiant, flowing red hair with a yellow, plush flower intertwined behind her ear. Her fair skin was complemented by her blushing red cheeks and soft freckles. She had large upturned green eyes and a slender frame. Aaron watched them, listening. He decided he would make every attempt to avoid Thor, but Tyr seemed as approachable as Asgardians seemed to come.

"Anything good?" she asked.

"No, not at all, Sjofn," he replied. "Unfortunately, everything is headed downhill quickly."

"What do you mean?" she said, concerned, taking a step closer.

"It means that no matter who leads us that all roads are leading to war. My father, either brother, it does not matter," he said, disheartened.

"Tyr, what do we do?" Sjofn asked.

"We wait," he said, closing the conversation. Sjofn was beautiful. Aaron couldn't help stare at her drawing green eyes, hiding behind wavy berry-red hair. Aaron was never one for freckles, but hers sprinkled along her cheeks changed his mind immediately.

The trumpet blasted again, signaling the entrance of the Most High. Aaron was the only one in the room who needed to cover his ears. The gods ended their discussions, each again lining up behind a chair at the table or in front of the chairs along the wall. Aaron noticed his former chair next to Asherah taken by another goddess, clearly a Duati, but he had no idea who she was. He settled for the last seat in a corner where he could see almost everyone in the room.

"Holy, holy, holy," the four heralds proclaimed, each from their respective corner of the room.

The Most High emerged from the same section of the wall as he had prior. He made his way to the throne, walking the three steps, and turning around toward the room. He gazed around, his annoyance clearly visible on his face. It was obvious he was hunting for someone, but wasn't finding them. Everyone knew who it was.

"Where is King Odin?" he asked. No one answered. With disappointment in his eyes, he raised a hand toward Dagon.

"Everyone please sit," Dagon announced, standing at the bottom step of the Most High's throne. Everyone sat, including the Most High. Only Dagon remained standing, stepping down so he stood off the stairs and to the side. He glanced over his shoulder toward the Most High, who directed him to proceed.

"We will continue now with two points of emphasis in today's assembly," Dagon announced. "The first will be the announcement to all that, by the decision of the Most High, as sworn by his own name, Odin is no longer in good standing with the Hall." And just like that, Odin, the original of all creation, the helper of bringing the universe into existence, was banished from the Shamayim. *Shit, I hope he knows what he is doing, kicking Odin out like this*, Aaron thought.

Dagon continued, "This dictates that Asgard will need a new king. Is this something that you Asgardians are prepared to address?"

An Immortal began to laugh, pointing at Odin's three sons all together. He was pale-skinned, with razor-short black hair and a thick, scraggly beard.

"Hades," Dagon called out. "This matter does not concern you."

"Tyr!" Hades belted back. "Lift your right hand and declare yourself the King." Tyr covered his wrist with his left hand, hiding his missing hand under his cloak.

"Baldr?" Dagon said.

Baldr rose from his chair, and after clearing his throat said, "No, I am not accepting the kingship of Asgard." Aaron watched as Baldr peered over at Thor. Aaron knew that look. It was a request for approval. Aaron felt sickened wherever he gave that look toward his father. *Like I needed his damn*

63

approval. Baldr then sat back down and raised his hand and gestured to his younger brother.

Arrogantly, Thor rose from his chair, raised his right hand, placing it on his chest, and said, "I, Thor, son of Odin, will be pronounced King upon my return to Asgard. Until then, I will speak on behalf of Asgard as King." Dagon lifted his hand to see if anyone had anything to say on the matter. Seeing no response, he lowered his hand and continued."For the second issue then, are you now prepared to speak regarding a treaty between Asgard and Olympia?" he asked. Thor shook his head, staring smugly toward Zeus.

"No," he answered. "I am not. I would like time as the new King to discuss everything back in Saggilmut." Zeus glanced toward the Most High, lifting his arms.

"Please," Zeus said. "This has gone on long enough. We all know if we cannot settle here that the likelihood of Thor--"

"Do not dare tell me what I will or will not do!" Thor yelled over Zeus. "You know nothing of me or Asgard." Zeus stood up from his chair, turning his back to Thor and looking directly at the Most High.

"Please," he said, directly to him, lifting both arms, palms skyward. Dagon placed his hands behind his back, and turned toward the Most High. The Most High waved his hand toward him, so Dagon turned around, pointing for Zeus to sit.

"We cannot make a new King settle a conflict that he neither started nor had time as King to discuss," Dagon announced. "We will reconvene in thirty days to allow time for you, Thor, to seek counsel. A hoopoe will be sent out to your provinces with specifics seven days prior. In closing, as we close every assembly, I ask you each if you have seen, or seen signs of the Unspoken?" *Unspoken?* Aaron thought. *Why the hell are you speaking about it then?*

"With that," Dagon concluded, "This assembly is completed. We will hope to see you all here to continue talks in thirty days."

Chapter 10 *Asgardian heritage*

Meanwhile, in Asgard, Odin had made his way back from Shamayim. He sat on his throne holding *Gungnir*, the King's spear, in hand. Still trembling with rage, he took a large swig from his horn of mead. Odin gazed around the sanctuary walls, staring at the large cut stones with various moss and shrooms attached. Modi, his grandson, had been watching him for some time, concerned something was wrong.

Odin seemed disturbed, cursing to himself as he took another swig of the mead in his horn. Modi decided he had better get his brother Magni to join him. Odin seemed to favor Magni, saying that he was a *real* warrior, while Modi was considered as soft as Bragi, the Asgardian poet.

Heading down the hall, Modi helped himself to a shroom growing from a small crevice out of the wall of the castle. The moss and fungi constantly grew along the walls. Tossing it into his mouth, he chewed, quoting aloud Buri, the first king of Asgard, "A god that keeps shrooms in his mouth, remains grounded."

He entered the dining hall where Magni was still sitting since earlier that evening, eating a red bean stew Modi had made for dinner.

"You gluttonous bastard," Modi said.

"What is it, *little* brother?" Magni said, blowing on the spoon. He had a red bean resting in his sandy-brown beard. Modi walked up, leaned over the table, and snatched the bean, tossing it in his mouth.

"Maybe littler," Modi said, chewing. "But older." Swallowing the bean, Modi continued, "It is Odin," he said, taking a peek inside Magni's bowl. "He is sitting on *Hlidskjalf,* and I am not sure, but something is wrong. I think it best we go and speak with him together."

"He is back already?" Magni said, shoveling a spoonful into his mouth. Another few beans landed onto his beard.

"And he looks crazy as Sheol, talking to himself. It is strange," Modi replied, reaching for the beans. Magni smacked his hand away, grabbing them off his beard, and tossing them in his mouth.

"Get your own damn beans off your own damn beard," he barked. Magni got up from the wooden bench, and with one final spoonful began walking the length of the long wooden table toward the door. Modi snatched the spoon out of Magni's bowl and shoved in a large helping before catching up with him. He searched for any hidden beans in his ruddy beard, but wasn't so lucky.

"My King," Magni called out to Odin, as the two entered the room. "You returned so early. I was told you all would not return until much later in the night."

"Children," Odin replied, with one of his forced smiles. *"Heil og sæl."*

"Heil og sæl," they both greeted in return. Odin stood up, then glanced back at his stone-built seat, *Hlidskjalf*, almost like a friend he was saying goodbye to.

Odd, Modi thought.

Odin put down *Gungnir*, the King's spear, leaning the wooden staff against the throne. Gliding his finger along the golden-edged tip. He then turned, letting it go, walking down the steps.

"I am famished," he said, rubbing his stomach.

Magni shook his head, "Sorry to hear that, because the only thing we have to eat is Modi's shitty stew."

"You might like it if you could actually taste it, instead of pouring on your beard, you *fif'l*." Modi beat his chest proudly, then pushed Magni aside, wrapping his arm around his grandfather.

"Is everything all right, my King?" Modi asked, observing his grandfather tugging at the corner of his silver mustache.

"It is now," he shrugged, putting his arm around Magni's neck, and leading them to the food awaiting.

"What do you think about going out hunting tomorrow in Myrkvior woods?" Modi asked, leaving the sanctuary.

"Sounds good," Odin answered. "We will see--not quite sure where I will be tomorrow." Modi wasn't sure what he meant, but he wasn't about to prod for answers.

Chapter 11 *Seventh ring*

Much later in the night, while laughing with Odin and his brother in the dining hall, Modi began to hear voices coming from the sanctuary. He took another drink of mead, then let out a deep and vicious belch. Shattering the ceramic cup on the floor, he rubbed his belly, proud of the amount he had eaten and drunk.

"I need to go see who is there," he said. "It sounds like the gods are back from Shamayim."

"Then it is time," Odin replied, raising his horn to his lips for one last drink before throwing it down and watching it burst in all directions.

Suddenly, the castle bells rang thunderously. The first, second...

"There will be seven," Odin announced. "I need to go meet everyone in the sanctuary."

Modi listened, counting each in his head. The bells' melodious clanging could be heard throughout all of Asgard village. For everyone inside the city walls, the final ring of the seventh bell, and a short pause of silence waiting for a possible eighth, felt like an eternity. Seven rings signified for all gods to gather in the sanctuary, while eight served as a call for defensive positioning, as there was an imminent attack. Modi hated the concept, but it was Borr, the king previous to Odin, that had instituted this under the belief that being summoned by your king should be met with the highest level of alertness.

"I must go see what all the fuss is about, my children," Odin said, dismissing himself from their company.

"It did ring seven times. We should go too," Modi suggested.

"Ohh no--to Sheol with that" Odin replied. "I am sure it will be nothing more than another exhausting report from Heimdall. Do not bother yourselves with the ramblings of a bored old guard."

"Will you come back when you have finished?" Modi asked. He could tell Odin was off. Something about his demeanor seemed too casual. Odin was never this nonchalant.

"If it is not too late, of course, I will. Now stay here and eat more. You boys are too skinny." He laughed, slapping Magni's back. Magni didn't move, having drunk one too many horns. He had laid his head on the table, passed out, letting his beard flow into the stew.

"I can practically see your heart beating through your chest." Odin laughed, walking toward the sanctuary. Modi left his brother at the table and trailed behind Odin, only stopping to make sure Odin hadn't seen him follow.

Entering the sanctuary, he noticed that most of the gods were already present. Bragi, Forseti, and Njord all stood side by side facing *Hlidskjalf*. Mimir and Loki spoke near the doorway. Vidar, Svetovid, Arawn, Camulos, Belobog☐, and others filled the room. Tyr entered the room, taking the first of five steps up to the throne.

"Quiet down" Tyr belted, waving his single hand. The crowd ignored him.

"Listen!" he hollered.

Modi remained in the back, watching. *Cannot be polite to Asgardians,* he thought, looking over the crowd.

"Shut it!" he exclaimed, angered. The gods slowly brought their rumble down.

"Thor, your new King, will be arriving shortly. He has summoned you all here as witnesses to his coronation. He also has called Odin to stand before him." The crowd erupted in disputes and outbursts. *My father--King?* Modi thought to himself. *The Sheol happened?*

"Odin," Tyr announced, with a hint of urgency.

"Watch your tone, son," Odin snarled, stepping forward from the crowd of gods. Odin's voice reverberated throughout the room. The room instantly became silent, eerily so. Odin stood facing the throne steps with his back turned toward Modi and the rest of the gathering. Everyone waited, expectantly.

Thor arrived, walking in from the foyer. He entered through the opened double-doors, smiling and greeting everyone, even the Viking men and

Shieldmaidens. Baldr entered by his side, waving and cheering his brother on. The crowd parted, carefully letting Thor through untouched.

He walked up the steps reaching *Hlidskjalf*. Thor grabbed *Gungnir* and lifted it skyward, waving it over the room. He leaned forward with a mighty roar, so vigorous that spit flew from his mouth and landed at the bottom step, while some clung to his bottom lip. The gods in the room exploded in cheer.

"Heil og sæl, Asgard!" Thor screamed. They returned the greeting with a collective, *"Heil og sæl!"* Tyr and Baldr stood to the side on the first two steps. Thor rested his eyes on his father standing before the throne. He took hold of the shaft of the spear in one hand, and pulled out *Mjolnir*--his hammer, intricately designed in Asgardian symbols--in the other, then took a seat on the throne.

"Odin, first in creation, step forward," Thor demanded. Odin obliged, taking two steps forward. He then lifted his arms, grabbing the collar of his furred vest. Modi's eyes lit. Odin only did that when he felt challenged or threatened.

"The Sheol is happening?" Modi mouthed.

Odin beamed directly at his son with his one eye, jaw clenched.

Thor proclaimed to the room, "By order of the Most High: you, Odin, are no longer in good standing at the Hall. You publicly embarrassed the Asgardian sect, disgracing us in front of our enemies. Now, because Baldr has stepped aside, then I, Thor, as the rightful heir to be king, will take the spear and throne as King of both the gods and people of Asgard." Odin glanced at Baldr, shook his head in disgust, spat on the floor, then looked back at Thor. Odin's face was flushed red, clearly fuming.

"And as King..." Thor paused. "And as Asgardian law dictates--I demand blood!" Thor shouted.

Odin burst into a maniacal laugh. He gripped his stomach, and slapped the side of his leg, laughing hysterically. He then pointed at Thor trying to catch his breath. "My son, Thor, always the zealot for Asgard and its laws." *The Sheol*? Modi thought, gripped with panic, unsure what to do.

In that moment's pause, Frigg, Odin's wife, appeared. She rarely attended the seventh bell ring meetings. Tears filled her eyes as she stared at Odin, but he did not return a glance.

He remained focused on Thor.

She turned her attention to Thor as well, "Son, please," she pleaded.

"Please what?" he chided. "Have I not been gracious? I am giving him a quick death. What more should he have to bear? Should he wander Saggilmut as a shamed exile? No, this is as honorable of an end that I can give to him. I have made my order, and what I decree is fated."

74

"Death," Odin proclaimed, turning his head toward the group. "You heard your new King. Do it."

Four large berserkers with battle axes drawn approached Odin to escort him outside the gate to the stump. There he would kneel, resting his face on a cold rigid tree stump, as a berserker would remove his head, then bring it back to Thor for validation.

"Remain strong, Frigg," Odin instructed with a wink, facing the four. He held out his hands for their chains.

"And father!" Thor yelled. Odin glared at him.

"I will take the battle to Olympus for you." Odin nodded at his son.

"For Asgard is fated to rule," Odin proclaimed.

"For Asgard is fated…" Thor answered.

Odin turned and caught Modi looking at him. He signaled him over. Modi shoved his way to his grandfather, trying to hold back tears. *Do not cry, you bastard. Gods do not cry,* he told himself repeatedly on the way, recalling his grandfather's tutelage. Reaching him, Modi wrapped his arms around Odin.

"Do not say anything, Modi," Odin commanded. "Just remember to be strong, be an Asgardian, and Modi--be yourself, son." Odin willingly followed the berserkers, led by Veles, the god ordered to complete all executions. They walked out of the sanctuary toward Odin's death. Veles smiled with his broken and missing teeth, excitedly. Leaving the sanctuary, he mumbled a song on the way.

"Send some of those damn birds out with a message to the other sects," Thor commanded Tyr and Baldr. "Tell them Thor is now King of the Asgardian and that Odin is dead. That should give them the message of who the Sheol I am." They both rushed out of the room, calling the Viking commander of the hoopoes to hurry and prepare them to fly, and take messages to the other sects.

Chapter 12 *A Spy among us*

Meanwhile, many of the Immortals and Duati gods remained in a corridor outside the Hall speaking. Aaron walked with Osiris, who had welcomed the Writer to join them. The two watched the friendly banter between Hades, Yama, and Horus. It was one thing to see gods that closely resembled mankind, despite their height, but the Sh'losh, with their animal heads, were something entirely different. Seeing Horus, a god with a bird's head, curse and yell, laughing at his jokes aimed at Hades, was baffling. It also helped that Horus was hilarious.

Osiris leaned near Aaron chuckling. "These three are never able to get together without arguing over who was better known on Earth as the *god of the dead*." Aaron watched, laughing to himself at the oddity of it all. It felt good to take a break from everything else, even if only for a short time.

"You two have been copying me since I became known among the *nethers*," Hades clamored. He then turned toward Aaron, then added, "No offense."

"None taken," he replied, unsure what Hades said that could have offended him. *A nether?* He looked at Osiris.

"Can I ask you a question?"

"Of course," he answered, turning his attention solely on Aaron.

"What is a *nether*?" he asked.

"Ohh, um, yes of course," he said, uncomfortably, scratching his head. "It is a term that most of us do not condone--not at all--that is used generally toward mankind. It is slang, referring to them as part of their nether region. Basically calling a person an ass."

"Damn," Aaron said with a smirk. "Maybe I *should* be offended?" He then recalled the tone in which Asherah had referred to him as one. *Makes sense,* he thought. *She really doesn't like me. Wonder why?*

"I have said it many times, and I will continue to shut you both up with it," Hades retorted, "But, who do the nethers on Earth even today most refer to as the god of death? Me. That is all the validation I need."

Bastet, a Sh'losh and one of the feline goddesses Aaron had seen earlier, approached Osiris, indicating with a nod for him to look over his shoulder.

Aaron drew in his lip nervously, as she had caught him gazing. Bastet's oversized cat-green eyes rolled behind her black fur.

Glancing back, Aaron and Osiris noticed Zeus standing with his hands together, waiting to speak. With him was Apollo, his son, as well as Jove. Athena, and another god that Aaron surmised was Ares. He remembered Ares being called the god of war, and compared to the other Immortals, he appeared like a warrior. He had jet-black hair and a fierce matching beard. A terrible scar from his forehead down over one eye and then to his chin. Ares seemed to be very interested in the two feline goddesses, openly staring.

"King Zeus," Osiris said, affirming his presence. "How may I be of service?" Bastet walked toward her sister Sekhmet, another feline goddess. Sekhmet was taller and even slimmer, with a face much fiercer, that of a golden-colored lioness.

Staring at Zeus, Bastet waited specifically for him to glance over, then rolled her eyes away toward Sekhmet. The two burst out laughing together.

"Well, with all due respect, I had hoped to speak in private, Osiris," Zeus insisted.

"Zeus, *with all due respect,* I should be halfway home by now. If it was not for these actual *nethers* holding me from my journey. I ask you to speak freely. I trust the Duati gods here with me as I hope you trust your own."

Zeus took a deep breath. He looked at the Sh'losh, pausing at the sisters, squinting with a tensed jaw. *He's obviously got a problem with them,* Aaron surmised.

Then, giving in, Zeus said, "Osiris, we share a very dangerous common enemy after today's events. I was told earlier by an Asgardian that, with Odin now banished from good standing with the Hall, he will be killed under their laws. This means Thor will have complete control, so there is nothing stopping him from attacking us."

"You mean attacking *you*," Sekhmet said mockingly.

"No, Zeus was right," Osiris agreed.

Jove announced to everyone, "Once Thor has taken control it is--"

"War," Sekhmet said. "Shit."

"And that is not just for us, but he will definitely come after you with everything he has after he decimates us," Zeus added. "We all know Odin is insane, but he was controllable to a degree as a king. Thor is not the same. He cannot be reasoned with."

"What do you propose?" Osiris asked.

"You do not threaten someone who is insane, but we cannot run from him either," Zeus answered. "We have to align our sects and be ready."

"And when does *your spy* say Thor will act?" Osiris asked.

"I do not know, but it will not be long. I have another meeting with the spy four days from now. He said he will be able to tell Thor's plan by then."

"How can you trust him?" Sekhmet asked, with a brow raised.

"It does not matter if he can be trusted," Osiris responded. "We have no choice but to prepare for battle. We can take this god's words with a grain of salt or as testimony, but it has little bearing on the truth."

"Truth?" Horus asked.

Osiris answered, "That if we do not prepare and Thor does attack, we will not last the thirty days the Most High announced until the next assembly. He has planned this since whatever happened with Vali." Osiris looked toward Zeus, who lowered his head, scratching the back of his neck. *Note to self; find out who the hell is a Vali*? Aaron thought.

"Zeus," Osiris said, "I want to be there with you when you meet with this source of information."

The two agreed, sharing the time and place, and afterward clenching their forearms. The Immortals parted ways, leaving through a wall and disappearing. *Really, what's so hard about a door*?

"Aaron," a voice called out from down the hall. It was Dagon, standing alone in the middle of the hallway. Aaron glanced back toward Osiris, like a boy being called by his mother.

"It was good to meet you," Osiris said, bowing his head gently.

"Yeah, you too," Aaron answered, and headed back toward Dagon.

"Bye, Writer," a female voice said. He turned around seeing Bastet waving at him.

Rotating her shoulders in a sarcastic flirt, she said, "I will see you later." Sekhmet grabbed her, and the two left laughing together.

"Uhm, yeah, later."

Chapter 13 *Let me explain*

After the gods had left, the Most High remained sitting on the throne in the Hall. Aaron returned with Dagon in the Hall, coming through the wall together.

"Not big on doors around here?" Aaron asked. Dagon didn't respond, but Aaron felt like he could see just a little bit of amusement on his face. *I'll break you down,* he thought.

"You must be tired," the Most High observed. Although Aaron was getting comfortable with a few of the gods, he was nowhere near that way with the Most High. His presence made Aaron's stomach queasy, as if he was in trouble, yet he was fully aware that the Most High had been nothing but kind to him.

"I'm okay," he answered, lying. In truth, he was rather hungry and exhausted.

"Sit down," he offered, waving to Dagon, who bowed then walked toward the table, picked up the closest chair, and brought it to the bottom of the stair.

"I assume you may now have a few more questions before you rest for the night?" the Most High asked.

"I have a ton of questions," Aaron admitted, walking to the chair and sitting. "Honestly, most of them are still about what I'm actually doing here, but I guess that isn't that important right now. I guess the only question right now is…" The flood of questions poured into his mind.

"What happened tonight? Why was Odin so mad? And what even started it? Why do the Asgardians have such a problem with the Immortals? Sorry, that wasn't at all one question."

"All fair questions," he answered, leaning forward in his chair with a gentle smile. "It may be best that I tell you the story that started it all. It was the last time I interfered with the gods. Afterward, I left them almost exclusively on their own, with the promise that they had the freedom to act. But with that freedom, dire consequences followed."

The Most High leaned back, tilting his head back to admire the ceiling briefly. It was apparent he was replaying the event in his mind, reliving the pain.

"It seems like you care for them all?" Aaron said, watching him.

He gently held his hands together. "Every single one." He paused for a moment, settling himself to begin. "Here is what happened…"

"This was very early in human history. It was before we had even decided to make use of writers, and before they had divided into sects. Zeus was once the beloved leader. He visited your world using the name Anu and claimed responsibility among the earliest peoples as the god of the sky and their heavenly father. He and Odin, who was still then known as Ahura Mazda, both coexisted in peace and even mutual respect, sometimes visiting Earth together and teaching mankind all sorts of things. It was beautiful to watch.

"The gods flourished, despite the occasional attempt to gain power and recognition by an outlier. Both Zeus and Odin stood tall, keeping stability between the gods. Through them, I saw that it was possible that all gods could live in harmony. They could teach people how to truly be good toward each other. That caring for each other is the best attribute one can have." *If only life could be that simple,* Aaron thought.

"Before men began to divide into tribes, claim lands as their own, and wage war against each other, they prospered by following the gods. But Vali, one of Odin's sons, was enamored with Aphrodite of the Immortal sect. She was passionate about seeing female intuition and sensuality become honored by early mankind. She often visited women all over the world, teaching them of the beauty and strength of their gender.

"Vali, the Asgardian prince, had taken to following her, listening to these teachings. Always hiding out of sight, he became obsessed. After a period of time, she caught him watching and became fearful. She found nothing appealing about him, and had turned him away numerous times before. Realizing that he would not leave her alone, Aphrodite warned her brother Ares, who swore he would confront him the next time." The Most High paused for a moment, then continued.

"The following afternoon, while at the Well of Ur on Earth, Aphrodite again shared her deeper insights with some women, as Vali concealed himself behind some nearby trees. Ares also hid nearby, waiting to see if he would come. Vali never noticed Ares and left his hiding place with intentions of violating her." Aaron waited silently for the story to continue.

"Ares stepped between the two to confront him. But Vali, removing a small dagger with a bone handle, lunged at him. The two entangled, and there in front of Aphrodite, Vali shoved his blade into Ares' ribs. Ares dropped to his knees, but Vali did not stop. He continued stabbing him even after Ares collapsed, lifeless. Fortunately, the women screamed out to the gods for assistance, or Aphrodite probably would have been killed right there as well." The Most High closed his eyes for a moment.

"Zeus, hearing their cry and knowing that the well was Aphrodite's favorite place to visit, immediately left his throne, accompanied by Jove. Arriving, he saw Vali tearing at Aphrodite's dress. Jove rushed, wrestling him off and throwing him onto the ground." Aaron could picture the scene in his mind, and a bile rose in the back of his throat.

"Seeing the ground soaked in blood and noticing Ares' body, Jove stepped toward Vali with the intent to kill him. But Odin, who had also heard the cry from the women, arrived and shoved Jove to the ground effortlessly."

The Most High paused, locking eyes with Aaron. Solemnly, he raised his hand in a hypnotic twisting motion. Aaron felt his own eyes close, as if his eyelids were weighted. "See for yourself, Aaron. Open your mind, and you will understand...everything.." Aaron felt immersed in the scene, in the powerful way that one experiences a waking dream.

"Stop!" Odin exclaimed, "What is happening here?"

"*Your* son murdered Ares!" Zeus asserted, clearly in anguish."

Standing between them, Odin reaffirmed his question, looking only toward Aphrodite, "I asked what happened here."

"My lord," Aphrodite answered tearfully. "Vali was--"

"Damn it, I just told you what happened," Zeus insisted. "What are you doing asking my daughter? This filth was attempting to rape her!"

Odin blocked Zeus, shielding his son. "Take your daughter and leave!" Zeus refused, demanding he be brought to the Most High for judgment.

Zeus immediately went to Aphrodite and clutched her tearfully, waiting. "We will get justice for Ares, my love," he whispered. She sobbed uncontrollably in her father's arms.

Odin then summoned two of his sons, Thor and Baldr, and the two sons arrived shortly after. Shocked at what they saw, they looked to their father frantically.

"My son, take *him* to Idunn," Odin ordered. He grabbed Thor and whispered into his ear.

Zeus was visibly furious. "To Sheol with you, Odin. You are not taking my son anywhere."

"I was not speaking of taking your son," Odin replied, pointing his sons to Vali. "Idunn can correct this, be patient."

"My son is dead, my daughter was abused, and you say to be patient?" Zeus replied bitterly. "You cannot take Vali anywhere. He must go to stand before the Most High for this."

Odin snapped, "How can you ever believe you can keep the respect of these people as a leader, when you retreat to the Most High for everything? I said I would bring a resolution to the matter. Just wait." Zeus remained quiet.

The three brothers left, and Odin took a seat on the well, as Zeus and Aphrodite clenched together, still on the ground. They waited silently and with enmity between them. With the evening dusk settling, Odin began to kindle a fire. Zeus and Aphrodite remained distant, whispering urgently to each other. He was unable to comfort his daughter who certainly felt a sense of responsibility for her slain brother. Jove remained standing near Zeus and Aphrodite, watching Odin.

"Should we attack him?" Zeus asked Jove, holding his daughter tightly.

Jove took a deep breath. "No, even if we could overpower him, he is not the one we want. We have to wait for Vali to return." As the hours passed, the wind raged, and the ground offered no warmth.

"Are you cold?" Odin asked of them.

"Do not even dare try to comfort us," Zeus growled, letting go of his daughter to stand to his feet. "You let Vali run off to find asylum, hoping the weight of his actions will not find him, but I swear by my own name that he will die."

"Horse crap," Odin replied with little consideration to the threat, still reclining on the ground in front of the fire. "Sit down before you and your son both end up in Sheol today."

Awake, but not awake--lost in a vision, Aaron realized he could feel and understand the thoughts and emotions of everyone involved in this riveting tale.

Zeus was fully aware he was no match physically for Odin. Odin, like all the gods at this point, had not experienced the concept of war. But he had observed how tribesmen on Earth were arising and pillaging others, and he began to learn about warfare. If men could murder each other on such a scale, so too might the gods engage in battle.

Neither Zeus nor Odin slept that night. Zeus played the situation and possible outcomes in his mind, while Odin lay near the fire relaxed, waiting for his sons to return. Aphrodite had fallen into a deep sleep once the adrenaline and anxiety had taken its toll. Jove took shelter against a small nearby tree.

With the sun rising, Odin's three sons arrived. Vali carried a small leather pouch slung across his shoulder. They circled Odin and began a discussion. Odin listened and responded, but Zeus again could not make out their words or intentions.

"Enough," Zeus hissed. "What are you going to do, Odin? We have waited all night on your proposal. What can you offer?" Odin looked at him, repulsed by his whining. He shook his head, making it clear that he was disgusted. Thor opened the circle, and took a few steps toward Zeus.

"We have a proposition," Thor said.

"To Sheol with you and your damn proposition!" Zeus thundered.

"We can bring Ares back from Sheol, and everything will be made fine again," Thor announced.

Aphrodite woke from her sleep upon hearing Thor's words. She wiped her eyes, stretching, disorientated for a moment. She searched Zeus' face to understand what was happening. Trying to stay composed, Zeus took hold of his beard.

"How is that possible?" he responded.

"Before anything else is said, first we ask that your daughter be given to Vali in marriage. He loves her, and their union can unite us all. She will be welcomed into our family and will learn our customs under the tutelage of Frigg." Frigg was Odin's wife, a beautiful goddess passionate about exploring and examining love and marriage.

Zeus didn't move. He was sickened, his throat felt dry and a pit formed in his stomach. Giving his daughter to these boorish gods appalled him.

"You bastard," screeched Aphrodite, with tears running down her face. She was not sure if her anger was aimed more at Vali for what he attempted to do, or at Thor for his absurd proposition. Zeus looked at Ares, then Aphrodite, unsure of how to proceed. Jove sat calmly near the tree, waiting for his friend to decide.

Odin watched his sons quietly, beyond frustrated, but he had given in to his son's strategy. He wanted to stop them, but not at the cost of risking their shame in front of the others. He believed public humiliation deserved death, so he chose to let it play out.

Zeus was paralyzed in thought. He felt as if time had paused. The seconds felt like an eternity, and no matter where his mind traveled, finding a positive outcome seemed impossible. All ideas ended with either death for Ares or the loss of his daughter.

"I'll do it," Aphrodite announced.

"No," Jove said emphatically, stepping forward. Aphrodite drew near and crouched in front of Ares. He had been a handsome god, black-haired with green eyes and a carefully groomed beard.

"I'll do it," she restated with more confidence this time. She then stood up and walked to her father, saying, "If they can bring him back, Father, then it is worth it".

"I do not know if it is, my daughter," Zeus whispered.

"Good then," Thor declared. "We will conduct the wedding today. Then tomorrow after the ceremony we will call him back from Sheol."

"No," Aphrodite answered. "You will raise him now. Then, and only then, will I agree to marry."

"I am not negotiating with you," Thor scoffed.

"That is where you are wrong," she said. "You will negotiate with me, or we can all draw weapons and kill each other today."

Thor ignored her and said to Zeus, "Do you want to side with her and die here now with your son, or will you accept my deal?"

Zeus knew his daughter. She would not succumb to Thor's demand even if faced with death. He found himself trapped again in an impossible choice. If he commanded her to follow Thor's instructions to marry first, she would outright deny him; but if he chose to listen to his daughter and demand Thor bring Ares back, he knew they would not leave there alive.

"Odin," Zeus called. "Surely you must see the devastation of killing my son. Please, all we are asking is that you bring him back as you say is possible. Then my daughter has freely said she would agree to this." The brothers looked toward their father, waiting for his response.

Zeus shook his head in deliberation. "Vali, bring him back first, then we can carry forth with the plans of marriage as agreed."

Vali cast aside his brothers' caution and decided to act now. He approached Ares and withdrew a small clay jar with a corked lid. Opening the container, he slid two fingers inside and pulled them out, now covered with a bright red cream. Only Odin had any real idea what the substance was.

Vali grabbed the dagger, still pierced between two of Ares' ribs, and pulled it out, tossing it aside carelessly. Kneeling before Ares, Vali then held him by the head and tilted his head backward, causing his mouth to fall open. He then stuck his fingers into Ares' mouth to get the red cream onto his tongue. Vali closed Ares' mouth and stood up, letting the head hit the ground.

"What was that?" Jove demanded.

Vali peered at his father for approval, and Odin nodded. "It is an elixir from Idunn," he answered. Idunn was a well-known goddess, and was among the first to begin learning the art of alchemy.

Before Vali finished speaking, Ares took a deep breath, gasping for air. His eyes were bloodshot, and he was panicked in the same manner as one who awakens from a nightmare. He sat up, but his wound still greatly hindered him, although the compound had already begun to heal it.

"Good, then it is settled," Thor said, beaming toward Ares with amazement. Thor tried to keep control over the situation, but was as bewildered as everyone else, having never seen such a thing. Only Odin had, but it was on a man, so he was just as astonished as the others.

Ares returned to his feet, grabbing the blade on the ground, and hid it in his sash before anyone noticed. Hurrying to his sister, he draped his arm over her for support and held his other hand over the gashes along his chest.

"Zeus," Thor announced. Zeus didn't hear him, still staring at his son in disbelief. He knew the gods were not immune to death, although they never died of natural causes.

"Zeus!" Thor exclaimed. "We fulfilled what was asked of us. So we will be leaving with Aphrodite—Now."Ares had heard all he needed from Aphrodite in the short time since he was revived. Glancing down at his wounds, he realized they had since closed and only scars remained.

Reaching into his sash, Ares took hold of the bone handle of the dagger. He peered back at Jove, signaling his intention, then lunged forward at Vali and slit his throat with one swift movement. The cut went deep, and blood spurted ferociously. Vali tried in vain to cover the wound with his hand, gasping for air. The blood streamed through his fingers and down his chest. Struggling to breathe, his eyes slid back inside his head. He collapsed lifeless onto the ground.

Chapter 14 *In the beginning of the end*

Staggering back seeing his brother now dead, Thor reached past his royal purple cloak, grabbing his hammer, *Mjolnir*. Jove sprinted at him, removing his trident strapped to his back.

Aphrodite was without her dagger and bow, which she normally did not carry on her journeys to the well. She rushed to aid Jove, now entangled with Thor. She leaped onto Thor's back, pulling at his beard and trying to gouge his eyes, while Jove cut into Thor's forearm with a swift stroke.

Odin leaped from a nearby rock formation, holding his spear high pointing at Zeus, but Ares had seen his intentions and cut him off, jumping and colliding mid-air. The two fell to the ground, and Odin immediately rolled over and changed course, running at Ares.

Baldr had stood axe in hand, circling Jove, but unwilling to throw himself into the fight. He looked for a vunerable opening to become exposed. Zeus held his trident in defense, watching them all fight.

Jove cut Thor along the forearms numerous times, but couldn't drive the trident into him. Thor clenched Jove's wrist and was much stronger. Jove, unable to move back to drive his trident, jerked and twisted, unable to break Thor's grip. Aphrodite was riding Thor's back with her arms wrapped around his neck. She had managed to slide her arm under his jaw and was slowly choking him with all her might.

Odin tackled Ares, and the two turned over entangled, rolling until Ares jabbed his dagger into Odin's shoulder, drawing him back. Ares quickly slashed the blade again, this time toward Odin's face. Odin tried to dodge, but it sliced down his face, splitting his eye. He would never see from that eye again.

The cut drove him off Ares. Thor, now turning a shade of red-purple from being choked, knew he could not sustain holding back both Jove and Aphrodite. He let go of Jove's wrist. Before he could react, Thor took *Mjolnir* and with both hands swung it into Joves' chest. Jove lost balance, falling flat on his back. Thor reached back, grabbing Aphrodite by the arms. Then, dropping to one knee, he whipped her over his head. Slammed to the ground, she immediately spun around to leap back at him.

Odin rushed Ares, lowering himself and taking another cut to the shoulder, but gaining both the momentum and angle. He drove his shoulder into Ares's chest and tore the dagger away from him, hurling Ares to the ground. Odin pushed forward, trampling Ares' chest, and purposely stomped his head with his sandals. Then he ran toward Zeus.

"Aaron," the Most High uttered softly. Aaron opened his eyes, surprised, looking around the Hall. He had that same disorientated feeling earlier when in a flash he was suddenly in the hallway with Asherah. He gripped his stomach. *Can't keep doing that*, he thought. *Probably going to vomit if I do it again.*

"What none of the combatants knew was that the women, watching the mayhem, had summoned me in prayer. I had given the gods control over Saggilmut, but never Earth. I governed the land--only allowing them to travel there," the Most High stated. "That is when I arrived. Odin, spear in hand, ready to kill Zeus. My first creation whom I loved so dearly, prepared to kill another. I was heartbroken for all of them, but so much more for him.

"What did you do next?" Aaron asked.

"We carried Vali back to Saggilmut and took time to give him a proper burial. I called a hearing for all those involved. After listening to both parties, we all made an oath in our own names to each other: *That no other conflicts would take place on Earth.* Idunn now serves me here in Shamayim with Asherah and Dagon for her manipulation of alchemy, which I have since outlawed among the gods. I have also closed direct communication between mankind and the gods. People deserve better from their gods. We tried to talk it out, but it was too late. A fire was kindled in Odin that, as you can see, has never gone out."

The Most High stood from his throne and walked down the steps. Aaron's hands instantly began sweating as he came closer. *Relax, relax, relax.*

"Dagon will both be your guide and guard in your travels."

"Travels? What travels?" he asked.

"Saggilmut, Aaron. Now there are many things you will not understand pertaining to Saggilmut, and that is totally understandable. Ask Dagon anything, and he will guide you. You will have full access to everywhere you see fit when you go." Dagon lowered his head in agreement.

"*Saggilmeet?*" Aaron asked. *I have to learn how to pronounce it*, he thought. *It's just embarrassing now.*

"Yes, but first I suggest we go to the Library," Dagon advised. "There you can learn some more about the three sects. I am sure the last few hours must have been a whirlwind for you."

"Yeah," he agreed. "It has been."

The Most High smiled. "Dagon will escort you to your room for the night. You will stay in the Library for no more than three to four days, then you will travel to Saggilmut. With all that you are about to see, I cannot have you remain naive to names and sects of the gods. I need you to be accurate." Aaron agreed and looked at Dagon, but

99

it all just wasn't sitting well with him. *Does he know what I do for a living? I don't think he can, and still ask me to do something like this.*

"So, I have to ask," Aaron said. "Once this is done, and I've written everything, or whatever--I mean, I know I'm dying and all--b-but I was wondering if you can just like...heal me and bring me back or something?"

"No," the Most High replied. "We have all made an oath that the gods will no longer do such things. Man has to learn how for themselves." *How to what? Stop death?*

Aaron reluctantly agreed and walked quietly toward Dagon, ready to go.

"Aaron," the Most High said.

Turning around, he answered, "Yes?"

"I am truly sorry to bring you into all this so suddenly, but more than anything, I am truly sorry for the accident."

"Me too," he responded, trying not to seem as dejected as he was.

With that, Aaron left the Most High and headed to his room. Dagon waved him toward another wall. Entering through, he paused. He was back home! The same small two-bedroom apartment he had lived in since he, his sister, and his mom had to find a place after Dad left them.

"I'm home!" Aaron sputtered.

"In a way," Dagon answered. "This is a replica built specifically for you. It is not your actual home. Your mother and sister are on Earth in the real one, of course. When you exit through the front door you will be within the Most High's castle again." Aaron didn't try to make any sense of it, rather just thankful to see a familiar place.

"Thanks," Aaron sighed, looking at the picture hanging in the hallway. It was of his mom and Sarah riding on a camel. He ran his fingers along the picture. *Miss you two.*

Aaron took the picture off the wall and flopped onto the old floral pattern couch, putting his foot on the wooden coffee table as he normally did. His mom always hated that.

"And Aaron, for what it is worth, I am sorry for what happened to you on Earth," Dagon said.

Aaron didn't reply; the ball in his throat was too large. He waved his hand toward Dagon, but focused on another photo on the coffee table.

"Wow, what a day," he said to himself. He had said that every day when he came home from work, but today was different. Grabbing his grandmother's prayer book that was collecting dust on the small bookshelf next to the couch, Aaron cracked it open. Randomly flipping pages, his eyes were drawn to the words, *You are to have no other gods before me. I am the Lord your God.*

Well, that takes on a whole new meaning now, he thought. He closed the book and laid his head on the couch, staring at the ceiling. *I'm going to die,* he thought, clutching the photo tight. He

began to sob, not for himself, but for his sister
Sarah, his mom, and even Tyler, her boyfriend, who
he secretly thought was a great guy.

Chapter 15 *The Art of War*

Early in the morning after the ceremony had been completed, Thor sat with *Gungnir* across his legs on his throne as King. Only his family remained inside the sanctuary, while outside many gods and humans were still celebrating. Music, shouting, and occasional fighting could be heard from inside the sanctuary, to his delight.

"Are you sure?" Thor asked, frustrated.

"Yes," Tyr answered. "I walked the area, he is gone." Frigg, Odin's wife, couldn't help but look cheerful that her husband Odin was alive.

"If you were not my mother, you would be in trouble" he replied with a playful smirk.

"What do you want to do with the bodies of Veles and the Berserkers, my King?" Frigg asked, trying, but failing, to hold back her smiling teeth.

"Baldr, you will ensure to bury them all before anyone can ask questions," Thor answered, "No one can ever find out Odin escaped. It would serve as an embarrassment to me, and the throne."

"We cannot let anyone outside of these walls find out or I will be shamed for his escape," Thor commanded. "And you are telling me there was no trace of him?"

"No, my king," Tyr responded. Thor leaned back in the chair, his hand holding up his head, his fingers massaging his temples.

"I am going to say this again: *No one will speak of this*," Thor commanded. "Wherever he went, we can assume he is no longer in Asgard. If anyone asks, he is dead." Thor rubbed his eye, letting out a long sigh. "Now, back to our conversation. Go get them. I want to send the spies today."

Tyr agreed, and called out for the captain of the Berserkers, waiting outside the sanctuary doors. Tyr instructed him quickly, sending him off to the homes of the gods, Vidar and Bragi. Thor had decided to send two spies to Mount Olympus to reconnoiter their land, looking for attack points and weakness.

"And you are sure you want to send Bragi, the *Poet*?" Magni asked.

"Bragi is no warrior, son," Thor admitted, "but he serves his purpose. If we can get him a single day surveying Olympus, he will be able to describe each brick, each window, and help us decide the best point of entry. That damn *poet* will tell us which gate we will need to go in through. And besides, he is going with Vidar." he added.

"One who does not shut up, and the other a mute," Magni scoffed.

"By oath," Tyr responded. "He does not speak by his own admonition. And, for as weak as Bragi is, Vidar will cover for him and then some."

Thor said, "Tell them I want their return in no more than one week." Tyr agreed.

Thor then said, "Tyr, make sure Camulos gets every damn last warrior from Valhalla prepared. This does not leave the room, but when Bragi and Vidar return from scouting Olympus, we will advance shortly after." Camulos was appointed by Odin to train the greatest warriors inside a walled section of the city known as *Valhalla*. Only the greatest of the Berserkers, Vikings, Rekkrs, and shield maidens, who had proven themselves on Earth, was accepted into the gates to cultivate themselves in the *Valhallians*.

"Let us go, my King" Magni pleaded. "You know you can trust Modi and me."

"No," Frigg argued. "There is no need to put yourself in harm's way unnecessarily."

"Father, please!" he insisted. Modi stood by Magni's side, eating a shroom, looking at his father. Thor stared into Modi's eyes, waiting. Modi stared back unmoved. He knew he could never break eye contact with his father. It was seen as weak, and he knew already Thor saw him as deliberate and tempered, traits not well suited for an Asgardian. He stared back, unwavering, then Thor grinned, and proudly slammed the blunt end of *Gungnir* onto the old stone floors.

"And here I was thinking my sons would be content just remaining in Asgard, and finding the next woman to lay with," he shouted to everyone. Modi wasn't interested in wasting his time on women like his brother, who was known to have different women consistently around his arms. Modi had a deep appreciation for Asgardian law. He, Tyr, and Sjofn would spend hours outside of the Asgardian gates, listening to Bragi and just talking.

Popping another shroom in his mouth, Modi asked, "What can we do, Father?"

Thor answered, "You will go to Nekhen in Duat, and listen to rumors there. Do not make yourself known. Odin was vilified there for attempting to recruit the Duati as an ally when he spoke to Osiris. We will not be as foolish as he was and believe they will take up arms with us, but we need to know if they have any plans to help Zeus and the Immortals."

"So you want us to just sit there eavesdropping?" Magni asked, crossing his arms.

"I expect you to do what the Sheol I say, boy!" Thor shouted. Magni unfolded his arms, looking at Modi, who had no answer, inspecting his next shroom.

"All cities appear peaceful from a distance," Thor advised. "You must get closer and speak to the natives. You will both strip yourselves of your armor and put on sackcloth. Cover your tattoos by rubbing your faces with dirt. I need to know if Osiris or any other Duati plan to align with our enemy."

Thor continued, "And take those damn braids off your beards. You must appear as nothing more than just another nomadic god." Nomad gods had turned from their sects and chose to roam the neutral sections of Saggilmut as wanderers. They had no alliance, no kingdom, and were treated no better than the livestock.

Thor then said, "Bragi and Vidar will return from their recon of Olympus in seven days, so you two need to make sure you are back before them. I need you both here for the attack."

Magni replied, "We will go after this meeting and prepare to leave by midday."

Eating his last shroom, Modi gazed into his empty hand, conflicted. *Fate*, he thought, *what a fickle woman you are. It would be nice to have a day where fate does not imply war.*

Chapter 16 *Fate*

"We need messengers sent to Guangdong," Thor said to Tyr and Baldr.

"Why would we send anyone there?" Tyr asked.

"The Sanguan Dadi," Thor said, beaming. "They have a large following that would fight for them. You tell them that if they help us conquer the damn Immortals, then we will help them overturn Osiris so they can rule Duat. You tell those bastards that, and they will lick the soles of our boots."

The Sanguan Dadi were a group of three gods that believed they could eventually become kings over Saggilmut if they worked together. They modeled themselves after the Most High, refusing to take names, and chose to be called by titles. Tianguan declared himself the ruler of the sky, Diguan claimed to be the ruler of land, and Shuiguan designated himself as the lord over the waters. They lived completely synchronized, working in absolute unison. Whatever one said, the other two agreed, wholeheartedly.

"I think they would know that we are lying to them," Tyr stated.

"And if they do, then they will not fight with us, so what? But *if* the Sanguan Dadi do believe we would be willing to help them take control over Duat from Osiris, then they just might fight for us.

Once we take control of Olympus, and they finally figure out we are going to be capturing control over Duat as well, it will already be too late for them to do anything about it. The Sanguan Dadi will help us, then watch helplessly as we take over Duat as well."

"I will go," Tyr said. "Loki can come with me."

"No, he is useless. I cannot trust him to stay on task," Thor objected. "Take Sjofn. Who knows? I have heard they are tree lovers like you two. Maybe you both can help persuade them." Tyr looked at Thor and nodded. He then glanced over at Modi, who was grateful his father hadn't found out he liked spending time with Tyr and Sjofn as well. It was tough to live up to his brother, who was so much more like Thor.

"You two had better leave soon, Tyr," Baldr said. "You are not bringing back information like the others. Thor needs you two to bring back an entire army." Tyr agreed.

"I will get Sjofn and leave for Guangdong by midday," he answered.

Frigg, and Thor's wife Sif, had been listening, arms intertwined, as Sif's golden blonde head rested on her mother-in-law's shoulder.

"Son, you have been king not even a full morning, and already we have our gods being sent throughout Saggilmut making preparations for battle. Why not just go outside to celebrate as the new king? Take some time with your wife to relax. Olympus can wait, my love."

"Mother, you know more than anyone, that even in his failing, my father only desired to fulfill the fate of Asgard. I have only the same intentions. Forget I am your son for a moment, and you would see that now is the best time. The longer we wait, the more they can prepare. They know I am coming, but I believe we can still surprise them if we do it soon."

"Thor," she said, in her calming tone. "I see you as both my son, and king. Although I openly admit, I see you as a son first."

Looking down the hall from the throne, she pointed and said, "Tell me what you see mounted on the walls?"

"Trophies," Thor answered. They were weapons, arrayed along the wall from the Saggilmut and Earth. The Asgardians collected weapons throughout history to display their dominance over anyone they came across in battle.

"Right," Frigg responded. "From all over the world, my son. We have brought the world in all its splendor to Asgard. Your father was part of that."

"I know, and I love him, but he could not stay here. He would have been slandered and mocked. I would be ridiculed as a weak king for not adhering to the strictest aspects of our laws if I let him live." Saying this, Thor reclined on the throne and rubbed his forehead, frustrated.

"I cannot come across as weak, mother," he added.

"I know, Son, and Odin would not have wanted you to." She let go of Sif and approached him, walked up the steps, then kneeling on one knee, placed her hands on his leg.

"Please know your father is proud of what you did," she said, tapping his leg. "That you chose the law over him. That you believe we are fated to rule, even if it means him losing his life. But things do not need to be so rushed, my love."

He lowered his hand from his hairline, resting it over her hands. "I do not want to bring the trophies of the world to Asgard. I want Asgard to be brought to the world. I miss him already, but the best I can do to honor him is by expanding this kingdom, his kingdom." His voice stammered, and Modi could hear the pain in his words.

"I may never see my husband again, and I accept that by your command." Frigg paused, covering her mouth, crying.

Bragi's singing could be heard as he made his way into the sanctuary. She quickly wiped her eyes, and kissed her son, who was wiping his eyes.

"I love you, Thor," she said, standing up and making her way back to Sif.

Thor responded, "And I, you."

Modi looked away, letting them have their moment. He pondered on one of the many tattoos on his right forearm. It was of a small pomegranate, opened, with its seeds bright and tempting pouring out. It served to remind him of a lesson Odin had taught him many times. He could still hear his voice. *"Life is no different than a pomegranate. Each seed within is to be enjoyed. In the same manner, each test is to be learned from."*

"You have a mission for me, my King?" Bragi asked, entering the room and taking a bow. As they spoke, Modi walked over to Tyr, hitting him on the shoulder to get his attention.

"Tyr," Modi whispered. "Can we speak before we leave?"

"Of course, come on" he replied. The two left the sanctuary.

It was still dark, nearly sunrise, and a cold wind blew. The stars were bright, giving a little more illumination, but it didn't matter. The city was still celebrating, with torches lighting their path.

Walking together, they looked at the gathering around the castle square. The celebrants were beating their drums, dancing on the wooden tables, and drinking from their horns. Tyr chuckled as he stepped over a man passed out along the dirt road, lying on his stomach naked.

"Quite a night," Modi said. Although he meant more about Odin, Thor, and the impending battle.

"Indeed," Tyr answered.

"Uncle," Modi said, unable to hold it in any longer. "Are we right? Should we be doing this?

You know I love my sect, but I cannot help but think we do not have to do this."

"Fate," Tyr responded. "How can we stop it? You are the grandson to the first creation of all the gods. If he was destined to bring all of Saggilmut to worship in Asgard, then it does not matter if we understand. Modi, we do not even need to agree with it. But I do not want to stand in the way of fate either."

"I will go because I have been commanded, but I cannot help but feel we are on the wrong side of fate," Modi answered.

"Time will tell, nephew," Tyr Replied.

Chapter 17 *Which side of the fence is greener?*

The following afternoon after the assembly, many of the Duati gathered at Horus' home in Nekhen, part of the Osiris plains and the capital city. The southern half of the Duati province was named after their king, while the north was known as the Kailash hills and home to their leader, Lord Shiva, who governed the region under Osiris' command.

Nekhen stood as a monument of Duati brilliance. The architecture was unique and diverse with its pyramids and temples scattered throughout. The city was built almost exclusively of saggilmut, the most prominent mineral found in their region, and the reason why the world was called Saggilmut, *heaven*.

If melted, saggilmut stone could be molded, reshaped, and hardened into almost anything. The Duati used the stone for nearly everything, from the buildings and structures, to their chariots, weapons, and armor.

Its properties allowed for a perfect reflection from light. When the founders built Nekhen, it was constructed in a manner specifically located to capitalize on the use of the sun's rays to beautify the landscape. Osiris' favorite pastime was to go to the city square and watch the sunrise. The surrounding buildings created a mirroring effect from the sun, and if he stood in the right spot, it appeared as if there were four suns rising in all directions simultaneously.

"I still cannot believe it. It has not even been a day since Odin's expulsion. Why would he attack so soon?" Horus, a god with a bird's head, wondered. He took a seat on the bench outside in the backyard of his home. It was the common meeting area for the Duati, since it was the largest home inside the city. It offered a large courtyard backfilled with garden fruits and vegetables ready for the picking. The Duati gods sat around a large table, which offered many of them in small saggilmut bowls.

Osiris had taken to living outside the city. To the south, there was a large plain he found serene. It was away from the noise of the worshippers. The people would line up outside his home at all hours of the day chanting, offering incense, and lying prostrate.

He loved them, but was vehemently against being worshipped with any praise at all. He felt it was *unnecessary* and *primal*. Nothing peeved him more than tripping over people lying prostrate in his lawn, as he picked fresh grapes from his vineyard.

"We should just let them both destroy each other," Sekhmet announced. "The Immortals are arrogant and prissy, while the Asgardians are arrogant and brash. They both are feces in their own way."

Osiris smiled, but remained silent. He knew how she felt about the Immortals. She never let a day go by without mentioning them, and how she wanted justice for what they had done to her and the other Sh'losh. The Sh'losh were first created by the Most High as Immortals. Considered as mixed breeds by Zeus and the others, they were forced to live outside of the Mount Olympus walls. After the conflict between Odin and Zeus arose, the Immortals became more stringent regarding anyone unwilling to devote themselves solely to their *civilized* customs. The Sh'losh, led by Sekhmet, argued against their policies, but it didn't matter. Zeus had decided all *the animal gods* needed to be sent away for peace's sake, because they would never fit in properly.

The Sh'losh sojourned during their great expulsion to various locations, but ended up on the Osiris plains, where they were accepted. Sekhmet, more than the others, took to the culture Osiris had created and donned a Duat inspired shoulder-length black braided wig.

"We must be careful, Sekhmet," Osiris stated. "The Asgardians are hunters. They have their eyes set on today's meal, but when they are hungry tomorrow they will set their eyes on us. Without our help, the Immortals will not be able to hold them back. And the way I see it, we would be next."

"Fair enough," she retorted, disappointed. "What do we do?"

Osiris stood up from the saggilmut-stone seat and addressed not only Sekhmet, but everyone. "We are going to wait until Zeus and I can meet with his spy in a few days and see what he has to say. I did not ask you all here to make plans today. I called you here to ask you to be aware. We should assume the Asgardians will send spies to gather information from us. For all we know, Thor may have already sent them. He might even ask us to fight in battle against the Immortals, just like his father Odin had. Either way we must be mindful."

Pangu grabbed his long flowing mustache that rested in his lap and began twirling it with his fingers.

"Osiris," he said. "If you are in one breath mentioning spies coming from the Asgardian, and in another discussing a meeting with one of these Asgardians with Zeus, I have to ask, how can we trust anything they may say at this meeting?"

"In the right hands, even false information is still relevant," Osiris answered.

"All right," Pangu continued. "And if we do find spies?"

"We should kill them," Sekhmet announced. "Then send them back to the Asgardian prepared to be buried. You know, to be respectful." Bastet lightly hit her hand against Sekhmet's thigh.

She mouthed breathlessly, "You are so bad." Sekhmet glanced back at her sister and winked.

"If they do send spies, then it would be wiser to just hold them and speak to them, but if it is necessary to keep our people safe, of course, defend yourself," Osiris advised.

"You know I respect you, Osiris," Sekhmet said, "but I just cannot agree on why we would fight with the Immortals. More importantly, why not fight with Asgard? Even if we did help them, they could never beat us in a battle." Ra, a fellow Sh'losh, chirped agreement at the words she was saying. He had the head of a bird, a small beak, and beady eyes that were always moving, studying his surroundings.

"Sekhmet, please," Pangu replied, trying to keep the situation from escalating.

"Please what?" she retorted. "Damn Zeus, damn the Immortals, and if Thor wants to end those bastards, then I say let him. The Immortals are a disease on this land. Then if that bastard wants a real war, I say we send them to Sheol. Let them keep fighting in death, and we can finally have real peace here."

Chapter 18 *Sekhmet's proclamation*

"We have lived in peace with the Immortals since we left," Horus argued.

"We did not leave," Sekhmet replied sharply. "We were banished. There is a difference." She turned her eyes toward Osiris, "And with all the respect I have for you, I refuse to even think about defending a place that did that to us." As she spoke, there was a growing murmur amongst the Sh'losh if she was right.

Toth, a long-beaked Sh'losh reclining in his chair, said, "I choose to side with Osiris, and the Duati gods after all they have done for us. Their love for us means more to me than any hatred for the Olympians." Osiris nodded, sitting back down. He respected Toth, and knew other Sh'losh did as well.

Sekhmet answered, looking at Toth, "Who said anything about choosing?" She then turned toward Osiris. "I ask you to do nothing. Do not enter the battle at all."

"Sekhmet, no," Osiris replied. "We cannot sit idly by and do nothing. Our best defense is with the Immortals."

Sekhmet raised her hands in complaint. "Well shit. I swear by my own name that I would go to Asgard myself and fight along with them if I knew Thor was going to be able to bring Olympus

to its knees. Osiris, I beg you to stay out of this."
The courtyard was aghast.

Bastet's eyes lit, and she stared at her sister in shock.

Osiris remained focused on Sekhmet. He didn't say anything; she had made her point. *What was left to say*? he decided.

Seeing that no one was challenging her, she continued, "Think about it. Why should we side with them and fight against the Asgardian? So what if Asgard wants to rule Saggilmut? What does that matter? What makes them any different than the Immortals, or even many of us? We talk and talk, but for thousands of years, we have sat here wasting our breath discussing how we would change Saggilmut for the better. The *nethers* forget our--"

"Damn it Sekhmet, do not call them that!" Pangu demanded, enraged. "You have said enough. You stand here and speak about revenge and nothing more."

He looked over everyone in the yard and continued, "They treated all of you Sh'losh terribly, abusive and even at times murderous, but do not take your advice from someone who would very likely do the same to mankind if given the chance."

"I would never do to a *nether* what they did to us, but if I did have my way, we would have been ruling Saggilmut ten lifetimes ago," Sekhmet replied. She sat down, content in her argument.

Bastet shook her head playfully at Sekhmet, as if disapproving. Sekhmet rolled her eyes, and the two broke out in laughter, breaking the tension briefly.

"Let me say this," Osiris announced. "I am asking you today to do the same thing I always do. Make your own decision, do what you believe is right, and be damn ready to live or die with the consequences. But I will be speaking with the four tribal leaders of the humans later today, asking that they would support me with an army."

"*Asking*? Why are you *asking* for the nethers support?" Sekhmet said. "You are the King, just tell them--"

"Enough!" Osiris yelled. "You have said enough. I will say this to everyone here; I do not believe Saggilmut will be won on the battlefield, but I do believe it can be lost there. I am leaving, so unless anyone has anything else to say before I go to the leaders?"

"I will go with you then," Toth said. Sekhmet glared at him.

Osiris announced, "Then it is settled. I will send out further information for another meeting after I speak with this *spy*, and after I have spoken with the tribal leaders asking if they will join us. *Em hotep*, my friends."

"*Em hotep*," they replied, calling for peace in concluding the meeting. Most remained nearby, eating and conversing about the looming threat.

Osiris grabbed a cluster of grapes and found himself a chair where the morning sun was now offering its heat. He ate them one by one, watching over everyone.

"I do not mean to cause any strife," Sekhmet said, standing over Osiris. "I have only the utmost admiration for you, even if we do not always agree."

Popping a grape into his mouth. "I know, my good friend, I know."

She nodded and left, exiting through Horus' home, holding her sister's hand on the way.

"I believe we have a serious problem developing with her," Toth said, turning a chair toward Osiris and sitting nearby.

Throwing another grape into his mouth, Osiris offered a half-smile. "I agree. What do you think we should do?"

Toth rubbed his hand along his beak, then said, "I believe she meant what she said. I can see her going to Asgard, and maybe even taking some other Sh'losh with her. I also do not think there is anything we can do to stop it." He held his hand out to Osiris, asking for some of the grapes.

Toth continued, "I cannot imagine having to draw a weapon against one of my own to defend the Immortals. They banished us, and now I should fight with them against my own? It seems surreal." Osiris separated a small bunch of grapes, handing them to Toth.

"Let us hope it does not come to that," Osiris answered. "My desire is that Sekhmet's anger does not get the best of her. I do not see her marching to Olympus with us, but I also hope she does not go there as our enemy."

"Do you think Asgard would accept Sh'losh in their ranks?" Toth asked.

"If they showed themselves willing to take up arms, then Thor would happily throw them on the front lines. They would be a means to an end."

Toth brought a grape up to his eyes to inspect it. Deciding it was good enough, he opened his beak and tossed in the purple fruit.

"I have always preferred the green ones, myself," Toth said.

"And here I was thinking you were so smart, green over purple? No way," Osiris said, chewing on one. "We should get going and speak to the tribes. I suggest the Nubians first."

"Agreed."

Chapter 19 *The home of Shiva*

"I do not care," Hades said, annoyed at Vulcan, who was trying to describe to him the property similarities between mercury and saggilmut. Vulcan was one of the few remaining renowned alchemists, after the Most High forbade it.

Mocked for his limp, which Vulcan received from an early childhood injury, he stayed away from others and spent his time studying the art. He refused a cane or walking stick, instead choosing to trudge along dragging one boney leg. Otherwise, he was muscular, spending much of his life practicing masonry, when he wasn't creating a new compound. His plain brown hair was always unkempt. He never understood the need for such *trivial* things as looking presentable, when a mere dab of one of his elixirs could lead goddesses to desire him.

"How can you not care? I do not get it, Hades," Vulcan insisted. "How can anyone not love the idea of how a drink of a simple elixir, or a little compound salted on someone's meal, could change the very thought patterns of whoever consumed it?"

"Because," Hades argued, "no one wants to be someone else's puppet. It is ridiculous and arrogant, like when you tricked Venus with your damn potion. You take away her right to choose you, but that is because you know she would never have chosen you damn *malaka*."

"Do not call me names," Vulcan answered. "You are just jealous, bringing up something from so long ago. I am not denying it. Shit, I got to marry the most beautiful goddess in all Olympus. It was worth it. And besides, she forgave me...*eventually*."

The following morning, after Odin's expulsion, Zeus sent Hades and Vulcan on a two day trip to the southern hills of Kailash. There, they were ordered to speak to Shiva and make an attempt to create an alliance with him. Although the Kailash hills were within Duat province, therefore under Osiris' control, Zeus decided to send them, fearing time was too limited to wait.

Hades agreed to go, since he was the only Immortal to have had any dealings with Shiva in nearly five thousand years. Hades had once gone to Shiva to purchase a guard animal. Hades had created a cave under the city of Olympus, tunneling it from his chambers in Olympus castle. He wanted something to guard the cave against anyone crazy enough to dare to enter.

Shiva created Cerberus, Hades' three-headed dog. Cerberus was specifically mutated by Shiva for him after years of studying alchemy. Vulcan had volunteered to go with Hades to try and recruit Shiva and the military he controlled. Vulcan was far more excited to meet a fellow alchemist, one that he had told Hades numerous times during the trip, was *on his level.*

Vulcan said, "Hades, how can you not care about alchemy? It teaches how to bend this damn world we are trapped in. You cannot tell me you are not even a little curious as to what compounds the Most High used to throw us together."

"No, now shut up, we are here," Hades stated, ending the conversation. The two approached the doorway of the small wooden cabin. Both gods were bewildered at the home. It was old and neglected. There were large gaps in the wall from the uneven wood used, allowing for them both to peer inside. The two windows in the front were grossly uneven and had no glass. The door frame was small and missing the door itself. Both gods would have to lower their heads to enter.

Standing at the doorway, Hades looked in and noticed the floors were of redwood, a bright bark from a tree indigenous only to the Kailash mountains. *At least the floor seems stable,* he thought.

"Shiva," Hades called out. No answer.

"Shiva!" Vulcan shouted, louder.

"I am here. Please, come in" Shiva replied from somewhere farther in the home. As soon as he stepped into the home, Hades was hit with a potent odor. It smelled of old fruit and stagnant water, making it difficult to breathe. Covering his face with his hand, he assumed Shiva must have been preparing some type of powerful elixir, because the smell was just horrendous. Despite the cool breeze coming in through the numerous gaps in the home, it still felt dank and humid.

"Is that Assam tea you are preparing?" Vulcan asked, unaffected by the stench. Hades glared at him, covering his face to hide the smell from reaching him.

From the other room, Shiva answered, "How is it possible someone with such a terrible sense of smell can be a fellow alchemist? Are you telling me you cannot even tell the distinct scent of Darjeeling tea?"

"Aha! So you have heard of me!" Vulcan boasted, jabbing his elbow into Hades proudly. *What a malaka*, Hades thought, following Vulcan. The two entered a cramped kitchen area with an iron stove in the corner and a small redwood table. The walls here had even larger gaps in them than the ones in the entry.

"I have heard of you, Vulcan. Nothing good, but yes, I have," Shiva responded.

"How did you know it was us?" Vulcan asked. Hades was thinking the same thing. How in Sheol *did* he know?

"I saw you," Shiva replied gently, closing the door to the stove and pointing out a large hole in his kitchen wall. His long black hair was braided down his silk robe. The robe was untied, revealing a tattoo of a snake wrapping around his body. The head settled near his collar, staring forward.

Hades didn't look at the hole. He was unimpressed with this *lord*, and his home. *Why would anyone follow him as their leader*? he thought.

"Shiva," he said. "You were there at the Hall the other day. I assume you know why we are here, then?"

"Have a chair," Shiva said as if he hadn't heard Hades' question. He pulled out an uneven wooden seat hidden under the equally rotted table. Vulcan sat down and began rubbing his lame leg. Hades slid into another chair, reluctantly removing his hand from his nose.

"Would you like some tea?" Shiva asked, as he grabbed the kettle. *I know he heard me. This old god is losing it.*

Hades shook his head at Vulcan, mouthing the word, "No." He decided if the tea tasted as bad as it smelled, he would be satisfied swallowing his own spit before drinking that shit.

Vulcan spoke up. "Yes, yes we would. Both of us...thank you." Hades looked at Vulcan and remained stone-faced, refusing to let him know how annoyed he was with him. *You Bastard*, he thought.

"Good," Shiva said cheerfully, "Because I had already poured it for you." He brought three cups filled to the brim to the table, holding them by their abnormally large handles. Taking a mismatching stool from under the table, Shiva joined them.

"Can I ask why you do not have a door?" Vulcan asked.

"Simple," he replied. "I love the breeze. And with it comes the most amazing smells from the nearby flowers."

Hades glared at Shiva with his brow raised. Something didn't seem right about him. Shiva seemed quite pleased with himself, drinking such a foul smelling tea.

Hades stared down at his cup. *I am not drinking this shit.*

"Shiva, you were at the Hall. What do you think about Odin's banishment from good standing?" Hades asked.

Shiva sipped his tea, then slowly placed the cup back on the table, leaving his hands on the cup.

"Be careful, it is hot," he stated.

Hades lifted his hands to signal he didn't know why he was being ignored. Vulcan shrugged and shook his head in frustration. Vulcan then picked up the cup and took a sip.

"What do you think about what happened with Odin a few days ago?" Vulcan asked, repeating Hades' question.

"It was to be expected," Shiva finally answered. "And to be honest, I am more interested in why you are here right now, and how that correlates to Odin. So, why are you here?" Hades moved the tea so the steam wasn't rising to his face. *He wants me to drink his tea, yet ignores me? I will give him one last chance* to…

"We are here because we all are in danger," Hades said. "With Odin now gone, Thor has taken the throne in Asgard. As we speak, he prepares the Asgardians for an attack on Olympus." Shiva took another sip of his tea, closing his eyes and inhaling the aroma.

"I will ask again..." Shiva said, pausing again to breathe in the tea's aroma. "What are you here for?" Shiva locked eyes with Vulcan, as if they were the only two in the room.

"Well..." Vulcan said, looking at Hades with a smirk. Vulcan then repeated Hades' exact words in a deliberate monotone.

"And why would you come to an old god like me for help?" Shiva replied.

"He is not going to assist us," Hades decided. Shiva didn't flinch at his comment.

Vulcan took another sip, then said, "Alchemy is a trade long lost. Together, we could greatly affect the war. The Asgardians have no real alchemists except Baldr, but with us together--"

"I have no reason to join *your* games. I appreciate you coming for the tea, but I have no reason to invest in an *Immortal issue*."

Hades stood up abruptly, ignoring his tea. "Damn it, let us go home now, so we are not wasting another moment here with this senile old fool."

Vulcan held his hand up, pausing Hades and mouthing to him, "Just wait."

"It is indeed beautiful outside," Shiva said gazing out of the crooked window. "The pomegranate trees are producing amazingly this year."

Vulcan gazed out of the window. "Right, they look good." He quickly turned to Hades with a menacing smile and mouthed to him, "Got him."

He then observed Shiva. "Are you sure you will not join us against the Asgardian? You do know how Zeus feels about those that disregard his invitations?" Vulcan took a large sip of the tea, then continued, "You know Zeus had his writer record it for all to remember the quote, *'It is not possible either to trick or escape the mind of Zeus*."

"If I did not know any better, I would take your words as a threat," Shiva passively asserted.

Chapter 20 *Tea and a conversation*

"No, Shiva. How can I threaten someone of *your* status among the gods?" Vulcan calmly offered. Shiva stared into his cup, nearly empty, then finished it off with one quick gulp.

"You both are welcome to stay as long as you like. I know it is a long journey back." Shiva glanced over at Hades and smiled, eyes widened, appearing surprised by his presence.

"It is wonderful to see you," Shiva said, tapping Hades on the shoulder. "Please have some tea before you go, my friend. I am sure you will love it. How is Cerberus? I miss him. He was one of my favorite creations."

Hades lifted both of his hands, dumbfounded. *You want to notice me now?* he thought. Hades shook his head in frustration. He'd had enough of the idle talk.

"All right, enough. Vulcan, it is time." Hades stood, bumping the table with his knees carelessly. Some of the tea spilled from his cup, which Shiva quickly wiped up.

"Waste of time," Hades concluded. He was disappointed by Shiva. *How could anyone respect this old tea drinking fool?*

Hades said, "When this is over with the Asgardians, I swear by my own name I will be paying you a visit." He took a step forward toward the door, but Vulcan stopped him again. Shiva shook his head, staring at Hades.

"You are always welcome back," Shiva said, placing both hands on the table and preparing to stand, only to stumble back onto his seat.

"How was your tea, Shiva?" Vulcan asked with a snicker.

Shiva's eyes widened, "What did you do, Vulcan? Did you poison me? You did! You poisoned me!" He sat back down and examined his empty cup.

Vulcan grinned, with a wink toward Hades, then said, "I believe you may have only another few minutes before you go to Sheol, my friend." Vulcan reached into his cloak and pulled out a small clay jar, waving it in front of Shiva.

He continued, "It is Eitr. I learned this mixture from a damn Asgardian, if you can believe it. I guess it makes sense, if you are unwilling to use your skills with us, that you die at the hand of our common enemy by their skills."

Shiva tried to rise from the table, but immediately collapsed on the hard, cold floor. He reached for his neck, and his breathing slowed until he could barely inhale. Eyes crossing, he tried to speak but couldn't push the words out.

Waving the clay jar slowly, taunting Shiva with it, Vulcan stepped over him and lowered the jar to his face and asked, "Will you join us for an antidote?"

133

Shiva shook his head slowly, refusing Vulcan. Hades stood, watching with his mouth open, shocked, but with a subtle smile. He looked at Vulcan, almost proud, but definitely with jealousy. *Damn it! I wanted to be the one who killed this old twit.*

Vulcan stepped away from Shiva and passed Hades, limping out the doorway. "Now we can leave." The two made their way back to the horses they had tied off down the road. Hades threw a soft punch in Vulcan's shoulder.

"I have decided you are my new hero, Vulcan," Hades stated, observing the sun. "Maybe I should learn more about all that alchemy crap you do. That was amazing. How did you get it into his drink?"

"He was so busy staring out of the window, he never even noticed," Vulcan replied. Vulcan scratched his beard, gazing toward the mountains. "I feel weird though. I have never actually taken another's life."

Hades put his hand on his shoulder. "I understand that it is not easy, no matter how you do it." After a few steps further, Vulcan came to an abrupt stop, dropped to both knees, and slumped his head.

Before Vulcan could completely fall, Hades caught him, lowering him gently to the ground. His eyes were rolled back in his head, and a white mucus foamed out of his mouth. Hades frantically searched Vulcan's cloak for the antidote he had waved at Shiva.

"That one will not work," a voice announced from inside the house. Shiva stood in the doorway, sipping the full cup of tea meant for him.

"I said I had heard about him, Hades. I told him what I had heard was not good. He never should have tested me. A *true* alchemist always has a good amount of Mithridatum in his stomach, just in case a fellow alchemist decides to try and poison him." Shiva leaned over and lifted an arrow he had hidden behind the doorway. He placed it in his bow and took aim.

"You tell him that when you meet him in Sheol," he shouted, releasing the arrow. Hades leaped out of the way, but not quickly enough. The razor edge grazed him, slicing his leg open. Sprinting away, leaving Vulcan's body on the ground, Hades ran until he was out of the bow's reach.

Looking back, he saw Shiva had already put the bow away and was holding the tea again.

The cut immediately became inflamed. A burning sensation crawled up his calf, reaching his knee before he even knew to slow. Hades stumbled farther from the house until he was out of view, then quickly pulled away his leather boots.

His heart sank. *Damn*, he thought. A small green-blue rash already festering around the wound.

"Damn alchemists," he muttered. "And here I was laughing at Vulcan's stupid limp. I may not even have a damn leg tomorrow." He staggered to the horses and fled.

Chapter 21 *The search*

Sjofn and Tyr, sent by Thor, had now neared the city of Guangdong, a three day ride by horse. It was home of the Sanguan Dadi. The gate-free city was the largest in the Saggilmut that thrived as a culture. The gods living there did so under the presumption that they were on neutral ground, and therefore were free to do as they wished, be with whom they wished. It served as a haven created by the three gods.

Each of the three Sangaun Dadi gods had become known and worshipped by mankind as lords over the heavens, the waters, and the Earth. Each with their specific authority.

The crown jewel of the city was the irrigation system, which resulted in four rivers flowing from each direction coming into the city and clashing into a magnificent geyser that reached well above the highest buildings in the city. Even from a day away the waters could be seen, rising to the sky before flowing back down to the city.

Guangdong was a marvel, but for Sjofn it was even more. Since she had never left Asgard, this was so vastly different. It was special. Not that she didn't appreciate the greenery in Asgard, but Guangdong was unique. As they drew near, she could see the diverse influence of every sect.

"From a distance it was amazing, but up close it is even more magnificent," she exclaimed. Her eyes lit up at the sight of the buildings. Each building was distinct, and the city seemed alive with energy. Compared to Asgard, where all the structures were made of the nearby woods and were no taller than the trees used to build them, this metropolis was intimidating, yet breathtaking.

"Tyr, you can see the Asgardian influence here in this one," she said, pointing toward a stone building with moss flowing over the walls. She drew near, picking off a radiant long-stemmed blue flower that was growing between two stones. Closing her eyes, she took in the smell. *Summer by the ocean,* she decided.

"Oh, how I hope to come here with you and Bragi. I do love our gathering spot, but a trip would be amazing," she exclaimed. "Even Modi would love it, right?" Taking the stem, she weaved it above her ear so it hung in full display.

"A *poet's* trip. That would be nice," he chuckled. "I wonder who might live here?" Tyr questioned, gazing at the Asgardian home, then continued toward the city's square. Seeing the fountain from a distance, he had decided and told Sjofn that it would be a good starting point to ask where the Sanguan Dadi lived.

The closer they got to the fountain, the more impressive it became. Even with the few remaining buildings blocking their view of the four rivers churning together, it was amazing. The sheer force of the water rising was unlike anything they had seen before.

Turning the corner of the last building between them and the geyser, Sjofn had to pause and absorb the spectacle of it all.

"How could anyone create something like this?" she uttered to herself in amazement.

"You are not from around here," a voice declared from behind her. Turning around, Sjofn saw an elderly god sitting against the building. He looked frail and tired, but had a mischievous grin, albeit missing a few teeth. His oval eyes shone over an extremely long silver beard that flowed in the wind

"Excuse me?" she asked, hoping to spark a conversation. She knew that they were supposed to hurry, but she had already decided she was going to meet some gods in the city. Gods that she could tell Bragi and Modi about. She despised the assemblies in the Hall of Shamayim, resolving long ago to never go back unless they were peaceful. This god was the first she had met in centuries who wasn't Asgardian.

"Sjofn, please, if he does not know where the Sangaun Dadi are, then we have to move on," Tyr prompted.

She understood that they were in a hurry, but she couldn't live with herself if she was not personable to others. She had accepted that some found her zealous approach to life a bit annoying, but since Tyr wasn't one of them, she planned to absorb all the joy she could on this trip. For all the love she had for Asgard, she found them a bit too aggressive for her liking. Even Tyr, who was considered one of the *softer* gods, was sometimes more of a brute than she wished.

The old god replied, "I said, you are definitely not from Guangdong. Those who live here do not observe the Shuiguan Fountain the way that you do."

"Am I looking at it wrong?" Sjofn inquired, thinking she was missing some meaningful detail because she was too mesmerized to notice.

"Like someone who values it," he explained. "Most that live here walk by it without taking notice. They never take the time to appreciate it."

"Oh my lord, I could behold at it all day, every day," she gushed, swiveling her head between him and the waters. "Back home, I have a particular tree where a few of us go and spend the day watching the leaves sway in the wind. It is the most whimsi--"

"Sjofn!" Tyr interrupted. "Please, we have no time for this."

She agreed, but first said to her new acquaintance, "My lord, I hope to return one day and find you here. I feel like you have a world of knowledge, and I know I would enjoy your company." The two shared a final smile, and she hurried herself to catch up to Tyr, who had already walked away.

Following him, she slowed, now directly in front of the geyser. Sjofn had to tilt her head backward to see its height. Tyr had moved past this view and hailed a nearby god.

Tyr waved down a young woman rushing by. "Excuse me, I see you are in a hurry, but the Sanguan Dadi? Where can I find them?"

"They do not live here in the city," she responded. "I believe they live outside of the eastern gate in the Observer's temple, a day's journey."

"You believe?" he asked curiously. "You mean, you do not know?"

"Not exactly," she answered, stepping away. "I have never been there myself." She nodded, then continued on her way.

Stopping another passerby, he questioned that goddess as well. "Excuse me, where do the Sanguan Dadi live?"

"Do you see *that* mountain? The closest one of the Kailash hills," she replied hastily.

"Yes."

"Over it, on the north side, there is an entrance marked with two torches; they are always lit. From what I understand, they are there at a temple called the Emperor's Palace." Without waiting for a response, she moved on.

Tyr paused, then called out to her before she had gotten too far, "Wait, wait! Someone else just said they lived out the eastern gate in another temple and you are saying north. You are saying they live over the mountain. Are you sure?"

Pausing from her walk, the goddess looked back at Tyr. "What do you want me to say? I am only telling you what I have heard."

"I am sorry," Tyr responded, waving her off with a smile. "Thank you for your time." He turned around, spotting another person to speak to. The city had no shortage of gods or humans nearby. There were celebrations, small dance circles, people eating and conversing with gods, foods being prepared. *Everyone seems so...busy*, Sjofn thought.

"Someone has to know for certain," Tyr muttered.

It is so quiet, Sjofn thought to herself, amazed by the absolute power as the water soared upward.

Unable to stay focused on the task, she asked Tyr, "The sound should be deafening, but it is no louder than that small brook we go to near the western walls. Curious right?" Tyr stopped to consider this.

"You are right. It is odd, Sjofn." Tyr answered, taking a deep breath. Watching him enjoy it, even if briefly, made her grin. *He really is one of the good ones*, she thought.

"I am sorry," Tyr said. "I do not mean to come off as a *fif'l*, you know that. But finding the Sanguan Dadi is really important and I cannot fail." He turned and approached another passerby.

"Some people are backward," an older god confessed, approaching Sjofn, grinning behind his salt and pepper mustache. He resembled the other god she met who had been sitting against the wall, albeit older. "They spend their time chasing their thoughts and ideas to make Saggilmut a better place. When in truth, they should spend their time letting Saggilmut change their thoughts. Then it will be a better place. God or no god, we have to learn to let go of this facade."

"Facade?" she asked.

"Control," he said. "We can barely control our minds. How many times a day do you have to dismiss some random thought, that if observed, would surely lead you to trouble? If we cannot even have a thought in our mind without other unwanted thoughts barging in, we are best served to just sit back and enjoy it all."

"Yes, that is right!" Sjofn clapped, looking at him. "That is so beautiful. I need to remember to tell my friends. But my friend and I here have a very important task. He is actually a very warm person. It is just that he has a lot of pressure he is dealing with."

Figuring she could at least start to help Tyr, she asked, "Do you know where we can find the Sanguan *Doodi*?"

"Dadi," he stated, correcting her.

"Ohh, I apologize. The Sanguan Dadi, right. Do you know where we can find them?"

Shrugging his shoulder, he sighed, "I am sorry. I have not seen them today. I am sure they are around here somewhere though."

"What do you mean, *around here*?" she asked excitedly. Sjofn could not help but think how great it would be if she would be the one to find them before Tyr did.

"I have heard they come around here on nicer days like this," he answered. "I believe they have been here every day recently."

"Thank you, my kind lord," she replied. Excited, she turned quickly to search for Tyr.

Chapter 22 *The city square*

"Want to know how they made the geyser so quiet?" another older god asked, staring at Sjofn.

She found it hard to ignore such a kind face. He was slightly overweight, and his soft brown eyes nearly closed with his warm grin. Deciding she could spare a little more time to enjoy his company, she answered.

"Why yes. Please tell me."

Leaning in closer, he whispered as if it was a secret. "It is the air surrounding it. Most of the gods think there is something in the water that keeps it quiet, but Tianguan, the Sanguan Dadi who rules the heavens, altered the elements within the air around it, removing the air's ability to pass sound. Amazing, right?"

"How could he control air like that?" she asked in wonder.

"That is *his* secret to keep," he said, smiling. "But if you lean over the railing here just far enough, you will struggle to breathe." Nervous and hesitant, Sjofn stood on her toes and leaned forward. She leaned her head as close as she could toward the water. Trying to inhale, she found it was impossible, as if she were underwater. Pulling herself back, Sjofn shook her head excitedly, mouth wide open.

"That is amazing!" she exclaimed.

"Thank you for pausing in your busy day for an old god like myself," he replied, bowing his head.

"No, thank you," she assured him, bowing much farther, still smiling. She stood back up and saw Tyr being given directions. She waved goodbye to the god, then turned to tell Tyr the amazing news she had heard.

Nearing Tyr, she couldn't help but grin. "The old god just told me that on days like this the Sangaun Dadi gather near the geyser. Maybe if we wait here, then they will come to us?"

Flustered, scratching his brow, he answered, "It cannot hurt. I have asked at least six different gods and gotten seven responses." She giggled, but realizing he was stressed, she stepped closer, gently rubbing the back of his neck. They had always been close, and he was one of the few that she could touch who wouldn't misinterpret her kindness for anything more.

"Damn," Tyr said, dropping his head. "Thor will kill me before any Immortal gets the chance, if I fail him." Sjofn's eyebrows lifted, because she was not fully sure how to interpret that. She had just watched Thor demand the execution of his father.

"Not *literally*, Sjofn," he said, trying to reassure her. "It is just that we are not close at all, and I do not want to let him down. I would rather not let anyone down. Asgard law is--uh...you know what? Forget it. I do not want you to worry. Listen,

Thor only gave me today to find them. Since we have to return within a week, we need to be there before Bragi and Vidar return from Olympus. The three day ride here, and another three back does not give us much time. We need to hurry."

"Tyr, why won't he wait? Why is he attacking at all?" If given the authority, she would prefer to melt all the weapons in Saggilmut. But Odin always met that sentiment with the rebuttal, *"If the gods did not use weapons, they would still pick up the stones to fight with."*

In frustration, Tyr asked aloud to anyone in earshot, "How in Sheol do you all that live in this damn city and not even know where the Sanguan Dadi live?" Most of the people nearby paid no attention and continued scurrying about.

"I know where they live!" a single voice proclaimed. Both Tyr and Sjofn instantly spun around to see the god who had spoken. He was dirty, unkempt. His clothes had holes, and the worn shawl draped over his head appeared to let through more sunlight than it blocked. His eyes were far apart and nearly closed, but his crooked smile melted Sjofn's heart. *I want to take these gods home and just look at them all day, they seem so gentle.*

"You know where they are?" Tyr repeated.

"Yes, if you travel out of the Nan gate, that is the southern gate, in case you are unaware, then follow the road to the Osan river near the Duati Crossing then--"

147

Tyr dropped his head, "Forget it."

"What?" he asked. "I am sorry, did I mishear? I thought you were asking where the Sanguan Dadi lived."

Tyr scratched his cheek. Sjofn knew when he did that he was finally getting perturbed.

Quickly, she said, "It is just that we have now been told that they have a temple somewhere outside all four gates of this city. We mean no disrespect to you, my lord."

"Why did you travel here?" the stranger asked.

"We are from Asgard," she answered proudly. "We journeyed for three days to have the ear of the Sanguan Dadi."

"I understand, and that is quite a trip, but that does not answer my question," he retorted.

Realizing that was true, she replied, "It is an urgent matter, my lord, and we cannot tell just anyone. Please do not be offended. I am sure you are quite special, but we are here on the authority of Thor, King and Ruler of Asgard, and must speak with the Sanguan Dadi soon."

Puzzled, the god asked, "Thor...king?"

Sjofn said, "Yes, Thor has been king for three days now, after Odin was removed from good standing in the Hall. I am sure you must have heard of that by now." Based on his expression, he hadn't.

"Well, anyway, we were sent here the same day Thor became king. My lord, we are short of

148

time, so if you really cannot help us find them, then I am sorry, but I must stay focused and continue my search."

"And you do not think talking to me is part of your search?" he asked, tilting his head to one side.

Never good with a confrontation, she faltered. "I...I…"

"I have heard some terrible things the last few days," he announced. "Very terrible things."

"What do you mean?" she asked, now torn between talking to him and following Tyr, who was walking off to talk to another.

The god knelt, grabbed some sand, and slowly stood back up. Grinding the sand with his hands, he let it filter out, letting the breeze guide it back to the ground. He appeared hesitant.

"I have heard that the problems between the Asgardian and the Immortals have finally reached their breaking point. I must assume that is why you two are here."

"Then you can understand why it is so important we speak to the Sanguan Dadi," she asserted.

"I wish I could help you, but I did not realize there were so many false ideas about where they live. I did believe what I told you. If that is not true, then I am of no use to you. Unless..."

"Unless what, my lord?" she prompted him.

"My nephew. He is an architect and a trusted servant for them. I am sure he can take you to them or at least help point you toward them properly, if you were willing to walk with me to him?"

Sjofn's soft green eyes brightened. She held up one finger to pause him and cried out, "Yes, that would be amazing! Let me go and get my friend, and we will gladly follow you to him."

Tyr agreed without hesitation, since he had not turned up any real leads. The three set out toward the northern section of the city, and approached a modest home hidden between two much nicer ones. The house was missing a section of the roof that must have fallen directly into the front yard.

"If he is an architect, then he is not too good at his job," Tyr whispered to Sjofn.

Chapter 23 *Are they even real?*

Opening the small gate, the old god called out, "Puren!"

A younger god hurried from the front door, bowing toward him. "Guowang, it is so wonderful to see you." He quickly nodded and smiled at the two Asgardians before looking back to the old god.

The two spoke to each other in some sort of foreign language. Tyr and Sjofn glanced at each other. It was unlike anything she had ever heard. She watched them intently, hoping that would help. It didn't. After a few words, the young architect turned to Tyr and Sjofn.

He said, "I am sorry, but the Sanguan Dadi do not meet guests any longer. Only those closest to them personally have seen them for centuries. I am sorry, but there is no chance they will meet you today, or ever. I thought everyone in Saggilmut was aware they had reclused themselves. I can share a message with them, if you are willing to tell me."

Sjofn didn't know what to think. *Did they ever go to the geyser and spend time there, as the old god had said? Did they live outside of Guangdong in some hideout? Why the mystery?* she thought. All she knew was that she didn't want Tyr to fail.

Sjofn was worried. "What should we do?"

Tyr shrugged. "Should we?" he paused, contemplative. "We did not come to sightsee. May as well tell them...I guess we have no choice." Tyr asked Puren, "If we tell you why we are here, when will you be able to go and speak to them?"

"Tonight, my lord," Puren answered calmly. "I must go speak to them on another matter, so I could bring your issues forth as well. You are welcome to remain here with Guowang until I return."

Tyr looked at Sjofn, searching for an answer in her eyes. She stared back, unsure of his thoughts. If she had her way, she would have told them everything. However, her father often told her, *The smile and trust you give to a neighbor will lead you into self-imposed trouble.* She didn't want to tell Tyr to *just* trust them, that everything would end up fine.

Let him decide.

Tyr shoulders dropped as he pondered his options. "Maybe I do not tell him, but follow him to their temple instead?" Sjofn didn't reply. He continued, "But if I got caught, then who knows how they would react to such a deception. If the Sanguan Dadi hide from their own people, then I am sure they would happily just kill me to make sure their location stays hidden." Sjofn nodded, listening, but refusing to speak. She didn't know what to say, and since he was ultimately responsible she thought it best to let him decide.

Tyr said, "If that is the case, we have no choice but to trust them, right?" She remained silent, nodding.

"Thank you for your advice, Sjofn," Tyr patted her shoulder.

Tyr told Puren everything pertaining to the impending war. He explained how the Immortals had long treated others, such as the Sh'losh, with grave injustices. And that the great King Thor would bring reprisal. Sjofn watched, excited as Tyr spoke with such conviction. *Huh, he is a bit attractive when he is passionate about something*, she thought.

Tyr explained that Thor had promised if the Sanguan Dadi joined Thor's plan to overthrow Zeus, that he in turn would assist them to usurp Osiris. And that they would be proclaimed Kings of all Duat. From the corner of her eye, Sjofn saw the old god grin and rub his hands together, as Tyr mentioned the Sangaun Dadi becoming king of Duati. Puren listened intently.

"I will tell them *everything* you have told me, *just* as you have told me," Puren assured them. The old god hugged him and shared a few more foreign words before Puren left.

"Thank you," Tyr said, relieved.

Puren turned to Sjofn and said, "Please, eat. Enjoy anything I have in my kitchen." Tyr watched Puren run off toward the city square.

"Has to be headed toward the western gate," Tyr whispered to Sjofn. "I knew it!"

They spent the remainder of the day and late into the evening on a large rock in the back yard outside the home. Sjofn saw no reason to sit in a home without a roof. *Might as well be outside*, she decided.

As the night carried on, Sjofn urged the old god to share more about himself and Guangdong. Instead, the old god sang songs, and Sjofn danced her heart out, humming along with the melody. Sjofn didn't comment, but she noticed that Tyr, normally disinterested in music and dancing, was swaying with the music that night.

Later, Sjofn raided the fruit basket in the kitchen and enjoyed the choicest ones that Guangdong had to offer. Some of these she had never seen before. Picking a bright red-orange fruit, she struggled to peel it. Inspecting it, she found no opening, nor stem to start from. The other two gods began laughing as she continued to struggle. Her face became flushed, partly because she was angry at being outwitted by a piece of fruit, and partly because she enjoyed watching them laugh, albeit at her.

"You...you stupid piece of fruit," she said, laughing. She studied it, still determined to open that damn thing no matter how long it took.

Well after midnight, Tyr and the old god had fallen asleep under the back door awning. Sjofn

154

was sitting against a rock in the middle of the yard, throwing the fruit against the wall of the home for what felt like the hundredth time. As it had every time previously, the fruit bounced, then rolled back near her, unharmed.

"I hate you," she said, holding it up eye-level, facing the fact that she couldn't win. It was the first thing Sjofn had ever hated. Dropping her hand to the ground, she forgot about the champion fruit as she gazed at the stars, some firing across the night. Her eyes became increasingly heavy. With each shooting star she closed her eyes for a little longer, until she couldn't keep them open.

"Hello," a voice said, waking up Sjofn from her brief slumber. Struggling to open her eyes, she realized it was Puren.

"Hey, Puren," she said, propping herself up. Lifting her hand, she displayed the fruit, "I cannot figure out how to peel this stupid thing."

"You do not peel it, you just take a bite and it dissolves in your mouth," he answered, kneeling next to her. "But Sjofn, you need to wake up. I spoke with the Sanguan Dadi." Shaking herself awake, she took a hesitant bite of the fruit. Her teeth instantly pierced the skin and the juicy fruit poured out, down her chin.

"Why, this is the greatest thing I have ever tasted," she exclaimed. She stared at the fruit, then said, "I am sorry for saying I hate you. I *adore* you." She took another bite.

"Did you hear me?" Perun asked. "I said I spoke with the Sanguan Dadi." His statement snapped her back to reality, and she sat up to reply, "And...?"

"They said you can go home *in* peace."

"Go home? Wait, why? They said no?" She dropped her fruit to the ground.

He continued, "Please, wake your friend and let him know. They said go *in* peace." Sjofn burst into tears and ran to Tyr, who had already awoken. She fell into his arms and he hugged her, patting her back.

"So, the answer is no, then?" he asked, still consoling Sjofn. Puren stared at him, emotionless.

"Did they at least offer a reason?" Tyr asked.

"Nothing," Sjofn shrugged nervously. All she could think about was how they had traveled three full days, and were now leaving with nothing.

"Please, my lord. They said go home *in* peace," Puren repeated. With that, the two stood up, agreeing to head back to where their horses were tied off. As they left the yard and walked down the street, Puren called for their attention. They stopped and heard him say once again, "They said, *in* peace."

"Do you know what he means, *in* peace?" Sjofn asked Tyr. He shrugged.

"They are not coming, so who cares if we go *in*, *out*, *over*, *or under* their peace?" he muttered.

Sjofn stopped, took a deep breath, then ran back toward the old god, still standing in the front yard watching them.

Hugging him, she whispered, "May we have a swift victory over the Immortals, so that you may be safe."

"I am sure we will," he responded.

Letting go of him, she picked up her fallen fruit and without wiping it off, she took a bite. She caught back up and grabbed Tyr by the arm, resting her head on his shoulder. They began their long journey back.

"Can we take a different way home?" Sjofn asked. "Maybe we can see some more amazing sights on the way.

"Absolutely," he answered, clenching her shoulder.

"Want to hear a poem I thought up about Guangdong?" she asked.

"Absolutely."

Chapter 24 *Read a book sometime*

"I just can't believe it," Aaron said, walking down the bright halls toward the library.

"I see this is troubling you," Dagon answered, a step behind him. After nearly four days in the library, Aaron felt antsy. He was tired of gazing into the same book all day, in the same chair, being stared at by Dagon the entire time. He wasn't the greatest conversationalist, Aaron decided. *I have to work on that. I can't have this stiff following me around. Have to break that wall and get him talking.*

"Of course it *bothers* me," he answered. "When you ask me what I think Heaven is going to be like, I'm thinking I can just somehow know what you're thinking, and we don't have to talk at all. What is that? Telekinesis? No, telepathy or something, right?" Turning through a wall and heading down another hallway, Aaron continued, "Or maybe I can just imagine being somewhere, and I'd instantly be transported. Heaven sounds so...boring, so old fashioned."

Shaking his head, Aaron walked through the wall, entering the library. He had finally grown comfortable with *the invisible wall trick.*

"Really though, at the very minimum, you could all make some kind of fast transportation, a car, train, *something*. But this book is telling me it's basically like the Wild West out there."

"Wild West?" Dagon asked, following Aaron through the wall into the library.

"Yeah," he answered, taking a seat. "You know? America back when cowboys were riding around on horses, before, you know--technology." He couldn't help but laugh at his joke. With a quick glance, he saw Dagon's fish face, unmoved. "I can't believe it. I'll have to ride a horse in heaven. Weird."

"*Saggilmut*," he corrected.

"Right, right, I won't call it heaven anymore; it's called *Saggilemeet*." He knew he was still mispronouncing. "I mean, I get what you're saying about electronics not being connected to spirituality and one's best self...*yada-yada*, but horses? It's just so, I don't know what the word is-- uninspired?"

Aaron took a seat in the room and sighed. The library was a small room, no larger than his bedroom. No windows or outside light. Aaron had yet to step outside, or even see a window. There were the same illuminating white walls he had grown accustomed to seeing. There were two chairs, facing each other, both made of a bright red wood with a soft cushion that Aaron looked forward to sinking into. Between the chairs stood a single red wooden stand displaying the only book in the room.

159

As he had done the other three days, Aaron grabbed the same black book and opened it. To a blank page. They were all blank at first.

"Okay," he said, settling himself deep into the cushion. "Tell me about the Unspoken." Immediately, letters began to flow onto the pages, filling the book with details relating to the *unspoken* gods.

Flipping through the pages, he said, "You do see the irony in their name, right?"

"It is not missed," Dagon replied stiffly. *He's so uptight, he needs to relax,* Aaron thought.

"And? Care to fill me in?"

"I assumed you would prefer to read about them, as it is clearly described on the very first page," he answered. Aaron clamped down on his lower lip. *Why read when you can just tell me?* he thought, staring down at the book.

Dagon scratched a gill on the side of his face then answered, "For the gods, the worst thing that can happen is to be erased, forgotten. Hence, when a god is shamed, they are punished by losing their good standing in the Hall, like Odin was. But to become one of the Unspoken means something altogether different. You will be sent to the worst part of Sheol upon death, erased from ever having another chance to gain your name again."

"How many are there?" he asked.

"Aaron," Dagon replied sternly. Aaron nodded, agreeing to be quiet and just read. Scanning the page, his eyes began catching the names. *Kaal, The Destroyer, usher of the deluge.*

"Wait, so Kaal brought the flood to the world?" Aaron asked.

"He is the son of Shiva, who is lord of the Kailash hill in Duat. Kaal, a rebellious one, took part in bringing the flood, or the ice age as some call it, yes," Dagon answered. "Your world's entire ecosystem is based on a program, a system. It was once managed on Saggilmut, but was moved here to Shamayim after their attack."

"So, the whole Noah and the Flood thing was real?" Aaron asked.

"Not exactly how you heard it, but yes, there was a flood. You know of the man as Noah, while other cultures heard the story of Gilgamesh. Other peoples in history have recorded different names and reasons why the gods chose to flood the earth. In all these stories you grew up hearing, there is often a shred of truth."

Aaron nodded in disbelief. *That's crazy*, he thought. *And here I was thinking all these religions were full of it.* He lowered his head and kept reading.

"Ishtar," he read aloud. "She sounds wicked."

"She is the worst of them all, Aaron. In the beginning, she was placed in charge over the Earth. She ran the weather systems, the ecosystem, and designed many of the animals still roaming. Ishtar was given special abilities by the Most High at the request of Odin. They thought she could be their representative on Earth, a loving ambassador. She was quite beautiful and wise, and we were all fooled by her. She turned against everyone, both gods and mankind. Not only did she give access to the system Kaal and others used to flood the Earth, but she was the one who planned it."

"And all these gods live in Saggilmut somewhere?" he asked.

"We do not know," Dagon answered. "It is possible she is in Sheol, on Earth, or hiding in a cave on the island of Baltia in Saggilmut. No one knows."

"And if we see her?" Aaron asked.

"If we see her, it means she probably meant for us to find her. Which means we are going to die and be sent to Sheol, or she has some manipulative plan we have already fallen into. She tends to stay a step or two ahead of the rest. A truly grave problem now that she has chosen to follow her evil inclinations." Aaron had heard enough about her. *Avoid Ishtar, check.*

"Let's just hope we don't ever run into her then." He continued randomly flipping the pages, looking for whatever caught his eye.

"Supay," Aaron read. "The demon, the initiator of human sacrifice." *Damn.*

Wandering the page of names, Aaron began reading over the names one after another.

"Mot, beginner of death. Kaal, Malsumis, Medjed, Buluc Chabtan." Aaron felt sick reading over some of the things they had done.

"And what? They're all just hiding around Saggilmut?" Aaron asked. Just the idea of running into any of them was frightening.

"As with Ishtar, the truth is, we do not know," Dagon admitted. "Saggilmut is a large place, but so is Earth. They have not been seen for at least two centuries. We have no idea."

"What if they are planning their next attack?" Aaron replied.

Dagon nodded. "Most of them are similar to hyenas, they have no leader. They will kill one victim and leave another. They burn one city down but walk through another unharmed. They are nothing more than chaos in god form. There is no reasoning to their madness."

"Alright, enough of *that* shit," Aaron declared. "Language?" Aaron asked. "How does everyone speak the same language?" The words erased from the pages, and new words began filling in. Aaron began reading intently, page after page.

"That's incredible!" he blurted. "So, our minds listen to whatever someone is saying in their language, and just decipher it into our own?"

Dagon nodded, "Correct, language is nothing more than one's thoughts processed into data in a relatable way. In Saggilmut, the mind of the one listening simply translates the data into their own native tongue."

"So everyone speaks and hears their own language, but we still perfectly understand each other?"

"Yes, although some phrases are not translatable, and there are some gods that have learned to bend and even break the system, creating their own language."

"That's pretty cool," he decided.

Dagon tapped his fingers on his leg, then said, "Now just imagine how much more you could know if you continued reading instead of stopping every few minutes to be shocked or amazed?"

"Do you know how often you make me feel dumb?" Aaron asked with a smile. Dagon didn't reply, he just stared at Aaron, scratching his gill.

Aaron buried his face back into the book. "I have a few words for you, but I'd rather not say them, since you're a god and all that."

"I assume they are not kind ones," Dagon said.

"Nope, not at all," he replied, laughing to himself.

"Good, then be quiet," Dagon replied. They both shared a chuckle, and Aaron got back to his studies.

Chapter 25 *The Meeting*

Four days after the assembly in the Hall, and as agreed upon with Baldr, Zeus traveled to the wellspring on the southern edge of Mount Hor. Zeus brought with him Jove and Neptune. They all had worn sackcloth garments with hoods, to avoid being noticed on their journey.

Waiting at the oasis, spear in hand, Jove glanced at the sun blazing down on them. All three gods had left their tridents back in Olympus, to avoid anyone recognizing them. *This damn thing, feels too light*, Jove thought, twirling it around a few times.

Both Jove and Neptune sat on a few large rocks near the well, but Zeus remained standing, leg shaking. He always appeared agitated when he was actually nervous. Jove ignored it.

The well was small and made of uncut stones. Next to it, a metal bucket was tied off to some nearby rocks that had collected dirt after years of neglect. No one used it any longer. The people of Saggilmut wouldn't dare travel outside of their own province, let alone to the middle of the country.

The region near Mount Hor was the only neutral territory in Saggilmut. Once designated by the Most High as his meeting place, now the area was desolate. This wasn't by the Most High's decree, but because the feuding kings demanded their people no longer travel to the mountain for his new moon festivals, when the Most High would visit.

The well was still littered with dead flower petals and various pots containing scented oils from all over the land. The aroma surrounded the well, carried aloft by the wind. Jove sat on the rocks, shading his eyes as he scanned the area, enjoying the freshness of incense lingering in the air.

Zeus paced nervously. He whispered to himself, moving his hands as if speaking to someone. Jove knew Zeus wasn't much for confrontations, unless he had the bigger army or an easy out.

"They are here," Jove announced, gazing into the distance. Zeus immediately turned his head westward toward Asgard province, which was nearly a two-day journey. Zeus saw Baldr riding in on a flaxen chestnut stallion. Svetovid galloped along beside him on a larger white stallion. Svetovid was an impressive god, tall with short, thick brown hair. He was one of the few Asgard gods that didn't keep a beard. He was greatly feared outside of the Asgardian province.

Baldr had deep russet eyes that even from a distance made Jove uncomfortable. Jove preferred judging others by their actions, but Baldr's bulging eyes had a way of making Jove feel that he enjoyed the battles between the sects. Perhaps he got excited

166

watching others die in front of him, Immortal or Asgardian; it didn't matter.

"Peace," announced Baldr, approaching Zeus.

"Yes, Peace to you," Zeus replied, headed to Baldr's horse. Baldr dismounted, extending his arm to Zeus. The two clasped forearms. Jove lifted himself from the rock and nodded toward Baldr, but wasn't comfortable with locking forearms with him. He instead walked away, taking another seat on a group of rocks a short distance away.

He was content with watching his king, listening, but respecting Zeus' position over him. Jove and Zeus often argued, but Jove would never disagree with him in front of others outside of the Immortal council.

Svetovid had remained on his horse a distance away as Baldr instructed.

"I asked you to come alone," Baldr said, motioning toward Jove and Neptune.

"And I see you brought someone yourself," Zeus answered. "Do you expect me to be so stupid as to have a sit-down with my enemy, and just believe we are…what, friends? You have to earn my trust, Baldr, not yet anyway."

"You are right," Baldr replied. "But I am here now to fix that. Svetovid does not know why we are really here. He is just protection."

Zeus pointed toward the rocks near the well, and they took a seat facing each other.

Zeus began, "Then I should first be open with you. After we spoke in the Hall, and you told me you wanted to meet, I then spoke with Osiris. He will be arriving soon, I am sure."

"You told him?" Baldr asked, troubled at the news.

"Yes, absolutely, and he has agreed to help defend my land. You do not think I will simply roll over and let Thor destroy everything I have built, do you?"

"Who else did you tell?" Baldr was now clearly uneasy. Fidgeting, he glanced back at Svetovid. Jove wouldn't dare show any emotions to incite Baldr to leave the meeting, but he enjoyed watching Baldr squirm at the news.

"Baldr, you seem nervous," Zeus chuckled, as he glanced back at Jove for assurance. "You asked to meet me, remember? You came to me. I had assumed you understood that when the dust settled, I will be the one left standing, not your brother." Staring at their shadows, Zeus continued, "I have done everything I can to keep your father Odin from taking my kingdom, and I will do the same against your brother."

"I understand that, but with Osiris' military, you have doubled in size," Baldr argued. He stepped away from the rocks, his fists clenched. "If the Duat ally with you, and my brother *somehow* loses, how can you guarantee to me that you both will not just mount your assault and attack Asgard?

168

I need you to take an oath that my kingdom will be safe from you and those Duati. I am not giving you any damn information without a guarantee I will be alive after all this."

Zeus didn't respond. Instead, he leaned back, placing his hands behind his head. *Damn it,* Jove thought. *I hate it when he gets cocky.*

Finally, Zeus said, "If you are on the battlefield, I am not making a single promise. I will not tell my gods or soldiers to hold anything back against you. Your safety is dependent upon you staying the Sheol off the battlefield. I recommend, if you want to live, that you find a way to avoid it altogether, but that has nothing to do with me. I can give you my oath that *when* we stop Thor's assault, I will not attack Asgard. I know that I can speak on Osiris' behalf in saying he would not attack. He wants us all to agree and work on a treaty. He is a bit of an idealist and naive, if you ask me."

"Fine," Baldr answered. "I am sure I can get my brother to leave me back in Asgard for some reason. They will need someone to be in charge while he is gone anyway. I just want to ensure my safety so that once this is done I am still alive."

Squinting, Zeus asked, "Do you mean alive, or *King*?"

Chapter 26 *I want what is mine*

"Yes, I want the throne," Baldr replied. "And I have the damn *rightful* claim to Asgard. You are already a king, so you should understand. I have had to stand off to the side, watching as both my father and now, even after only a few days, my brother waste their time in needless fighting. I can make Asgard what it is supposed to be. Why? Does that *bother* you that I am using all the tools laid before me?"

Zeus smiled. "Not at all. I like knowing where everyone stands. So, Baldr, what news do you have for me then? Or did you drag me out here for nothing more than to dream with you of killing your own brother?"

Baldr glanced over to Svetovid. He was sitting on his horse, spitting on the ground at a small lizard running under his horse.

"What an idiot," Baldr decided, shaking his head. Looking back at Zeus, Baldr spat on the rocks and continued. "Thor was proclaimed king immediately on our return to Asgard. Shortly after, he sent emissaries to Guangdong to find the Sanguan Dadi. They have an army behind them, so if the messengers can get them to somehow join Asgard in the fight then you are going to have a serious problem on your hands. And that is even with Osiris' military behind you."

"Damn," Zeus replied. "How long before you know if they are with you?"

"It is no less than a seven-day trip back and forth to the city, so we expect their return within another few days."

Zeus stared off into the sky, then asked, "And if they, for whatever reason, actually do join with him, how long before you plan to attack?"

"As soon as possible," he answered. "In less than thirty days Thor wants to go to the next assembly that the Most High called as the King of gods, ruler of all three provinces. He is not like my father. He will not wait centuries, just to trip himself up. Thor is coming with everything immediately."

Jove leaned back against the rocks. He let the idea of Thor ruling Saggilmut seep into his mind. *No way that can happen*, he thought. *A mindless savage. He would treat anyone that was not Asgardian like shit. I assume they think the same about Zeus, after banishing the Sh'losh. I guess all of Sagiglmut does. I cannot see anyone fit to run this world properly.* Jove watched Baldr and Zeus, frustrated, listening in.

Zeus said, "Then I want to meet again one week from today to get any new information. By then these messengers should have returned from Guangdong, and Thor should have more of a plan developed. Then you and I will be able to hopefully plan against him."

"Yes, that sounds good," Baldr answered, "I will send a Hoopoe the moment they arrive back with further information. On that, I swear."

Zeus nodded his agreement. "I think Neptune should go with you when you return today. He can remain outside of your walls hidden, just to ensure there are no surprises. I have to be sure that if Thor decides to attack, I will have some notice. And no offense, but I trust my gods over you at this point." Baldr raised his hands in a gesture of surrender.

"Fine," Baldr answered, clearly upset.

"Just out of curiosity, what happened to Odin?" Zeus asked.

"Thor tried to have him killed, but he escaped."

"Really?" Zeus asked in disbelief. "Why kill him?"

Baldr shrugged. "Asgardian Law dictates. It does not matter anymore. He is gone now, but I can tell you that we want him dead as much as I am sure you do."

Zeus scratched his beard and glared at Jove wide-eyed. *Why would he lie about that?* Jove thought. *Finally, something I can believe.*

"Thor tried to have his own father killed," Zeus repeated.

Baldr said, "I thought after all these years, you would have known by now. Thor is not the type to be reasoned with. He believes in Asgard and our laws, maybe to a fault."

"And scouts? How many scouts were sent to Olympus?" Zeus prodded.

"Scouts?" Baldr repeated, glancing at the sky, and rubbing his chin. "To my understanding, there were no scouts sent out yet."

Zeus seemed skeptical. "Really? The mighty Thor sends his gods to ask for help, but not to recon his enemy's land?"

"Every breath Thor takes is for the glory of Asgard. He is loyal. Maybe more so than any other Asgardian. But he is also an idiot. All I can tell you is the main attack will occur sometime in the morning, probably before the sun rises. Like a typical raid, once we get into your gates, then they will do what they do best--lay the city to waste."

"How many?" he asked.

"A half a million from Valhalla," Baldr answered confidently. "The best-trained warriors this world has ever seen."

"We have Spartans," Jove replied, smiling. "But please, keep going." *There is no way those Vikings make it past the Spartan defense.* As commander of the Immortal army, Jove believed that Thor could be held off. But more than him or Thor, Jove believed it was up to Zeus more than anyone. *If Zeus was willing to put his ego to the side and listen to me*, he surmised.

173

Baldr continued, "Thor is simple, Zeus. He is going to attack one point of your defense until it snaps. Then, it is over."

"He must have *some* tactics. Even he is not stupid enough to come right at my walls head-on? Tell me he has not found the Unspoken, or has some alchemy concoction he will unveil?"

"For what?" Baldr answered. "Thor believes he will roll over your forces. That you are all soft and unwilling to get down in the mud and fight. That you are too *civilized*." Zeus bent over and picked up some dirt, rubbing it in between his hands.

Baldr added, "And even Thor is not deranged enough to think he can tame the Unspoken. They are a bomb that would blow up both sides." It was the first time in their conversation that Jove completely believed what Baldr was saying.

Svetovid, still on horseback, rode around Baldr and Zeus, pulled up near Jove, and dismounted.

Staring at him, Svetovid smirked, "How are you, my *friend*?" Shaking his head, Jove understood that he was trying to provoke an argument. Jove gripped his spear and returned the stare.

"I am well, and you, *friend*?" Jove replied sarcastically.

Svetovid said, "I assume you are both here to discuss your surrender? It is the only thing that makes sense to me. Bunch of delicate bitches, if you ask me."

Unwilling to back down, Jove answered, "I am surprised anything makes sense to you." Jove crossed his legs, leaning back on the rock, relaxed. He wanted to show Svetovid that he wasn't afraid. He refused to be bullied, even if it meant losing his life to the much larger god.

Svetovid leaned in and whispered, "You know I could kill you right here, and I could not care less what Baldr thought."

"You can try," Jove replied, glaring up at him while shielding his eyes from the sun.

"Be careful," he warned Jove. "We Asgardians have a law under the Norse philosophy. If a stranger insults you twice, we can walk away. But if a foreign god slanders a third time, then I have the duty to bury them."

Jove rubbed his thumb against the edge of the spear. It was cold to his touch, despite the heat of the day. "With all due respect, despite being an Immortal, if I had to die, then I would die good and old, lying on the grass overlooking Saggilmut from the mountain I call home. And despite your lack of hygiene, I hope you will die at a ripe old age surrounded by loved ones, and doing whatever it is you see fit for yourself."

Svetovid laughed mockingly, "That silver beard tells me you are old already." Jove didn't reply. Calmly, he twirled his beard in his fingers. *What a malaka*, he thought.

Chapter 27 *Family Business*

"Zeus," Neptune called out, breaking up their deep discussions. "Zeus!" He shouted again, this time getting his attention. Zeus clearly understood why Neptune was calling for him. Osiris had arrived, along with a small team of Duati gods.

Osiris rode in on a glistening chariot led by two black stallions. He stopped near Jove, Neptune, and Svetovid. Osiris leaped off, signaled back toward his Duati gods, then handed the reins to Horus, who was next to him on the chariot. Ra was on horseback next to the chariot. Osiris walked straight toward Baldr.

Without warning, he bypassed Zeus's extended hand, grabbed Baldr by the neck with one hand, and pulled out a dagger, placing the tip along his neck. The blade's edge immediately drew a single drop of blood. Before Svetovid could react, both Ra and Horus had their spears aimed at him. Toth and several other gods held bows with arrows already locked on ready to fire at any one of them. Jove remained on the ground, relaxed, watching Osiris to see what he had planned next.

"Hear me now and hear me well!' Osiris barked at Baldr. "I know you have sent spies to my land. Thor's sons no less." Baldr closed his eyes, flinching, expecting Osiris to kill him.

His color rising, he whimpered. "I d-did not know. I have no idea what you are talking about."

"Liar!" Osiris insisted. "Now, because of your foolishness, one of Thor's sons is dead and the other is waiting to join him in Sheol."

Jove leaned forward to see Baldr's reaction. Baldr's eyes were bloodshot, but he didn't react, despite hearing that one of his nephews had been killed.

Osiris continued, "Why did you send them to my province? What business does Asgard have with us?" Baldr glanced over at Zeus.

Zeus said, "Baldr just told us that he was unaware of messengers or spies sent anywhere except Guangdong." Osiris didn't move.

Baldr added, "I had no idea. I did not know of any plan to send them. Thor must have se--"

"Liar!" Osiris roared again. "I give my oath in my name, if you are lying--"

"I-I am not l-lying," Baldr whispered, behind Osiris' grip. Osiris pushed his blade a little farther, drawing another drop. Then, after a sigh, he relented and took a step back, still gripping the blade.

Baldr bent over, gasping for air and massaging his neck. Ra and Horus raised their spears. Neptune's brows raised as if entertained by it all.

Baldr, still trembling, said, "I am h-here to help. I did not know you were coming before Zeus told me after arriving, Osiris. B-But even if I had known, I would have come either way. If you are allying with Zeus, then I am here to help you, too. But I cannot help with what I do not know." Osiris didn't reply. Instead, he glanced back at his group.

"Which one is alive?" Baldr asked, wiping the blood with his fingertip.

"Does it matter?" Osiris responded, taking a seat on a large rock near the spring. "Have you two already discussed their attack plans?"

Zeus answered, "Yes, before you arrived, Baldr had begun to tell me Thor's plans. We also agreed to meet here again in another week, so Baldr can update us with any new information."

"Seven days?" Osiris asked. "You believe the Asgardians would not have already mounted their army and be halfway to Olympus by then?"

Zeus shook his head and answered, "No, I do not think so. The Asgardians are waiting on word from messengers sent to the Sanguan Dadi. There is no way they are going to move until Thor knows if they are willing to join them or not."

"Damn it," Osiris said to himself. "They can be easily persuaded and have plenty of warriors at their disposal. We *have to* assume they will agree."

"Why would they?" Zeus asked. "What is in it for them? They are Duati--your gods, Osiris. Control them."

"I do not enslave my gods; it is their choice," Osiris answered. "And I know Thor can dangle the prospect of ruling Duat over their heads. If the Sangaun Dadi believe he would help them take over the land, then they are in. They want to rule, plain and simple. Removing you from the equation, Zeus, only betters the odds of their ultimate goal to rule. With both of us out of the way, then it is only them and Thor left to rule. Much better odds."

Zeus asked, "Are you willing to battle against your own, Osiris?"

Osiris said, "I will fight to keep the peace. I am not fighting against any one person like you are, Zeus. I am fighting against *anyone* that believes they should rule alone using an iron fist. Anyone that believes they should have absolute control, especially if they plan to take it by the sword."

"I will send a hoopoe to both of you the moment we know if the Sangaun Dadi have joined them," Baldr assured them.

Zeus said, "Then I believe we are done until we can confirm whether they are fighting or not." Baldr agreed and extended his arm toward Osiris.

"Wait," Osiris said, signaling back toward Toth. Still, a distance away, Toth turned and signaled toward the grove of trees.

A moment later Magni emerged from behind a trunk that was marked with a large triangle. He was blindfolded, and his hands were tied behind his back. Seth, who was holding him steady, untied his blindfold and pointed him toward Baldr. Magni sprinted toward his uncle, struggling to keep his balance.

Baldr left his horse and ran toward Magni. Jove followed on foot, using his spear as a walking stick.

Reaching Magni, Baldr embraced his nephew tightly. Then he grabbed Magni's head with both hands, kissing his forehead. Magni looked bewildered at what he was seeing.

"Baldr, what are you doing here?" he asked. Baldr stepped around him to untie the rope binding his wrists.

Baldr explained, "I learned of your capture and quickly set up a negotiation with them for your release. Have you seen your brother Modi?" Jove was amazed how quickly Baldr came up with the lie, but didn't say anything. *That is family business*, he concluded.

"Not since we got separated. From what they told me, Modi is dead."

With tears in his eyes, Baldr replied, "Do not worry. All that matters now is we were able to mediate your return, and that you are safe." Svetovid rode up to them trailing Baldr's horse. Both Baldr and Magni mounted, and with Svetovid, the three began their journey back to Asgard.

"I will see you soon, old god," Svetovid taunted.

"I hope so," Jove waved mockingly.

"Stop!" Zeus ordered. "Are you forgetting someone?" Neptune galloped to join the three and nodded to them.

"What is happening?" Magni asked.

"I will explain on the way," Baldr said.

"I bet you will," Jove jabbed, heading back toward Zeus and Osiris.

Osiris, Zeus, and Jove talked late into the evening about what Baldr had revealed. They discussed war strategies, and Osiris agreed to have his armies prepared to travel within one week.

Chapter 28 *Man in Heaven*

"Crap," Aaron said to Dagon. "Mount Olympus is amazing!" He had finally finished his fourth day in the library, and Dagon led him through the Crossing to the mount. He stood to the west of the glimmering city, admiring everything.

"And you are sure you did not want to go to Asgard first?" Dagon smirked.

"Yeah," he answered, with a sarcastic thumbs-up. "I'm sure." After his meeting with Thor at the Hall, he decided he would visit Asgard last of the three sects. He'd rather put off Thor's insults and threats as long as he could.

"The castle is right near the tower," Dagon announced as they headed down the trail leading toward the gate. The white stone tower rose twice the height of the matching stone walls that wrapped around the city. Aaron couldn't see the city beyond the walls, but the tower was more than enough for him. He imagined what the view must be like from up there.

"That's incredible," he said, mesmerized.

"It is," Dagon agreed.

They made their way to the western gate. Aaron kept his eyes on the tower until the walls captured his attention. They were made of white limestone, each block being tall and broad. He imagined himself standing on Dagon's shoulders, then figured that each stone was both higher and longer in dimension than them together.

"Tell me how many people live here again?" he asked.

Dagon gazed at the top of the wall, clearly struck by its beauty. "Nearly five million people live within the walls."

Incredible, he thought. *How could Thor ever get through these walls?* He couldn't help but ponder how the walls midway up must have stayed so pristine. *Somebody must risk their lives to clean up there*, he surmised. *Poor guy, I know the feeling.*

Aaron felt like he knew the layout of the city through the maps and descriptions from his time in the library, but to see it in person was something altogether different. He stood at the arching western entrance, mouth agape.

Dagon said, "Remember what the Most High said, You are here to observe. You cannot interfere, or I am unable to protect you."

"I got it," Aaron said. He was too enthralled by Olympus to concern himself with Dagon's warning.

The entrance through the western walls was a single door. It stood tall, and was made of red bark. The door's hinges were made of saggilmut stone, latching the door to the white-stone arch frame. Getting closer, they saw two Hoplite soldiers with bows staring down at them from high on the walls. Dressed in golden armor and helmets, they looked at Aaron oddly. They probably knew he didn't fit in.

"Open up," one commanded. Aaron placed his hand on the massive bark door. It was rigid and grooved. He thought it was ugly compared to the smooth stones of the wall.

"Is this wood from the trees of Kailash?" he asked. Dagon nodded. Aaron was proud of having remembered that detail. The tree bark was renowned for being impervious to an axe, and could only be worked after being melted like clay. Once hardened, the material was nearly impenetrable. *So cool*, he thought, unable to tear away any of the bark from the door.

A piercing steel on steel sound rang on the other side of the door. Aaron pulled back his hand. *That's enough of that*, he decided, startled by how loud it was. The door opened just enough for the two to be confronted by Mercury, wearing his winged helmet.

"Am I to assume this is the Writer?" he asked Dagon.

"Correct," Dagon answered. Mercury moved aside, waving them in, opening the city's door wider for them.

"Come in," Mercury announced. They walked through the entry and Aaron stopped to take in the city. The first thing he noticed was the apartments built directly into the city walls. From the outside, the walls were stone. But inside the city, they were backed by endless rows of apartments, walkways, and balconies.

There appeared to be no individual homes at all. Only tall, white-stoned apartments, row after row of highrises mirroring each other. Outside many of the apartment windows there were displays of flowers, incense, and statues for various gods. Dagon, trying to hurry Aaron along, pointed toward a small white cobblestone style road between the apartment buildings, but Aaron didn't notice as he continued to be enthralled by the impressive city.

There were small bridges scattered throughout the highrises, spanning window to window over the narrow roads.

"Aaron," Dagon said, taking another step forward.

Aaron watched as city residents enjoyed their day. Many stood at their doorways, while others hung halfway out of their windows, talking to others doing the same. Each row of apartments had oil lamps lined up between the doors. *No electricity, weird*, he thought.

"Aaron," Dagon said, a little more sternly.

"One more second," Aaron answered, walking through the arching entrance. Once Aaron had passed the archway and was inside the city walls, he stood in a large plaza. At the center, a fountain with pots and cups nearby. A group of people were gathered there, drinking its waters and conversing amongst themselves. He watched them, studying how people acted in heaven. They seemed like regular people, laughing and enjoying themselves, although their taste in clothing was dated. *Stereotypical Roman garb straight out of my school books*, he thought.

Deciding it was time he followed *his nanny*, he continued along the city roads. They were filled with small shops, eateries, and people performing shows. One was reading poetry, while another pair stood face to face, arguing. *Democracy*! Aaron thought, laughing to himself.

Despite the city's impressive size, there was something special about being there, something *more.* As he let his eyes wander, it appeared as if the people he saw were enjoying themselves. They didn't seem like they were in any rush or preoccupied. They seemed happy, content.

Walking toward Zeus' castle, he noticed just how narrow the stone roads were. The buildings on both sides restricted the view more than when he was at the plaza. And the columns in front of each doorway shrank the roads even more.

"There's no way I'd walk from one side to the other," he announced, gazing at a walkway connecting two opposing windows near the top of the highrises.

Dagon chuckled in response. "It is not that bad. They are safe."

"No way," Aaron insisted.

Chapter 29 *A pig in the air*

Crossing the roads, Aaron noticed what appeared to be endless rows of apartments. Beautiful smooth buildings, one behind the other, seemingly going on forever.

"It's like a maze," he said, astonished. "And from what I remember reading at the library, there are only three entries, right?"

"Yes, there is no doorway on the eastern wall. It was bricked up a long ago," Dagon answered.

"You've been here before?"

"I *am* a Sh'losh," Dagon said. "Remember, you read about how we were created as Immortals, but told to leave Olympus for being so different. This was our home before we were banished."

"Oh crap, I'm sorry. I'm an idiot, I forgot." Aaron's heart rode up into his throat. He hated making others feel bad, even if he had nothing to do with it. He had remembered reading about the tragic history of the Sh'losh, but hadn't connected it to reality. Everything still felt dreamlike.

"It was a long time ago," Dagon assured him. "They bricked the eastern gate after we left to symbolize we were never welcome back. It does not matter anymore. I have no plans to return--this is no longer my home."

"And where's home now?" he asked quickly, trying to move away from the subject of the banishment.

"Shamayim, for now," he answered. "The Most High agreed I would serve him for a while longer. When I am released I hope to be accepted in Duat."

"Can I ask what happened? Why do you have to serve him?" Aaron ventured. He knew he shouldn't have, but he gave in to curiosity.

"Of course you can," Dagon replied. "But are you asking as the Writer or as a friend?" *A friend?* Aaron thought. It felt nice to hear that Dagon thought so highly of him. He had hoped they were getting closer during their time in the Library, but it was hard to get a read on him.

"A friend," he replied proudly.

"Then as a friend, I chose not to tell you," Dagon explained. Aaron rolled his eyes, annoyed. Dagon seemed smug about it, making it even worse.

"Well, I'll just shut up then," Aaron announced.

Dagon placed his hand on Aaron's head, "Maybe another time." Aaron glanced up at the massive hand plopped on his head, *He is so weird.*

"Deal."

The two walked silently through the stretch of the apartments. Aaron just watched everyone, taking it all in. *This might be a nice place to live when I die*, he thought to himself.

The idea of being nineteen and thinking about his impending death didn't sit well, but he tried to face it with a sense of humor. He thought about Sarah, and how he wished she could have been here with him, seeing everything. Despite hating his job, he loved being able to see Sarah every day. She was his *Sarah Bee*, he took pride in being the best older brother he could.

She must be worried sick about me. I must be laid up in the hospital with tubes everywhere. I need to let her know I'm okay, and that she is going to be fine without me. He knew he was lying to himself. He wasn't going to be fine, and he knew she wasn't either. But the lie helped him push on for now.

As they approached the tower, the apartments gave way to a large open city square that displayed both the tower and the castle at its center. The square was crowded with thousands of people singing, dancing, and praising the gods. Others were lying on rugs, burning incense, and lighting candles.

One man chanted praises, "Hail Zeus," repeatedly as he held a small swine in the air in one hand and a knife in the other. Aaron turned his attention from the man and his sacrifice to a woman holding a basket of fruit over her head, praising the gods for their yields.

Aaron and Dagon made their way through the crowd.

"Why are they doing that?"

190

"What? Worshipping?" Dagon asked.

"Yeah," he said, baffled. "I mean, it's like they don't know they're in Heaven or something. Shouldn't they know that Zeus isn't *the* God anymore?"

"Some do not," he answered. "Many people here have been inside these city walls for thousands of years. He is all they know. Ever since the Most High blocked us gods from visiting Earth, many people have chosen to stay here with them. They have never left these walls, Aaron." Aaron remained silent as they continued toward the castle. He was too busy looking around at everyone. He didn't want to ask. He didn't want to know any more.

"We are here," Dagon said when they reached the walls surrounding the castle. The wall had a large ungated opening in front, allowing for open access. People were gathered around the wall, shouting repeatedly, "Hail Zeus!" toward the castle.

Entering the castle, Aaron marveled at it all. Like the city, the inside of the castle was built with white perfectly cut blocks. Walking down the two steps from the entrance, Aaron entered a large foyer and saw two hallways. One headed north and the other east. Athena towered in the room, motioning people toward the eastern hall.

Aaron and Dagon quickly learned from her that Zeus had left with Jove and Neptune. She informed them that they were expected to return sometime the next day. Aaron was not quite ready to begin traveling to visit the Duati, a three- to four-day journey, so he decided they would wait.

A large burly god entered, catching Aaron's eye. He was much larger than the other gods. He wore the same white satin garment as the others but stood out, not only by his size, but the tattoos covering his arms. He had many of the same symbols that Thor and the other Asgardians had.

"Why would someone like him be here?" Aaron asked. Dagon shook his head, uncertain. Aaron approached the god, who stood easily double his height.

"Hello," Aaron announced loudly. The room was already noisy with all the people inside, but the god quickly noticed him.

"Hello, can I ask your name?" Aaron continued.

"You may. My name is Dadga," he replied. He contorted his face into a large smile that even his full brown beard couldn't hide. Despite his protruding eyes, he appeared kind and warm.

"Dadga, right. Of course," Aaron said, trying not to give away the fact that he had no real idea who he was. "What are you doing here in Zeus' castle?"

Chuckling, Dadga replied, "Zeus' castle is open to all Immortals. He lets us use various study rooms here in the eastern hall for classes. Today I am teaching a real passion of mine, gardening! I am headed there now, if you two are interested. This class is all about growing the perfect tomato."

"No," Aaron explained. "I mean what are *you* doing here? Aren't you Asgardian?"

Nodding his head now, understanding the question, Dagon grinned even wider. "I left Asgard," he said proudly. "I simply never fit in there. I am not like them. I take no pleasure in fighting, drinking, and cursing. I am no Viking. I love my gardening, and speaking of things that *actually* matter. I had only a few friends there, but most just ridiculed me every day."

"And Zeus accepted you here?" Aaron asked, biting his lower lip. The lingering thought of what Zeus had done to the Sh'losh came to mind.

"He lets me live in the province as long as I do not reside in the city. I also get to teach others how to take care of their gardens, and no one mocks me."

Leaning closer toward Aaron, his demeanor turned a bit more serious, and he said, "Am I completely accepted? No, but am I ridiculed for not being tough enough, as I was in Asgard? No, not to my face anyway. I will accept what I can have at this point."

Smiling again, Dadga clapped his hands together. "I must go teach a class now. Would you care to join me?"

Chapter 30 *Reincarnation?*

Aaron approved of Dadga's idea to go into the class, since they were waiting for Zeus anyway. He and Dagon followed Dadga through the first door. There must have been a few hundred people already waiting for him, sitting on the floor. The walls were hidden behind large bookshelves that had no space available to place another book on.

"Wow, you need to charge admission," Aaron joked. Dadga grinned, made his way to the center of the room, and immediately started giving his introduction--leaving Aaron to find somewhere to sit while he waited for Zeus.

Aaron decided today wasn't the day to learn about gardening. If he had his way, tomatoes and whatever else someone desired would just manifest in his hand. *That is what heaven should be like*, he thought. He decided to find someone to talk to instead.

He scanned the back of the room, watching for someone to make eye contact.

"Bingo," he whispered to himself. "Dagon, stay here. I'm headed to the back over there to, you know, interview and do my job." Dagon agreed, remaining by the door and listening intently to Dadga. Aaron worked his way to the far side of the class.

"Hello," he said to the young woman who had locked eyes with him. She looked at him again and half smiled, but appeared more interested in Dadga's lecture now.

"Hi, I'm the Writer," he said, expecting that to grab her attention.

"That's wonderful." He was losing her. She didn't seem at all interested in talking with *the Writer*. "Can I speak to you for a moment?" he asked, expecting her to say *no*, since she seemed cold toward him.

He pegged her at about his age. Petite, she had wavy blonde hair twisted in two braids on one side, and the rest was free-flowing. Her lips were bright and full. It took only an instant for Aaron to imagine what they must have tasted like. He didn't want to let his mind wander, but she was attractive. He was surprised he had the nerve to speak to her at all.

Glancing back again at Dadga, she said, "Today is not my day to learn about tomatoes, I see." Aaron felt like dirt, and he turned to walk away, letting her get back to her biology class. He was content having at least given it an effort.

But then, suddenly, she replied, "My name is Sophia, and yours?"

"Aaron, my name is Aaron," he said excitedly. It was nice to finally hear the voice of a normal person instead of a god. Especially someone like her. Sophia motioned her hands to lower his tone. Aaron covered his mouth, acknowledging his bad manners.

"So, you know what *the Writer* is then?" he asked. He didn't know how else he could start a conversation. Talking about the weather just seemed too *Earthly*.

"Yes, I've learned a great deal about the writers. As a matter of fact, do you see him?" she asked, pointing at an older bald man who was sitting cross-legged and listening diligently to Dadga.

"Yeah."

"He was one of the first writers ever. He was the first to write about Hestia, if you can believe it." Aaron shook his head in disbelief, strictly for appearances, since he had no idea who Hestia was. *Learn about Hestia--check.*

"That's incredible," he said, taking another glance at him. "Sophia, I have to ask, what's it like being here? I mean in Sagglemet?"

She erupted in gleeful laughter, covering her mouth to muffle the noise. "You mean *Saggilmut?*" she corrected him, still laughing.

He couldn't help but chuckle, but mostly out of awkwardness. *That word is going to be the death of me.*

"Being dead is amazing, Aaron. You should try it sometime," she said, still snickering to herself. "Okay, let me explain, or at least try."

"All Writers that come here are normally alive on Earth when transported. You are living, right? I mean you're still alive on Earth?"

Not wanting to tell her that he was here with an expiration date coming soon, Aaron played along with her question. "Yes."

"Well, that's because at some point while living here in Saggilmut you chose to cross over and be reborn on Earth. Every time someone is living on Earth it is because they were first here and chose to go back to Earth. I have been to Earth countless times. I have already gone as nearly every race you can think of, some no longer even exist." Aaron didn't know what to say. He never thought to ask these questions in the Library. *Reincarnation, huh? Which religion had that one right?* he thought.

She continued, "I'm thinking I might go as an Indian again next time. It's been so long since I went as one, and I haven't visited Rishikesh in forever, it is so spiritual there. The Hindu people are so nice, too. And the food, the food is amazing."

Aaron was scratching his forehead, still trying to grasp the concept. "You're saying I'm a reincarnation of...what, myself?"

"Let me try again," she said. "Aaron, you have a soul that you were given from the beginning of the world. Your soul, like mine, is forever. It can live either here or there, but you can only be in one place at a time. So each time you choose to live there on Earth, your soul is, in a sense, born again

197

as it leaves here. When you come back here to Saggilmut, you return with all your new memories and experiences."

"I can't remember what I ate for lunch yesterday. How can I have been living forever?"

"I have memories from every single one of my lives on Earth. In Saggilmut, you can recall memories from your past visits to Earth. That's why I was trying to learn how to grow tomatoes. It's something I never trained on yet."

"Why don't we take our memories with us to Earth, then?"

"*Why?*" she repeated, "Because when the Most High designed both worlds, he did it with the concept of *forever* in mind. When you chose to go to Earth, you lose all your memories and knowledge for that period of time you're there. There's something beautiful and real about experiencing things for the first time, that makes it worth doing again and again."

"Who am I then?" he asked. Somehow he had hoped she knew him. She smiled and nodded, watching his face contort in this new revelation.

"You're Aaron," she replied. "*For now.*"

"It sounds like a person can do whatever they want, then, on Earth since--"

"Not quite," she said, halting his train of thought. "A soul will always have some punishment for its actions. That's what Sheol is for."

"Sheol? Like *hell*?" Aaron asked.

Chapter 31 *Sheol*

Sophia moved her chair a little closer to Aaron, then in a softer tone, said, "Yes, *Hell* is an actual place. It is where the soul goes when it dies here in Saggilmut."

"You die in Saggilmut?" *Damn*, he thought. *I should have studied this in the Library.*

"We can only die of unnatural causes. That's why everyone is so nervous about rumors of the war coming. If we die here, then we go to Sheol, and there's no return from there. No more Saggilmut, and no more visiting Earth. Death on Earth is temporary, but death in Saggilmut means you go to Sheol forever."

I wonder what happens when you die in Sheol? Aaron thought, but decided not to ask. *Maybe another time.*

"What's it like in Sheol?"

"It depends where the Beast marks you to go. He determines where each soul will be sent. There are good cities like Elysium, but from what I have heard, most of the land is desolate, scary. The gods used to be allowed to travel there to visit the dead thousands of years ago, before the Most High forbade it. They told us terrible stories about it. They also said those down there lose all track of time, mindfulness, and sense of peace. They said, unless you're sent to one of the good cities, you will end up in torment forever."

"Wow," Aaron was stunned and terrified. He stared at a space on the floor, thinking about everything she had said. *That's bullshit.*

"Why would the Most High make such a place like Sheol then?" Aaron was openly distraught. Sophia reached out, touching his forearm.

"He didn't," she answered. "He gave control over all realms to the gods, except his home in Shamayim. The gods here in Saggilmut are responsible for making it what is today, not him. The same for Sheol, it was the Beast and other gods ruling Sheol that have made it terrible as it is. Thankfully, the Most High banished the gods from Earth so that Ishtar, who used to rule it, can't anymore. So good or bad, everything that happens on Earth is the fault of those living there."

A rush washed over Aaron. *These gods must be crazy,* he thought. Why wouldn't they keep everything peaceful? He knew some of the answers after reading those four days, but hated the idea, *power.* Aaron despised the destruction the gods were doing, all in the desire to gain more power.

"It may be hard to grasp from your perspective as the Writer because there's so much," she said, "but Saggilmut is normally a fairly decent place when all this fighting isn't hanging over our heads. Sometimes there have been lulls, and those are quite nice. Earth can be a beautiful place too, if you learn to see it in the right way."

"Well, crap," he chuckled aloud, "I wouldn't know. I feel like my life hasn't been exactly sunshine and rainbows. It's been hard. It kinda sucks actually, except for my mom and sister. They're like a piece of heaven to me."

The notion of leaving them alone on Earth to fend for themselves rushed into his mind. It mocked him. The sinking feeling that he was here in paradise, while they were struggling without him back home, made him sick. He felt guilty, even if it wasn't his choice.

He could feel the tears welling inside, his heart slowly making its way up into his throat. Shifting his attention to the doorway, he saw Dagon, his only *friend* now. Gazing at him, he studied his gills and restless fish eyes as he was entertained by Dadga's antics.

Just then, a god walked past Dagon in the hallway. The ill-looking being appeared to be shocked at seeing Dagon. He scurried off furtively.

"I'm sorry, Sophia," Aaron said, drawn to the god's eerie presence. "I have to go, but I hope I can find you once this class is done, so we can talk more."

"I would really like that." She waved goodbye, turning her attention back to the instructor. Aaron rose and made his way through the students interrupting many, but apologizing as he went. Heading for the door, Aaron pointed at the hallway.

Rushing up to Dagon, Aaron asked, "Did you see him? Who was that?"

Dagon, still listening to Dadga, replied, "I believe that was Ahriman, but to be honest, I was more interested in learning about the tomatoes, so I was not paying attention."

"Right, right, tomatoes," Aaron agreed. "So, where did he go?"

Chapter 32 *The dungeon*

Dagon turned and led Aaron down the hallway, stopping only at the next door on the other side of the hall. "I saw him go in here."

"I'm sure it's nothing, and he's probably not doing anything wrong. It's just in my head, but he creeped me out. And even if I do die, I'd be right back here in Saggilmut anyway," Aaron said, shrugging off his fear.

Dagon shook his head. "Not quite that simple. You would be transported to the Crossing of whichever sect you belong to and no longer be an unbiased writer. I would prefer not to have to answer to the Most High for that."

"Do you know what sect I am?" he asked, intrigued.

"Not a chance I am telling you." Somehow Aaron knew he wasn't getting the answer he wanted.

"Well, either way, you have to protect me, and the Most High did say I could go anywhere, right?"

"Yes," Dagon answered.

"Cool, let's go see what's up with the creepy god that walked by you." Aaron grabbed the handle and pulled at the door. It wouldn't open. Pulling harder, he cursed under his breath. He grabbed it with both hands and yanked as hard as he could.

"It's stuck."

Dagon moved Aaron's hand, shaking his head. He then gently pushed, and the door opened. There was a short stone stairwell.

"You do enjoy making me look stupid," Aaron teased.

A single torch hung on the wall provided just enough light to see the bottom step. Walking down the stairs slowly, he paused when he heard a loud grunt coming from the bottom of the stairs.

Any sense of humor disappeared. Caution overrode Aaron's desire to rush and see what the sound was. With each step he crept down, the light from the hallway dimmed.

Reaching the last step, he heard a loud pounding sound followed by several guttural coughs. It was then that Aaron realized what was happening. Someone was being beaten. That was the sound of a fist connecting to flesh.

"Should we go?" Aaron whispered.

Matching his tone, Dagon advised, "You can go anywhere you please under my protection."

"Right," Aaron said, trying to build up his confidence. He stood upright from his slight crouch and turned the corner to see what was happening, bolstered by his newfound sense of security.

There, inside the room was Odin, stripped of all clothing except a small loincloth that was barely hanging on. Ahriman had him in chains, his arms raised and locked over an iron beam above his head.

Odin's feet dangled and scraped along the floor. He would have been able to hold himself up, but he seemed too weak to stand. Purple bruises, red wounds, covered by dried blood coated his body. He was struggling to breathe, coughing up blood as he tried. Ahriman stood near him, not far from the bottom step.

Ahriman slammed his fist into Odin's stomach. Odin's head hung low as he gasped for air, coughing, and wheezing. Ahriman watched his struggles with awful pleasure. He balled his fist again and landed a blow on Odin's jaw this time.

"Weak!" Ahriman yelled, shouting so close that his spit sprayed onto Odin's face.

Odin planted his feet and tried to stand, but he fell backward and the chains caught him, dangling him. He tried to spit out the blood pouring from his mouth, but it dripped off his lip onto his chest.

Odin stared straight down, his eye patch near his feet. Aaron had seen enough. Trusting in his protection, he took a step forward from the shadows into the dim light from the candles that clung to the walls behind Odin.

"Stop!"

Ahriman looked back, startled, but after noticing who it was, scoffed, "You are most definitely in the wrong place, nether." Dagon emerged from behind Aaron, instantly stopping

Ahriman in his tracks. "What in Sheol is this? What are you doing here?"

Dagon did not respond to Ahriman.

"Remember, I can only protect you as long as you do not intervene," Dagon whispered. Aaron couldn't see how that rule would matter until right then. He recalled what the Most High had told him. It wasn't his place to choose sides, *but to record the truth*. He felt powerless.

"Why are you doing this?" Aaron said, hoping to stop the thrashing, or at a minimum slow it down. Ahriman paused before he answered, clearly admiring the work he had done to Odin's body.

"Whatever you think you know of him, know that this piece of feces deserves everything he gets from me and then some."

Without warning, Ahriman turned and drove his fist into Odin's ribcage. The sound of a rib cracking was only muffled by the grunt Odin made.

"He has been a plague on the gods, and now I have been tasked to bring retribution." Ahriman then backhanded him across the face.

"This isn't right," Aaron insisted.

Ahriman glared at him, then turned, squared his feet toward Odin, and began pummeling his body. Stopping only to catch his breath, he turned back.

"Keep talking, nether," he said, his chest heaving. "You talk, I hit."

Aaron froze. He knew he was not going to get through to him. Anything he did would only result in Odin's continued pain.

"Dagon?" Aaron begged, mortified. Dagon shook his head, unable to do anything.

"I was wrong about Zeus," Aaron screamed, "and I will make sure everyone knows it." Ahriman smiled, showing his decayed brown teeth. Then he turned and grabbed Odin by his beard.

"You hear that!" he bellowed at Odin. "Looks like I am in trouble." Laughing maniacally, he reached back and drove his fist into Odin's lips, still holding his beard with the other hand. Aaron realized that by being there he was only making matters worse.

"Thor is right. Zeus and his gods have to go." Odin raised his head and locked eyes with Aaron. His saliva mixed with blood dribbling down his lips onto his beard.

"He will vindicate me," Odin said quietly with great effort.

"C'mon," Aaron said to Dagon, walking by him and heading up the stairs. "It's time to get out of here."

Chapter 32 *The son's return*

Baldr returned the following evening with both Magni and Svetovid. On the way from Mount Hor, Baldr convinced them he had met with Zeus and Osiris after receiving a message from a hoopoe. It read that he was to meet them there on amicable terms to have Magni returned. Magni struggled to believe the story, but it didn't matter. He was home and his brother was dead. He wanted blood.

Nearing the village entrance, Svetovid, clearly tired from the trip, grunted something to Baldr, and rode off toward his home. He still had a good half-day ride before he could board the small boat he had hidden at the coast. Svetovid and many other gods made their home in Rugen, an island just off the coast of the southernmost part of Asgard. Collectively the islands, known as Szczecin, were governed by Lord Belobog, under Asgardian rule.

Magni was still in shock and ignored Svetovid's departure. He needed to know what happened to Modi. Just thinking about his brother's body in the possession of such filth bothered him. He glanced back at Neptune, still trailing them from a distance.

"We should kill him and send his head back to Olympus," Magni said.

"No," Baldr said. "Zeus does not suspect us, so for our attack, we have to remain patient."

Something about Baldr's tone didn't sit right with Magni. He just had too many answers, Magni concluded, but decided against challenging him. *Another time.*

Magni watched as Neptune rode off, disappearing into the darkness.

"I will kill you. All of you," he whispered to himself.

Entering the gates, Magni and Baldr rode toward the castle. The closer they got to the heart of the city, the more they heard the sound of festivities. Riding up the dirt roads, Magni grabbed a shroom dangling off a wall. *Modi loved these damn things*, he thought, inspecting it. He took a bite but promptly spat it out. *These things are gross.*

Turning a corner, Magni slowed his horse. A large crowd had gathered around the market square. Normally, crowds of this size meant the King was among them and was spending time with his people, probably drinking.

Tying their horses to the pole near the city square, Magni and Baldr went to see what the fuss was about, since it was on the way to the castle. It wasn't long before they saw Thor drinking from a large horn as liquor escaped from the sides, seeping onto his cloak. The crowd cheered him on, screaming "Long live Thor!"

"There he is!" Magni yelled, waving, but unable to draw his attention. Pushing people out of the way, Magni called out to his father several times, but couldn't be heard above the crowd. Baldr stayed behind Magni, following more slowly, apprehensively. Magni noted his odd behavior.

Shoving one last person to the side, Magni screamed out, "My King!" Thor grinned at his son, threw down his horn, and shattered it, to the delight of the people. He took hold of his son.

"Magni, my son. *Heil og sæl*," he said, muffled by his son's shoulder. The crowd cheered louder, seeing their king so joyful.

"How did it go, son? I imagine you two have plenty to share." He let his grasp on Magni loosen a little, but Magni held on even tighter.

"Son?" Thor asked, looking down at his face. Buried against his chest, Thor could feel Magni sobbing.

Thor scanned the crowd.

"Where is Modi?" Magni heard his father call out for Modi, and it broke him.

Magni cried loudly, but the music and singing in the market drowned him out. Men played their lyres, flutes, and tagelharpas while others drank, screamed, and howled at the night sky. Some women danced in circles with their arms interlocked, while others lifted their hands, waving them in rhythm.

In the midst of the festivities, Thor grabbed Magni's beard, staring into his eyes.

"Modi?"

Magni wanted to speak. He wanted to tell him he would get revenge, but the lump in his throat was too large; the pain of letting his father and brother down was too great. Thor's eyes watered as he pulled Magni into an embrace.

Thor looked to Baldr. He gestured him closer and clutched him, as well. Thor wept quietly. Magni squeezed his father's fur cloak. He wanted heads. He wanted death!

After a long pause, the three gathered their collective breath. Thor gestured and they moved away from the other people. He pointed toward an empty alley, and Baldr led the way through the crowd.

They put on celebratory faces and hugged, shook hands, and cheered to avoid the impression that anything could be wrong. Thor raised his arms, pumping his fists in the air to encourage the jubilee for the villagers. Magni wanted to drop to his knees, but would not allow himself to appear so weak or broken in front of the people.

Entering the shadows of the alley, Thor grabbed hold of both of Magni's shoulders. "What happened, son? What happened to Modi? Damn it, I should not have sent you two."

"Father, I am sorry!" Magni gathered his thoughts and continued. "Right before we arrived at Nekhen we saw a large gathering at Mauna Kea Hills and decided to go and scout it. There was a mixture of Duati and nomad gods eating and drinking, so we thought we could safely blend in. We listened for information, just as you said, until Horus and Toth spotted us."

"And what happened to your brother?" Thor repeated.

"We had no idea they had spotted us," he said, flustered. "They must have made plans with the other gods to prepare to kill us. We noticed too late that they had already recognized us, and tried to escape. We agreed to run and meet down the road near Mount Hor, trying to lose them. We were separated." Magni paused and took a deep breath.

"That was the last I saw of him. I was surrounded by Horus and many others. I fought them, but...they surrounded me and I lost. They tied me up and brought me to Nekhen, where they covered my face before we entered the city. After that, I lost track of time and where I was, until I saw Baldr at Mount Hor, and they released me."

Baldr quickly spoke up, "A few nights ago, I received a note with the Duat seal on it." Baldr's leg shook violently as he continued, "The letter stated that I needed to go to the wellspring by Mount Hor alone and without telling anyone, if I wanted to bring home both Magni and Modi. It was not until I arrived that I saw Zeus and the others there, and learned of what happened to Modi. My King, I am sorry I acted without your permission, but--"

"Where is his body?" Thor demanded.

Baldr stuttered, "M-My lord, I have n-no idea. I simply received the message and--"

"DAMN IT!" Thor erupted, furious.

Chapter 33 *A King too staggered*

Thor stared, eyes bloodshot, at his brother Baldr. "Obviously, they do not see you as a threat, since they called for you to have this meeting instead of me. You will ride to Nekhen, where Magni said they took him, and find Osiris if need be. Speak with whoever you must, to bring back my son. Do not come back until you have retrieved his body, so he may be sent to Sheol properly."

"Yes, my King," Baldr agreed. "I will leave first thing in the morning."

"Did you just call me your king or your brother?" Thor asked.

"What?" Baldr answered, confused. "I called you my King, of course."

"Then if your king asks you to gather the body of his dead son, why would you put it off even a single moment?" Baldr bowed. He gave a brief hug to Magni, and headed back to his horse to begin his journey to Duat.

With their arms across each other's shoulders, Thor and his son went into their stone castle, deciding to fill their horns with the finest mead. They went up the castle stairs, exited onto the castle wall, and found themselves a spot to sit overlooking the village. The day was calm, without the wind they often felt at that height.

Once they sat down, feet hanging off the wall, they sang songs, drinking heavily and watching the villagers continue to celebrate their new king. Thor rested his hand on his son's shoulder. "I am proud of you."

Magni hit his father's chest gratefully. It felt good to have a father who cared as much as Thor did.

After a number of trips for more mead, the two were heavily inebriated. Having saved each other from falling off the wall more than once, they agreed it was time to make their way back to the village for more refreshments. Their sorrow was only outmatched by their desire and capacity for drink.

Staggering, Thor and Magni held each other upright as they entered the city square again. Unlike the first time when they headed up to the castle gripping each other for emotional support, this time it was more for physical support. Thor lifted his horn to his mouth and found it empty.

"I am going to get a-another," Thor said, almost incoherently. Magni was slumped against the most well-known tree in Asgard, the Yggdrasil tree. The large ash tree earned its name as the tree of life, because that was where all three former kings of Asgard gave their speeches to the people about Asgard laws, their way of living.

"My King," a voice called from a few steps away. As he turned around, Thor's bleary eyes lit as his head wavered.

Both Tyr and Sjofn were now standing in front of him and Magni. They had returned from Guangdong! Thor struggled to his feet, then embraced them simultaneously, taking them into his arms. Tyr was clearly confused, but appeared happy to receive such a welcome from Thor. Magni remained slumped against the tree, fighting to keep his eyes open.

"My King," Tyr proclaimed nervously. As he tried to form words with his lips, nothing came out. Magni surmised that whatever he had to tell Thor wasn't good news. But no matter what it was, it couldn't be as bad as what Magni had told him previously.

Unable to hold his head up, Thor tried to speak. His words were garbled, barely audible. The mead had finally taken its toll.

"Did you hear him?" Sjofn asked Tyr.

"I heard him, but did I understand him? No, I do not speak *mead*." Laughing, Tyr grabbed the empty horn from Thor's hand.

"I am going to cherish this trip forever, Tyr," Sjofn whispered. "Even if it did not end up well for us regarding the Sanguan Dadi."

"Unfortunately, Thor just said that Modi is dead," a feminine voice said from above Magni. Magni's head was heavy as he lifted it to see who had spoken. *Sekhmet!* The feline goddess was propped on the lowest branch of Yggdrasil.

"Sekhmet? W-what are you doing here?" Sjofn asked. She reached for the small dagger hidden under her waistbelt.

Sekhmet looked at her, shaking her head."No need for that, young one," she purred.

"How did you get in here?" Tyr demanded. He stepped in front of Thor and Sjofn.

"Your guards," she said, pointing down at two Vikings lying on the ground, passed out in a puddle of their vomit.

"Huh, interesting," Tyr said.

"We came to speak to Thor, but I see that may not be possible tonight." Thor's eyes had closed, and Sjofn struggled to hold him upright.

"*We?*" Sjofn questioned.

"Yes," Sekhmet answered, as she lowered herself off the branch and approached them. "There is a group of us outside the gate. The rest made camp a half day's journey north of Tunda's Forest and are waiting for the signal. They have sage to repel Tunda, so I am sure we will be fine," Sekhmet said. Watching Tyr nervously glance back at Thor, she added, "Unless you want to open the gates for us all?"

All sects stayed away from the woods in fear of Tunda. An alchemist from the beginning, she had learned methods of manipulating scents and fragrances to lure those passing by into the forsaken woods, where she killed them in sacrifice to herself. Others had tried to hunt her down in the past, but never returned. Tunda and the gods allied with her were the only Unspoken that the three sects had located with certainty.

Tyr said to Sjofn, "Go to Baldr's home and wake him. Let him know what is happening, and ask for his guidance." She rushed off to get an answer.

"What do you want with Thor?" Tyr asked, now bearing the brunt of Thor's weight alone.

"We want to join your cause in killing Zeus," Sekhmet said. "You know what they did to my clan. That is why we are here. To pledge ourselves in the battle against him."

"How many of you are there?" Tyr asked.

"Enough to make some waves," she answered with a smile. "Ra, who will join us in a few days, will inform the Duat council during their next assembly that we will fight with you. We hope he brings others." She took a step away, apparently repulsed by the strong smell of alcohol on Thor.

"So, when is it? When do we go to Olympus?" she asked.

"With all due respect," Tyr said, with one brow raised. "But there is little chance you will get any information from me. If your group wants to fight with us, then I would welcome you, but I am not the king. He will have his say when he recovers. I am sure you can understand my hesitancy."

"Of course," she replied. "Fair enough, but all of you must know that Asgard alone is not enough to overrun Olympus. It is isolated, fortified, and the walls will be teeming with archers. They have easily half a million Hoplite soldiers on the ground as well. We can help."

Sjofn returned, short of breath. She told them both that Baldr was not there. Nanna, Baldr's wife, told her she had not seen him for nearly four days, but that he had left to do something to help the war efforts. In response, the three concluded that with Thor inebriated and Baldr gone, the best course of action was to wait until morning.

Tyr and Sjofn took two trips, carrying first Thor and then Magni to Thor's chambers. Magni lived too far for them to carry him home. They decided some pillows near Thor's bed would have to suffice for the night. Magni opened his eyes only long enough to see Sjofn carrying him.

"Hey! I always knew you wanted me," he mumbled. Then the weight of his eyelids and head bested him once again.

After settling Thor and Magni for the night, Tyr and Sjofn went to get some rest for themselves.

While Magni slept, Sekhmet returned to her group with what little information she had been given, and a promise that she would go back in the dawn. Neptune, who had been sitting alone in the grass, leaning against a rock outside the walls, saw Tyr and Sjofn return without anyone from the

Sanguan Dadi. But when he saw Sekhmet leaving the gate, he chose to follow her instead of returning to Olympus.

Chapter 34 *It's settled then*

The following morning, Magni awoke with his head pounding. He sat up, rubbing his eyes. Staring around the room he realized he was on the floor of his father's room. Struggling to his feet, he saw Thor lying on his bedspread, stirring awake as well. Thor was still wearing his askott-húfa on his head and his goatskin boots.

Magni rested his hand on his temples, and tried to recall the night's events that concluded with him laying at the foot of Thor's bed. Thor was clearly struggling to remember the last night, as well.

Seeing Magni, Thor covered his face. "Damn Osiris, he is responsible for Modi's death." Rising awkwardly from his bed, Thor waved Magni near. "Damn Zeus too." Sif, Thor's wife, remained sleeping on the other side of the bed as the two staggered to their feet and left the room.

Tyr sat waiting in a chair down the hall with a view of the bedroom door. Seeing Thor and then Magni stumble out of the room, Tyr leaped from his chair and approached them quietly.

"My King," he said gently. Magni, rubbing his temples and still suffering, was grateful for Tyr's lower tone.

"You are back?" Thor responded haltingly. "Good, what did they say...to our request?"

"They refused to even meet with us. We sent a message to them, but--"

Dismissing Tyr, Thor squared his shoulders and said, "I am not going to let them slow us down. Gather everyone in the war room. I am ready to move forward."

"My King, if I can have a moment of your time. Something else happened last night you need to know about."

"*Last night*?" Thor questioned, scratching his head.

Tyr answered, "Last night during the celebration, Sekhmet approached me."

"She was here? Inside *my* village?" he said, eyes blazing. Magni listened as well as his headache would allow.

"My King," Tyr said gently, trying to calm him. "Sekhmet said she and other Sh'losh want to fight alongside us when we raid Olympus."

"Why would they do that? Where are they now?" Thor asked.

"Some are outside of the gate, but the main party is camped near Tunda's Forest. She said they want revenge for being exiled."

Thor glanced back at Magni as they walked down the stairs toward the dining hall. "Did you see her out there when you and Modi were spying and got attacked?"

"No," Magni replied. "I did not see her there at all."

Thor said, "Good. If they are willing to fight for us, then go and prepare a place in the outer rooms. They will be guests in our province, not outcasts."

"Yes, my King," Tyr agreed.

Thor smiled and placed his hand on Tyr's shoulder. "Well, damn, after last night I am glad to be hearing some good news. Go now, and ring the bells for an assembly. I will be there later in the afternoon. I want Sekhmet there as well." Tyr agreed and headed back up the stairs to the belltower.

Thor and Magni continued slowly toward the dining hall. Magni could smell the meat being prepared in the dining hall. He knew the cook was Frigg by the scent of the herbs. Lamb stew, he surmised. *A good hangover cure.*

"This has gone on long enough, it is time to move forward with the attack," Thor said.

Chapter 35 *In Peace*

Later in the afternoon, Thor and Magni entered the war room together. Bragi was already there and had drawn various angled layouts of the city of Olympus. Vidar sat in a corner with his head slumped down, fighting sleep. Numerous gods had gathered around Bragi's drawing and were reviewing possible entry points, weaknesses, and where the Sh'losh may be best served in the siege. Sekhmet brought her sister Bastet, and stood over the table discussing possible strategies.

Collectively, the Asgardians welcomed their king, "*Heil og sæl.*" Bastet and Sekhmet looked at each other and tried to avoid any facial expressions that might seem offensive, but Sekhmet couldn't help but smirk at the odd sounding Asgardian greeting.

Thor did not respond to seeing her there. Instead, he walked directly to the map. "This is good, Bragi," he said.

"Thank you, my King. It was not a problem. We were able to stay near some trees and--"

"I said, thank you," Thor said, louder. Bragi tightened his lips.

Studying the drawings, Thor continued, "Given the height of the walls, we are not getting over those damn things easily. Tell me about the entrance. It is *just* a door?"

"Not *just* a door, my King," Bragi answered. "There is a single door to the three entrances into the city, they are all the same. Made of Kailash bark, and the hinges are saggilmut stone. They can only be opened from the inside. I think our best option would be--"

"We cannot send over such a large group using ladders," Thor said. "And Kailash bark, we are not getting through that. Now the saggilmut hinges on the other hand, *that* is our weakness."

"How so?" Magni asked. "It's saggilmut stone, that is--"

"Broken when it is struck by another refined saggilmut stone object." Thor hit his hands together excited. "I want all the saggilmut we have in the province gathered at Yggdrasil and melted down immediately. A single weakness, no matter how small, can be the fall of a kingdom. That is our entry point. we will take out the hinges at the southern gate." He turned to Tyr. "And the Sanguan Dadi?"

"My King, we never found them," Tyr said dejectedly. "We went to the city square and asked, but no one knew where they lived. Not a single person in that damn city could tell us where they were. We tried, my King. I am sorry."

"Did you go to the Shuiguan Fountain?" Sekhmet asked. Thor looked at her with irritation. She could feel Thor's eyes, but ignored him. It wasn't her fault he had issues with her posing a question. The attack on Olympus was bigger and more important than his ego.

"Yes," Tyr answered. "We spent quite a bit of the day there asking both gods and nethers. No one knew where they lived, bunch of fools. It was as if each person there totally made up their answers, and--"

"If you went to the fountains, then you would definitely have met them," she blurted, unable to hold back any longer.

Tyr glanced at Sjofn across the table and shrugged. "They were not there, I am telling you."

Sekhmet said, "And I am *telling* you. They are *always* there."

"We asked everyone we saw," Tyr stated. "No one could lead us to them, and they did not introduce themselves, that is for damn sure."

Bastet patted her sister, then said, "What my sister is trying to say is that the Sanguan Dadi do not have a home. They do not have temples or anything of the sort, no matter what you were told. The people in the city are taught different legends, so that the Sanguan Dadi come across as omnipresent. It is a trick, a facade. They live as paupers, there near the waters."

Tyr, shaking his head, responded, "I understand what you are saying, but--"

"I met them!" Sjofn realized. "I mean, *we* met them. Sekhmet and Bastet are right! I *knew* there was something different about that old god sitting in the corner playing with sand in his hands. I had that same feeling about another god near the water, too. And I think the old god that brought us to the home was another one."

Tyr asked, "Guowang?"

Sekhmet replied, "That *is* one of them. Guowang is not a name, it is a title for those living in Guangdong. It means *king*. What did he tell you?"

Tyr, mouth open, was clearly replaying their time with him. Sekhmet looked at Sjofn, who was staring at the ceiling, thinking.

"Nothing useful," Tyr decided. "He brought us to an old home with a nearly collapsed roof. It belonged to a younger god he knew, named Puren. He claimed to be an architect for the Sanguan Dadi, although his shitty home made me think he was lying. He said he could not take us to them, but could deliver a message. We just--"

"And the old god was there?" Sekhmet asked.

"Yes, we just sat there, waiting together after Puren left," he said.

"He was one of them," Sekhmet said. "Puren is not a name either; it means *servant*. He worked for them. Do you remember what they told you?"

"With every breath I seem to forget something. I cannot remember," Tyr said, staring at Sjofn.

"Memories are all we have," Sekhmet said. "A person without a memory is soulless."

The others stared at Tyr and Sjofn as they considered what they could remember. Sjofn described her memories.

"We sang songs, he listened to my poems, and we laughed a lot. Later in the night, after falling asleep, Puren woke us up and insisted we leave..."

She paused and added, "And he wished us well, saying, go peacefully."

"Peacefully?" Sekhmet questioned. "Do you mean *in* peace?"

"Yes! I remember that, because it came across so odd. Also, while there, I did eat this amazing--"

"It means they are *with* you, Thor," Sekhmet said, grinning widely. "I do not know what you said, but the term *in* peace means they are willing to join us." Sekhmet winked at Bastet.

"How do you know this?" Thor asked.

Sekhmet said, "Because when we were exiled by Zeus, my sisters and I first went to Guangdong. It is a free city, and we thought we could live there away from the sects and their turmoil. We all became *purens* of the Sanguan Dadi. We learned how they operate and spoke with them all the time. Bastet and I eventually left, but my other sister, Mafdet, chose to stay."

Sekhmet turned toward her sister and shared a wistful smile.

Thor raised his fist and yelled, "Well damn it! Let us not waste another moment. How can we notify them?"

"Hoopoes will drop a message at the fountains, and one of them will get it," Sekhmet offered.

Thor said to his brother, "I am sure it will take them a few days to prepare and another two days to travel to Olympus. Tyr, go with Bastet, and send a hoopoe telling them we will be attacking in five days at dawn. I understand they may not be ready to join us immediately, but we will need them to join us sometime that day. How many warriors do you suspect they have?"

"At least two hundred thousand," Sekhmet said.

Grinning, he replied, "That is more than I expected, good. We will have Zeus' head hanging on a post outside of the walls before the Duati even arrive there. That should be enough motivation for them to turn around and go home."

"You are right. There would be no reason for them to fight, if he is already dead," Sekhmet agreed. "Zeus does have a secure room in his castle though," Sekhmet added. "That room is nearly impregnable, and if we are unable to stop Zeus from getting inside it, then he will be safe until Osiris arrives."

"What is it made of?" Magni asked.

"Kailash bark, layered in saggilmut stone."

"Shit," Magni said, glancing down at Bragi's drawings.

"Then it is settled," Thor announced. "Once we get in those gates, you Sh'losh must make your way to that room, ensuring he does not get in. The Valhallian warriors will be right behind you."

"Fair enough," she agreed.

"And what do you know about Modi?" Thor asked, studying her expression.

She raised her brow, then asked, "Your son? Not much. I do not see him here."

"You do not know, then?" he said.

"What am I supposed to know?" Sekhmet scanned the room again, making sure he wasn't there.

Thor then commanded, "Everyone leaves the room except Sekhmet. You stay."

Chapter 36 *Sekhmet and Thor*

Without a word, everyone quickly left the room. Sekhmet rotated her head, getting in a decent stretch in case Thor decided he was going to test her. Under her cloak, Sekhmet folded her arms behind her back near the dagger in her waistbelt. It almost felt like it was calling for her.

With everyone gone and the door shut, she crossed her arms. "How can I help?" The animalistic side of her was heavily on guard.

"Tell me the truth; Do you not know about what has happened to my son Modi?" he asked.

"I do not."

"Swear upon your name," he demanded.

"I, Sekhmet, swear on my name that I do not know anything you are asking about your son. I have not seen him since the last time he and Magni attended an assembly, and we both know that was some time ago."

"All right, fine," he said, holding up both hands in mock surrender. "What happens when Zeus is dead?" Thor asked. "Do you think Osiris will simply welcome all of you back to Duat?"

"Baltia," Sekhmet said. "Osiris is honorable and forgiving, but this is too much to forgive, even for him. We have decided to travel to the island of Baltia once Zeus is dead. I am not here for whatever cause you have; that must be clear to you. We share a common enemy, and I am sure you know the saying; *the enemy of my enemy is my friend.* You do not need to trust me, but you can trust my hatred for Zeus. He mistreated and abused my friends for no reason other than being alive."

She continued, "Listen, your timeline is perfect. The Duati are going to take at least four days to gather their military and get to Olympus once they are alerted. If we move quickly, then by the time they are able to reach Olympus it will be too late. And if we kill Zeus before their arrival, then as you said, there is no reason for Osiris to put his people in harm's way. You kill Zeus, their fight is over."

"Straight through the southern doorway. We will break down that damn doorway and flood in. There will be nothing they can do to stop us once we are inside." Thor punched his fist into his other hand. "Finally, fate is with us!"

"As soon as Ra arrives, we will leave then?" she asked. "He may bring more gods with him to fight alongside us."

"Fine," Thor agreed. "Because you have sided with us, I will wait for him to make his journey here." Thor extended his arm. "Then the plan is settled. Come, join us for some mead and food."

"If I can invite the other Sh'losh outside of the gate?"

"Sekhmet, as far as I am concerned, once you agreed to fight with us you are all Asgardian. They are most welcome." He was sincere. She could sense his child-like excitement and respected his acceptance.

"Then if that is true, *Heil og sæl,* Thor. I will send a hoopoe to those others near Tunda's Forest as well." She grasped his forearm, embracing their shared respect.

"And *Heil ok sæl,* to you, Sekhmet."

Shortly after, both Sekhmet and Bastet returned to the gates and told the group everything that had occurred.

Unknown to Sekhmet, Neptune still remained hidden in the bushes, listening to the two feline goddesses. He heard Bastet explain the war strategy, the attack on the southern gate, and that the Sanguan Dadi would be joining Asgards' assault.

Neptune remained unseen in the grass as the Sh'losh sang and cheered, hollering at the night sky as they made their way to Asgard. He crawled back to the road, staying out of their view. He then untied his waiting horse and quickly rode to Mount Olympus to inform his king that the attack would occur in just a few days.

Chapter 37 *Bread of heaven*

After they left Olympus, Aaron and Dagon traveled to the Duat province by horseback. Those two lessons in summer camp when he was thirteen paid off, Aaron thought numerous times along the journey. Nearing the city of Nekhen, Aaron saw that the city was made of saggilmut stone, its walls reflecting the sun.

"Amazing," he whispered. Each building distinct from the next, the stone cast brilliant reflections around the city. A series of pyramids stood tall. As Aaron rode in from the north, the city reflected the light skyward, making it appear as if the city gave light to the sun as much as the sun gave light to the city.

"That is the most beautiful thing I have ever seen in my entire life," Aaron said.

"It is just melted stone reshaped," Dagon scoffed. "I find *life* to be the ultimate beauty, and--"

"Whoa there big guy," Aaron replied. "It's just an expression, and can I tell you that the way you used the word *just* is wrong?"

"Wrong? You are less than two decades old and are trying to teach me how to speak?"

"In this situation, yes, I am," Aaron said, sitting up straight on his horse. "A person who says the word *just* before anything is doing nothing more than belittling it. I have *just* a million dollars, or, I'll *just* go and jump off a bridge. I hate that word. It takes away the meaning and value of things."

"You seem to be adamant about that."

Aaron pumped his fist in the air. "Especially now that I know I have *just* another few weeks to live."

"Has anyone ever told you that you are a wise young man?" Dagon asked.

"No, no they haven't," Aaron answered, feeling proud.

"Then you should keep working at it. Maybe one day someone will."

Aaron laughed.

They made their way to Nekhen, and headed to Horus' home. Dagon explained that his home had stood in the heart of the city as a hub for everything that happened in Duat. Having shared hoopoes, and after confirming a meeting for today, Aaron looked forward to meeting with Osiris to see what his plans were.

On the way through the city streets, Aaron caught the smell of fresh bread. Its distinct aroma took him back to his grandmother's kitchen. Every Friday, she had prepared fresh bread for him and Sarah when they visited during the summer. *A loaf never made it through the night*, he was proud to say. Thankfully, Bubbe always made two.

"Hey, do you mind if we go to find out where that smell is coming from first?" Aaron asked.

"I am sure we can, if we hurry," he agreed.

"Not that I'm not grateful to you for preparing such *great* meals for us." Aaron held up a small bag full of various nuts, shaking it sarcastically.

"Spoiled," Dagon said, shaking his head at Aaron. "You have been spoiled rotten."

The two laughed and followed the aroma to the next alleyway. Aaron noticed a man outside in his front yard, pulling out a pan of baked loaves from a time-worn stone oven. There was a small sign nailed to a crooked wooden pole next to him: *Fresh bread, made daily.*

"Excuse me, are you open?" Aaron inquired, savoring that perfect smell as he lifted his head and inhaled deeply.

The man was too busy to pay Aaron any attention. "If it's cooked, then I'm open, my friend. I suppose you would like some fresh from the oven?"

"That would be so kind of you, sir." The man took two loaves of flatbread, wrapped them in a small cloth, and handed the package to Aaron, still mounted on his steed.

"Enjoy, my friend," he said, nodding his head proudly.

Aaron inspected the bread. It was crispy on the outside. But the real test, as his grandmother always said, was when it was ripped open. Aaron pinched the end and tore at it, revealing a steamy-soft inside. *Now that's bread!* he thought.

Looking back at the man, perplexed, he said, "Sir, I have to ask, you're in heaven, right?"

Without pausing, drawing another pan of fresh loaves out of the oven, the baker answered, "*Heaven*? Haven't heard that in a while, but sure, that's the idea."

"Then why are you baking bread?" Aaron asked. Ripping off another piece, he inhaled the delicious steam as it rose. With a quick lunge, he took a bite into the warm bread, perfectly moistened in the middle.

"Have you even tasted it yet?" the baker asked. Dagon grinned at the baker. He seemed amused that he wasn't the only one getting to take playful shots at Aaron.

"Yes, sir," Aaron mumbled as he chewed. "It's delicious." *The hint of garlic, it's perfect,* Aaron thought.

"You like it then?" the baker asked.

"Yeah. Don't tell my grandmother, but it's better than hers." He pulled off another piece and took a bite.

"Now you understand why I make it then?" he said. "A person who is passionate about their craft can find *heaven* in doing it. So in actual *heaven*, why wouldn't I do what makes me the happiest?"

Aaron, still chewing, realized he had ignored him. The man smiled and winked, then turned and went back to his business.

Leaving the baker, Dagon asked, "What would you be doing if you were back home right now?"

Laughing to himself, Aaron answered, "Probably messing with my sister, of course."

"Miss her?" he asked.

"A lot," Aaron admitted. "It kinda sucks." The thought took his appetite away. He opened his bag of peanuts and shoved the rest of the bread inside.

"I am sorry, Aaron, I did not mean to--"

"It isn't your fault. It isn't anyone's fault that I'm dying. Honestly, that's part of why it's so hard, because I have no one to blame. There is no bad guy to be angry with, it's *just...just*--there's that damn word again."

Chapter 38 *Sh'losh divided*

The two made their way through the small streets toward Horus' home. Turning the corner, Aaron was taken aback. There was a small crowd gathered in the yard around the front entrance. Taller than most, Osiris stood on a single step leading to the door. He was holding a small black cat in his arms, stroking it.

"Cats in Egypt, that really is a thing," Aaron said.

"You never heard what happened on Earth when the Persians went into battle against Egypt using cats?

"Uh-uh," Aaron said.

"Another time," Dagon replied. "Remind me to tell you about that battle." Aaron agreed, hoping to remember to ask him later.

Standing next to Osiris was Horus, Toth, and a man in a colorful headdress clapping exuberantly. He was staring at something happening in the crowd in the front yard. As they got closer, Aaron could see a circle of people formed around Shiva. The people cheered him on as he danced wildly.

"Seems like we arrived just in time for the party!" Aaron exclaimed, throwing his hands up and moving to the beat from two male drummers near Shiva.

"Appears so," Dagon agreed, still watching Shiva flapping his arms and spinning. The two approached the door, making their way through the crowd, captivated by his dancing.

Reaching the single step, Aaron waved, trying to get Osiris' attention. Osiris saw his signal, smiled, and gestured him over.

"Welcome," Osiris said, reaching forward. "I am glad you are here." Aaron grinned and locked arms with him. He couldn't help but look back at Shiva, now leaping in the air, twirling around.

"*Tandav*," Osiris said, clapping to the rhythm. "The dance, it is called *Tandav*. Quite beautiful, right?"

"It is," Aaron replied. "It really is."

"Join us," Osiris said, pointing toward the front door. "We are all headed to the back yard for a meeting." Aaron followed him inside.

The inside of Horus' home was beautiful, decorated in satin purple curtains and colored three-dimensional hieroglyphics running across the top of the wall.

"They tell the story to remind me where I am from," Horus said, standing behind him. "You see that image there? That is me," he said, pointing to a figure in the corner of the wall that was quite obviously him.

Then, pointing to another symbol of a character holding a spear, Horus continued, "That one there is Seth. Most of the symbols tell stories of countless debates and fighting between us. It is not something I am proud of, but as you can see in that image there," he pointed at another section of the wall showing them together, "And the fact that he is here today sitting at my table, that we have reconciled. We can never forget our past, Aaron, no matter how bad it was." Horus paused to adjust his left eye patch. "Life experiences help us to purchase wisdom."

"What was the fighting about?" Aaron asked.

"There is only one reason any fight ever happens: ego. In our case, we both suffered from that disease, so that made it all the worse. Thankfully, though, that was a long time ago, and we both have a tad more wisdom now."

"Wisdom from life experience?"

"Exactly," Horus replied.

Gesturing toward the back door, Horus said, "Come, let us go to the back yard before they start without us." They walked out to a courtyard covered in flowers and various plants. A fence surrounded the yard, made even more secluded because of the tall bushes attached to it.

Already seated around the large circular table were Osiris, Ra, Pangu, Shiva, Seth, and several others. Many other gods sat in chairs spread throughout the yard. Baldr stood with his hands folded in front of him, waiting near the back doorway of the courtyard.

Standing in the four corners of the yard were four gods wearing white shrouds that veiled their entire bodies, including their faces.

"What are they?" Aaron asked, nodding toward one of the shrouded gods, as he took a seat between Osiris and Pangu. Dagon stood in the corner of the courtyard with his hands folded.

"Servants," Osiris answered.

"You have other gods serving you?" he probed further.

"Only today. I know it may seem odd, but they are here for a reason. They have a purpose, Aaron." Aaron didn't say anything but was perplexed, seeing them with their faces covered.

Pangu left the table, putting his hand on Aaron's shoulder, greeting him, "*Em hotep,* my friend." Aaron gave an awkward smile. He didn't understand what Pangu had said. For whatever reason, it didn't translate for him.

"Okay, you know I have to ask. What does that mean?" Aaron conceded.

"Glad you asked," Pangu calmly stated. "Not many would ask in a place like this, full of gods. It simply means *peace to you.* It is our greeting here in Duat."

Ra rose from his chair. "Brothers, may I speak?"

Slowly, everyone turned their attention to him. "Since our last assembly nearly one week ago, you all heard Sekhmet share her point of view on fighting with Thor. I ask you again; how can we as Sh'losh defend Zeus after what he did to us? I know many of you gods agreed with her, that we should be fighting *against* the Immortals instead of for them."

Ra's falcon eyes pierced into Osiris', then he continued, "I ask that you all consider this again. The Immortal's imperialistic manner may not be the aggressor today, but it will be tomorrow. They may ask for our hand today for help, but tomorrow they will step on our necks. Look at what they did to my people! How can we be expected to join them after such persecution? I would like you all to rethink your ideas and join *us*."

"Brother," Shiva said loudly, "I already told you all what Hades and Vulcan did, when they came to my home just a few days ago. How they tried to persuade me to join their cause and go to Olympus and bring my army to fight for the Immortals. How Vulcan tried to poison me when I told them I was not interested. Let me be clear. I cannot side with you and Sekhmet to fight against Zeus, because that means I would be fighting against Osiris. But as the leader of the Kailash Hills and those within my area, despite being under Duati rule, I will not fight along with the Immortals after what they tried to do to me in my own home."

Shiva continued, "Osiris, you are my King and I wish the best for you in this battle, but those from Kailash will not take part in this conflict, on either side." Osiris nodded as Shiva sat back down. Shiva grabbed a small cup of tea he had near him, sniffed it, then took a sip.

"Wait!" Osiris commanded, lifting his hand. "Ra, before Shiva spoke, did you say *join you*?"

Ra, still standing, nodded. "Yes, I did. Sekhmet and others have already left for Asgard, but there is no reason we all cannot go. It is not too late." Everyone in the courtyard gasped. Aaron felt the same discomfort he had when Odin was railing against the Most High. He wished he were somewhere else, anywhere else.

Ra glanced around, then continued, "All of you have been nothing but gracious to us Sh'losh. For the Sh'losh who are fighting with Thor, we would ask for one more act of kindness: That once Zeus is dead and is in Sheol, you let us pass through your land so we can travel to Baltia. Every god that went with Sekhmet to Asgard knows that they are not going to be welcomed back to Duat by you, Osiris. But this is something that must be done. Zeus needs to be punished for what he did to us."

Mortified, Pangu asked, "What has Sekhmet done? What have *you* done?"

"Those of you here today are the last gods we would ever want to stand against," Ra assured them, "But for the justice of my gods who suffered under his tyranny, we have no choice."

Ma'at, a Duati and wife to Toth, spoke out from her seat, "You know nothing of justice. How dare you mock such a beautiful concept with the hate and anger you spew. Your actions will lead to many unnecessary deaths, Ra. Maybe your own."

Livid, Ra glared at her and responded, "And who are you to judge me? You speak of justice. It is easy to talk about forgiveness when you were not the one who suffered."

"My husband Toth was, and he would never do something so unbecoming!" Toth scratched his beak, then took his wife's hand with a proud gleam.

Osiris stood up and declared, "I believe it is best that you leave. And anyone joining you in going to Asgard, you may leave now without incident." In response, Ra stood, gently placed his chair under the table, and left. No one else followed.

Chapter 39 *The final days*

Osiris watched Ra depart, then glared at Horus, Seth, Anubis, and the other Sh'losh who were sitting together.

"And you three? Will you be joining him?"

Horus responded, "I am a proud Sh'losh, damn proud. But now, thanks to you, I am also a Duati. You fight, I fight." The other Sh'losh in the courtyard echoed his support.

"Besides," he added, "This is *my* house. I live here, so *you* would have to leave." Shiva charged over to him, giving him a playful hug.

Sobek, an intimidating god with the head of a crocodile, chuckled to himself. He stood up and began walking toward the door, following Ra.

"Are you sure?" Horus asked. Sobek stopped, nodded, then left. No one spoke.

"Baldr," Osiris said, glancing at him where he stood in a corner. "To what do we owe this pleasure?"

Taking a step forward, he replied, "I was sent by Thor to ask for Modi's body, so we may give him a proper burial."

"So, no new secrets?" Osiris asked, prodding. "No new information about your brother you care to share with us all?"

"I have none," Baldr answered. "The moment I returned from Mount Hor, he sent me here. I give you my oath in my name that when I return, you will receive a hoopoe with any information I have."

One of the servants shrouded in white approached Baldr, holding up and offering one of the glasses of wine the servant displayed on a silver tray.

"Get away from me," he said, rejecting the servant's offer. The servant said nothing, but held the tray out closer.

"I said, get away from me," Baldr repeated. The servant silently backed up into the corner.

Baldr continued, now talking to everyone, "What do I gain from lying to you all? I need your help to become king. I would not jeopardize that by hiding anything."

"Why not just serve your brother?" Shiva asked, sipping his tea.

"Because he is a fool!" Baldr thundered. "I am the fated one to rule Asgard. He stole it from me. Now I am here for his son's body, like a damn servant. I would happily tie him to my horse and drag him back for his stupidity of serving his father so blindly, putting him in harm's way."

The same servant approached Baldr again.

"What is wrong with you," Baldr said. "Are you deaf?"

"Servant, please," Osiris said sternly. The servant walked to the table and placed the tray in

247

front of Shiva. Then he returned to his corner, arms folded.

Osiris shook his head, then said, "Baldr, one day the spy, the next an ambassador. Must get confusing for you to know which face you are supposed to wear each day." Tapping the table with his hand, he continued.

"I will send Modi back respectfully to Asgard when *everything* is finished."

Baldr grimaced, then said, "Osiris, it is--" But before he could continue, a loud cawing came from the sky, silencing him. It was a large bird, holding something in its beak.

The winged messenger dropped a small piece of rolled-up parchment onto the table.

"Hoopoe?" Aaron asked, having read about them. Shiva nodded, picking it up and inspecting the scroll briefly before handing it to Osiris. The letter had a red-wax seal. It was circular, and inside was a double-peaked mountain, the right slightly taller. Osiris picked up the scroll and tore away the seal.

"What is happening?" Aaron asked Shiva.

"It is a letter from Mount Olympus," he answered, pointing at the seal.

Osiris read the message then gestured to the hoopoe, which flew away afterward. Osiris leaned back in his chair deep in thought. Whatever was written had turned Osiris' attention away from Baldr. He tossed the letter to Pangu.

248

"It is time you leave, Asgardian," Osiris proclaimed. Baldr stomped out the courtyard without a word, walked through the house, and disappeared through the front door. Pangu had read the letter as he waited for Baldr to leave, then handed it to Toth. Osiris rubbed his hands along his shaved head.

"Brothers, the time has come. Olympus has learned that the Asgardians will be attacking in only a matter of days. We have to prepare and leave immediately."

Toth cried out, "We may already be too late!"

"You are right," Osiris said. "Listen, nothing has changed. In the same manner that Lord Shiva has stated he cannot commit his gods to fight alongside us, each and every one of you must make your own choice. I am King, but I will not demand any of you fight for a province that is not your own. We will ready ourselves immediately."

Osiris took a deep breath, then added, "Those coming to Olympus need to be at the northwestern shore of Lake Ronkonkoma by midnight tonight. We can discuss everything else on the way. Does anyone have anything that needs to be said before we end this assembly?"

Toth stood up. "I do."

Osiris responded, "Please."

"I am ready to both fight and die to keep the Duati safe. I hope I am not alone on this. I understand that Osiris stands here and says you all must make a choice, but for me, there is none to make. If Asgard is allowed to take Olympus, they will undoubtedly continue here to Duat afterward. As a Sh'losh, I am not happy about defending Zeus, but I am more than willing to fight alongside all of you."

"Thank you, Toth," Osiris replied. "Shiva, I respect your decision." He reached out and clasped forearms with his fellow Duati.

Looking at Pangu, he pointed at him. "I need you to go inform the four tribes. Thankfully, they should be ready, since we already warned them."

Osiris continued, "Friends, we do not know every Sh'losh that left with Ra. I ask that you Sh'losh, before we leave at midnight, mark your helmets and armor with the Duati seal so we can make the distinction. I understand that Ra and whoever is with him are our brothers, but..." Pausing, he scanned the courtyard.

"Either way, we all know what must be done to keep Saggilmut safe. *Em hotep*!"

"*Em hotep*!" they responded loudly.

Aaron approached Dagon, "We need to go to Asgard now."

"It will take us three days," he answered. "Based on the letter Osiris just received, we will need to rush, or they will more than likely already be marching to Olympus."

Aaron held up one finger, asking for a little time. He ran over to Osiris, who was talking with Toth and Pangu.

"Osiris, can I bother you for a second?" Resting his hand on Aaron's shoulder, Osiris led him a few steps away.

"Of course," Osiris said, focusing his attention.

Aaron wanted to tell him Zeus wasn't who he thought he was. He wanted to tell him about everything he saw with Odin being tortured, and about Ahriman. Aaron knew that simply saying anything could get him in trouble with the Most High, since he was not supposed to interfere at all, but he wanted to tell someone, anyone who would help.

"Yes Aaron?" he prompted.

Losing his courage, Aaron said in a low voice, "Nothing. Just b-be safe."

Chapter 40 *Asgard*

It had been three long days riding on horseback, and Aaron and Dagon were finally nearing Asgard. They had fallen far behind Ra, Sobek, and Baldr. Early in the trip, they could see the trio in the distance, but by nightfall the first day they had disappeared ahead on the trail. Aaron decided they were so much faster because they were far more experienced riders and didn't need to stop to use the bathroom nearly as often as he did. Bouncing around on a horse for hours was rough on his bladder.

"That is Asgard," Dagon announced, pointing toward numerous smoke columns rising skyward not far in the distance, behind a moss-filled stone wall.

"It's huge," Aaron said.

"It is," Dagon agreed.

"But they refer to it as the *Village*? That, my friend, is a *little* larger than a village. Don't they know what *a village* is?"

"Asgard began as one. It grew into what you see now as gods came joining the first Asgardians. The kings kept the name."

The city was the polar opposite of Olympus, no highrises or clean white stone. Aaron couldn't find one home any higher than a few stories, they were made of various misshapen stones and wood.

Aaron did notice two large buildings, both gated on opposing sides of the city. "What are those?" he asked, pointing at them to Dagon.

"The one near the large tree there is the castle. It is Odin's--I am sorry, it is *Thor's* home now. The other there is Valhalla. A training camp for many of their warriors." Aaron decided it was best not to say he knew what Valhalla was, because everything he understood from it came from watching movies. Dagon wouldn't have been impressed.

It wasn't long afterward that Aaron noticed the aroma of meat cooking. *Someone is having a barbeque*, he thought. His stomach immediately reminded him that the various nuts and now-stale bread just weren't cutting it anymore.

But it was the sounds coming from Asgard that gripped him more than anything else. The beating of drums and war cries were vicious and erratic the closer they got. Asgard was ready for war, and anyone nearby knew it.

Outside, beside the city walls were thousands of shirtless bearded men preparing for battle. One large group was painting their wooden shields bright blue with various symbols. Other men, standing together in their group, were painting theirs yellow with different designs. There was also a group of women doing the same, using a bold red. Many even had their faces painted to match. Aaron

253

glanced silently at Dagon, curious to know who they all were.

"Over there are the Rekkrs," he said, pointing at one group. "And those are the Berserkers. The color of their shields indicates which group they belong to."

"And the women?" Aaron asked.

"They are women, Aaron, but they would just as soon slice off your head for calling them that. They are shieldmaidens, and they are incredibly fierce." *Stay away from Viking shieldmaidens--check.*

The warriors shouted and raised their arms as Aaron rode by. One blew into a horn, producing a deafening tone. Aaron covered his ears, blocking the intense pitch. Fortunately, the blast didn't last long, but Aaron's ears continued to ring as they entered the stone city walls.

Entering the eastern gate, Dagon grabbed Aaron by the shoulder, leading him through the crowd toward the castle. Being led like a child, Aaron couldn't help but think about his little sister. Now he knew how she felt whenever he held her hand, leading her around in public and making her jog to keep up. *I'll never do that again to her*, he thought, chuckling. Then the looming thought hit him: *I'll never have the chance to do it again.*

Despite the Vikings' crowded frenzy of banging drums, shoving, and screaming at one another, Aaron couldn't drown out the rushing thoughts of his mom and sister. He could see Sarah, from a few years prior, covered in makeup after she found their mom's purse. He could almost feel his mom's hug, which she *forced* on him when he came home after work. She knew he was working his ass off for the family. He knew it bothered her that she didn't earn enough, and that he had to work so hard at such a young age to help them. His throat tightened and he couldn't swallow.

"I can't leave them," Aaron said, unsure who he was even speaking to. "They need me."

He had reconciled that his life wasn't exactly where he thought he'd end up a year after graduating, so whenever the doctors did finally choose to pull the plug, it wasn't going to be a big loss for human history. But he was a good brother, and Sarah could use him around for a few more years. His mom was going to miss him, too, but he couldn't help worrying about how she was going to find the extra money his work had provided for the bills.

"Damn!" he shouted, tensing his entire body, but no one heard. Even Dagon, still leading him, paid no attention with all the other voices nearby.

The notion of being an important writer shrank in comparison to the thought that he wouldn't be there for them. *Who would Sarah become? Would she even remember him in another year or two? Would Mom marry Tyler? At least*

Tyler could maybe help, he thought. *He was a supportive guy*, a *good man*.

"I'm going to ask the Most High if he'll let me go back," he declared, mostly to himself. Dagon turned to him.

"You can ask him anything," Dagon said. "However, you have to be ready for an answer you may not want."

"It just sucks, because I understand that Earth sucks. You do get used to it, and it can be fun for sure, but to die and then come *here*?"

Aaron shook his head, "Even in death, we haven't seen the end of war."

Dagon looked at him in confusion as they entered the castle foyer.

"Plato," Aaron remarked. "It's a play on a famous quote from the philosopher." Seeing that Dagon had no idea what he was saying he stopped himself. "Never mind."

Dagon led him into the crowded sanctuary where he expected to find Thor sitting on his throne, but he wasn't there. He led Aaron through the timbered hall with vaulted ceilings and then into a dining hall. The hall was filled with both gods and Vikings. They were eating, drinking, standing on tables, and celebrating. Everything that Aaron would have guessed Vikings did at dinner.

Aaron quickly spotted Sekhmet and Bastet standing on a table, arms around each other, singing loudly for the crowd. They had colored their faces in war paint, similar to many of the Vikings in the room.

The two continued to wander the castle, watching everyone eat and enjoy themselves before the march to Olympus, but they were unable to find Thor. Dagon touched Aaron's shoulder, pointing him to Sjofn, who was standing near two goddesses who appeared to be related.

"That is Thor's mother, Queen Frigg, and the other is her sister Freya. Between the three, they may know where he is," he advised. Aaron gave him a quick thumbs up to avoid speaking aloud. He glanced at Frigg and Freya. They were both tall and slender, with strawberry blonde hair that fell to the small of their backs. He dreaded speaking to Frigg, knowing that her husband was imprisoned in Olympus with Ahriman. As they approached the goddesses, Aaron wanted to pull away from Dagon's grip and run. He hated this madness, this war, but most of all he hated knowing what he did about Odin.

They walked over and stood directly in front of the three. Aaron raised his hand tentatively, feeling as if he was a student trying to get his teacher's attention. For a moment, he thought Frigg must have been purposely avoiding him, as it appeared that she made eye contact. Sjofn spotted him, and with a welcoming grin, she nudged Frigg toward him.

Frigg glanced at Dagon, offering a gentle bow, then turned toward Aaron and smiled."*Heil og sæl,* Writer."

Clueless to what she said, he attempted to respond, "*Hel oag seel.*" Knowing he had butchered it, he mouthed the words, "I'm sorry" to her. She laughed aloud, without concern for his apology.

"That was sweet that he tried," Sjofn offered.

"It can be best translated to mean *health and happiness.* It is our greeting here in Asgard," Frigg explained.

Aaron nodded, feeling like an idiot for the lame attempt, then simply replied, "Thanks, you, too." He felt even more stupid the moment the words came out. "*Thanks, you too?*" *Makes no sense.*

"I like this nether." Frigg smiled. "What are you doing here, Writer?"

"Thor, we need to speak to Thor," he answered.

"Of course," she replied, "And may I say, I am glad you are here to record everything. I do not want history to view Thor becoming the sovereign ruler of the realms as anything other than what it is."

"And what's that?" he asked.

Leaning in so close her breath tickled his face, she whispered the word, "Fate," then smiled.

Rising again, she spoke to Dagon. "He is on the castle walls. I believe you are familiar enough with the layout?" Dagon gave a single nod.

Aaron waved as they left the goddesses, ventured down another hall, and up a flight of steps. Reaching the top of the castle, they exited a thick wooden door that led onto the castle wall. Taking the first step out, Aaron immediately felt the wind rush against his face.

Crap! With a quick shiver, he turned his head toward the inside of the village walls to escape the gusts and was amazed to see a field of warriors. The walls themselves couldn't contain the horde, which flowed out of the four gates into even larger masses.

Chapter 41 *War celebration*

"How many people are out there?" Aaron asked, following Dagon on the wall. Aaron had never seen so many people in one place. He wasn't sure he had seen that many people in his entire life. Every street was packed with people; there was an energy in the air. Asgard knew their king was ready for a battle.

"I cannot say," he answered. "I would estimate perhaps three million, if not more."

"Damn." The villagers were enjoying themselves in festivities like they hadn't a care in the world. Like they had already won.

"Why are they celebrating? I'm nervous, and I'm not even fighting. Crap, I'm nervous *for* them." *And everyone else for that matter*, he realized.

"Fate, Aaron. They believe fate is on their side. Fate can be a powerful force in someone's life," Dagon said.

"What do you mean?"

"One may have faith in something bigger than themselves, fate being it for these Asgardians. But if the outcome does not match where they placed their faith, then clearly it may be ill-suited, or nonsense. They may be acting out of ignorance or stupidity."

"Aren't ignorance and stupidity the same thing?" Aaron stood to Dagon's side so he could block the wind.

"Ignorance is not knowing. Stupidity is being aware of what you believe may not be true and choosing to believe in it wholeheartedly anyway."

"Are you saying Asgard is being stupid or ignorant, then?"

"Neither. To an outsider like me and you, it can appear as either. Only they know if their belief in this fate of ruling is grounded in truth or fiction."

"You know, you're a pretty smart god sometimes." Dagon took hold of Aaron's head, shaking it lightly.

"And you are a decent student."

Aaron turned his attention back to the broad walls. He saw Thor, not too much further, inside one of the many watchtowers with a few other gods he couldn't quite make out.

The stone room gave them concealment, except for the doorways on each side of the room opening to the wall. There were a number of small windows that allowed them to peer out in all directions. The moss grew all around the tower and the walls.

Reaching the door, Aaron paused, taking shelter behind Dagon. He still wasn't keen on speaking to Thor but found courage with Dagon by his side. From outside, it appeared they were finishing up a meeting.

Aaron didn't recognize any of the gods as they passed from the doorway back onto the wall. Most were holding drinks, singing as they stumbled along. Aaron did notice Baldr in the middle of the group.

"Right, right!" Baldr exclaimed to a god Aaron didn't know. "Thor said I will stay and act as king regent while you all go…" Aaron couldn't hear anymore with the noise and wind. He kept walking, but looked back and saw Baldr spilling his drink as he strutted, pumping his fist, and shouting toward the warriors below on his way back to the party.

"Baldr's staying back?" Aaron said to Dagon. "And he's happy about it. Doesn't seem very Asgardian of him."

"You cannot mention that you saw him in Nekhen," Dagon stated.

"Oh, I know, no *interfering*," Aaron said, making air quotes. He sincerely wanted to *interfere*, but wasn't about to do anything that could incite Thor.

Chapter 42 *Know your position*

Aaron and Dagon walked under the cover of the watchtower, and Thor glanced over at them. Next to him were Magni, Tyr, and two other gods Aaron didn't know.

"Forseti, I trust you can handle it," Thor announced to the brutish god standing near Tyr. The god smiled at Thor proudly, despite missing half of his teeth. He turned and headed toward the door. "You are my eyes and ears!" Thor added.

Forseti quickly spun around, struck his chest once with his fist, then continued on his way out without missing a step. Watching him leave, Thor gestured to Aaron to come in.

"Ah, nether," he said, his voice echoing inside his horn while he took a large drink. "I see you and fishhead found us." Aaron peeked at Dagon to see his reaction. Dagon folded his hands in front of him and turned his attention to the crowd he could see through a small window.

Tyr walked toward Dagon, extending his left arm.

"Always good to see you," Tyr said. Dagon accepted his welcome. Thor shook his head at Tyr, turned back around, and leaned against the stone wall. He stared out through a small window toward the crowd. The window was almost too high for Aaron to see out.

"So, what's the occasion?" Aaron asked, nodding toward the crowd.

"We are celebrating," Thor replied. "Tomorrow we go to battle."

"So you have a *party*?" he asked, closing the distance between them.

"What better reason is there for warriors to eat, drink, and enjoy themselves?"

Seeing Aaron's confusion, he continued, "You cannot understand, Writer. To you, death is where life ends. That makes it something to fear."

"This whole dying and going to Saggilmut thing is new to me. Now I learn that when someone dies here, they go to Sheol. I don't know what to think of death anymore. What does it mean for you?

Taking a drink from his horn, Thor said, "I saw my brother Vali murdered. Then, for thousands of years, I saw those responsible get away with everything, while the Most High did absolutely nothing to gain retribution for my family. And then, he kicks out my father for *nothing*." Aaron, not knowing what to say, just listened.

Taking another large drink, Thor continued, "Aaron, death is not to be feared, but respected. If I die and go to Sheol, then so be it. I will still fight in there to ensure that the fate of Asgard is achieved."

"Fight in Sheol?" Aaron didn't know what to make of it. "What happens if you die there?" He didn't know why he asked Thor that question, it just

264

slipped out. But luckily, Thor didn't seem to be annoyed.

"A nightmare," he answered. "Death in Sheol begins the true eternal nightmare." Aaron didn't understand, but Thor's shaken tone was enough to make him realize he didn't want to know more.

Thor continued, "We are celebrating because we are going to correct all this. Soon Zeus, that *fif'l*, will be in Sheol, and I cannot wait."

Aaron mouthed at Dagon the word *fif'l* with a shrug. Dagon silently said the word *fool*. With a quick nod, Aaron turned and prepared to listen to Thor continue, but he was drinking from his horn again.

Aaron glanced at Magni. His eyes were bloodshot, with dark bags. He probably hadn't slept in days.

"I hate to ask," Aaron said cautiously, "but is it worth it to you? I mean, risking everyone's lives? Your son, brothers. I think that--"

"What is it you *do* exactly, Aaron?" Thor said.

"I'm not sure what you mean," he said. "What I *do*?"

"Job," he stated. "What was your job on Earth?"

Aaron immediately felt uneasy. He glanced at Dagon, but saw he wasn't going to get the help he wanted. He wanted to leave. A sense of shame came over him like a dark cloud.

Aaron answered, "I'm not sure what that has to do with anything. Right now I am the Writer, and--"

"What was your job?" Thor asked again, sharper.

"I am a j-janitor," he answered. "An elementary school janitor." Seeing Thor's brow raised, he knew the look he was receiving. It was the same face all of his old friends made when he told them.

Now, in front of a king, he had to see it again.

"You wouldn't get it," Aaron said under his breath. There weren't many options for a nineteen year-old who needed to earn money quickly for his family. A lump formed in his throat, and he was sickened to imagine what Thor must have thought of him. The lowest form of nether trying to talk to *him*, a King.

The thing was, he enjoyed the job, even if others mocked him for it. It brought in enough to cover the rent and then some. More importantly, it let him work at Sarah's school, and she thought it was great seeing her big brother during the day, so he loved it.

"So then, *janitor*," Thor replied in the exact tone Aaron had hoped he wouldn't. "How about you scrub floors, and I'll lead my people? Someone who does not truly know their position in life is often quick to offer advice to those far wiser and more established. I do not mock you for what you do, Aaron, but do not give advice when you do not know what you are speaking of. These matters are *above* you."

Aaron certainly heard enough. The knot in his throat was trembling, and with little ability to hold it back any longer, he nodded and left.

Passing through the door and walking back along the wall, Aaron found the wind had become even more chaotic. He was glad because it seemed to take away his shattered nerves as it blew from both sides, almost pushing him over. Nearing the doorway leading back into the castle, he felt a hand rest on his shoulder. It was Tyr.

"Listen," Tyr said. "My brother cares. He cares about his family, his gods, and his people. He is loyal to a fault, if there is such a thing."

"There is," Aaron offered. "When you hate everyone else that isn't in your circle."

"That may be true, but he believes this can bring peace to Saggilmut, and that is something we have not had since...well, ever."

"His own *insane* version of peace, and what about you? Do you think killing Zeus is the answer?" Aaron folded his arms, it was damn cold up there.

Tyr gripped his stump, massaging it, then said, "I lost my hand protecting my family. I wish there was another way to bring peace to this realm, but until one presents itself, I will stand by my brother."

Aaron didn't know what to say. Nothing he thought he could say would change anything. Tyr smiled and turned back, walking toward Thor.

"You seem kind-hearted, Aaron," Tyr said. "I am sure you would enjoy spending time with Sjofn, and a few others of us one day, when this is over."

Such a nice god, surrounded by a bunch of-- but it wasn't worth it, he decided, stopping himself. Aaron looked at Dagon, "It's time we go."

"Olympus?" Dagon asked.

"Yeah, we should get there before Asgard makes their way."

Chapter 43 *Sun Setting, Bows Rising*

The following evening, Aaron and Dagon returned to Olympus. Entering through the southern doorway, Aaron noticed it had the same layout as the western entrance he had seen when he first came. The same style fountain and shops, and similar highrises.

The difference was in the atmosphere. Instead of people in the plaza enjoying themselves, there were rows of Hoplite soldiers holding spears and shields. Rather than people hanging out of their balcony windows chatting, most were blocked. Those that were open showed more Hoplites with bows. Along the route to the castle, the streets were filled with soldiers lining the cobblestone road.

Aaron's stomach turned and his nerves were unsettled, yet he was ready to go to sleep, exhausted from the night's travel. He didn't know what he should be feeling. How should one feel before a war? Is there a *right way* to feel? He worried, but after everything that he'd seen, he no longer knew which side he was more worried for. Nothing felt black or white, right or wrong. Everything was so confusing.

As he reached the city square, Aaron noticed Jove, who was pointing out positions and advising the commanding Hoplites. Jove held a long golden trident and a body-length shield. The shield was decorated with the same two-peaked mountain design that was on the seal from the message sent to Osiris.

Athena stood at the tower's entrance, speaking with Mercury. There was a tangible panic in the air. Taking a deep breath, Aaron found some solace that he wasn't the only one panicking. Conflicting emotions showed on all of their faces.

Except for one group. Thousands lined up together in a military formation. They were dressed differently than the Hoplites. They wore dark crimson tunics, carried saggilmut stone shields, and had spears that were taller than themselves. Unlike the others, they showed no fear in their eyes. They were calm, prepared.

"Who are *they*?" Aaron asked, pointing toward the warriors.

"That is Ares, there," Dagon answered, pointing to the god at the front of the formation. "And those are the Spartans. They are the only people to ever have successfully hunted and killed some of the Unspoken."

"Damn," Aaron said, with admiration. "God-killers."

"God-killers, indeed," Dagon echoed.

Near the castle's entrance, Dagon stopped at the doorway where Aphrodite and Poseidon stood, blocking anyone from entering.

Aaron tapped Aphrodite's elbow and spoke her name.

Her eyes lit up with warmth. "Aaron!" She tapped Poseidon's arm. "Let him in. He is our *special* guest."

Aaron smiled, unsure why someone like her would be so kind to him. *Wish girls back home were as kind*, he thought. She and Poseidon both moved aside for Aaron and Dagon to step into the foyer.

"Think Zeus is in the study where Dadga taught?" He had hoped to bump into Sophia. He worried over her, hoping maybe she left Olympus and became reincarnated as she had wanted.

"No, no, that is the eastern hall," Dagon said. "I believe Zeus would be in the council's chambers. First door on the right along the northern hall."

Aaron agreed and they walked toward the north hall. He glanced over toward the study, but there were far too many people there for him to try and spot her. *Be safe*, he thought, thinking about Sophia. He wasn't sure who he was talking to. W*as that a prayer? I know she can't hear me, so why would I even think it?* The more he thought about it, the more baffled he became. *Am I just talking to myself?* Made sense, since he never felt like his prayers were heard.

Entering the room, Dagon went to the corner, folding his hands as was customary for him. The room wasn't large, and had only wooden walls.

Nothing special, Aaron thought. Except for the colossal map spread over the table in the center of the room. The gods gathered there were in deep discussion over possible strategies and scenarios. Aaron couldn't make sense of any of the terms they used: *flanking*, *funneling defense*, and *phalanx defense*. He was lost.

On the map were various scattered pieces, representing each province's forces. Zeus stood, listening intently to his son Apollo debating strategies with numerous other gods around the table.

Aaron was shaken, startled seeing Hades. He was pale, sweating as he sat in the corner. He was wearing a long white robe with a hood draped just above the top of his tired red eyes.

Aphrodite, who had followed Aaron into the room, leaned close to Aaron and whispered, "He is dying. We believe he has no more than a day or so left."

"How? What happened?" Aaron asked.

"From what he told us, he was attacked by the Duati, Lord Shiva, who also murdered Vulcan. Hades and Vulcan were sent to the Kailash region to ask for help from Lord Shiva. He has a good sized population that could have fought for us. Instead of just saying no, or even saying nothing at all, Shiva tricked them. He invited them inside his home and poisoned Vulcan. Thankfully, Hades refused. He tried to save Vulcan, but Shiva shot him

272

with an arrow. Can you believe that? Like Zeus always says: *You can never fully trust these other sects.*"

Aaron was at a loss for words. He recalled how, in Nekhen, Shiva had given a very different account of what had occurred.

"Who's that with him?" Aaron asked, hoping to change the subject.

"That is his wonderful wife Persephone," she answered. The beautiful black-haired goddess sat next to her husband with her two hands wrapped around his hand. Zeus, seeing Aaron in the room, waved him over.

"Aaron, I am glad you chose to be here during this grave time. I want you in the tower with Jove, where you can watch these savages scatter like cockroaches from a candle."

Aaron nodded, encouraged by the idea of being in a place that would allow him to see the battlefield. He was grateful Zeus would think about him, but a more pressing thought lingered in Aaron's mind: Odin.

"Thank you, and that sounds great," he replied, placating him. Taking a deep breath to bolster his confidence, he said "But I would like to ask you something, if that is okay?"

"Yes, of course, but please make it quick," Zeus replied. "I really must prepare."

"I was hoping it could be somewhere private?" he said.

"I am sorry, but that just is not possible today."

Aaron stood on his toes and very quietly said, "I know about Odin in your dungeon."

Zeus looked at Aaron, dumbfounded.

Chapter 44 *Ahriman*

"I am sorry, what?" Zeus asked.

"I *saw* him. I saw Odin," Aaron assured him, hoping to drop the facade, though his hands were trembling. He did it behind his back, trying not to come off as scared as he was. After a quick mental pep talk, Aaron continued, "Just a few days ago. You were the first one I came to see when I arrived here to Sagglemet- Sagleg-"

"Saggilmut," Zeus corrected.

"Anyway..." With Dagon's presence, he felt emboldened. "When I first came here, while waiting for you in the castle, I saw Ahriman walking by in a strange rush, so I followed him. I saw him beating the shit out of Odin."

Zeus grabbed his son Apollo's tunic, signaling for him to join them in the conversation.

"You need to show me, Aaron," Zeus commanded.

Zeus had a sense of urgency that appeared to have gripped him. He was nervous. Aaron led the two Immortals with Dagon trailing. Both Aphrodite and another goddess Aaron didn't know watched curiously, but returned to their discussion at the table.

Without speaking, Aaron led Zeus to the foyer and along the other hallway to the same stairwell. He half-heartedly believed that Odin would be gone. That Zeus would take him for a fool.

But as they made it down the stairwell and turned the corner, they found Odin still hanging on the post by a chain locked around his arms, his feet dangling.

A disturbing mixture of blood, sweat, and dirt covered his body. Aaron looked away, frustrated, and sickened. He had never seen anything like that. He was shocked at how much worse Odin was. Both sides of his battered chest were blackened to a purple hue. His hands were missing fingers, the bloody stubs lying on the ground under him. Gashes covered his body.

Ahriman had clearly been toying with him, holding death over him mercilessly.

Ahriman stood in front of Odin, but hadn't noticed his visitors. With his back facing the stairwell, Ahriman was whispering to Odin. He held a machete in his hand, pressed against Odin's chest.

Without pause, Zeus pulled his small dagger from his cloth waistband and thrust it directly into the back of Ahriman's neck. With first a grunt, then gurgling sound, Ahriman dropped to his knees. Odin lifted his head just enough to watch Ahriman take his last breath. Zeus withdrew the blade then stepped away, letting the lifeless body slump to the floor.

Dagon had removed his sword from his sheath, gripping Aaron's shoulder, but Zeus slid his blade back into his waistline without pausing to wipe it.

He turned and called to Apollo, "Go now and get Asclepius and Epione from the medical chambers!" He placed his foot on Ahriman. "Have them take this piece of shit and throw him off the northern cliffs. He will not receive an Immortal burial. I want Odin taken to a bed in the chambers and his wounds tended to."

Apollo quickly responded, "Yes, my king," and turned to run, but Zeus called out again.

"I still want Odin in chains and guarded," he commanded. Apollo grunted his reply and rushed up the stairwell.

Zeus drew a deep breath and looked back at Odin. "Asclepius and Epione are the best medical experts in Saggilmut. They will take good care of you."

Zeus sighed. "I am sorry Aaron. I did not know."

Odin's chin rested slack on his collar. Except for his chest rising and falling with each breath, he appeared lifeless.

Zeus took off the purple robe that was draped over his white cloak and covered Odin. Zeus then dropped to his knees, searching Ahriman's corpse. Finding a set of keys tied around his neck, Zeus tugged them past his head and stood up to unlock the shackles. Inserting then turning the key, Zeus watched as Odin collapsed to the ground.

"We had better leave him," Zeus said.
"Trying to move him could cause more pain."
Aaron stood, frozen in place. His medical training was limited to Band-Aids. They waited together silently.

Zeus paced until Apollo returned with the two gods, Asclepius and Epione, who brought a carrying board to lift him with. Dagon moved forward to help them lift Odin and gently lower him onto the wooden gurney. The two medics rushed him away as quickly as they came in.

"Damn it, Aaron, I am sorry," Zeus said once again. "A king cannot offer excuses and must know what his subjects are doing."

Aaron glanced at his shaky hands then offered some reassurance. "You can't know everything. I'm just glad you acted so quickly to help. I wish Thor would have seen you help him. Maybe it would, I dunno..."

Zeus asked, "Did you tell Thor that Odin was here?"

"No," he answered. "I haven't said anything to anyone."

"Thank you. It is not always easy to manage a kingdom, even less so when you have these savages making their way to attack you and your way of life. Listen, you are more than welcome to return to the war room, but I really must leave to return there now." Zeus reached out and clasped Aaron's forearm.

"Thank you again," Zeus repeated as he quickly headed up the stairwell. Aaron and Dagon followed more slowly. As they started up the stairs, Aaron paused; he had never seen anyone killed before. He had attended funerals, but that wasn't the same. Even though Ahriman was evil and probably deserved to die, Aaron still felt bad, even queasy.

"How soon do you think Asgard will be here?" Aaron asked Dagon.

"As early as tonight's sunset," Dagon answered. "They will most likely attack either at dawn or dusk, when the sky creates limited visibility."

Aaron looked around the foyer at the surrounding chaos. The noise and tension of the situation bothered him. He wasn't only nervous for them anymore, he was anxious for himself. Death was real. *Anyone can die*, he thought.

"Let's go to the tower now," Aaron said. "Maybe get some sleep before everything goes crazy." He didn't need sleep; he needed quiet.

"Are you sure? You do not want to get something to eat first?" Dagon offered. Aaron shook his head, and the two made their way to the tower. Aaron walked past Ares, deep in conversation with a goddess. He overheard him refer to her as Nike, but he didn't have it in him to care. Who knew if she would even be alive tomorrow? *Everyone I've been learning about could be dead soon.*

Entering the tower, they saw a stairwell wrapping around the inner walls ascending to the top, but on the opposite side was a small iron elevator.

"Oh, thank you!" Aaron said, seeing the elevator. They stepped inside, closed the door, and with a pull on the latch, the turnbelts rushed them up to the top smoothly. Walking out of the tower, they found the view was incredible. Aaron could see the ocean to the north and all the beautiful land southward. Off in the distance, Mount Hor was on full display illuminated by the sun's rays.

"What's that for?" Aaron asked, pointing toward a silver trumpet mounted on the wall.

"Various things, but let us hope it is used today to declare the end of the battle," Dagon answered. Aaron moved to the eastern side and gazed down at the rows of tall buildings.

He wondered where Sophia was and if she was scared.

"Ever been up here before?" Aaron asked.

"No, it was built well after we left."

"Can I ask what it was like? I mean, being kicked out and everything." Dagon faced the sunset and considered Aaron's inquiry.

"Are you asking as the Writer or as a friend?"

With a smile, Aaron replied, "A friend."

"In that case, no," he answered with a chuckle.

"You jerk," Aaron said, resting his head against the wall. "You do like trying to make me feel stupid."

Dagon walked over and placed his hand on Aaron's head. He glanced up at the massive fingers draped over his head.

"As a friend, you can ask me again when everything is done," Dagon said.

Aaron nodded in agreement, "Deal."

Chapter 45 *Let it begin*

This night was warm. There wasn't a cloud in the sky, and the stars were abnormally bright, offering decent visibility for the archers. The Hoplite archers were aligned along the four walls of the city, bent on one knee, peering over the finely cut stone battlements. They had been there all night, unmoving, watching for their enemy.

Beside each shooter was a quiver holding twenty additional arrows, and behind them, a barrel of arrows ready to replenish as needed. In addition, a small flame remained lit between each bowman, ready to set their arrows ablaze with a small canister of pitch before firing.

The sun was not ready to rise yet, but Aaron began to wake, stretching on the cold floor of the tower.

"You good?" he asked Dagon, who was sitting, legs crossed, staring down at his feet.

"Of course," he answered. "Asgard will be attacking soon."

Finishing his yawn, Aaron peered over the battlement, "How do you know that?"

"Remember, a warrior attacks in the dusk or dawn," he replied.

"I'll take your word for it," Aaron said, stretching his arms over his head. Then he jumped back, startled, as he saw Jove already on the tower in full armor, standing nearby and looking over the land.

"Holy crap!" Aaron shrieked. Dagon covered his mouth, laughing. Jove quickly glanced back, nodded toward Aaron, then turned back around and continued watching the south.

"Have you been here for long?" Aaron asked, walking to his side.

"Yes, all night," he answered.

Aaron hoped he hadn't snored. He'd feel terrible if the enemy had been able to sneak in because Jove's attention was on his snoring.

Leaning against the battlement next to Jove was his trident, his helmet resting over the three prongs. Near his feet, he had a basket filled with different colored flags.

Aaron wiped the last bit of sleep from his eyes. "I wish I had known. I'd have stayed up with you." He joined Jove at the wall and rested his head against the battlement, surveying as far as the night sky would allow.

"What are those for?" Aaron asked, pointing at the bright yellow flag in Jove's hand.

"Each colored flag and movement I will make with them means a separate order for everyone on the ground."

Jove was slowly mouthing silent orders and moving his hand. He was rehearsing for when they attacked.

"Nervous?" Aaron asked. "It looks like you're practicing."

"As a god, speaking to a young man, the answer one may expect me to say is, of course not." Jove took a deep breath. "But the truth is, yes. I care for the Immortal way of life. I care for the gods inside my province, and I care for the people. I just want to protect it the best I can."

Jove's sincerity was clear.

Aaron said, "I can't say I know what you're going through, but I get that you're trying to be ready." Dagon joined them, placing his sword against the battlement near Joves' weapon.

"I hope you won't have to use it," Dagon said, joining them in peering over the land.

"I do, too," Jove replied.

"Asgard will come from that road, there," Jove said, pointing out the single dirt path from the city doorway went a ways before it disappeared into a row of trees, obviously planted. They were in nearly perfect rows, and lush. They could easily hide thousands of Vikings.

"Just past those trees the mountain descends," Jove added. "So we truly will be unable to see them until they reach past the treeline onto the battlefield."

"That close, huh?" Aaron asked.

Jove replied, "A city on a hill can be well defended, but it can also be extremely vulnerable. I just want these people safe; they do not deserve any harm."

"They deserve to live in safety," Dagon replied. "We all do."

"Think you can defend Olympus from Asgard?" Aaron asked. Having seen the Asgard warriors, and now the massed Hoplite army spread around the city, he couldn't tell which side had more.

Jove raised his index finger, then pointed as he spoke. "We have three entrances. A spy told us they will attack only at the southern entrance, but I cannot abandon the other two doors. So I made sure to place plenty of Hoplites on the western wall just in case, and the northern side is already heavily defended." Aaron turned and walked across the tower to peer over at the northern archway for himself.

"That's it?" Aaron said, unimpressed. The number of Spartans seemed insignificant.

"Those are the Spartans," Jove replied. "They can defend that entry against all of Saggilmut if need be."

"So if they're so great, why not put them at the southern doorway?" he asked. Jove looked at Aaron, shaking his head.

Turning back around again to face the treeline, Jove answered, "You have the makings to be a great battle strategist, but apparently, a terrible king."

"What do you mean?" Aaron asked, confused.

"That was my advice as well," Jove answered. "It only makes sense to put the Spartans there at the southern doorway, since Poseidon informed us that they planned to attack there, but a king will always get his way." Aaron winked at Dagon, proud he had thought up such a smart idea.

Dagon stepped near Jove, placing his hand on his shoulder. The two shared a few words, too quiet for Aaron to hear. He watched, confused. He had thought that it was a foregone conclusion that *all* the Immortals must have hated the Sh'losh. He decided it best he didn't say anything further on that topic.

"Who's leading them?" Aaron asked, pointing to the sea of Hoplites formed up at the southern plaza.

"Neptune is leading the soldiers at the southern entrance, from *inside* the walls. Another one of King Zeus' *wonderful* plans. Inside the plaza, we have one hundred thousand soldiers with him. Using these flags, I will be able to tell Neptune when to send reinforcements to the other hundred thousand just outside the walls."

On the other side of the southern doorway, in a square formation, stood thousands of Hoplites. They stood ready with their helmets, breastplates, and their blue skirts. Each held a spear and shield.

"So you'll signal him, and Neptune will just keep sending more soldiers, trying to stop them from ever making it to the entry?"

"Sounds simple, right?" Jove answered. "We have to hold the entrance until the Duati arrive, because if Asgard does get through the doorway, we all know it is going to be nearly impossible to hold them back from surging into the city and destroying everything. They will attack the castle and...well, I would rather not think about that."

"When do the Duati arrive?" Aaron asked.

"We sent them a message urging them to come as soon as possible. I know Osiris well; he will rush to our aid. He is truly an honorable god, but even still, no earlier than midnight tonight, given how far away they are."

"And where's Zeus?" Aaron asked.

Jove shrugged. "I assume he is already in the safe room, but I do not know for certain. The door guarding the room was built of layered Saggilmut, so it is solid. He can stay in there until Osiris arrives. It is probably better that way."

"What do you mean, better?" he asked. Jove was taking some sort of jab at Zeus.

"He is our king, Aaron, and we Immortals have indeed prospered under him, but..." pausing to choose his words carefully he continued, "No one is perfect, and I would say, maybe he does not handle pressure well." Judging by his face, Aaron knew he struggled to find the proper wording, that Jove felt much stronger about it than he let on.

Aaron decided not to push the issue and rested his head on his folded arms, leaning on the battlement. He, like Jove, trained his eyes on the treeline, watching, waiting silently.

A cold breeze began to pick up, pushing at Aaron lightly. Moments later, the wind rose and became unrelenting, bending the tops of the trees ruthlessly. Aaron, who had raised the school's flag each morning, knew that when a wind like that came from the east, it meant the sun would follow shortly behind. *They attack at dawn*, he thought, replaying Dagon's words.

Suddenly, a sound much louder than the rush of the wind began to rise from the south. The blaring noise was coming from where the road dipped downhill past the trees, out of view. It grew increasingly louder, filling the air. Aaron knew that sound. He had heard the Vikings make it, using their horns when they were painting their shields outside of Asgard. Battle horns.

Hearing the growing blast of the horns, along with now thunderous roar from within the trees, Jove held up a white flag and waved it in circles above his head. The archers along the southern wall dipped their arrow tips into the pitch, and waited for his command to light them.

"Asgard has arrived at Olympus," Jove announced.

Chapter 46 *Enough talking*

The shrill and roar grew louder, painfully earsplitting. The deafening clamor disoriented the Hoplites outside the southern walls and left them gripped in pain, tensing in agony. Hordes of Vikings hammered their shields, shaking the trees.

Aaron plugged his ears, but it didn't help much. The terrible sound carried throughout the city, shaking candles and torches off the walls. Pottery from balconies shattered on the street, and small walkways between buildings crumbled. Aaron was certain that all the Immortals inside the city were now fully aware that Asgard had arrived.

Then, in a single moment, it all stopped. Aaron could still hear it in his mind, still feel it reverberating in his bones. Slowly he uncovered his ears, still hearing a muffled ringing. There was blood on his fingertips. He felt dizzy, like the world was spinning. Aaron placed one hand on the wall for balance, waiting for his mind to stop whirling. He wasn't alone. Both Jove and Dagon were bent over, collecting themselves.

Next, a blinding light erupted in the sky. Aaron lifted his hands to block its radiance as Dagon grabbed him, shielding him from the glare. Aaron caught a glimpse before Dagon's cloak covered him. In the sky, he saw countless arrows with fire tips lighting their flight toward Olympus.

"Holy shit!" Aaron screamed, from under Dagon's protection.

The arrows struck like hail in the city, bursting into fires. They pierced through apartment walls and shattered windows and doors, starting fires in many of the highrises. The Hoplite archers, formed along the walls, dropped onto both knees behind the battlements.

Following Neptune's command, the Hoplite soldiers in the southern plaza raised their shields. Those who were distracted by the light suffered the rain of fire, and many died.

The second wave of arrows soared through the otherwise still-dark sky. A third, then a fourth, and fifth. The sky brightened like the sun at noon with each onslaught. After each additional volley, more fires ignited around the city.

Jove held up the red flag, waving it side to side. The archers on the southern wall lit their arrows and began firing toward the treeline beyond the battlefield. Some arrows fell short of the trees, while others flew beyond them and into the Asgardian army waiting on the other side of the mountain slope.

The arrows streamed in both directions, racing past each other on their way to their intended targets. The fires throughout the city forced people to flee their homes, and they rushed past their Hoplites protectors in a panic. Many of them tried to make their way to the castle for sanctuary.

A single Asgardian horn sounded again. Three short bursts, then silence. The volleys from the treeline ceased. Jove waited, letting his archers continue firing. The Hoplites loosed arrow after arrow.

"Why did they stop?" Aaron asked. No one responded.

Jove anxiously reached for a mustard-colored flag and waved it in the sky. Seeing his signals, the commander on the walls ordered the archers to halt. After a few last shots, most landing short of the trees, they ceased.

A complete hush followed, except for the cries of the wounded Hoplites being tended to. Smoke rose sporadically around the city.

~*--*--*~

The Hoplites outside the walls watched the trees, waiting for what was next to come.

The land fell calm, for a moment.

The first of the sun's pink hue emerged.

Together, with their colors ripping through the air, thousands of Vikings, axes and colored shields in hand, charged through the woods. Their battle cries tore into the hearts of the defenders in front of them.

"Shields!" the Hoplite captain commanded. The front line of Hoplites placed their shields overlapping each other, slotting their spears firmly in between. They faced the horde of Vikings storming toward them, axes flailing.

Tyr, holding his silver-tipped spear, led the first charge, running faster than all others.

Although several Immortal arrows landed near him, he continued charging directly toward the center of the first row of Hoplite shields. At a full sprint, he screamed a battle cry at the nervous warriors, jumped over their shields, smashing away their weaker spears with his, then drove his hungry blade deep into his first Olympian. His spear pierced through the breastplate. Tyr wretched out his weapon, tearing open the poor victim's chest, then cast his eyes toward his next opponent.

Thousands of Vikings followed behind Tyr in a classic wedge formation. Widening Tyr's crack in the defense, they swung their axes against the Hoplite shields, smashing through, penetrating rows deep into the soldiers from the original point.

Tyr thrust his spear into the face of a soldier. The tip pierced his skull, scraping the back of his helmet. Without pause, he let go of the handle, grabbed a horn from his waistbelt with his free hand, and blew two short blasts. Before the soldier's body hit the ground, Tyr put his horn back, caught the spear's shaft, and yanked the blade from the crushed head. He turned and kicked a Hoplite, shattering his ribs and launching him into the group behind him.

A second wave of Vikings emerged, surging toward the small opening created by the first assault. They ran with even greater ferocity, battle axes and machetes at the ready.

Whooping with demented fervor, the second group smashed into the Hoplite ranks forcing the gap wider. The small breach grew larger with each fallen Hoplite.

"Axes!" Tyr commanded. With one swift movement, the massed Vikings all lifted their axes, then synchronized violent blows against the Hoplite shields, cracking many of them. The blades of the axes proved too sharp for the thinner, lighter shields. With each stroke they drove deeper into the weakened Hoplite defense.

Deep within the sea of spear-thrusting Hoplites, Tyr sounded the horn a third time with another two short bursts. Leaving his spear buried within his latest casualty, Tyr reached for a nearby sword. Without hesitation, he slashed an enemy soldier from the neck down, opening his torso. The wound was horrific, releasing the soldier's innards onto the battlefield before he died. The dying soldier raised his head in time to see Tyr's blade swinging toward him. His head rolled.

"This is just awful," Tyr said aloud to himself. "Shoddy craftsmanship. I need my spear back."

This third wave summoned by Tyr's horn brought forth Ra, Bastet, and other Sh'losh--

charging forward leading thousands of Berserkers in their spear-tip formation. They forced the gap even wider, violently twirling their axes and slashing mostly Hoplites, but not slowing down when they struck one of their own accidentally. Bastet leaped, driving her sword into a soldier's chest, then grabbed his sword, and with one quick slice, separated a Hoplite from his legs. She turned and leaped onto a soldier's back, drawing her razor-sharp blade across his exposed neck.

Chapter 47 *The King watches*

Jove, watching his defense being devastated from the middle, waved a red flag toward the southern archway. Neptune signaled back, then commanded his soldiers to open the doorway, to push out reinforcements through the exit.

"Already, *damn*," Neptune said, pointing to the Hoplites at the arch. "Send out the first legion." Opening the door, thousands rushed out in eight columns to bolster the rear of the Hoplite defense.

Near the center of the battlefield, Tyr and Bastet had created a small gap between them and the nearest Hoplites. The defenders were hesitant to attack.

With the doorway opened, Neptune signaled to Jove, pointing at himself, then with all his fingers extended, he pointed at the two gods shredding the Hoplite forces. Jove motioned for him to remain where he was.

"He *wants* to go?" Aaron asked.

"Asgard is moving quickly, but we cannot afford to send our gods out to the fight too soon," Jove answered, signaling Neptune once again.

Neptune tossed his hands in the air, clearly frustrated, then ordered his soldiers to close the door.

From the tower entrance, Zeus commanded Jove: "They are overrunning us. Do something!" Aaron looked back, startled to see him there.

Jove responded, "We have to let this play out. It is far too early to send more soldiers out there. We expected this."

"Expected *this*?" Zeus roared. "You *expected* them to run through us like this? What kind of commander are you?" Jove didn't respond. He moved to the northern side of the tower and waved his blue guidon.

"What are you doing?" Zeus demanded. His face was red in anger.

"Calling for the archers on the northern wall to get their asses to the southern." Jove hustled back to the southern side of the tower. Zeus reached out, grabbing Jove by his cloak.

"You *need* to do more!" Zeus commanded fiercely.

"What would you suggest?" Jove said calmly, staring into Zeus' eyes. "You thought we could simply push them off the battlefield? That they would hear your mighty name and fall to their knees in fear? They do not respect you, let alone fear you."

Shaking his head, Jove reached up and removed Zeus' hand. "We have to hold them back as long as we can. Now let me pass, so I can try to help us hold our ground." Zeus let him go with a shove. Jove sent new signals down to his forces. He waved the red guidon at Neptune again to add reinforcements.

Jove signaled to the commanders on the wall to continue firing into the treeline. The archers steadily fired volleys into the trees, but it was impossible to tell if they were hitting the Asgardians through the thick foliage.

"Just have them aim at the Vikings on the field!" Zeus ordered.

"I am not willing to have them fire into the crowded battlefield. Especially since the majority are our soldiers."

"Jove!" Zeus stepped toward Jove.

Jove sharply raised his hand, fist clenched and shaking. He struggled to avoid lashing out. His eyes showed rage and his jaw locked shut. Zeus stepped back, releasing a string of curses.

Chapter 48 *Jove and Tyr*

On the battlefield, Bastet slammed into a
Hoplite, pushing him to the ground and driving his
own sword through his neck. Encircled by a group
of four soldiers, she lunged at the nearest, grabbing
a dagger from her boot and sliced deep into his
neck. Then she turned toward the other three. Their
weapons trembled in their hands.

Tyr sounded the horn again to alert another
wave of warriors. He quickly put it away and
plunged his spear into an onrushing soldier. Tyr
lifted his spear, flinging the body across the
battlefield toward Ra and Sobek. Tyr peered back,
watching as another roaring legion of Vikings
rushed through the trees, hungry for battle.

Despite the Hoplites firing their arrows
toward the oncoming Vikings, very few were hit,
and they were able to maintain their pointed
formation. They pierced deep into the middle of the
Hoplite force, driving their wedge relentlessly. The
Hoplites outside the formation were unable to get
close enough to join the fight, and those in the
middle were being slain by the savage warriors.

With each death, the incursion grew larger
and more defined.

Jove focused squarely on Tyr. He studied
him as the Viking thrust his spear into yet another
Hoplite.

"Have to stop him," Jove whispered, loud enough for Aaron to hear.

Jove motioned to the southern wall captain, pointing directly at Tyr. He gave very distinct flag signals. Aaron didn't want to interrupt. He watched as Tyr severed an arm from a Hoplite, then looked back at Jove, who was still waving his flag. Finishing his last movement, Jove placed both hands against the wall and watched.

The commander signaled Jove, then after a series of commands, the nearby archers aimed at Tyr.

Tyr slashed at another soldier, then stuck his spear into the ground as he prepared to sound the horn. Before he could bring the horn to his lips, Bastet kicked him onto his side. Tyr flipped over to his back, pointing his horn toward her.

"What in Sheol!" Tyr demanded.

She held a stolen Hoplite shield over her head. Stowing the horn, he rolled toward a nearby soldier and pulled out a small blade from his belt. Tyr thrust it into the soldier's forearm, exchanging the blade for the Hoplite's shield. Tyr curled low to the ground, covering himself as Bastet drew close, still holding the shield above her head.

Bastet slashed with her sword, dropping a soldier to the ground directly in front of Tyr. With the shield protecting him, he blew his horn, calling for the next legion of warriors.

Several Hoplites approached Tyr as he lay on the ground covered by the shield. Trying to get closer, they all took turns swinging at Bastet, who stood over him.

The captain on the southern wall signaled back to Jove.

"Damn it!" Jove shouted.

"What are you doing? Fire!" Zeus ordered.

"They are waiting for a clear shot at Tyr. I will not fire on our soldiers," Jove argued.

"Damn it, Jove, look at him!" Zeus insisted. "We need to stop him blowing that damn horn."

"No!" Jove cried out. "Not like *that*. I will not sacrifice these men--"

"Give me the guidon right now," Zeus demanded, holding out his hand.

Taking a step closer, Jove glared at Zeus, furious. He whispered, "You might want to rethink your choices right now. I *believe* it is time you go back to the castle."

Zeus stared back, fists clenched.

"How dare you?" Zeus said, slowly reaching back to unclip his trident.

"Are you planning on killing me?" Jove said, eyes still locked. "Or can I get back to commanding our forces?"

Zeus glanced at Aaron, shaking in anger. Then he turned and stormed out through the door.

Chapter 49 *The crack opens*

The next wave of Vikings charged ahead into the deep crack in the Hoplite defense. Sjofn and Sekhmet, both holding bows, came forward to the front of the treeline. Thousands more Viking archers formed up by their sides. Without command, each took a knee and fired arrow after arrow toward the battlegrounds.

Sekhmet took deadly aim at the Hoplites on the wall, dropping one after another. The Asgardian archers shot into the combatants without concern for hitting their own. Raining down on the Hoplites, few of the arrows struck other Vikings.

Many of the warriors continued wielding their battle axes despite the stray arrows that pierced into their backs.

Bastet and Ra were nearing the middle of the battlefield, helping the Asgardians cut through. They were fighting shoulder to shoulder, ripping deeper into the ranks. Ra spent furious energy by taking extra slashes on those he had already killed as they fell to the ground.

Tyr, just ahead of the two Sh'losh, continued leading the charge. He moved gracefully, cutting down defenders in front of him, switching weapons from victim to victim, artful with his footwork, as if he were dancing.

Tyr ripped loose a soldier's spear, kicked the fighter back into his own men, then threw the spear, impaling him and a soldier behind him, before swinging and dropping another. Tyr leaned forward and roared ferociously at his opponents.

Watching Tyr's frenzied attacks from on the tower, Jove seemed as overwhelmed as Aaron was.

Aaron glanced over at Dagon, who watched the battle silently, emotionless, as if it weren't happening at all

"Damn this!" Jove yelled, striking the stone battlement with his fist. He took off running to the northern side of the tower. He waved his signal flag, then threw it down, ran back near Aaron, and scanned the battlefield, locating Tyr again.

Jove said, "With Zeus out of the way, it is time to test *our* theory and see if the Spartans can hold them off from breaching the entrance. Now we just have to hope Ares can get them to the southern doorway before they force their way inside."

Aaron turned and jogged over to the northern side. He watched as Ares and the Spartans raced in a full sprint south.

"That's going to take them all day," Aaron said, watching them rush down the main center road.

"Let us hope not," Jove said. "I doubt we have that long."

Jove signaled Neptune to send another group of ten thousand outside the walls. Neptune ordered

302

the door opened, and the Hoplites quickly surged forward. As the wooden door opened Neptune surveyed the battle and watched as Tyr removed a soldier's arm, flinging it upward. Tyr's face was drenched in blood, none of it his.

Once more, Neptune gestured at Tyr, but Jove signaled back, refusing to allow him onto the field. The two exchanged another signal before Jove disregarded Neptune's insistence.

As Neptune glanced back at Tyr and the battle, it was already too late. Tyr had already leaned back with a spear in hand, holding his other arm forward for balance.

Tyr launched the spear with such force that it flew through the air with almost no arc. Aimed perfectly, the blade pierced deep into Neptune's chest, and he dropped down onto the cobblestone road.

Neptune reached for the shaft, gasping for air his lungs couldn't draw. A group of soldiers leaped to the ground to render aid, but he waved them back.

"D-amn nethers, get...away...from me," Neptune muttered. Trying to remove the spear, he quickly gave up, dropping his arms to his side. Glancing at his trident on the road beside him, Neptune grunted in frustration. "Never even got to use the damn thing," were his final words.

The soldiers quickly closed the doorway, not allowing any more reinforcements to move out.

Smiling, Tyr brought the horn to his lips and blasted it again.

Chapter 50 *Knock, knock*

Past the treeline and down the hill, Thor stood in front of the legions of Vikings, preparing to send them to join their comrades. Watching the backs of another group disappear over the hill, Thor placed his arm over his son Magni's shoulder.

"Ready, son?"

Wearing bright red face paint, Magni hit his chest. "With everything I am."

"Remember, son," Thor said. "Bring the fire of Sheol with you, but do not take them all. Save a few for me."

"Father?" Magni whispered. "I am sorry that I could not be there for Modi. It *is* my fault he died. I lied. We did not run from the Duati after being chased. The truth is, we did not know that they had *already* spotted us. They brought us liquor. Bottle after bottle of--"

"No, no, no son, do not for a moment blame yourself," Thor assured him. "Blame *them*, and I promise you that those responsible are next."

"Thank you, Father," Magni said. Thor glanced up the hill, listening to the sound of the battle raging.

Thor hit Magni in the arm. "Forget what I said. When you charge up the hill, you tear every last one of them down." With a fanatical grin, Magni nodded. After a final pat on the shoulder,

Thor turned and walked toward Svetovid, who waited farther down the hill on one knee.

Tyr's horn blasted again, calling for Magni and his legion of ten thousand. Magni lifted his axe off the grass, and with a scream, rushed forward leading his warriors toward the enemy. Rushing past the last few trees, Magni slowed as he saw the sea of Hoplite soldiers across the field.

Magni led his spearhead formation of Vikings forward through the now well-established gap. Reaching the middle of the field untouched, he hailed Bastet and Tyr much farther ahead, close to the gate. Magni's first stroke gutted one Hoplite.

Tyr continued slashing the Immortal line with each blow. He picked up an abandoned Hoplite spear and quickly shook it, watching it flex as he did so.

"Weak and flimsy!" he shouted, casting it aside and piercing another soldier. "I have to go and get mine. Damn it, Neptune. Give it back!"

Tyr grabbed his horn, blowing one short burst followed by two longer. Then, quickly taking a step toward another Hoplite, he swung the horn, smashing the soldier's helmet, collapsing him to the bloody ground. Tyr picked up the fallen soldier's sword and fought on.

After hearing Tyr's horn, Bastet turned and shouted, "Finally! I have been waiting for you to blow that command all day!"

All the Asgardians warriors in the field closed the gaps between one another. They moved and shifted until they were able to form two lines of Vikings right up the middle of the field. The two lines stood back to back, facing toward the surrounding Hoplite soldiers.

Both Ra and Magni sprinted together through the narrow space between the two lines, racing toward Tyr, who was now near the Olympian gate. They dodged various Hoplite blades being jabbed toward them from behind the Viking lines. The gruesome path was littered with the dead, dying, and severed body parts from both sides.

Inside the treeline still firing arrows, Sekhmet howled in excitement hearing Tyr's horn.

"Is it time?" Sjofn asked.

"Yes it is! Time to open that damn gate," Sekhmet said, grinning.

Tyr glanced at the gap through the middle of the battlefield. He then blew four short blasts on the bloodied horn.

Svetovid, a giant among gods, rushed forward with his Bogatyr warriors, all wielding saggilmut stone-tipped axes. The Bogatyrs charged into the fray, swinging at anyone in their reach. Many of the Vikings were forced to dodge the barbarians' deadly blades.

Blitzing through the opening, Svetovid and his axemen soon reached Tyr and the others. As they arrived, Tyr swung viciously on a soldier whose back was turned. The blade drove down through his helmet, splitting him nearly in two.

Panting, Tyr looked at Svetovid and demanded, "What are you waiting for? You are the one with the saggilmut stone-tips! Go and open the gate." The Bogatyr warriors rushed toward the large gate, hacking down the hapless soldiers in their way.

Tyr and Svetovid reached the gate while Magni, Bastet, Ra, and the Asgardian warriors established space around them.

"Remember," Tyr said. "Hit the hinges!" Svetovid raised his axe far over his head and with both hands, drove the blade against the top hinge. As the giant pulled the axe skyward again, there was barely a scratch.

"It is going to take some time!" Svetovid yelled.

"Damn it," Tyr replied. "You need to hurry up!"

From the tower, Jove watched Tyr shredding through his defense. Jove once again signaled the archers to target Tyr. With a gesture from the commander on the wall, the archers aimed. They simultaneously fired down into the warriors, killing many.

One arrow drove deep into Bastet's leg, dropping her to her knee. Taking hold of the shaft, she moved it carefully but gave up after a shriek, shaking. Svetovid glanced over at her, but undeterred, rained another blow on the gate hinge.

Sekhmet, after burying an arrow into another soldier, glanced through the gap and saw her sister in pain. Sekhmet screamed for her archers to take down those Hoplites firing on the gods near the gate. She sharply drew back her bowstring, locking in an arrow.

She looked down the straight arrow and saw a single Hoplite archer already aiming toward her sister. They released in unison, and as his arrow found its mark in Bastet's neck, Sekhmet's pierced between his eyes.

Bastet folded to the ground, dead.

"No!" Sekhmet screamed. She dropped her bow, falling to the ground sobbing. She pummeled the grass with clenched fists as she cried aloud, calling for her sister.

"I am sorry!" Sjofn shouted from behind a nearby tree, "But I need you!" Unable to reply, Sekhmet held onto the grass, squeezing it tightly--trembling.

"Please!" Sjofn cried out.

Sekhmet raised her head, eyes locked shut, inhaling the cool air. Taking a long breath, Sekhmet released a scream from deep within her. Then, taking a series of deep breaths, she opened her tear-filled eyes and grabbed her bow.

"Sekhmet!" Sjofn called out.

"I am fine," she replied, taking aim and firing. Sjofn watched, lowering her bow and staring at Sekhmet. Sekhmet's tears streamed down her face. With each arrow loosed, she screamed with rage. Sjofn was fearful of her; Sekhmet appeared unhinged.

Chapter 51 *Unstoppable Force; Immovable object*

Near the gate, Tyr had created a grisly jumble of bodies around him, and he dispatched another Hoplite before turning around, spear in hand, ready for more.

With a bone-jarring *whack,* Svetovid took another swing on the top hinge.

Tyr noticed Bastet had collapsed with an arrow in her neck. Glaring up toward the archers responsible, he stumbled back. The soldiers above were preparing to heave a large boulder over the wall.

"Move!" Tyr shouted at Svetovid and his warriors nearby. The massive stone plummeted to the ground, crushing a single Viking as the others scrambled clear. The archers on the wall continued dropping smaller boulders at the attackers near the gate. Tyr glanced at Bastet's crumpled body again, then peered down the now-closing gap running down the center of the battlefield.

"We are out of time," he said to himself.

"Help me move this damn rock!" Svetovid yelled. "It is blocking the gate!" Magni, Ra, and a group of warriors rushed forward to assist. The bowmen had rolled another rock into position and were preparing to heave it over.

Near the treeline, Sekhmet drew back her bowstring then fired. The arrow soared true, toppling a Hoplite off the wall and plunging him down to the city street.

"Aim for the wall! Hit the ones moving the stones!" she commanded.

Sekhmet, Sjofn, and the other archers fired furious salvos at them, forcing them to seek shelter behind their rocks.

Tyr stood up straight, not fighting or even protecting himself. He was exhausted. He dropped his latest weapon, a Hoplite sword, and reached into his waistbelt to pull out the horn.

Svetovid ordered some of the Vikings to protect Tyr.

"Tyr, what are you doing?" Svetovid yelled, giving one last push and rolling the boulder out of the way. No answer. Svetovid quickly turned back, took hold of his axe, then continued his attack on the gate's hinges.

Whack!

"We need this damn gate open," Tyr said to himself, staring into the sea of fighters. Swords and spears hacking and cutting, blood spurting, and screaming. The howls of rage and pain all blended.

Tyr raised his horn, first inspecting it. With a deep breath, he sent out seven sharp blasts.

"Bring them all, brother," he whispered.

A tremendous battle cry roared from beyond trees. Then the trees began to tremble, shaking violently as Thor emerged answering Tyr's battle horn. He was followed by all of the remaining gods and waves of Asgardian warriors.

Thor screamed furiously, running with *Mjolnir* in hand and *Gungnir* strapped across his back. Reaching the gap created by his forces, Thor stood upright, chest out, marching through, inspecting his warriors, patting them as he walked toward the gate.

An arrow gashed him along his arm, a spear slashed the back of his neck, but nothing deterred him in the least. Dodging an oncoming arrow by leaning to one side, he smirked.

He raised his hammer in the air. "Fate!"

One Berserker fell back onto him after a Hoplite spear gashed him, but Thor quickly grabbed his warrior by the back of the neck, pushing him back to the line.

"Fight!" Thor commanded. "Your king fights with you!"

Finally reaching the gate, Thor patted Tyr on the shoulder, "Take a break, brother." Tyr nodded, but was quickly back in the battle, engaging with two soldiers, slamming one with the blunt end of a spear before turning and driving the blade into the other's gut.

Thor approached the gate and watched Svetovid take another fearsome swing at one of the latches. He had smashed the second latch, but was slowed by an arrow stuck in his thigh. He continued to attack the third hinge.

"Move!" Thor commanded, raising his hammer.

Looking back, Svetovid shouted, "Who would dare tell me--" Noticing who it was, he stopped himself. He raised his hand, then continued, "It is all yours."

With his first swing, Thor displaced the third hinge, and the gate toppled over, falling inward and opening the city to the Asgardians. After a second swing, the heavy Kailash bark door toppled forward, falling flat onto Olympus' cobblestone road.

Beneath the arch, Thor pointed his hammer toward Olympus castle. He shouted at the thousands of Hoplites massed in front of him with their spears drawn. "You would fight for a king who hides! Who would not lead you into battle, but rather--"

Mercury shouted over him, pointing his sword. "Do not for one moment dare speak ill of King Zeus. You think you--" Thor threw *Gungnir,* piercing Mercury's chest, driving him into the fountain behind him. The water immediately flowed red.

Ares, followed closely by his Spartan army, rushed past the fountain, spear and shield ready.

"For Olympus!" Ares yelled.

"For Olympus!" the Spartans echoed, charging past him toward the archway. The Immortal gods and Hoplites near the southern gate moved aside to let them pass.

Thor waved forward as many warriors as he could before the Spartans had time to set themselves. The Vikings poured through the gate and fanned out in every direction.

"Blockade!" Ares commanded. His Spartans surged forward to impede the Viking raid. They barricaded the entrance, lowered their shields and overlapped them into a perfect row, and slotted their spears between each shield, ready.

Thor clenched his hammer and led his gods into the clash with the Spartan defense.

Chapter 52 *Thor and the Spartans*

"They're in!" Aaron yelled to Jove.

"Not quite yet," Jove answered, and he left his position and ran to the western side of the tower.

Aaron watched as he frantically waved the guidon, then threw it down in frustration, and rushed back to the southern side.

"The Spartans have them at a standstill. We have to hold them there," Jove said.

"What did you tell them at the western wall?" Aaron asked.

"I just ordered every soldier at the western gate to exit the castle walls, race to the south, and *hopefully* flank them."

"Think it will work?" Aaron asked, peering over and seeing the soldiers flood out of the gate and rushing south along the wall.

"No," Jove decided. "Not for long enough. Even if the Duati do arrive as early as midnight, I do not believe we can keep them out of the city for that long. Our best hope is that the Spartans hold the southern gate, and the Hoplites that I sent from the western gate can flank Asgard, and keep them occupied as long as possible."

"What if they find out the western gate is open?" he asked. "Or even the northern?"

"It is a gamble, Aaron," he stated, "But we are out of time and options."

"So that's it?" Aaron asked, concerned. "They're getting in?"

"Yes," Jove answered. "I do not think we can stop them now. I wish we had been able to place the Spartans outside of the southern gate as I had advised." He paused for a moment, then added, "It does not matter anymore."

Jove waved another colored flag toward the eastern walls, then finally stopping for the first time since morning, he approached Dagon. They spoke to each other, forearms locked, then Jove turned toward Aaron. "You need to stay here to remain safe, son," Jove said. "Dagon will protect you. At this point there is no reason for me to be here on the tower. I have now sent all of our forces to one gate." Jove picked up his helmet and trident and after a nod, he ran toward the door leading to the elevator.

Aaron surveyed the area. Many of the highrises were now in full blaze from the fires, as Immortal citizens ran along the streets in panic. And as he watched the two sects battle at the southern gate, he felt the sun blazing down on him from the high point of the day.

At the southern gate, the Spartans had forced the invasion to a standstill. Even Thor struggled to move against their determined resistance. He swung his hammer, striking and denting a shield, but in quick reply a spear thrust from between the shields

317

gashed Thor's arm, and a new shield was quickly rotated in.

"Damn it!" Thor thundered, taking another swing and pounding into a Spartan shield. The defenders' shields were piled over each other with spears pointing in all directions, making it impossible for the Vikings to advance.

"Let me try!" Tyr yelled. He wrestled his spear from Neptune's body lying on the road. He thrust it into the crevasses of the shields, aiming for the eyes behind them, but with slight movements, the gaps closed, fending off his jabs. A spear stabbed out from another opening, slashing Tyr's shin and forcing him to step back in pain.

Svetovid slammed his axe on the top layer of shields, but the shields remained unyielding. Two Spartans at the rear of the defense rose and quickly fired two arrows before disappearing behind the shield barricade. One arrow dug into Svetovid's shoulder and the other grazed Ra's helmet.

From behind the Spartans, Ares drew his spear. Keeping a loose grip, he pressed his thumb gently against the staff, lifting his opposite arm, and aimed at Thor. Staring over his hand, Ares took three steps forward then launched the spear. Before Thor had time to react, Svetovid lunged forward in front of Thor, shielding him as the spear pierced through the giant's back. The two looked down at the bloody speartip now touching Thor's breastplate.

Svetovid dropped to his knees, reaching out for his king's forearm. Thor took hold of Svetovid and guided him to the ground, as the other gods continued their steadfast assault on the Spartan defenders.

"You bastards!" Thor roared as he stood back up. He stepped toward the blockade and prepared to swing, but a Spartan blade thrust from behind the shield sliced his shoulder, causing him to pull back. Thor quickly switched the hammer to his left hand, and leaped forward, swinging ferociously onto the top of a shield, shattering it into pieces.

Chapter 53 *Sjofn meets some friends*

On the other side of the battle, Sekhmet and Sjofn had pushed forward from the treeline with the archers. They stood at the rear of the battlefield, firing arrows and dropping defenders from the wall. Sekhmet, the faster and more precise of the two goddesses, seemed to take solace for her sister's death by watching the Hoplites disappear off the wall after each volley.

Sjofn's quiver had long been empty, and she had resorted to pulling arrows from the ground or the dead. With each shot, Sjofn's aim grew worse. Her hands trembled and tears filled her eyes. With a panicked breath, Sjofn loosened another arrow and dropped another archer off the front of the wall.

"Damn it," she whispered to herself.

"What is wrong with you?" Sekhmet yelled.

"Oh, uh, nothing," she said, quickly lowering herself for another arrow.

"I said what *is* wrong?" Sekhmet prodded, burying another arrow into a soldier.

"I do not like hurting anyone," she whimpered. "I never did."

Sekhmet stopped. "Good, because we are not trying to *hurt* them." She loosed another arrow. "We are trying to *kill* them." Sekhmet slung her bow behind her back, and pulled out a spear from under her cloak.

"I am moving forward," Sekhmet declared. "I am *done* standing here in the rear of the battle. You stay here with the archers."

Sjofn didn't respond. Instead, she picked up another arrow, took aim, and fired off-target. "Oh, thank you," she said to herself.

She watched Sekhmet run through the gap, headed toward Thor. Sekhmet leaped over the Vikings into the ocean of Hoplites, and Sjofn watched as Sekhmet created a storm of blood and severed limbs with lightning slashes of her spear.

"I wish I was like you," Sjofn whispered to herself.

She grabbed another arrow. She thought about being home in Asgard. Trying to psyche herself to fight harder, she asked herself, *What if they were attacking my home? How would I fight? I need to fight as if protecting Asgard!* But it didn't work. It *wasn't* the Immortals attacking her sacred Asgard--it was her attacking their sacred Olympus.

Taking aim, she fired another miss. *Oh, thank you.*

As the battle raged on, in the midst of the noise and turbulence, Sjofn heard a gentle voice behind her say, "Hello, need some help?" She turned, startled, grabbing at her chest. Her tears had smeared her war paint.

She grinned. It was Guowang with the two other gods she had met in Guangdong near the fountains. They were covered in armor, riding on horseback with countless more behind them flowing along the trail back down the hill.

"It *is* you! You *are* the Sanguan Dadi!" she cried out. With tears now flowing, she added, "I had no idea that you were--"

"Perhaps we can better reintroduce ourselves another time," he said, interrupting her. "Where is he?"

"Thor? He is through the gate, but it appears we have been stopped there now," she answered.

"What about the western and northern gates?" he asked calmly.

"I do not know," she answered. "King Thor commanded we attack straight through this one." She pointed at the southern and saw Sekhmet. She held a soldier's arm in her hands, swinging it over her head as she roared.

Guowang turned to the other two gods. "I will remain here with our friend. They seem to have enough warriors here, so leave me our bowmen and take the rest. You two will lead your troops around to the western gate and begin your assault there. Do not stop to fight. Ride past anyone in your way. If it is too heavily guarded, go and scout the northern next. Get us inside!"

Nodding, they rode off with the myriad of Samurai warriors galloping behind them. Guowang leaped off his horse just as an arrow struck a short distance away. He waved his bowmen forward.

Stabbing his oversized shield into the grass, he crouched behind it, waving Sjofn over as well.

"Sjofn, my name is Tianguan. Take a moment to collect your peace here behind my shield. Let my warriors continue the attack for you." Then the old god pulled out a small fruit from his pouch. "I brought this for you."

Sjofn smiled, "Thank you, but I cannot just sit here. I am sorry. I must go and inform my King you are here. I will be right back."

Sjofn wiped her eyes. She rushed forward to tell Bragi, who was at the rear of the battle, to pass the news of the Sanguan Dadi's arrival forward to Thor. She picked up a stray arrow and fired it, hitting a Hoplite in the back of the leg before the soldier swung on a Viking. The Viking turned around, then swung his axe and finished the wounded soldier with a blow to the neck.

"Bragi!" Sjofn yelled, trying to get his attention.

Bragi thrust his double-edged axe, fending off an attack, and replied, "What?" Deflecting his opponent's sword with the haft of the axe, Bragi reared back and swung again, this time burying the edge into his enemy's collar.

"What?" he shouted again. He deflected another spear and delivered a kick to the soldier's shield, sending him to the ground. "Damn it! I said, *what*?" This time he looked back.

Sjofn was sprawled on her back in the grass, with an arrow driven into her belly. He gave off a menacing war cry and rushed toward her, erratically flailing his axe at those in his way.

Reaching her, Bragi glanced at the arrow buried deep. Her green eyes were empty, void. Her bow rested on the ground near her, and her hand clutched a small purple flower.

Not long after that, the Sanguan Dadi rode right past the Hoplites defending the western gate and headed off to flank the Asgard military. The Sanguan Dadi smashed through the unprotected western gate, pouring into the city unopposed. The two gods galloped, with a flood of Samurai with them, toward Thor at the southern entrance.

From on the tower, Aaron watched them.

"You are going to protect me, right?" he said to Dagon, bottom lip drawn into his mouth.

Dagon nodded and assured him, "I do." The two on the tower watched the Sangaun Dadi and their army flood into the streets and rush toward the southern plaza where Thor and the gods struggled, unable to pass the Spartan ranks.

Chapter 54 *Unwelcome Guests*

Aaron stared down at Ares and the Spartans, who were holding back the Asgardians at the gate. Jove and Athena stood behind Ares now, watching with weapons in hand.

Ares repeated his order, "Step!" In one swift movement, the entire Spartan line in unison rammed their spears forward, then took a step forward while remaining perfectly hidden behind their shields.

Thor just missed a spear to the eye, and backed up in frustration. He looked past the impenetrable shields and saw Ares pacing back and forth, spear in hand. Staring at Ares, Thor swung, shattering another shield, but was gashed along his arm, and another shield replaced the opening.

Thor swung again, bellowing, "I *will* stand in Olympus as King! Damn these nethers!" He slammed his hammer against the Spartan defense, lifting a shield off the ground with the impact. Before the Spartans could react to replace the shield, he spun again, crashing his hammer into the same shield, widening the opening. Tyr rolled forward, jabbing his spear into the gap, plunging it into the neck of an unlucky Spartan.

At that moment, the Sanguan Dadi arrived at the southern plaza, crashing into the Immortals from behind. Their horses broke into the Hoplite formations, trampling Jove and Athena. The

Samurai warriors threw small pouches that exploded, spraying shards of saggilmut stone into the crowds of soldiers. Ares dove out of the way of a Samurai's blade, then flung his dagger and buried it into the back of the rider's head.

The Spartan defense crumbled. Many of the rear defenders turned to engage with the Sanguan Dadi's forces, while the Asgardians poured through the now broken Spartan defense. The Vikings howled, running in all directions. They rushed past the plaza and poured into the streets, entering into the apartments, running up the balcony stairwells, and breaking through windows.

"We are in!" Thor exclaimed, raising his hammer. Tyr, Sekhmet, and the other gods nearby approached him.

"I am taking the Sh'losh to the castle," Sekhmet said.

"Sekhmet," Thor said. He pointed to an apartment door against the southern wall. "That will be our stronghold. Bring any news you have there." She agreed, and signaled her group onward.

Inside the castle, Zeus forced his way through the crowd as he headed to the Infirmary. He moved down the packed hallway, trembling as he took hold of those in the way and pushed them aside.

"Move!" he screamed, but his order was drowned out by other shouts of panic. There were simply too many to provide a way for their King to pass easily. Zeus' elbows struck his people as he neared the end of the hall. Finally reaching the door, Zeus slammed it shut and leaned against it. He held his shaking hands together.

"Asclepius!" he called out.

There was no answer. The small room was unlit, dark. The torches and candles were snuffed. He walked slowly, guided by a window offering just enough light to navigate the room. There was an eerie silence.

"Asclepius, I need Odin in chains, right now!" Zeus turned the corner into another row of patient beds. Nothing.

The darkened room was empty. It was *never* empty.

"Asclepius," he said again, but in a lower voice. He walked past the beds and rounded a corner where there were a handful more beds against a wall.

There, slumped against the white stone wall, was Asclepius. His body was crumpled and his head folded forwards. His snake-entwined staff was planted into his gut.

Zeus stumbled back then fled the room, headed back down the hall toward the secure room. No longer giving commands to move, Zeus pushed, driving his elbows into anyone in his way. He picked up a man that was blocking him and flung him through the doors into a crowded study room.

Finally arriving at the foyer, Zeus tried to hurry to the northern hall, shoving a woman out of his way. She fell, and as her head slammed onto the marble floor, the sound of the impact was enough to make him pause.

He looked down at her as she stared back up at him in horror, blood flowing from her forehead. Others knelt, offering help to the woman. In her hand, she held a small ivory idol of Zeus. He shook his head, unsure what to do.

Hera, Zeus' wife, grabbed her husband from behind, startling him.

"Zeus!" she cried out. He quickly grabbed her hand and continued, passing the woman. Zeus and his wife pushed through the northern hall toward the secure room. He held up his hand, shoving anyone who got in his way.

"Your King demands you move!"

Arriving at the secure room, Zeus grabbed the handle and slid open the heavy door. Hades and Persephone were already inside, lying down in the middle of the floor. Hades lay sweating, shaking as Persephone wiped his forehead with a cloth. Dadga stood over them both. Zeus and Hera stepped in, and he slid the door closed, locking the large bolt.

Zeus collapsed to the floor. Hera stood over her husband, rubbing his back as he struggled to catch his breath.

Chapter 55 *Unlock the gates of...*

"Are you all right, Hades?" Zeus asked, leaning against the door.

"He has not moved in hours," Persephone answered. "It is only a matter..."

"Damn," Zeus said. He and Hera rose from the floor, and they walked over to Hades. Hades stared emotionless at a pillar in the middle of the room.

Zeus knelt, taking Hades' hand, "I am sorry, brother." Hades turned his eyes toward Zeus.

"As am I," Hades whispered, his lips barely moving.

Zeus said, "They are breaking inside now anyway. It is only a matter of time for all of us."

"And the Duati?" Persephone asked.

"Even if they rushed, they would not be here until late tonight," he answered. "It is just too late for us."

"What can we do then?" she asked.

"Nothing. We can wait...that is all we can do now," he answered. "I went to the infirmary. I wanted to kill him. To kill Odin for everything that is happening, but.."

"But?" Persephone asked.

"He was gone, and Asclepius dead. He killed him." Hera placed her hand on Zeus' shoulder. Zeus looked back at Hades. "Damn Odin for *all* of this."

"Zeus," Hades whispered, barely audible.

"I am here," he replied.

Hades said, "My King, I-I did it for Olympus." He paused, taking a breath, "For protection."

"I know, everything you did was--"

"No," Hades said, panting. "Listen."

"What? Did *what* for Olympus?" Zeus pressed.

"In m-my chambers--down the hall." Taking another breath, he continued, "The Unspoken." Zeus turned toward Persephone, confused.

"What did he say?" Zeus asked. She shook her head.

Dadga backed up, mortified, "He said, the Unspoken."

"In m-my room there is a t-tunnel--that leads to my c-cave. Let Dagda take me--so we can unlock t-the door. I...I will unleash hell on the A-Asgardians."

"Not only the Asgardians," Zeus insisted. "They would just as well kill our own. We cannot control them."

Hades replied, "The choice is yours. B-but if we will not last the night...then here is a chance to slow them down--or maybe even--"

"How many?" Zeus asked.

"Twenty, I f-found twenty."

"Damn, this is dangerous," he said. He glanced over at Hera, who shook her head.

"I do not want any part of it," she said. Zeus watched Persephone as she stared at her husband.

"Let the Unspoken out," she said quietly. "Better *they* destroy the city than that filth doing it now."

Zeus nodded, then with a pat on his chest, rose to his feet. "We will open the cave. This offers at least a chance to make it through the night."

He turned to Dadga and said, "I need you to take him. Move quickly." Dadga sighed, then lowered himself and hoisted Hades onto his shoulder.

"Thank you, King Zeus," Dadga said. "For letting me into your gates, despite being a foreigner." Zeus nodded, and they walked to the door.

Zeus unbolted the doors and Dadga went out, carrying Hades. Zeus watched as Dadga moved carefully up the northern hall toward Hades' chambers. The halls were still crowded with people and gods searching for safety. Zeus' face fell as he saw the panic in his people.

"*Malaka*," he cursed.

He grabbed a man and pulled him inside the room, then commanded the others, "Get in! Hurry-- *hurry!*" The people trampled each other, fighting their way inside. The room quickly filled as they poured in. Zeus watched as the woman he had pushed earlier entered. The room quickly filled, while others still outside fought to come in.

"Damn it!" Zeus slid the door shut, pushing countless hands away and locking the rest out. "I am sorry!"

Outside the castle, the Asgardians forces, now with the Sanguan Dadi, were overwhelming the city. Vikings laughed and shouted, proudly beating their chests, as they ran through the streets, randomly entering into highrises and setting the city ablaze.

Thor remained at the gate, filling the plaza with a Viking song of victory, as he waved his warriors through the fallen gate. Tyr stood on the other side of the arch exhausted, blood covering his armor and sweat soaking through his garments. Ares hid inside a home, standing near the window as he kept his eye on Thor. Athena stood near Ares, watching him by the door and waiting for his command.

Chapter 56 *The doors opened*

Sekhmet led the Sh'losh toward the castle, hoping to stop Zeus from entering the secure room. She rushed into the castle entry with her spear dripping in blood.

The people in the castle foyer erupted in panic. Jove, already there, was waving people from the hallway into the room for safety.

Jove noticed Sekhmet, Ra, and the others watching him. Jove's head dropped as he let out a deep sigh. The attackers walked in and stood in the middle of the foyer. Sobek grinned with his crocodile teeth, gripping his sword tightly, waiting for Sekhmet's order.

"I understand why you are here, but let these people go find safety," Jove requested.

"And you may go with them," Sekhmet answered. "We have no issue with you. There is no need for you to die today."

Jove pushed more people from the foyer, telling them to run down the hall, before responding, "Look around you, Sekhmet. This city is falling to ruins because of the insanity of one god, and you are helping him! You do not have to do this."

Shaking his head, Ra answered, "Then it is indeed settled. You can die with them."

"Wait!" Sekhmet commanded, stopping Ra. "Jove, please. You have always been supportive of us. Just go, it is not too late. "

"You are right; it is not too late," Apollo said, emerging sword in hand from behind them, blocking the entrance doorway. Ra turned to face him, as Sekhmet and the others faced Jove.

With the foyer now nearly empty, Jove shouted, "You think it ends with Zeus' death? Do you really believe Thor will wash his hands of Duat, and dance his way back to Asgard? This only ends when Thor is either king over *all* Saggilmut or dead."

Sekhmet yelled back, "You minimize Zeus' wickedness! It was not simply a delusion of grandeur. Because of him, my people were killed, beaten, and exiled. No, this is not the Olympus that I will accept standing among the gods. When Zeus is dead, yes, *you* can rebuild it better and more glorious than anything that roach now hiding in the walls could ever imagine." Jove held his trident, watching Sekhmet's eyes as she stared into his, neither of them moving.

Only a short distance away, Dadga entered through a hidden door inside Hades' chambers and traveled through a dark, cold cavern. Dadga rushed, still carrying Hades until they reached a locked doorway.

Hades whispered, "T-The keys are around my neck." Dadga gently laid him down on the hard sand and removed two small keys tied together on a string, one silver and the other gold.

"Wait," Hades said. Dadga froze, eyes wide. "When you open this door, you must run to the secure room."

"All right," Dadga agreed. "I am not that fast, but we have to try, right?" Hades watched him tremble as he brought the key to the door.

"Wait," he said once again. "Let me open the door. You c-cannot outrun them with me...slowing you. I want you...to leave. I'll give you t-time."

"What? No!"

"Y-Yes," Hades insisted.

"Are you positive?" Dadga asked. "You do not have to. We can--"

"I am dead either way," Hades said. Dadga gave in and grabbed Hades under his arms, stood him up, then leaned him against the wall.

"Thank you," Dadga said. He patted Hades on the shoulder, nodded, then raced back down the cavern.

Hades waited until he could no longer hear his labored panting from the dark tunnel. Shaking, he inserted the key, turning it until the door opened. He fell to the floor, unable to support his weight any longer. He took the deepest breath his body would allow, blew it out, and threw the keys toward the center of the room. Cerberus, his faithful dog, approached him with all three heads whimpering.

"*Kathizo*," Hades said. Cerberus sat at Hades' command.

He heard the sound of chains falling to the ground from inside the room, the Unspoken were released. Amid subtle murmurs, he heard them picking up their weapons that he had piled beyond their reach when they were chained, taunting them. Hades closed his eyes, as he heard them approach.

"Good dog," he said, lying on the ground. He could only feel them all run past, except one. Sensing a presence hovering over him, he turned to see which one would kill him. A small hand with long dirty nails reached toward his neck, and he felt a swift breeze at his throat, a brief gush of blood, then nothing.

Chapter 57 The *Unspoken arrive*

Dadga ran as fast as he could, making his way toward the secure room. He came to a halt in front of Jove, who was still standing in the foyer.

The much larger Dadga grabbed Jove by the arm, "We all have to run, now! They are coming."

"Who?" Jove asked, keeping his eyes toward the Sh'losh.

"The Unspoken!" Dadga cried out.

Jove was horrified. "What?"

"What?" Sekhmet said equally panicked.

A shriek erupted from the end of the hallway where Dadga had come from. Then another, and another, until they became indistinguishable from each other, sounding like one long scream of terror. Both Jove and Dadga stared down the hallway.

Sekhmet watched the two gods' faces, since from the middle of the foyer she couldn't peer down the hall.

She said, "I do not want to hurt you Jove, but--"

"It is them," Dadga said fearfully, more concerned with Hades' doorway than Sekhmet's threat.

Surging from Hades' chamber door was first Supay, a pale dark-eyed god. Following him was Kaal, waving Hades' head as a trophy. Following them were Malsumis, Shinigami, then Buluc

Chabtan. The screams became louder as people in the studies saw them moving past the doorways. As they headed down the hall, one by one, the Unspoken entered into the studies, weapons drawn, as more screams poured out of the rooms.

"Please!" Dadga insisted, clutching Jove by the neck. "The secure room."

"We have to fight. We have to stop--"

"There are at least twenty of them!" Dadga cried.

Jove glanced back at Sekhmet, shaking his head. "This is not the time, Apollo, get out of here!" He and Dadga hurried down the northern hallway.

Sekhmet walked forward to see for herself and peeked down the hall. Amidst the crowd, she caught a glimpse of Buluc Chabtan's war headdress. He was holding a man above his head by his arms, then with a swift jerk, tore both limbs off, dropping the man to the ground. Behind him were another group of Unspoken, each hacking and slashing anyone in their path.

"We need to move!" Sekhmet commanded. She turned toward Ra, who was still facing Apollo.

"Are t-they really there?" Apollo stuttered at Sekhmet.

"Wait here and find out," she blurted, "but we are leaving."

Apollo turned and ran out of the door. The Sh'losh followed, quickly exiting the castle.

Sekhmet grabbed Ra's arm. "Apollo will lead us to Zeus. Even Zeus is not wicked enough to leave his son to die in the streets." Ra agreed, and the two followed behind Apollo from a distance. Sekhmet gestured to the others to choose another direction.

Chapter 58 *The open door*

Reaching the door, Jove and Dadga met Poseidon, who was already banging on the door, trying to get those inside to let more in.

"Can they hear us?" Dadga asked, frantically pounding the door and looking down the hall.

"Of course they can. I do not know why they will not open the door," Poseidon answered.

Dadga continued slamming his fist, shouting, "Open the door! It is me, Dadga!"

Persephone slid the door open. "Hades?" she asked at Dadga.

Dadga shook his head, "I am sorry."

The crowd in the hall surged into the room. Apollo rushed in as Jove shoved in as many people as he could, before going in himself. The room filled, suffocatingly tight. Persephone was unable to slide the door with so many blocking.

Kaal, holding his large red mace, entered the hall and locked eyes with Persephone.

"Jove, Zeus!" she screamed. "Someone help! They are here!"

Zeus rushed over. Reaching the door, he shoved a number of people from the door's sliding path and out of the room. He gripped the door and tried to slide it, but too many remained in the way. He peeked out of the room and saw Kaal with his filed brown teeth, dripping in blood, grinning at him.

Kaal swung the mace, exploding a man's head against the wall. Some Unspoken hurried down the hallway, while those in the rear took the time to kill everyone in their way.

"Move!" Zeus demanded, still trying to shut the door. Kaal clubbed a woman in his way, showering blood on Zeus and the floor.

"Trident!" Zeus shouted to his wife. Hera grabbed it from the wall, handing it over the crowd to him.

"No!" Jove shouted, but he was too late. Zeus thrust the trident into the people blocking the door, dropping them to the floor.

"Shut it!" Zeus screamed at Dadga, as he took another swipe. Dadga tried to slide the door, but there were still too many in their way. With the door nearly shut, Zeus helped Dadga and gave it one final push despite the arms and hands blocking from the other side.

"Ahhh!" screamed Dadga. His ankle was caught.

"Damn it, move!" Zeus yelled at Dadga. Opening the door slightly, Dadga slid his leg in, but it was too late. Kaal shoved his mace between the door and the frame. He smiled, shaking his head, scolding Zeus for trying to keep him out.

"You cannot outrun your fate, my King," Kaal said mockingly.

Standing behind Kaal, Supay sliced his machete through the narrow opening. He struck a man's head, driving the blade midway down. He then jerked the blade out and took another swipe, this time slicing into Dadga's forearm.

Dadga tore his arm away, and Jove made another attempt to slam the door, but Kaal's mace blocked him again. Supay swung his machete, and both Zeus and Jove let go of the door as they dodged the blade.

Kaal and Supay slammed the door wide open and began swinging wildly in the room. Led by Supay, the rest of the Unspoken followed and began killing in a frenzy. One Unspoken sang as he rammed his hand into a man's chest, ripping out his heart.

Many of those who had crammed into the room now tried desperately to escape, but they were cut down by the Unspoken.

"Zeus!" Hera screamed in horror.

"Everyone follow me!" Dadga ordered. He grabbed the King's hand and brought it to his shoulder. "Follow me," he repeated, whispering directly to Zeus. Zeus nodded and grasped Dadga's shoulder. Dadga rushed forward, holding his arms out in front of him. He took a blow from the mace to his chest, but kept charging ahead, pushing everyone, including Kaal, away from the doorway.

Slamming both Supay and Kaal against the wall opposite the door, Zeus, with Jove and several

others, hurried up the northern corridor. Dadga
stayed, blocking Kaal as they escaped with the
crowd. Dadga pummeled Supay, until a blow from
Kaal's mace to his head dropped him. He collapsed
lifeless near Persephone, who was already dead.

Zeus ran, holding his wife's hand, and
headed down the hall toward the rear doorway of
the castle. Rushing through the kitchen, the gods
followed their king, leaving the castle from the
northern hall. They ran together through the secret
King's gate, hidden behind a bush near the castle
walls. Running down the street, they stopped near a
series of columns, hiding from groups of Vikings
and Samurais who were entering into a highrise.

"Father!" Apollo shouted, waving him into
an abandoned street-level apartment. Zeus, Hera,
Jove, and Poseidon ran inside, and Apollo slammed
the door behind them, leaning against it.

"We are safe here," Apollo announced.

"I am glad we designated this place a safe
house!" Hera said.

Sekhmet and Ra, perched on the castle wall
after following Apollo, watched them enter the
abandoned apartment. They leaped onto the street
and stayed low as they ran forward, then hid behind
a set of columns in front of a neighboring apartment
door.

Chapter 59 *Like a Rat in a Cage*

"We are going to need help," Ra said. "There are too many of them inside."

"I have no interest in killing *them*," she retorted, staring into the window, "just *him*." They hid, lowering themselves behind the pillar as a group of Immortals ran past.

"Sekhmet," Ra said, kneeling. "There are too many. We *need* help."

"Fine," she answered. "I will go to the southern gate and find Thor. You wait here." She turned to leave.

"Wait," Ra said quietly, stopping her. He had noticed Diguan galloping by with a squad of Samurais.

"Sanguan Dadi," Ra said, pointing. "They can help us." Sekhmet nodded.

Trying not to draw unwanted attention, she picked up a small stone from the road and threw it, hitting the side of Diguan's helmet. He quickly stopped, scanning the area angrily. His jaw dropped when he spotted Sekhmet waving.

Diguan dismounted, gestured to his Samurai, then crept toward the two gods.

With the sun setting, his silhouette blended with the shade cast by the buildings.

"My Sekhmet, my favorite Puren," Diguan said with a smile. "Bastet's letter told me you were with Thor. It is so good--"

"Zeus," she said, pointing toward the doorway. "He is in there hiding."

"You *know* that?" he asked.

"Yes," she replied. "You stay here with Ra so I can notify Thor and the others."

"Why not just attack now? We have help," Diguan said, pointing his head toward his Samurais. Sekhmet saw that he had no more than ten, and raised her brow.

"Not enough," Ra decided. "Jove, Apollo, and Poseidon are with him. We need some *real* help."

"I will go there to find Thor," Diguan said.

"I will go," Sekhmet said. "I know where he is. He is near the southern plaza in an apartment. They are using it as a stronghold."

"All right, take my horse," he offered.

"Thank you," Sekhmet said, touching his hand. Keeping low, she hurried to his horse. She grabbed the reins and jumped on, riding off and turning down a cobblestone path.

Within the city walls, Olympus was all but won by the Asgardians. The Hoplites' defensive hold had faltered and they were spread thin fighting throughout the city. The weakened Spartans struggled to guard the castle's main entrance.

Thor and his son leaned against the wall inside the apartment, waiting to learn news of Zeus' whereabouts. Tyr sat on the floor humming an old Viking melody. Bragi stood near the entrance, looking away from the sunset, and Vidar was lying under the table fiddling with his knife.

Thor watched the contrast grow as the sky became darker, and the flames engulfing much of the city brightened.

"We should be out searching for him!" Magni blurted. "This is crazy for us to just wait here."

"No, son," Thor said. "Zeus could be anywhere. We cannot assume he is in his secure room. We have to wait. That roach could have hidden anywhere in this damn city. If we focus all our attention on one room and he is able to escape, then we will have a bigger problem on our hands. Once the Duati get here, we need to throw Zeus' head at their feet. They will leave then."

Magni shook his head. "But this is--"

"There!" Bragi called out, pointing toward Sekhmet galloping toward them. He opened the door and waved to her.

"Over here," he said, stepping halfway out of the door. She quickly leaped from the horse and dashed into the room.

"I know where Zeus is!" she exclaimed. "He is inside an apartment behind the castle with a handful of other gods."

"We will follow you then!" Thor announced, reaching for his helmet.

"Good, there is another thing though. The Unspoken are roaming the city."

"*What?*" he asked.

She continued, "They are here. I do not know how, but they are."

"All of them?" Thor asked.

"I do not know," she said. "I saw enough of them." Scanning around the room, she asked, "Where are the other Sh'losh?"

"I sent a few to scour the city for Zeus," Thor said, "but they could be halfway to Baltia for all I know."

Reaching back, she grabbed the small grip of a dagger in her waistbelt. "Do not ever insult my gods again. We are here fighting with you, and you have the nerve--"

Tyr held up his hand. "Relax, please. He means no harm."

"Right, calm yourself," Thor said, opening the pantry and glancing in. He pulled out a bottle of white wine and took a large chug.

"Piss! What is this, flower water?" Shaking his head, he guzzled the rest, then shattered the jar on the floor.

"I will not *calm* myself," she retorted.

Thor said, "Everyone prepare now. We leave shortly. We cannot afford to be slow, as it may well be our last opportunity to find that bastard. We must kill Zeus before the Duati arrive, or we are going to have a lot more trouble on our hands."

Picking up *Gungnir,* he continued, "Bragi, you stay. I need you here to keep our stronghold."

"Yes, Poet," Magni said, laughing to himself. "Sing a dirge."

Tyr grabbed his helmet and spear, then approached Bragi. "My favorite days are when Sjofn, you, me, and Modi would go to the large rock just outside of the Village. Sitting there quietly meditating, as you and Sjofn read your poems and acted out your play. It is just us two now, and it may be meaningless with them gone, but I would--"

"That is not meaningless at all," Bragi replied, smiling. "Those moments, those conversations...they encapsulate the best of life. I am glad you would still want to continue enjoying those."

Thor whispered to his son, "You did well today."

Biting a nail on his finger, Magni responded, "Thank you, father." He spit the nail to the ground and took hold of his weapon.

Thor approached Sekhmet and rested his arm on her shoulder. "I meant no harm regarding the other Sh'losh. As I said in Asgard, you are one

of us now. Are you ready, my *Asgardian* sister?"
She smiled.

"I am."

"Lead the way," Thor commanded, opening
the door. Sekhmet sprinted out, and Thor and the
other gods quickly followed.

On the tower, it was nearly too dark for
Aaron and Dagon to see.

"They're moving!" Aaron announced,
pointing toward Thor and Sekhmet where they
stood near the doorway. "We gotta follow them!
C'mon."

Chapter 60 *A Street Fight*

As Thor ran down the street, Ares watched from inside the apartment where they were hiding. He gripped his spear and shield as he neared the door.

"They are moving," he said to Athena. She put her silver helmet on and took hold of her spear.

"Let us go and slaughter those bastards," she said fiercely.

Ares opened the door slightly and peeked out. There were soldiers on both sides still fighting and running through the streets. He heard the screams from the apartments above him, but saw no one to stop them from following Thor. He readied his spear.

He whispered, "All right, it is dark enough now that we can follow them, and they should not be able to see us, but we will still keep a good distance. I just need one good throw, and I'll impale that son of a bitch."

"I am ready when you are, Ares," she answered.

"Go!" he said, opening the door. She crept forward, but stopped behind a column in front of the highrise.

Staring at the Asgardians as they ran, she said, "We just need to be careful of their nethers running around, and we should be fine."

Ares followed her and stepped out of the house, but was immediately toppled over. He fell, rolling onto the street, losing his spear and shield near the doorway. Looking up, he saw Mot, a tall Unspoken with a horned helmet and a broad scar down the center of his face.

Glancing back, Athena raised both hands to defend herself, but it was too late. Mot had already swung his club, hitting her chin. She fell backward onto the road. Ares watched as she crashed to the street, her head turned toward him, lifeless.

"Damn you!" Ares yelled. Mot smiled as he admired his work.

Ares rolled to his knees, but before he could stand, Mot swung hard, battering him to the ground. Mot lifted his club and swung again. Ares raised his arm over his head to defend himself, taking the impact on his hand.

Crack!

Ares rolled backward, flipping onto his feet, gripping his broken hand.

~*--*--*~

Tyr glanced back, hearing the shattering of Ares' hand. "Thor!" he shouted, pointing back toward Mot and Ares.

Thor stopped, staring back and smiling. He took a few steps closer, entering into the light provided by a fire burning above him in a highrise.

"Kill him, Mot," he murmured. "That scum killed Vali, my brother."

Mot again slammed the club at Ares. Ares lifted his arm again, bracing, and the blow immediately shattered his wrist. With a maniacal laugh, Mot raised his club to take another swing.

Ares used his undamaged hand to pull out his bone-handled dagger. He lifted his right arm again as a shield, and Mot struck hard. The hit smashed his fingers, leaving them dangling from his battered hand. Before Mot could attack again, Ares lunged, slicing a gash along Mot's arm.

"Thor," Sekhmet barked, "We must go!"

He didn't react.

She reached out, grabbing his arm, "We have no time for this. You know the Duati will be here at any moment." He grabbed her neck and shoved her against the wall, holding his hammer pressed against her head.

"Do not ever touch me like that!" he shouted. As he saw her grimacing, he pressed harder. "If you are with us, I am glad, but if you ever try and handle me, we may have problems." She closed her eyes, angry, then she nodded the best she could. Thor relented slowly, releasing her. The two stared at each other until Thor turned to his brother.

"Tyr, Vidar, you stay here. See to it that Ares dies. Either Mot kills him, or you do."

Tyr's lip curled up, "Vidar, come." Tyr tapped the end of the spear against the road excitedly and jogged toward Mot and Ares. Tyr and Vidar drew within a bow's shot and watched Ares as he tried to figure out how to kill the much larger, stronger god. Thor and the others continued with Sekhmet toward Zeus' hideout.

Vidar clapped softly, drawing Tyr's attention, then tapped Tyr's spear and pointed at Ares.

"No, my mute friend," he said. Tyr then lowered himself to the street and folded his legs, placing the spear along his legs and watching. "I will not kill a god when they cannot give me their full attention. I will wait." Vidar shrugged and stood over him, watching the two gods brawl.

"How can you let Tyr and Vidar just stay and kill Ares? We will need their help with Zeus." Sekhmet asked.

"You said he was with only a handful of gods, right?" Thor asked. "Then trust me, we are fine."

~*--*--*~

Ares managed to grab hold of his spear with his remaining good hand. Mot whipped the club, slamming it against Ares' shoulder and launching him back. Ares held his broken hand close to his chest, wincing in pain.

Mot twirled his weapon at Ares' head, but Ares jerked back out of reach. Mot leaned forward, swinging at Ares' legs, but Ares leaped and thrust his spear, piercing deep into Mot's chest.

As Mot stumbled back, Ares launched his spear. It penetrated Mot's stomach, forcing him back and pinning him to the highrise wall. Mot cackled, looking at the pole jutting from his gut. He lifted his head skyward and belted out a long raspy howl. The sound carried, but was cut short by Ares slashing his blade across Mot's neck.

"You know what Mot's scream means, right?" Tyr asked as he walked behind Ares.

Ares spun to face him. "No, but I assumed it meant he was *very sorry* he chose to challenge me." Ares reached back and shoved his dagger into Mot's head. As he twisted it out he added, "*Very* sorry."

"It means more are on their way," Tyr said.

"He was not so bad," Ares said. "A few more may even be fun."

Tyr shrugged, then leaned over and whispered to Vidar, who promptly ran toward the stronghold apartment where Bragi remained.

"Do not worry," Tyr said. "It is just you and I."

"Are you going to let me get my spear?" Ares asked calmly, sliding his dagger into his belt.

"Of course," Tyr said, "You are a god of war for Olympus. I am a god of war for Asgard. This should be fun."

Ares brought his damaged hand to his forehead, and with a half salute, turned and ripped the spear from the wall. Mot's body slid to the ground.

"And look, a fair fight. We are single handed," Tyr said, raising his arm and displaying the gold cap over his missing hand. Ares lifted his swollen hand, smiling.

"True."

The two gods clashed their weapons.

Chapter 61 *Night in Olympus*

The night sky gave little visibility for the battle raging on. Only the fires burning around the city offered any real assistance.

"We are almost to Zeus," Sekhmet said. She led Thor and Magni, turning down a narrow road behind Zeus' castle.

Thor glanced up at the rows of highrises lining both sides of the road, "Rats, they live like damn rats."

Sekhmet slowed her run, pointing them to Ra and Diguan, who remained hidden. The gods approached Ra and knelt in the shadows. Sekhmet pointed at the three dead hoplites, piled on top of each other at Ra's side.

"We are collecting now?" Sekhmet whispered, lightly prodding the bottom soldier with her spear.

Ra kept his eyes on silhouettes showing in the window of Zeus' apartment. "They got in my way." Diguan lifted his hand with a closed fist toward his Samurais.

"Who is in there?" Thor asked.

Ra said, "Zeus, Jove, Apollo, Poseidon, and Hera."

Thor noticed the ten Samurai, "Are they with you?"

"Ready and waiting," Diguan replied.

"Bows?" Thor asked.

Diguan nodded. "Strapped to their horses."

"Too damn easy. On my mark," Thor commanded. "Have them light the tips. Time to let Zeus know we are here."

Diguan signaled his Samurais to use a small flame burning from an apartment nearby. As directed, the ten began cutting small pieces of cloth from their garments and wrapped them around the arrows' heads.

Thor looked at Sekhmet and said, "We are going to smoke them out with the arrows. You and Ra post yourselves there on the west side of the door, so when they try and get out they will already be surrounded."

"Understood," Sekhmet said, and with a nod, she and Ra moved.

"And Sekhmet," Thor said, halting them. "Do not engage any of them until Zeus comes out."

She nodded her agreement, and the two set off, staying in the shadows as they worked their way near the doorway. They crouched behind a fallen pillar.

Thor pulled a small leather pouch from his belt and tossed it onto the ground near the Samurais.

"Tell them to pour it on the tips of their arrows. It was my celebration mead for when I held Zeus' head, but this will suffice." Diguan signaled to his warriors, and they each poured some of the liquor onto the tips. With a last glance at Sekhmet, Thor smiled.

"Light them," Thor whispered to Diguan, who gestured to his Samurais. They all held their arrows over the fire, then formed a row and aimed.

Using the shadows for cover, two Unspoken, Kaal and Shinigami, approached the ten from behind. Shinigami, a thin god with wild long black hair, drew two short-bladed swords from inside his sleeved robe.

At the southern plaza, Tyr and Ares held their spears, blades scraping against each other. Both were cut and nursing wounds given by the other. Both were exhausted, panting.

Ares struck Tyr's staff then lunged. Tyr dodged and swiftly left Ares with a laceration below his eye. Ares shook his head, frustrated, then brought his blade up, again leaning it on Tyr's.

Next, Ares hit Tyr's spear away then sprang forward, thrusting low. Tyr, unable to move quickly enough, took a gash along this leg. Tyr swiped back, slicing open a wide cut on Ares' arm.

Before Ares could set his blade, Tyr swung his. Tyr leaped forward, kicking Ares to the ground. Tyr jabbed his blade toward Ares' head, but Ares deflected it with his broken hand, driving the tip into the road.

Ares swept his spear, taking Tyr's legs from under him and dropping him to the ground. They both slowly struggled to their feet, staffs lowered, Ares shaking his head.

"You would make a great Immortal," Ares said, tightening his grip on the spear.

"Is that an offer?" Tyr said with a smirk.

"No," Ares replied. "Not at all."

Chapter 62 *Duat*

Ares thrust his spear, but Tyr dodged and kicked Ares to the ground.

"You know," Ares said, rising back to his feet. "This whole one-handed thing is going to take me a little while to get used to."

"No rush," Tyr replied. "You will have all the time you need in Sheol." He bolted forward, jabbing his spear, but Ares blocked.

Suddenly a bright light beamed into Tyr's eyes, blinding him momentarily. He stepped back from Ares, held up his arm, and glanced toward the light from the southern plaza. Ares rolled backward onto his knees, then watched Tyr's eyes. Ares didn't move, and he focused solely on Tyr.

Horus, the Duati, was on horseback at the southern entrance, holding a Saggilmut-tipped spear. A fire above the arch reflected brightly off of his breastplate.

"I hope we can continue this at another time?" Tyr said, stepping away. He turned and sprinted down the road in the direction Sekhmet had led Thor. "I have to tell Thor," Tyr told himself. "Sekhmet said they were behind the castle. I will start there."

"I would prefer not to continue this at all," Ares mumbled, exhausted, watching Tyr disappear into the darkness. Ares stood up and raised his spear, resting it on his shoulders. He watched as Pangu, Yama Anubis, and many other gods joined Horus at the southern plaza. A flood of Duati tribesmen rushed in behind them, each wearing their unique tribal colors. They circled the plaza center.

Osiris entered on a chariot made of Kailash bark. He halted the two stallions leading him at the center of the southern square. He stepped off surrounded by Nubian tribesmen, all holding their full-length wooden shields and wood-carved spears. He stood, wearing a saggilmut-stone helmet, chest plate, and leather boots. Following him on horseback were the Sh'losh, Toth, Kek, and Heqet.

Osiris spotted Ares and raised his hand in greeting. Then, looking past the Immortal, he noticed Mot, the Unspoken Ares had killed, and his jaw dropped.

"Horus!" he shouted. "Tell the tribal leaders the Unspoken are here. They must ready themselves for a long night." Then focusing back on Ares, he saw shadows behind him becoming figures. With the flames burning on the second-floor window over Ares, he saw two Unspoken, Supay and Buluc Chabtan, emerge with weapons in hand.

"Oh no," Osiris mumbled to himself.

Frantically grabbing his shield and spear from the chariot, he yelled, "Toth, Horus! You two come with me." He pointed to Yama. "You stick to the plan. I want Zeus found. Search everywhere!"

The three gods rushed through the surrounding tribesmen toward Ares to stand against the two Unspoken.

Osiris ordered Toth and Horus, "You two go after Chabtan. I have Supay." The two agreed. As they all reached Ares, they both unclipped their spears. Osiris wielded his double edge spear.

"How is your night going?" Osiris asked.

"To be honest, shitty," Ares said. "But I think things are looking better now."

Supay held two double-sided axes in his hands. Twirling them, he lunged and slashed at Ares, but Ares rolled, dodging the blow. Supay spun around and swung both axes against Osiris' shield. Osiris stayed low, letting the shield take the brunt of the attack. Supay lept back toward Ares and threw one of the axes. Ares, unable to move in time, took the blade in his shoulder. Supay ran at him holding the other axe above his head, but Osiris intervened, tackling him to the road.

The two rolled around until Supay was on top. Supay took hold of the axe with both hands, pushing the blade down against Osiris' chest. Osiris struggled to hold the axe back. The blade slowly forced its way past Osiris' armor, piercing into his chest. Osiris grit his teeth, trying to push harder. He roared, as the axe cut deeper into his chest.

Suddenly, Supay's grip loosened, and Osiris shoved the axe from his chest. Supay toppled over to the side of the road. Ares stood over him. His spear lodged in the back of Supay's head.

"Thank you, Ares," Osiris said, blowing out a deep breath.

Meanwhile, Chabtan swung his axe, but was parried by Horus' staff. Toth sprung forward, thrusting his spear into Chabtan's chest. Chabtan stumbled back, then Horus swung his staff across his face, knocking off his headdress.

Chabtan fell back, slamming against a wall, where only a few steps away, Aaron and Dagon stood.

Aaron, frightened, reached for Dagon's cloak. "Wrong turn! We took a wrong turn!"

"You must be someone special to have Dagon here protecting you, boy," Chabtan said, wiping the blood from his lips. Chabtan turned toward them, then threw his axe at Aaron before charging.

Dagon covered Aaron as the blade dug into his back.

Horus hurled his spear, piercing Chabtan's back and throwing him to the road. Toth ran past Horus, then leaped and drove his spear into Chabtan's head, pushing until the blade pinned his skull to the street.

Horus and Toth ran to Dagon, who was still covering Aaron with his arms. Without a warning, Horus pulled the axe free, tossing it to the ground. Dagon lowered his head, grunting in pain.

"Oh my god, D-Dagon...are you okay?" Aaron stuttered.

"I am fine," he replied, wincing.

"You saved my life!" Aaron grabbed Dagon's hand. Dagon peeked over his shoulder, trying to measure the wound.

"How is it?" Dagon asked.

"You will have one spectacular scar," Horus replied. "Not *losing your eye scar,* like me, but a pretty decent one, nonetheless."

"Are you all right?" Osiris asked, approaching the group with Ares.

"Yes," Dagon replied. He leaned against his spear as a crutch.

"Good," Osiris said. "I will make sure the Most High knows about what you did."

Osiris continued, "We need to find Zeus. Any ideas?"

"From what I know he should be in the safe room," Ares said. "It is a good place to begin the search."

"Right," Osiris said. "You and Horus go join up with Yama, and he will make sure you have all the gods and warriors you will need. Toth, you and I will work our way around the castle, and we can all meet at the castle entrance."

"Sounds good," Ares said, and he and Horus ran back toward the southern plaza.

"Aaron," Osiris said. "You do not have to be here, son. You and Dagon should go to Pangu at the southern entrance, and let him put some warriors around you. They can protect you."

Aaron said to Dagon, "What do you think? You're the one that had an axe in your back."

"You are the Writer, Aaron," Dagon grimaced, clenching his jaw. "You cannot write what you do not see."

Aaron nodded. "Thanks for the offer, King Osiris, but like my friend here said, I have to see how this all ends."

"Then I want you two to stay with me, at least. The city is not safe for you to be walking through," Osiris said.

"Deal," Aaron decided.

Dagon nodded, hobbling on his spear. "Thank you, Osiris."

Chapter 63 *A safe house?*

Hidden inside the house, Zeus sat on the wooden table, his face down toward his lap. His wife Hera sat beside him, rubbing her neck gently. His son Apollo sat against the wall with his eyes closed. Poseidon leaned against the wall, looking out of the window as Jove stood waiting for an answer from Zeus.

"So?" Jove said, pushing for a response. Zeus remained silent.

"We cannot sit here simply assuming we are safe. The Asgardians are no doubt searching door-to-door by now. It is only a matter of time." Zeus sat, contemplatively fiddling with his hands. Hera watched her husband silently.

"And what would you have me do, brother? The best thing we can do is wait and hide," Zeus said. "Once the Duati get here--"

"Listen to yourself! You are the *King*. Your people are outside and need you," Jove insisted. "Thor will find us hiding here like rats and have our entrails wrapped around the city walls long before Duat finds us." Zeus listened but didn't speak.

Jove's body shook. "We need to make a choice, Zeus. We can go out there and fight, or we can make our way to the northern gate and leave the city to link up with the Duati, then return with them in force," He added, "If we stay here, then we will die, and so will your people...*our* people."

"Which would you have me do?" Zeus asked, standing up from the table, glaring at him.

"We must leave now to the northern gate," Jove said. "We can go through and leave the city, then follow the travelers' road. There is no doubt the Duati will use that road to get to the southern entrance. Maybe if they see you alive, they will fight for us. *If* it is not too late, already."

"I agree with him," Hera said. Zeus nodded his agreement, biting down on his lip.

"Get ready!" Jove commanded as he surveyed the room.

Suddenly, ten flaming arrows flew through the window. One drove deep into Poseidon's shoulder, knocking him to the floor. The others landed around the room, sparking fires throughout the apartment.

Apollo stomped out a small fire near the table, but Jove grabbed his arm. "It is too late for that! They know we are here!"

Jove pointed to Poseidon and Apollo, then commanded, "We will go first and lay to waste whoever is out there. Get ready!" He turned to Zeus. "After we succeed, we will call for you and Hera, then we leave to the northern entrance. Be ready." Zeus gave a thumb of approval.

Apollo helped Poseidon back to his feet, then yanked the arrow from his shoulder. "To Sheol with every last one!"

"Damn them all!" Poseidon yelled. "I give my oath, I will get revenge on those that started this!"

The three gods lined up near the door. Apollo looked at his parents, blew out a short breath, turned the knob, and they rushed outside to the street.

Apollo was immediately confronted by Diguan, Thor, and Magni. Poseidon at first headed in the opposite direction. Startled, he jabbed with his trident at Sekhmet, but missed. At the same time, Jove saw the Samurai archers being slaughtered by two Unspoken, Shinigami and Kaal. He turned, joining Apollo to face the three other gods.

Ra swung at Poseidon but was blocked, and Poseidon thrust, stabbing Ra with one of the prongs from his trident and driving it deep into his ribs. Ra fell back, dropping to his knees.

Magni swung his axe. Apollo dodged but was unable to evade Thor's hammer, which struck his stomach and threw him against the wall.

Magni leaped forward, slamming his blade against Apollo's shield. Apollo stumbled backward, hitting his head against the wall.

Jove stepped between the three opposing gods and Apollo. "Damn you for this, Thor!" Jove shouted. He slashed his trident, but Thor leaped back. With a swift step, Jove lunged again, gashing Magni's shoulder.

The Unspoken, Kaal, slipped unnoticed behind Diguan. Kaal pummeled his head with a series of blows from his mace, and he collapsed to the ground. Shinigami rushed forward, grabbed Diguan by the hair, and rammed his sword into his neck repeatedly, roaring in delight with each thrust.

Magni heard a muffled groan and glanced back to see the two Unspoken still attacking Diguan's corpse.

"Father!" Magni screamed, nearly falling forward. Thor quickly stepped near his son and raised his hammer toward the two Unspoken. He and Magni stood between the Unspoken and Jove. Jove held his trident aimed at both Thor and son, but looked past them at Shinigami, who was holding up Diguan's head proudly.

Sekhmet thrust her spear at Poseidon, stabbing through his chestpiece. She twirled, swinging for Poseidon's neck. Poseidon blocked, and the two weapons clashed. She spun in the opposite direction then swung again, gashing his neck. He stumbled back, bleeding but refusing to let go of his weapon.

Sekhmet rose from her fighting stance, lowering her weapon.

"You can leave, just run," Sekhmet said, motioning her head down the street. "I am not here for you." Poseidon felt the blood flowing through the cut in his breastplate, then the wound on his neck.

"You would let me go?"

"Why die here?" she said. "You know it is too late for Zeus, but there is no reason *you* have to die with him." Poseidon glanced at Jove, who was crashing weapons with Thor, and then at Apollo propped against the wall, holding his head in pain.

Poseidon lowered his weapon and walked past Sekhmet and Ra, then hurried down a dark alleyway and disappeared.

Chapter 64 *Jove and Thor*

Thor studied the two Unspoken, then glanced at his son Magni. With a sigh, he turned toward Jove. "You are in my way."

Jove shook his head. "It is not too late to leave."

Thor pulled his spear *Gungnir* from a sheath on his back. He stared at Jove, grinding his teeth, holding both hammer and spear. He glanced back at Kaal and Shinigami and spat toward them. "They are not my enemy. But you...you damn smug Immortals sure as hell are."

Thor twirled his hammer and readied himself to fight Jove. He raised his spear, blocking Magni from fighting alongside him. "This Zeus imposter is mine."

Magni stepped back to let his father take the fight. Magni looked at the Unspoken, but they had turned away as if uninterested.

"A god like you can never rule, Thor," Jove said. "You lack compassion for anyone who is not *your own*."

"When I am done," Thor sneered, "everyone will be *my own*."

Jove shook his head. "Coexistence is the answ--"

Thor slammed *Mjolnir* against his chest and roared. He rushed at Jove and lunged with *Gungnir*.

Jove thrust back with his trident. The two weapons crashed together, sparking. Thor struck Jove's face, driving him back.

Jove tried to lift his trident, but Thor, the faster, smashed his hammer down on it, shattering the three prongs like glass. Immediately swinging again, he belted Jove across the chest. Jove fell back against the wall. He spat blood onto the ground, shaking his head.

"You are a better fighter than me, I will give you that," Jove said, raising himself to his knees. "Do you do anything in Asgard besides drink and fight?" Thor quickly struck *Mjolnir* across Jove's face. Jove spun, landing on his back in the road. His right eye instantly swelled shut.

"You hit…" Jove muttered, smiling with blood in his teeth, "like a nether." He rolled, pushing himself onto his feet again.

Thor smirked. "You have the heart of an Asgardian. I will give you that." Jove rose and pivoted against the wall to prop himself upright. He took off his dented helmet and tossed it to the ground.

Jove took a deep breath. "Heart of an Asgardian? I will take that as a compliment. As long as you do not say I have the *mind* of one."

Jove chuckled, coughing up blood. He peered at Thor with his one good eye and asked, "You would rather kill me and walk through this door for *your* kingdom than to try and help your own son?"

Thor looked toward Magni and struggled to stay composed. Magni was surrounded by Kaal, Shinigami, and Kalma, a goddess holding a short double-bladed scepter. The three gods relentlessly gashed at him, piercing his side, then slashing his face. After a quick cut along his leg, Magni fell to his knees. Taking a deep breath, Thor turned to face Jove.

Thor stepped toward his son but froze when Kaal drove his blade under Magni's ear. Thor's hands shook as he watched his son fall to the ground. He spun back around to confront Jove.

"He will die a hero of Asgard! But as for you, I will take you and Zeus, remove your heads, and drink my mead from your skulls!"

Thor thrashed *Mjolnir* deep into Jove's chest. Jove fell back and collided with the wall of the apartment where Zeus and Hera hid inside. He dropped to the street, barely moving.

Jove gasped for air as he watched Thor approach the door.

"But I want you to watch me kill your spoiled king first," Thor said, his hand resting on the door handle.

Apollo crawled slowly over to Jove, and the two collapsed together there in the road, helpless.

Chapter 65 *The Two Kings*

Thor opened the door and stepped inside the smoke-filled apartment. There, he found Zeus standing behind the table and holding his wife. Hera gripped Zeus tighter.

"You know, my son is now dead right outside this very door," Thor announced, tapping his spear against the white wall. "My other son lies dead somewhere in Duat, and my father..."

Shaking his head, Thor said, "Well that is another story." He stepped closer to the couple. "You know? It was all worth it, just to be here in front of you like this."

Thor watched Zeus, waiting for a response. Zeus stood motionless in the swirling smoke.

Thor continued, "Fate is a funny thing, Zeus. It gives and takes. I know that Osiris is coming, and I am glad he is. Because over the last few weeks fate took more than I care to bear, but today it is giving me double. Fate is handing me two kings. You saved me a trip to Duat, my friend. Normally, fate is not so...loving, but today she smiles on me."

Zeus released his wife's hand, pushing her away slowly.

"Do not kill me in front of my wife. Please, I beg you."

Thor gazed at Hera, scratched his blood-spattered beard with *Mjolnir*, then said, "A coward asking for a respectful death?" He drew a breath through his teeth, then shrugged.

Thor pointed at the door, "Get your weapon. Let us go outside."

"And my wife?" Zeus asked.

Thor hit his chest. "She will not be touched."

"Your oath?" Zeus requested.

"I do not think you are in any position..." Thor stopped himself, stepping closer and glaring eye to eye with Zeus. "On my name, she will not be harmed." Zeus nodded, then turned and grabbed his trident. He looked once more at his wife, then walked past Thor toward the door.

Thor clenched his teeth, enjoying the hopeless manner in which Zeus moved.

Zeus moved through the doorway into the street. There he saw Jove and Apollo lying beside each other on the cobblestone. He turned and raised his trident at Thor.

Thor spoke calmly to Hera. "I will be right back, my lady." And with a wink, he walked out the doorway.

"No!" Thor commanded Sekhmet. She had already raised her spear and was approaching Zeus. She stared at Thor and hissed in anger.

She took another step toward Zeus, but Thor raised his hammer and said, "You would not be here without me. I will handle Zeus."

Sekhmet stomped her foot and her eyes watered, with a growl she stepped back. "As long as I see him die for what he has done," she said.

"And he will," Thor said, raising one brow as he stared at Zeus.

"Thor!" Tyr cried out, running from down the road. Tyr stopped, startled by Zeus standing against Thor. He stared intensely at his brother. Thor knew--Tyr's eyes told him. So did Jove.

Osiris had arrived.

"Help me stand," Jove said, raising his arm. Apollo, who had managed to get to his knees, helped him sit up.

"Who said we are done?" Jove mumbled to Thor.

Thor smiled and replied, "Like I said, the heart of an Asgardian." Jove wavered and fell back to the road. He turned himself over and managed to get to his knees unaided.

Thor raised his finger to Zeus, delaying their battle, then approached Jove. Still kneeling, Jove lifted his weapon, now only a broken staff with shards of the trident clinging to the pole.

Jove attempted a slow, weak swung at Thor. Without flinching, Thor let it strike his waist. He laughed, jerking the shaft from Jove's hands. He tossed the weapon aside and thrust forward, smashing his hammer into Jove's face.

Jove folded once again, collapsing onto the street.

"Are we done now?" Thor asked mockingly.

Zeus, hoping to catch him off guard, attacked with his trident, but Thor swatted it away.

"*Really?*" Thor said, tossing his helmet away. Zeus jabbed again, but Thor stepped aside and barreled his shoulder into Zeus, toppling him over. Thor raised his hammer and took a half step, feinting a rush at Zeus, but stopped sharply. Zeus flinched, holding his hands in front of his face, obviously shaken.

Thor relaxed his battle stance and squared his shoulders, chest out.

"And *this* is your king?" Thor said with obvious disdain.

"Enough!" shouted Toth with a gesture from Osiris. The Duati warriors filled the road behind Osiris as he faced Thor, Zeus, and the others fighting. Osiris dismounted and walked toward them, Aaron and Dagon trailing behind.

Chapter 66 *A King's entrance*

Osiris lowered himself from his horse and signaled to Aaron to stay where he was. He walked toward the two kings with his spear and shield in hand. Sekhmet glared at Osiris as he approached her. He stopped in front of her.

"Did you get what you wanted in all this death?" he asked.

"Zeus is still alive, so then the answer is no," she stated.

"I am sorry that you gave in to your anger," he said softly. He tapped his spear onto the road. "Move or die."

She didn't move.

Thor hailed Osiris, "I am glad you are here! You saved me a trip to Duat. Sekhmet the Asgardian, let him pass. Let him come and *talk* with Zeus and I." Sekhmet gritted her teeth, then stepped aside.

Thor quipped, "What was that saying you Immortals taught all your people? *Two birds, one stone,* or something like that." Thor dropped his shoulders into his lower fighting stance.

"You have a choice!" Zeus yelled. "You do-_"

"Choices are for those who believe they hold power over fate," Thor retorted. "Fools."

"Then change your fate," Osiris said, nearing both. "It is not too late."

Thor smiled, "The wisdom of Osiris. Thinking he could ride all this way from Nekhen where my son was killed and talk me into a treaty? Damn that, and damn *you*."

Thor glanced over at Zeus, who was still on the ground. He spat toward him, then rushed at Osiris. Osiris planted his foot firmly and took the first strike from *Mjolnir* on his shield. The vibration rattled through his body. Osiris jabbed his spear from behind the shield, but Thor deflected it off *Gungnir*. Thor swung his hammer again, but Osiris blocked with his shield. He thrust his spear again, gashing Thor's leg.

Osiris kept his head low, eyes on Thor from behind his shield.

Zeus stood up and swung his trident wildly at Thor. Thor blocked with his spear, batting Zeus' weapon to the ground. Thor shook his head scoldingly and leaped at Zeus, kicking him, launching him back against the wall. He spun around and rushed Osiris, swinging his hammer at the shield.

The hit forced Osiris' arm above his head. Thor kicked Osiris in the chest, toppling him. Osiris quickly rolled onto his knees, pointing his shield and eyes at Thor.

Thor stepped closer and Osiris moved the shield and thrust his spear at Thor's neck. Thor

dodged, spun, and slammed his spear against Osiris'
shield. Thor plunged *Mjolnir* into the shield. Osiris
shifted his shield to the side, gashing Thor's arm
with his spear, then rolled away and retreated
behind his shield.

Thor stepped back from Osiris and jumped
at Zeus. He raised his trident as Thor's spear
slammed into it. Thor thrust *Mjolnir* into Zeus'
chest. Zeus fell onto his back, releasing his grip on
his trident.

Thor raised *Gungnir* toward Zeus. "DIE!"
But Osiris lunged, plunging his spear into Thor's
back. He jerked it out and cut along Thor's
shoulder.

Thor spun around and delivered a series of
hammer swings, each blocked with Osiris' shield.

Osiris jabbed his blade at Thor and the edge
cut along his neck. Osiris snapped his spear back
and held his shield tightly in defense. He remained
low to the ground.

Thor glared at him and shouted, "Did you
travel all the way here to hide behind your shield?
Fight!"

Osiris didn't move.

Thor took a half-step toward Osiris, but
quickly changed direction, leapt and swung his
spear at Zeus.

Zeus parried with his trident, and the two
weapons crashed together. Thor slammed his
hammer against the trident, breaking the staff in

two. He then immediately thrust *Mjolnir* into Zeus' chest. Zeus collapsed onto the road and rolled to a halt near some rubble from a highrise.

Thor turned back to Osiris and swung his hammer upward, hitting the shield and deflecting Osiris' arm skyward. Thor twirled and smashed into the shield again. Osiris lost his grip, letting the shield fly into the air. It landed in the street and rolled away near Sekhmet's feet.

Osiris lunged forward and cut Thor's cheek. In return, Thor plunged *Gungnir* deep into Osiris' shoulder.

Thor yanked the spear out and blood flowed. He thrust his spear again, but Osiris rolled to the side and buried his spear into Thor's abdomen.

Buckling, Thor stumbled back, looking down at the spear. Dropping his weapons, he clenched the pole with both hands and pulled it out.

Tyr, seeing the attack, lowered his spear and his head.

"Damn...good move," Thor said, dropping to his knees. Osiris stood up and took a deep breath. He glanced back at Sekhmet, holding her spear and trembling as she stared at Thor.

Zeus staggered to his feet behind Thor. Holding the blades of his trident, he drove the three prongs into Thor's back.

"You die!" Zeus yelled.

Osiris stepped closer and pushed Zeus back. He raised his hand and Zeus took another step back.

Osiris crouched in front of Thor, wrapping his arm around his neck and letting him down onto the road gently. Osiris whispered a few words into his ear. Thor nodded, smiled, and murmured, "I appreciate that." Osiris patted his chest, then rose to his feet and took a step back.

Thor stared up at the sky and saw shades of pink and orange emerging, a new day. He turned his face toward Tyr, closed his eyes, and released his last breath.

"What did you say to him?" Zeus asked.

"It does not concern you," Osiris said.

Tyr let go of his spear, letting it fall to the road. With his head slumped, he approached Thor, bypassing the two kings.

Chapter 67 *A spoken treaty*

Tyr lowered himself to one knee in front of Thor's lifeless body and rested his hand on his brother's chest. "I must return him to Asgard."

"What? How dare you even--" Zeus said, looking for a nearby weapon.

"Of course, take him," Osiris said softly.

Zeus raised his voice. "How can you--"

"There are few things more tragic than someone dying far from home," Osiris said, folding his arms. "He will be taken home. They all will."

"Thank you," Tyr responded. He rose to his feet, then pulled the battle horn from his belt. "Never thought I would…" Tyr shook his head, then blew a series of piercing blasts. They reverberated throughout the city, echoing down the streets.

"The Asgardian army has been called to gather outside the southern entrance," Tyr announced. "I demand you sound your trumpets and sheath your weapons, as well."

Zeus stepped forward, holding the sharpened end of the broken trident, but Osiris grabbed him by the arm.

Osiris said, "You heard him. Sound your trumpets. It is over." Zeus' eyes bulged as he stared grimly at Tyr. Turning his glare at Osiris, he spat on the road, frustrated.

"Fine," Zeus growled.

Osiris called out to Toth, "Sound the trumpet. We gather at the western entrance." Toth pulled a silver horn from a small leather pouch strapped to his stallion and blasted a series of short deafening notes.

"The Unspoken?" Osiris asked, "How are they here?"

Zeus shrugged. "I do not know." Tyr agreed.

"All right," Osiris said. "Once Asgard leaves these walls, we will stay to comb the city for them."

Zeus watched as Tyr eased Thor's body over his shoulder, then asked, "Is it over? I mean *really* over?"

"I cannot promise that," Tyr said. "I will not be the one taking the throne to replace him. Baldr will rule, and I will continue to obey the will of the king. We will see what Asgardian Law has to say on the matter."

"Baldr?" Osiris asked. "Why him?"

Tyr said, "Both of Thor's sons are now in Sheol. He is the next in line."

"Wait," Jove said, struggling to stand. Jove stumbled forward, bending over and picking up *Mjolnir*. He handed it to Tyr.

Osiris placed his hand on Tyr's chest and asked, "May we speak alone?"

Tyr chuckled and said, "It has been a rather long day. I cannot lie; I'd rather not."

Osiris lowered his arm. "Please, we *need* to speak."

Tyr replied, "Unless you wish to kill me or put me in chains, then I am leaving. I am tired." He walked on, carrying Thor over his shoulder and holding *Mjolnir*.

Tyr stopped to speak with Ra and Sekhmet. "I am sorry we failed you." He continued walking. Ra slid his weapon into its sheath. He stepped over to Magni, lifted his body onto his shoulder, and followed Tyr.

"Sekhmet?" Ra said. "Are you going to be all right?"

She tugged on her whiskers. "I am done. Done with all of you." She looked at Zeus, her hands shaking. "If Osiris were not here you would be dead! And soon, no matter what, you *will* be." She turned around, donning her hood. She trudged down the street, fading into the darkness.

Ra's head sank to his chest, and with a deep breath, he carried Magni and *Gungnir*, following Tyr.

Osiris jogged to keep pace with Tyr. "Please," Osiris said. "I will not apologize for what has happened, but you must know about Baldr. After Odin's banishment, I met with him and Zeus at Mount Hor, and--"

"It does not matter," Tyr said. "Your words are meaningless in Asgard court, so unless someone

Asgardian was there, whatever you tell me holds no power in Asgardian law. It--"

He replied, "Svetovid was there, and he--"

"Is dead," Tyr stated. "Baldr will be king. Just keep yourselves prepared. Baldr is not a warrior. He will not lead us to battle. He is the type to have an alchemist visit your wine cellar, if you understand what I mean."

"And what if Baldr does *not* become king?" Osiris asked. "Is there a chance for peace then?"

Tyr stopped. "Enough! It sounds to me as if you are threatening my brother, and that is something I will not listen to. I am not a conspirator! We are a monarchy, Osiris, and Baldr will be king." He turned and started to move away.

Osiris reached out, clutching Tyr's shoulder. "I know you to be a god of honor and good judgment. If you want peace, *true* peace as you spoke of at the Hall during Odin's banishment when everyone laughed at you, then we need to try, tired or not."

"I was a fool," Tyr said.

Osiris said, "Not at all! Listen, all I ask for now is that you discourage any of Baldr's plans. Just try to hold him off from any type of attack."

"You expect peace?" Tyr asked. "I think it may be a little late for that now."

"Tyr," Osiris said, and his voice changed as he pleaded. "Go home. Mourn and care for your dead. I will ensure that we bring every one of your lost warriors to the northern gates of Asgard. I beg you, stop him from acting as quickly as Thor did."

"I will not make any oath," Tyr insisted, "But...how can I know you will not attack us?" Tyr asked.

"Because if that was my plan, I would not be speaking to you now," Osiris said. "I heard you in the Hall. You believe in peace, and I believe in *you*."

"All right, all right, fine," Tyr said. "I will try. Are you done now?"

Osiris smiled and gestured for him to be on his way. Tyr sighed and continued southward toward the fallen door. Ra followed silently, carrying Magni.

Osiris hailed Apollo. "The trumpets must be sounded calling for the battle's end. We must gather all remaining soldiers at the eastern entrance. And we must sweep the city for the Unspoken."

Tyr directed the remaining Asgardians to collect as many of the dead as they could, and they left the city through the southern arched entrance. Walking through the gate, Tyr glanced at Hades' head that dangled from a rope against the wall.

Outside, Tyr and Ra walked the battlefield, stepping over bodies. They trudged down the hill to the iron wagons they had used to transport weapons. Thor and Magni were laid side by side, arms folded over their chests. Bragi placed his green cloak over their heads, and they began the journey back to Asgard.

Before he left, Tyr returned to the battlefield and found Sjofn, her face resting peacefully. He knelt before her and carefully withdrew the arrow from her body. Tossing it aside, he noticed the purple flower in her hand.

"You are such a peculiar one," he mumbled, before gathering the flower from her fingers. He slid the stem over her ear and through her hair. The flower brushed against her temple. Sliding his arms under her, he lifted her and stood up.

"Maybe we can take a long way home," he whispered to her.

Chapter 68 *When Does It End?*

The afternoon was cloudless, bright, and blue. The hunt for the Unspoken within the city had found six of their bodies, but the rest remained to be accounted for.

Ares leaned against the southern archway examining his shattered hand. Aaron watched him from the Plaza. Although he was disgusted by Ares' disfigured hand, he couldn't help staring. Dagon sat near the plaza fountain, getting the gash on his back tended to. Aaron noticed Jove when he passed the fallen door outside the southern gates. Aaron was watching as various gods separated the bodies into three groups.

With a pat on Dagon's arm, Aaron gestured toward Jove. For the first time since arriving at Saggilmut, Dagon waved him to go ahead unguarded. It felt good to have someone who would do such a selfless act, as Dagon had done. His dad used to say he would take a bullet for him, but when he later left Aaron and the family without a cent, Aaron found his dad's words to be empty. But Dagon was different. Dagon cared, not only in word, but in action.

"All the dead are now in Sheol?" Aaron asked as he approached Jove. Seeing the thousands of bodies scattered about on the field, Aaron felt sick to his stomach. He watched as the Immortals and Duati sorted the dead into groups, placing them in piles. The Duat removed the Asgardian dead on wagons, preparing them for the trip to Asgard.

Aaron clutched his stomach as a Hoplite picked up a severed Asgardian arm, pulled an axe from the lifeless grip, and tossed each into separate wagons.

"The dead?" Jove asked. "Yes, the dead go to Sheol." Aaron paled.

Jove pointed toward the castle. "Maybe we should get you out of here," he said. "Zeus should be starting the public assembly soon. It might be a good idea for you to see what he has to say."

"Yeah," Aaron answered, closing his eyes. "That's a good idea, but I'm definitely going to throw up." He rushed around the corner, back inside the city walls, and found an isolated spot. His stomach instantly knotted and he vomited. He closed his eyes and tightened his hold on the wall as his stomach churned, and he retched again. Gasping for air, Aaron spat to clear his mouth. Hearing a step behind him, he glanced back and saw Dagon standing near him.

"Get the hell away from--" Another rush of vomit spewed out. Aaron lifted his head, struggling to breathe. "They're all dead, just gone. I can't believe it." He wanted to cry. *How could the gods let this happen? This isn't love. This isn't right.*

"It is heartbreaking. We gods must do better," Dagon said. Dagon stepped toward him and hid Aaron from the crowd in the plaza. Jove rushed up behind them.

"Are you all right?" Jove asked.

"I-I am done. I think I'm done," Aaron said, finally taking a deep breath. He wiped his eyes and stood up. He did feel a bit better. With a gesture from Jove, the three began walking toward the castle.

Aaron's stomach sank again. Throughout the city there were bloodstains, bodies yet to be gathered, and dismembered limbs. "How can all of you fight like this?" Aaron asked. Jove gestured for Dagon to answer.

"When someone believes their principles are more important than someone else's life, we always end up here," Dagon said.

"What do you mean?" Aaron asked, lifting his head at the brilliant sky, avoiding the carnage on the ground. It didn't help much. The highrises were smoldering, and bodies hung from shattered windows.

Dagon explained, "What I am saying is, Thor believed in his version of the truth so much that he was willing to sacrifice others to achieve it. His principles surpassed the value he placed on life. A god that would demand the lives of others to fulfill their beliefs is not a god worth following. Thor never once worried about the lives of those now lying dead. In the end, his twisted desire to rule became a god to him, a false god."

"With Thor dead, do you think it's over?" Aaron asked.

"I cannot say that and feel comfortable," Dagon said. Aaron's gaze fell on a dead Hoplite, armless, slumped against the wall. His eyes teared up.

The rest of the walk was silent, and Dagon and Jove placed their hands on Aaron's shoulders.

Near the city square, the masses had gathered for their king, who would be out soon. The people of the city had covered the castle grounds with flower petals and poured oils onto the road. The air was filled with the aroma of lavender. Smoke from clay altars rose as the people celebrated, dancing and waving their hands, exalting their gods.

Jove led Dagon and Aaron through the revelers until they finally reached the steps to enter the castle. Aaron stopped there and scanned the crowd.

Jove stooped to speak to Aaron. "I do hope you are okay. I am sure Zeus will be out soon, and I assume afterward you should be free to go back to Shamayim to get some rest before you begin your writing. You can feel free to wait here, or you can join me in the castle. I will go and check on him."

"I-I'll stay here, thanks," Aaron answered. Jove patted Dagon's shoulder and smiled at him, then entered the castle.

"I didn't get to thank you for what you did last night," Aaron said, looking up at his bodyguard.

"It was my job," Dagon replied, shrugging it off.

"Well, either way, thanks."

"You can pay me back one day," Dagon said, staring off into the crowd.

"Of course, anything," Aaron said, perking up.

"One day, when my service to the Most High is finally done, you can treat me to some bread and tea in Nekhen." Aaron offered his arm, and the two clasped forearms.

"As friends?" Aaron asked.

"As brothers." Dagon almost smiled, gently pushing Aaron.

Chapter 69 The *disagreement*

Waiting outside the castle entrance, Aaron peeked inside the doorway, having heard murmurs coming from the foyer. Many Immortals were approaching from the northern hall. The gods walked by the people gathered in the foyer. All of them had volunteered and were on their hands and knees wiping the blood from the marble floor. Apollo emerged from the doorway first, to the joy of the crowd. He pumped both fists above his head, rejoicing.

His cheers to the masses gathered excited them even more. Jove followed slowly, still clearly nursing his wounds. He offered a brief wave before taking his position near Apollo by the castle entrance. The roar of the crowd grew louder as each god appeared through the castle door. They aligned themselves one after another on the stairs, descending into the crowd.

Finally, Zeus emerged and presented himself with Hera by his side. He wore a Saggilmut crown reflecting the sun's rays, a pristine white toga with a purple sash around his shoulders, and held a new trident made of pure gold. He smiled, waved, and pointed out various prominent men and women in the crowd.

After extended applause and chants praising him, Zeus eventually hushed the crowd. With a few final exaltations and hand gestures, they finally settled down enough for him to speak.

"Would anyone care to hear how we won the battle?" Zeus shouted, holding his hands in the air. The onlookers erupted into roaring applause, whistling, chanting, and praising their king.

"Maybe we should just go wait in the war room with the Duati," Aaron said. He already felt sick, but hearing Zeus' boasting made him feel even worse. Dagon signaled, and the two backed out of view inconspicuously and walked toward the back entrance of the castle.

Entering through the back door, they headed down the freshly cleaned hall. Aaron bit his lower lip, feeling flustered. Dagon nudged him, but Aaron waved him away, preferring silence. Dagon nudged him again a little harder.

"Speak your mind," Dagon whispered.

"I just don't get it," Aaron blurted. "I mean, why is everyone so happy? How can they celebrate when they still have dead people in the streets? That's insane."

"Because they worship him more than they love others," Dagon said.

"That's crazy. How can anyone love a god, then treat others like crap?" he asked, frustrated. "So, because they *worship* him, they can ignore reality, pretending like everything's fine? That's moronic and dangerous. They should be grieving for the dead, no matter the sect!"

"You are correct, Aaron. They are denying the gravity of the situation, instead believing that, since their god is *benevolent,* they need not care about anyone who is not with them. They have oversimplified it to good winning over evil."

"Then they're no different than Thor!" Aaron insisted. "He believed in his stupid philosophy so much he was willing to go to battle over it. These people believe in Zeus so much that they don't care about others' lives. Celebrating after any war is sick."

"But that is how faith works, right?" Dagon said. "You believe in something greater than yourself. Then you have to ignore your feelings to place the faith's ideology first?"

"I guess, but I'm not like that." Aaron said, shaking his head, "I'll never have faith in something enough to treat it as more important than people. That's just ridiculous."

"And that makes you a good person, Aaron. The fact that you care, truly care for others, is why you were selected."

"Selected? Who picked me?" he asked. "I remember one of the first things Asherah said to me was that she didn't want me to be the writer, so I--"

"I did," Dagon stated, "and the Most High agreed."

"Then why can't gods like Zeus care for..." He paused, stopping at the entrance to the war room.

"What?" Dagon said, studying Aaron.

Aaron looked at him with a squint. "You already knew Thor and Zeus were like that. That they cared more for their ideals than they did for people. You wanted me to see through them and their bullshit?"

"Aaron, unfortunately, the books written on Earth about the gods have not always been accurate as you have been told. We cannot afford the dangers of what has happened on Earth with religion and theologies to happen here. I asked for the Most High to select you, because you care for all the right things. I believed in your writing before you ever set foot in Shamayim because of who you are. I watched you care for your mother and sister. You put people first, even above your own viewpoints. That is rare."

"So many of these gods are nothing more than egotistical jerks," Aaron decided.

Dagon placed his hand on Aaron's head. "If only if there was a writer that could see past the fact that they are gods and write the truth of what he sees, and the truth that caring for others should come above all things."

Dagon's words made him feel better. "Yeah, if only there was someone to write something like that." He opened the door for Dagon, waving his hand as a butler would, and the two entered the war room.

"Aaron," Pangu said with a smile. He was sitting in a chair.

"Pangu," Aaron said. "Good to see you."

"I am glad you are safe," Pangu said.

"Yeah, me too." He stuttered to correct himself. "I mean, I'm glad you're safe, too."

"Sit down, relax," Pangu offered. Aaron sat, then scanned the room and noticed that everyone in the room was Duati, except Ares and Aphrodite.

"Shouldn't you be outside?" Aaron asked Ares.

"No," he answered sharply.

"Definitely not," Aphrodite added.

Aaron noticed her leg was shaking. Unsure if he should ask why they weren't outside, or why they both seemed so upset, he ended up staring at them until his mind wandered.

"Are you okay?" Aphrodite asked, after a moment.

"Oh. Oh yeah, I'm good," he said, coming back to reality. "Sorry." She smiled briefly, but something was clearly bothering them. Then Aaron realized that none of the Sh'losh were there.

"Where's Toth--Horus? Where are all the Sh'losh?" he asked.

Osiris offered a half-smile, but before he could answer, Aphrodite spoke up.

"*He* still will not let them in," she said in disgust. "After everything they did for us." Aaron's mouth opened in shock.

"Zeus? No way," he mumbled loud enough to be heard in the otherwise silent room.

"That is why Ares and I are here," she said, leaning her head on Ares' shoulder. Aaron looked at Dagon, who didn't make eye contact.

Osiris said, "They are gathered outside of the southern gate, burying Bastet and others." Ares added, "It is better they have some of their own time anyway, rather than have to deal with Zeus' insane rationale."

"I can't imagine," Aaron said, mortified. He glanced at Aphrodite and played her words in his head, *after everything they did.*

Osiris said, "I understand your frustration, but I honestly believe that right now may not be the best time for the Sh'losh. They have a lot to deal with. After their argument and the split between siding with Thor and Zeus, they need time to mend. Sekhmet is outside the gate right now burying her sister. I cannot imagine the pain she must be going through. But thankfully, they are a strong group, and have their own values that I believe will help them get through this even stronger than before."

"Forever the optimist," Ares said in a monotone.

"Is that a bad thing?" he asked.

Ares sat up in his chair. "No, not at all. I just wish I shared it with you."

The room quieted, and no one spoke. Osiris stared at the pieces representing the armies on the table, Thor's piece knocked over. Aphrodite rested her head on Ares' shoulder with her eyes closed. Aaron tried to stay awake, but the long night bested him as he slouched deeper in the chair, yawned, and dosed off.

Chapter 70 *A proposal to end the war*

"Long night, Aaron?" Apollo said, waking Aaron from a short, but deep sleep. Raising his head, he wiped his eyes and noticed drool on his shirt.

"Seriously?" he said to himself, wiping it off. Now embarrassed, he saw Dagon staring at him with a knowing grin.

"Welcome back," Dagon said, laughing to himself far more than Aaron thought he should have.

"*I hate you,*" Aaron replied, giving Dagon a playful jab.

"The ceremony is over," Apollo announced as he sat on the far side of the room, facing everyone else. "King Zeus will be here soon."

Rubbing a hand across his eyes, Aaron sat up. *A little bit longer would have been nice*, he thought. He yawned and shook it off. *I wonder if gods drink coffee?*

Aaron leaned over to Dagon. "After this, I'm ready to go back to the Library. Might as well get started on my writing *homework*."

"I believe you are right," Dagon said.

Zeus entered the war room, but stopped, shouted back, out of the door, "You tell Saturn and Venus, they had better come to see me later today!" He and Jove entered. Zeus stepped toward the center of the room, clapping and singing, spilling wine from his cup. The city's celebration could be heard inside the room even after Jove shut the doors.

Aaron said to Dagon, "The city sounds so different now."

"I do prefer music to the sound of violence myself," he replied.

"Yeah, me too. Do you think it'll stay this way? I mean peaceful?" he asked.

Dagon frowned. "I do not know. It is never that simple when it comes to the coexistence of different gods."

That doesn't sound hopeful at all, Aaron thought. But before he could say anything, Dagon touched his hand for silence, nodding toward Zeus.

"Aaron," Zeus said merrily. He had been heavily drinking, Aaron surmised. "I am happy you are here, my friend." Zeus brought a chair to the map table. He sat facing the others, then waved Apollo over to join them. He looked at each of the gods in appreciation. Osiris sat with Pangu and Yama to his side, as Jove took a chair next to Ares and Aphrodite.

Zeus addressed the Duati, "First, thank you. I can honestly say, without your help, we may not have been as successful. We owe much of our victory to you. I will be sure to repay you for your kindness."

Osiris, stroking his goatee, replied, "Thank you for your words, but we have everything we need, thank you. We only ask for your continued hospitality as we gather the fallen Asgardians. It will take us several trips to deliver them all."

"And thank you for that," Zeus said. "I would have thrown them off the cliff near Seychelles Beach and let them rot. That might not have gone well with those bastards."

Osiris agreed, "We are happy to serve as a mediator during this time, until we can all come together in the Hall. We should work toward building a truce, and maybe we can finally move forward."

Zeus leaned back, crossing his arms. "Do you, King Osiris, truly believe it is over? We must ask ourselves this from the Asgardian perspective. Are they going to accept this defeat? Can they possibly *move on*? We know them better than that. This is not over, their idiotic take on fate would never allow for it to be over."

Pangu twirled his long mustache and said, "If we all work together, I am sure a truce can be made."

"You say that because their attention is not focused on you," Zeus argued. "Their swords and axes are aimed at *us*. I am sure you will be next if they ever do finally destroy Olympus, but let us be honest. Their gods are foul, and their people emulate them. They cannot be taught peace because their entire sect is built on self-indulgences. They do nothing for the glory of their sect. Everything is built on selfish lusts and war. Do you believe they will ever be *cultured*?"

"Not *your* culture, no," Osiris said. "But if you mean, can they create their own culture that does not demand a war, then I say yes. We can be amicable." Aaron watched the two, intrigued.

He whispered to Dagon, "I see what you mean. It never is that simple to get along, I guess." Dagon nodded, disappointment clear on his face.

"I wish that were true, Osiris" Zeus argued, "but I cannot live in your false reality. The only way this war undeniably ends is with Asgard either ruling all Saggilmut or being stopped once and for all."

"What in Sheol are you proposing?" Pangu asked.

"Look outside at my people. Because I have provided a good life for the Immortals, my people are content and orderly. They are structured and do all for the greater glory of Olympus. They do not make fools of themselves and live wildly, acting as if fate is on their side, like Asgardian nethers. We can give that to them. I can bring a civilized lifestyle to those--"

"Be clear with your words, Zeus. Do you wish to attack Asgard?" Osiris demanded.

Chapter 71 *The cycle continues*

"Look," Zeus said, rising from his chair. "They will never allow us to have peace. They are primitive in thought and uncivilized in action. For centuries, we have tried to teach them, and they are no different, still barbaric. If we leave them to their own devices, they will attack again and one day succeed. Then what? Yes, Osiris, I do say we need to attack them. Help me root out these savages."

Aphrodite, squeezing Ares' forearm, insisted angrily, "You said the *same* thing, using the *same* words when you expelled the Sh'losh. Our cultural differences do not--"

Zeus retorted, "Even the Sh'losh, despite being part animal, are more civil than the Asgardians! But…" He stared at Osiris. "Look at how they repaid me for sending them into exile instead of killing them. Those bastards attacked me with my enemies!" Zeus took a deep breath. "We are the gods! So I ask you, who do you pray to for help? I will no longer stand by waiting for Asgard to adopt our ways, and I will not live another night worried that I may have to be subjected to theirs."

Jove waved his hand for attention. "My King, I think we are best served if we focus our attention where it is most needed. The real question you seem to be asking is if they will attack again or if peace can be achieved with them. And I do believe peace is--"

"No, I am not asking that at all," Zeus interjected. "I am *certain* they will attack again. My friends, I am asking if you will join me to stop them from ever invading our provinces again. Will you join me in a siege on Asgard to end this, once and for all?"

Aaron felt sickened by the thought of seeing any more dead. *Please say no to this lunatic*, he thought. He looked at Osiris and the other Duati, hoping they could talk some sense into him.

Yama glanced at Osiris and said, "You see? This is why we should have let them both just destroy each other. Both sects are filled with such foolish gods. Any time someone's belief is more important than life itself, others die."

Aaron hid his smile, thankful for his response.

Osiris stared at Zeus intently.

Pangu spoke up, "Zeus, we came here as defenders and that is where it ends. Their king is dead, and Baldr can be swayed much easier than Thor. We do have a chance for peace. Now all we need to do is wait until we meet in the Hall at the next assembly, and if we--"

Zeus blurted, "Baldr is manipulative! We cannot trust anything that comes from that snake." He stepped to the map on the table and pointed at Asgard province. "Listen, these savages have no

406

real king. Whoever sits on *Hlidskjalf* is only the tip of the arrow that the damn Asgardian Law and savagery use to aim with. This is our chance to break the entire arrow."

"I will not take part in any of this," Ares announced. Aphrodite nodded in agreement.

"What?" Zeus replied in disbelief. "Those bastards once killed you! I saw you lying on the ground, and now you would stand against me and protect them from justice?"

"Yes," Ares assured him. Tilting his head toward Aphrodite, he continued, "Father, we respect you as King, but this is wrong."

"Are you all blind?" Zeus roared. "Baldr turned on his own brother. He will do the same to us. If we wait long enough, he will--"

"Baldr will not be king," Osiris announced, standing up and staring at Zeus. "He is not the rightful heir to the throne. As a monarchy, the law demands that Modi will be king." Zeus snorted at the absurdity of the statement.

"What?" Aaron asked. "H-He's dead, though. He was killed. Y-You know that."

Osiris shook his head at Aaron. "The Sh'losh caught him and his brother wandering near Nekhen. They were spying out our lands, talking to the gods, asking questions. They did not exactly *blend in*. So the gods watching those two spies did what anyone would do to truly weaken an

Asgardian. They got them both drunk and waited for them to pass out."

Zeus argued, "Then they will attack you next if you ever let him go. All the more reason we must attack them now."

Osiris sighed. "No, you misunderstand. Baldr came to Nekhen after he met us both at Mount Hor. You were there, Aaron, remember, at Horus' house?"

"Yeah, I remember him there. He came and asked you for Modi's body. You kicked him out."

Osiris explained, "Right, Baldr traveled to Nekhen on the command of his brother, trying to claim Modi's body. But, as all fools do, he could not stop himself. He spoke openly about killing Thor and wanting to rule. He shared his true intentions and hatred for his own Asgardians. What he did not know was that Modi heard everything. Modi was in that courtyard with us, Aaron, listening to everything."

"He was one of the masked servants! He was covered in the mask so we didn't know," Aaron exclaimed. Osiris winked.

"Holy crap," Aaron said, stunned.

Osiris continued, "I told you that they were there for a reason, Aaron. After hearing Baldr for himself, Modi openly made an oath on his own name that he would ensure that Baldr would pay for his treachery, and that as king, he would be more open to conversations of peace."

"Do not be naive," Zeus argued. "He was saying whatever it took to be released."

"It is worth the risk," Osiris stated. "And no god breaks an oath on their own name, no one. Modi learned something that day that he had not known before." Zeus tugged at his beard in obvious frustration.

"What is that? What did Modi learn?" Aphrodite asked.

"What I would hope we all know in this room," Osiris said, staring at Zeus. "That no one sect is perfect. That each god makes their own choices. That we owe it to the people here in Saggilmut to do everything in our power to always try for peace." Zeus turned his back to Osiris and grabbed a red figurine from the map on the table.

Zeus turned and held it up for everyone to see. "You see this piece? It was first used for Odin. For thousands of years, I have stared at this thing with disgust. Then, for only a few days, the piece I worried over was that one *there*." He pointed toward another red piece, one holding a hammer skyward. "Now with Thor gone, I will have to deal with some *other* red piece. You see? It does not matter who they have in charge. They are not worth the stone used to make these pieces. Please, I ask you to reconsider before it is too late."

Osiris asked Zeus, "Is there anything else? If not, I would like to assist in transporting the dead back to Asgard and pay my respects to Bastet and the other fallen warriors." Zeus tapped his hand along the wooden table, then threw the figurine against the wall.

"Then peace to you, Zeus," Osiris said. He looked at Jove, Ares, and Aphrodite. "And you, as well." He signaled the other Duati, and they all stood up and headed for the doorway. Pangu smiled at Aaron and waved goodbye.

"Wait," Zeus called out to Osiris. "Please, meet with me here once more, before you leave for home. Can you at least agree to that?" Osiris looked at Pangu, who agreed with a shrug.

"All right," Osiris decided. "It will take a few days, of course." Zeus raised his hand to wave them off. As Osiris and the others left, the room was left in an awkward silence.

Chapter 72 *the Truth*

Leaving the war room, Pangu leaned into the other two Dauti and sneered. "I told you Zeus was a fool. He is the type that buys a fish, takes it home, cuts off the head, then claims to be a fisherman."

Osiris laughed, despite his frustration. He wrapped his arm around Pangu's shoulder. "We did not come here for Zeus, nor for the glory of being recorded in the writings of Aaron. We came for *them*." Outside the castle, the three gods found the entire city celebrating. Osiris smiled, appreciating the joy that engulfed the city.

Yama listened to a woman singing loudly from her seventh-story window. He grabbed Osiris by the shoulder and echoed her in a girlish pitch, "*Zeus, the savage slayer, struck down the mighty Thor.*"

Osiris pushed Yama playfully. "This is *their* day. A fool seeks honor."

Jove had followed three Duati gods out of the castle, and called out, "Wait! Osiris." They stopped.

"I just wanted to say thank you, to all of you," Jove said. "Had it not been for you, I know we would not be here today." He touched Osiris' shoulder, "I owe you my life. And whether Zeus ever acknowledges it, he does as well."

Pangu locked forearms with Jove. "I take payment in the form of cleaning my home, my old friend." The four shared a laugh, and Jove waved as the Duati headed toward the southern entrance.

Meanwhile, inside the war room, Aaron was leaving to return to the Library.

"Aaron," Aphrodite said, rising from her chair and walking toward him.

"Yes?" Aaron spun around, raising his eyebrows. He wanted to leave, but she was far too kind for him to ignore.

"I am glad you are safe," she said, offering Aaron her hand. He reached and took her forearm.

"I cannot imagine what you went through," she said. "To have seen all that you saw. And now to have to write it, knowing that all of Saggilmut will read it and learn of what happened."

"Yeah," he answered chuckling. "I'm kinda a big deal."

"Can I ask you to do something?" she said in a lower voice. She peaked back toward Zeus. *She doesn't want to be heard*, Aaron thought.

"Yeah, of course," he said. "But it really depends on what it is. The Most High told me that--"

"Be honest," she stated.

What was she hoping to gain for this? He nodded and loosened his grip on her arm.

Aphrodite squeezed tighter. "Aaron, I mean it. Be honest. You know the damage that has been done by writers on Earth as they blindly recorded whatever the gods told them. Those books have caused more deaths and brought more wickedness than the Unspoken could ever have hoped to achieve. Even Ishtar's flood to the world caused less damage than the deceit spread in the pages of those books. If you are not honest, or were fooled in your time here in Saggilmut, then I fear the same effect can happen here as on Earth. Does that make sense?"

"Right, no pressure," Aaron replied. He wanted to leave, and turned toward the door but stopped. He felt an urge to tell her. With a deep breath, Aaron whispered, "If I'm going to be honest; the *truth* doesn't exactly make your king look...uhm, that great." He watched for a reaction.

Immediately regretting his decision to say anything, he added, "Listen, I shouldn't have said anything. I am--"

She said, "Good, then you saw the truth. The truth cuts deeper than any blade ever could."

"Okay," Aaron said, unsure how to take her comment. She let go of his arm and went back toward the other gods. Aaron turned to leave again, but Jove blocked the doorway.

"I was just thinking about you," Jove said.

"All good things, I'm sure," Aaron responded automatically. That was a habit he picked up from his mother, as he had heard her say it many times.

"It was," Jove said. "Ares just mentioned earlier to me something that I had yet to honestly ponder. You are the first person to come here from Earth to write for the people here in Saggilmut. All the other prophets came, took what they saw, and shared it with those on Earth. You are writing for us here. That is amazing."

"Yeah, it's weird," he agreed. "I mean, everyone here in Saggilmut is either a god or a person who can remember all their past lives. I'm literally the dumbest person in this entire world, yet I have this insanely big task."

Jove laughed. "Even if that is so, I am glad you were chosen."

"Thanks," Aaron muttered.

"Heaven's Bible." Ares offered with a smirk as he came up behind him.

Crap, Aaron thought, realizing he hadn't thought about it like that.

"Yeah, I'm the man." Aaron smiled awkwardly and pumped his fist in the air without emotion.

"So, are you heading back soon?" Jove asked.

"Yeah, I am leaving now. I have to get back to Shamam...Shayamam-"

"Shamayim," Jove said, patting him on the shoulder.

"Right, yeah there," Aaron said, giving up on his pronunciation.

"I wish you the best, Writer," Jove said, moving aside to let Aaron pass. "And Dagon, I heard about what you did, taking that axe in the back. I do hope the Most High learns of your heroism. Maybe it--"

"Thank you, Jove," Dagon said, "but you know I did not do it to have him reduce my service time. My punishment time to serve the Most High is justified. I deserve it for what I did."

Jove replied, "Anyway, I hope to see you back in Saggilmut soon."

Dagon and Aaron again turned toward the doorway.

"Aaron," Zeus called to him. Aaron, almost at the door, turned with a sigh. *I'm never getting out of here.*

"Please do not tell me you are leaving?" Zeus said. Aaron wanted to. All he wanted was to get away from Zeus. Hearing Zeus talk about attacking Asgard had left a bad taste in his mouth.

He bit his lower lip. "I think it is about time I maybe check on a few things and head back to the Library to get writing, I guess."

"But it is already getting late, and it may not be time to start writing quite yet. I believe there will be more for you to witness." Aaron's stomach sank.

Zeus raised his hands proudly. "I am sure you do not want to write a story without an ending."

Chapter 73 *The best defense...*

After everything Zeus had just said to the Duati, Aaron had to ask, "You're going to attack the Asgardian?"

"I am," Zeus proclaimed. "We will begin to plan today, with or without the Duati." The other gods in the room seemed just as shocked as Aaron was. Aphrodite's glance at Aaron helped him understand what she had meant before. *Everyone in the universe needs to know this god is a real jerk*, he thought.

"What about Modi and everything Osiris said about a possibility of peace?" Aaron asked.

Zeus grimaced in disgust. "Empty words. Osiris is *malaka*, a fool. Do not get me wrong. I am grateful he helped defend us here, but he is delusional with his notion that peace is attainable. He and the other Duati will not support us in our attack, and for all I know, they might turn and defend Asgard! So I will not tell him any of my plans. I will wait for them to go back to Duat before I attack." Zeus paused. "You see this, right? We cannot stand idle and let them rebuild Valhalla to attack again."

In response, Jove peered at the corner of the ceiling. With a deep breath, Jove said, "My king, let us--"

Zeus thundered, "Are you trying to talk me down from defending my people? Damn it, Jove, if there was anyone who would side with me against these beasts, I thought it would be you!"

Jove stepped toward Zeus, clenching his fist. "Do not dare for even a moment to imply that I will not defend Olympus. Look at my face." He pointed to his blackened eye. "Let me ask: would you charge at Asgard with your trident in hand? Or should we move your throne into the secure room as you hide, waiting for me to return with proof of victory? All the choices you make are for your own glory, and I will not fight for your fame."

"Get out!" Spittle flew from Zeus' mouth. "I killed the very god that gave you that damn mark on your face. You dare stand against me with such disrespect?"

Jove stood still.

"Did you hear me?" Zeus demanded. "Are you challenging my authority?"

"I do hear you," he said softly. "And unfortunately, because of your pride, yes, I do challenge you. I demand an election so the people can decide." He glanced over at the other gods. "Ares, Aphrodite, you are both my witnesses. I am calling for the council to put together an immediate election between the King and I. This has to end."

Zeus laughed. "You have no chance to strip me of my rule, after what I have done for these nethers. You will never be seen as anything more than my shadow. And I promise you this, Jove: After this election, I look forward to banishing you from my kingdom."

"We will see," Jove retorted. "You hide behind this mask of defending Olympus, but the truth is, you hate anyone different. You hate the Asgard gods the same way you hate the Sh'losh. Not everyone is like you, Zeus, that is the beauty of choice! So if I lose the election, you do not have to worry about banishing me. I will leave of my own volition."

"And I will leave with him," Ares proclaimed.

"So will I," Aphrodite agreed.

Zeus chuckled, staring at Jove's one open eye. "The people will vote tomorrow. Aphrodite, my daughter, before you go and pack your belongings: as your king, I command you to have the election council prepare for tomorrow." She agreed.

Zeus continued, "Once the votes are tallied, you three can join the other animals I sent out of my pure kingdom." Jove stormed from the room. Aphrodite tearfully followed, with Ares behind her.

Aaron said to Dagon, "Well crap, looks like we're not leaving yet, brother. C'mon." They left the castle to observe the festivities.

Aaron sat on the castle wall, high enough to see the ocean of people in the streets. The crowd sang songs of praise as smoke columns from offered sacrifices rose as high as the tower.

"Do you think Zeus would really go to Asgard?" Aaron asked.

"Yes," Dagon said. "I do."

Dagon's facial gills were pulsating. That was his tell, he was flustered.

"What?" Dagon asked. "Why are you staring at me?"

"Can I ask you a serious question?" Aaron asked, still staring at him.

"Yes." Dagon waited.

"How do you breathe with a fish's head?"

"*I hate* you," he laughed. Aaron shrugged and gazed into the crowd.

"Do you think there is a way we could find out if Sophia is okay?" Aaron said.

"Absolutely," Dagon said. "I see the god Saturn, right there. Let us go and ask him if they have begun a census."

Chapter 74 *Election night*

Zeus celebrated with everyone in the city square until nearly dawn. He drank, danced, and told the story repeatedly to the devoted crowd of how he delivered the fatal blow, thrusting his mighty trident into the weaker Thor. The people circled him, worshiping at his feet, while others prayed loudly as they took hold of his robe. After finishing another cup of wine, he finally felt satisfied for the night.

As Zeus wandered back toward his castle, he paused to place his hands on the heads of those he encountered, whispering subtle blessings in his name to them. People gathered near the castle steps began chanting his name. Apollo, who also had been out all night enjoying the festivities with his father, waited at the top step.

"Hail Zeus!" they cheered.

Zeus faced the crowd, raising both of his hands to hush them. That only led to louder chant and applause.

"They love you," Apollo observed.

Zeus blew a series of kisses, then signaled again for them to quiet. Slowly a hush fell over the revelers.

When they finally silenced, Zeus pointed to a kneeling woman near the bottom step. She continued calling out to him in adoration. He waved for her to join him on the top step. She raised herself, trembling and crying joyfully as she approached him.

"M-my king," she whimpered fervently, reaching the top step. "I w-worship you." Zeus took a moment to calm her, then turned her to face the people.

Zeus proclaimed, "Every thought, every choice, and every action that I have made is for beautiful people like this woman. And I give you my word that as long as I am your king, it will always be this way." The worshipers exploded into a frenzy. He whispered to her, gently waving her back down the stairs. Tears streamed down her face as she rejoined the crowd.

He offered one last wave, then disappeared into the castle with Apollo.

Putting an arm around his son's shoulder, he burped. "Too much wine." Apollo grinned.

"I may have had a few too many, as well." They both laughed.

Zeus said, "Come to my chambers in the morning, son. We have much to discuss regarding Jove."

Apollo, chuckling to himself, asked, "Of course. Would you like sweet or dry wine brought with breakfast?"

Zeus belched again. "If I have another cup, the people outside might see their king fall out of his window in a stupor."

"Tea it is then," Apollo said, turning down the hallway toward his room. Zeus headed to his chambers, singing one of the songs of Thor's defeat he had heard earlier in the evening.

Zeus entered his dark room and called out for his wife, "Hera, my dove. I hope you are awake because I am feeling--"

"She is dead," a husky voice whispered from behind the door. Twisting around, Zeus saw a hand moving, but the rush of cold steel piercing his stomach gripped him. He fell backward to the floor, his head against the end of his bed. Seeing only a portion of the handle outside of his abdomen, he realized he couldn't pull it out.

"You lied," the voice said. Zeus closed his eyes, trying to focus his attention despite the pain. He placed his hands over his stomach as blood soaked his white robe. Zeus' head spun. He rested it against the bed rail. Struggling to stay alert, he raised his eyes to see his killer.

Odin stood over him.

Odin's face was battered and caked with dried blood. His eye socket was blackened, and a trail of the blood traced down into his beard. His mouth opened with missing teeth, and he laughed maniacally. Odin wore one of Zeus' many robes, this one crimson with the Immortal signet over his left breast. Odins' hands, missing fingers, shook uncontrollably.

"I was going to leave," Odin muttered. "Once I killed Asclepius, I was content with running off to Forsaken woods, Baltia, or..." He paused, thinking. "But it was you, Zeus. It was you, standing in front of that damn nether, Aaron, pretending to be a hero. Fooling him, making him think you saved me. I would never expect you to have been honest with the Writer. You care too much about your name, but it was the way you stood over me. So arrogant, so smug. I just could not shake it from my mind, you know?"

Zeus' eyes began to roll back. Odin grabbed his face, slapping him to keep him awake.

"And when I heard you say you sent my son Thor to Sheol..." Odin swallowed, wincing in pain. "It sickened me, but I knew that staying was the right choice."

"It was not me," Zeus mumbled.

"Zeus!" Odin said, acting shocked. "You would not be lying, would you?"

"Osiris," Zeus whispered, struggling to breathe. "Osiris."

Odin leaned closer to Zeus and whispered, "Thank you for telling me the truth. I knew *you* could not be the one to kill him." Odin stood over him, staring with his broken grin as Zeus took his last breath.

Chapter 75 *Morning in Olympus*

That morning, Apollo came to his father's chambers holding a small silver tray. It held two small cups and a kettle of sweetened green tea. There were also two bowls, one of purple grapes and the other of green olives, which Zeus enjoyed. Apollo knocked, waited, then knocked again.

"Father?" Apollo said, opening the door. "Obviously someone had too much to--" He stopped, dropping the tray to the marble floor. The cups shattered, and the grapes and olives rolled across the room. Apollo rushed to the foot of the bed, where his father lay lifeless with the dagger deep in his belly. A puddle of thick blood surrounded him.

Apollo let out a panicked scream for help. Two servants from down the hall quickly arrived. One froze at the doorway in shock.

"He can't die!" the petite servant shrieked. "Zeus can't die." The other ran out to find help from the infirmary.

Down the hall, a shirtless Ares and Pluto, a much shorter god with wildly curly golden hair, were about to leave for the pools near the northeastern section of the city. Hearing the servant's shriek, they sprinted toward the sound. Nearing Zeus' room, Ares and Pluto saw the frightened servant at the doorway.

"What?" Ares said, rushing to her. "What is it?"

"Ares!" yelled Apollo, from the bedroom. Ares looked into the room and saw his king slumped into Apollo's arms.

He pointed at Pluto and said, "Shut the door!" Pluto shooed the servant away, slammed the door, and pressed his back against it, his face ashen.

"What happened, Apollo?" Ares asked.

Apollo struggled to answer, his voice shaky, and his speech incoherent.

"Apollo," Ares said, grabbing his arm, shaking him. "What happened?"

"I-I do not know," he finally answered. "I just walked in and he was h-here." Ares searched the room. He checked under the bed and pushed back the curtains. Noticing a lump under the blanket, he reached to move the blanket, forgetting about his broken hand. He winced as he pulled it back in pain. Then he used his other hand, just a pillow.

Seeing Pluto still leaning against the door, Ares pointed to the closet on the other side of the bed. "Open that." Pluto cautiously pulled open the door. Inside he found a goddess, bound and covered, her hair escaping the head covering. It was Hera!

Pluto dropped to his knees and tried to untie the linen cloth knotted behind her head. Suddenly, her body twisted and jerked. She was alive!

425

"Blade!" Pluto said, struggling. Hera's muffled cries added urgency. Ares grabbed a small ivory statue of Zeus holding his trident and handed it to him.

Pluto cut through the cloth with a single swipe. Hera opened her eyes but still contorted her body in terror.

"It is only me, Hera. You are safe," Pluto said as he carefully sliced the mouth gag off.

Her eyes scanned the room from Pluto to Ares, finally resting on her husband, still being held by Apollo. Hera laid her head on the closet floor and sobbed. Pluto quickly cut off the rest of her restraints and lifted her into his arms. Ares cautiously drew near her.

"Hera, my Queen," Ares said softly. "What happened?" She struggled to form words through her tears.

Pluto rocked her delicately, and they all waited for her to collect herself. Finally wiping her tears, she took a deep breath and held it for a moment. Hera closed her eyes and slowly let the breath out.

"Odin," she whispered. "It was Odin." She told them how she entered the room as he hid inside waiting. How he had bound her, telling her she would be a widow because of the torture Zeus and Ahriman had inflicted on him in the dungeon.

"He s-said I had to tell the Writer," Hera concluded, "or he would come back."

Apollo and Ares wrapped Zeus in his blanket, leaving him in the room. Pluto remained with Hera comforting her.

Ares ran to the tower, shoving people aside until he reached the elevator and slammed the lever, which rushed him to the top. He grabbed the silver trumpet and blew a series of blasts, signaling for an emergency council meeting.

He threw the horn down and dashed back to the castle, headed to the war room. By the time he arrived Aphrodite, Jove, Apollo, and Saturn were already waiting. Aaron was sitting in the corner staring at Ares.

"He is dead!" Ares yelled. The others looked at him then at each other in confusion.

"What are you talking about?" Jove asked.

"Last night, Odin killed him," Ares said. "He bound the Queen and left. She is safe."

"Wait," Jove said. "Who? Who is dead, Ares? I do not understa--"

"Zeus is dead," he stated more slowly. The others rose from their chairs, speechless.

"Odin? Odin killed Zeus?" Jove asked. Ares nodded grimly and told them the rest as other gods arrived, how Apollo had found Zeus dead, and of finding Hera inside the closet.

"What happens now?" Aphrodite asked the group. Aaron watched Jove to see his response.

Chapter 76 *A New King*

"Hera should be made ruler," Apollo submitted to the group of gods.

"No," one goddess stated. She was pale with red hair and wore a golden necklace of two scales. "We must have an election designating a new ruler. That is our law." Aaron listened intently, still unsure who many of the gods were.

Another goddess stood and agreed. "Dike is correct. We already had an election planned for today. We must follow through." A murmur rushed through the room.

"An election?" Apollo asked. "Someone challenged my father's authority?"

"It was me," Jove announced. "I called for an election and planned to be placed on the ballot against Zeus. I would never hope for harm to come to him, but you must know, Zeus wanted to invade Asgard. I disagreed, and we argued. That is why I challenged him. I still request that my name is on the ballot, and I hope to be elected as King, but if anyone wishes to run for the position, including Hera, then I would welcome it."

Dike added, "According to our law, we must have a king elected by sunset of the day of a king's death. Until then the throne falls into the hands of the council. Yet, there is no need for the council to act today regarding Asgard, or any other matter.

Therefore, we will move forward with the election and let the new king or queen be chosen."

"Jove should be King," Aphrodite said.

"Will anyone seek to challenge Jove in the election?" Dike asked. She surveyed the room, but no one spoke out. After a brief pause, she proclaimed, "Then by the law of Olympus, established by the first king, Zeus, it is decreed that Jove be declared King of Olympus. All witnesses present shall serve as validation by declaring 'we see,' and shall further bear testimony to this truth from here on."

Dike looked at Jove, then announced, "Is there anyone here who sees that Jove is the sole elected representative seeking the throne?"

Collectively, everyone agreed, "We see."

She proclaimed, "Then it is done." She continued, "Then it is hereby decreed that Jove is both god over the Immortal people and the King over the Immortal gods. Is there anyone who sees?"

The group again pronounced in unison, "We see."

She concluded, "Then it is done. You, Jove, are King." Some of the gods came to congratulate him, while others left the room, heading to Zeus' chambers.

Aphrodite asked, "My King, when do we announce to your people of Zeus' death and your election?"

Jove sighed. "A king's first news to the people should not be so downhearted, but in this situation, the sad truth will provide better fruit than a joyful lie. We will call an assembly for tonight at sunset."

Ares asked loudly for all to hear, "King Jove, do you still feel the same about attacking the Asgardians as you did last night?" The others awaited his answer.

"Even more so now," Jove insisted. "We cannot let Odin's actions cause more bloodshed. Odin acted alone. He alone must be punished." Aphrodite clapped her hands together in agreement.

"How do you know Odin acted alone?" Dike asked.

"Baldr, the traitor of Asgard," Jove said. "He told Zeus at Mount Hor that Odin was to be killed according to their laws but escaped. They want him dead as much as we do."

Apollo added, "That does make sense, Odin could also have killed our queen, but he left her to tell the story. He was acting in revenge for the torture my father did to him, nothing more."

Aphrodite asked, "My King, would you like messengers sent to the other sects?"

"Not yet. This is all too new," he said. "I do ask that you send a rider to Osiris privately, who by now should be on his way to deliver some of the dead to Asgard. Tell him we must meet with him on his return trip. Once I speak to him, we will tell the others."

"Yes, my King," she replied.

"Do send a message to Shamayim to inform the Most High. We need to push the next assembly closer," he instructed.

"Yes, my king."

Jove said to Aaron, "I believe there is more to witness, my friend. Maybe you should wait a bit longer before returning to the Library."

"Of course," Aaron said. "I'll hang out around the city until Osiris comes back."

"Should we go see Zeus' body?" Dagon asked.

"No. I'll talk to Queen Hera and Apollo, I guess, but I don't think I need to go see it all." Aaron stared at the floor, gripping his stomach. "I hate all of this."

"Want to go outside for some fresh air?" Dagon offered.

"Yeah, that sounds great." The two left the war room and headed to the foyer.

Aaron turned to Dagon. "Can I ask you a question?"

"Of course," he answered.

"With Jove as king, do you think there can be peace now?"

"Yes," he answered. "Yes, I do."

Aaron chewed his bottom lip. "Okay, well at least that's hopeful. I guess we'll see."

Dagon rested his hand onto Aaron's head gently and the two headed outside.

Chapter 77 *One change in a new direction*

The following night, the Duati returned for their second cluster of the dead. They set camp for the night outside the southern walls of Olympus. Having received the message from Jove that called for a conclave, Osiris and Pangu headed for the castle, leaving the Sh'losh in charge to collect the dead.

"To think," Pangu said, staring around the city walls, "not too long ago this city had over a million combatants fighting each other. Unbelievable." They walked silently, saddened by the carnage still evident around the city. The walls were littered with thousands of arrows still dug in. Some people were celebrating on the roads, dancing, and burning incense, while others had passed out. Osiris grimaced, seeing a group of women mobbing a shirtless god. He held one in his arms, kissing her.

"This city is filled with the mixture of death and life," Osiris said as they entered the castle walls. "It is as if sometimes we gods are less intelligent and more childish than these humans."

"*Only sometimes?*" Pangu said in jest.

"Hello there," Aaron said, from his perch on the castle wall. "I'd imagine you're here for the new king."

"New king?" Pangu asked. Aaron and Dagon moved to the ladder and lowered themselves.

"Crap," Aaron said to himself, watching the steps on his way down. "Forget I said anything. I'm an idiot, sorry. I hope you all had a safe trip."

Pangu looked toward Osiris and repeated, "New king?" Osiris shrugged. Aaron reached the ground and approached them, happy to see them.

"I thought you were leaving," Osiris said, grasping forearms with Aaron and nodding at Dagon.

"I wish," he said with a grin. "If it's not one thing, it's another, I've learned."

Pangu said, "Speaking of one thing or another, we are here because we received a message from Jove. Based on what you just said about a new king, and the fact that this letter has the king's official seal, is it fair to say there was an election here in the short time we have been gone?"

"It's more than that, and I can't say another word, but I'll go with you two to speak to the *new* king," Aaron said.

As they entered the foyer, Aaron marveled at how pristine it was. Like there had been no battle at all. The castle was eerily silent, except for a muted conversation in one of the studies. In the foyer, two Spartans guarded the hallway leading to the war room.

Aaron said to the taller of the two, "The King wanted to talk to these gods."

Ignoring Aaron, the Spartan said to Osiris, "We were informed you were coming. I ask that you go to the war room, and we will notify the King you have arrived." Aaron sized up the Spartan, feeling disrespected.

"Not a chance," Dagon whispered, nudging him toward the war room.

"What do you mean? I could whip him. I took wrestling in high school. If I--"

"Nope."

Aaron glared at Dagon sarcastically. "Well, maybe if he didn't--"

"No."

"If you trained me, then I would--"

"Not a chance," Dagon insisted. Aaron turned and shadowboxed a few jabs into Dagon's stomach.

"You gotta see me in the ring. I'm no joke," Aaron assured him. The four walked to the room and sat, quietly waiting. The Duati seemed tired, probably because they had not stopped since leaving Nekhen to come and protect Olympus, Aaron surmised.

After a short time, Jove arrived with Aphrodite. "Pangu," Jove said, smiling. The two locked arms then hugged.

Osiris awoke and raised his head. He stood, and the two gods clasped arms.

"Thank you for coming," Jove said, gesturing for them to sit. He grabbed a chair and sat directly in front of them. "The Sh'losh, are they still with you?"

"Yes, they are outside the gate, probably getting some rest before loading more of the dead," Pangu said.

Jove stood up and summoned a Spartan guard. He spoke to him quietly, then he sat back down, folding his arms.

"We must wait. I sent for a Sh'losh representative to be here." Osiris and Pangu shared a glance.

Osiris smiled, "I am content to get a little more sleep."

Aaron rested his head on the chair, studying the ceiling. It was the first time he had been bored in a long time. *Bored is wonderful*, he thought.

A few moments later, the Spartan knocked on the opened door and moved aside for Ra and Toth to enter.

"Please, have a seat here." Jove pointed at two seats near Pangu. They all sat in a row, facing Jove. "Zeus is dead. He was killed last night." Their eyes widened.

He continued, "No matter how you felt about him, we Immortals loved him. He was our king. But, I did not ask you here to console us for our loss, or to simply share the news. I asked you here for something else. The first is to officially thank you as the new king of the Immortals. Without you, all Olympus would have been lost to

Thor. I know this, and..." Looking directly at Aaron, he continued, "*You* will ensure all Saggilmut knows this, as well." Aaron nodded his agreement.

Chapter 78 *Out of the chaos comes...*

"How did Zeus die?" Osiris asked.

Jove explained about Ahriman, Zeus, the torture, and Odin's escape.

"And where is Odin now?" Osiris asked.

Jove shrugged. "We do not know. But what we do know is that Odin could have killed Queen Hera, but let her live to ensure Aaron knew the truth. That Zeus was part of Odin's torture, and in an attempt to avoid being written as a wicked god in Aaron's eyes."

Looking at Aaron, Jove continued, "He cared how you would describe him in your work. It was important to him that he remained revered and honored. He spent his entire reign promoting himself as perfection, as this symbol of benevolence. As the new king, I will not make the same mistakes."

Pangu stood up and placed his hand on Jove's shoulder. "There is no one better, brother." Seeing the admiration of the two sects, Aaron leaned toward Dagon, holding up his fist playfully.

Dagon glanced at the balled hand. "What?"

"We are celebrating King Jove. You gently bump it with your fist."

"Why?" Dagon asked.

"Will you just tap it?"

Dagon punched Aaron's hand.

"Damn," Aaron whispered, "not so hard next time!"

"And you wanted to fight that Spartan outside the door?" Dagon rolled his eyes.

Toth rubbed his beak and said, "Jove, please tell me you did not call us here to try and sway us into attacking Asgard? I understand that Odin's actions were egregious, but--"

"No, no," Jove answered vehemently, holding up his hands. "Odin acted alone; he will pay for his sins alone. We will send huntsmen to find him. I did not ask you here for that."

"Then, what?" Osiris asked.

Jove turned his chair toward Toth and Ra. "As King, my first new order will be to reinstate the Sh'losh as full citizens. I am sorry that I was unable to defend all of you during that time, but I will damn sure correct it now. You are welcome to return to Olympus if you would like to come home."

Aaron beamed at Dagon, excited, but Dagon seemed stoic and disconnected from what Aaron thought was wonderful news. Confused, Aaron glanced at Toth and Ra to check their expressions. They both appeared equally subdued by the concept of a return to Olympus after all these centuries.

Toth rubbed his beak again. "I think the sentiment is most kind. I do perhaps wonder--"

"Wait," Osiris interrupted. "*Even* those that attacked alongside the Asgardian? You would welcome them all back?"

"Yes," Jove said. "I cannot fathom walking in your shoes, having been shunned and tormented as you were. I was there, Ra. I argued for you all, but what does it matter? In the end, you all suffered so much, and watching you leave out of the eastern gate made me sick. It made a lot of us sick. Many Immortal gods left because of that situation, not just Sh'losh. I stayed because I believed I could make Olympus better. I tell you this, I know war never leads to peace, and what was done to you all is not easily forgiven. Seeing a beautiful god such as Sekhmet filled with anger breaks my heart, I can only hope for reconciliation. This will be our first step."

Ra winked at Toth and said, "I submit to you, brother. I listened to Sekhmet and followed my foolish anger, but never again. Besides, they say you are the smart one."

"Are you sure?" Toth asked.

"Yes," Ra said. "Whatever you decide."

Toth took a deep breath. "Thank you, Jove, but no." He turned at Osiris, "You accepted us. Duat is our home now. I ask you to forgive those that battled alongside Thor and let us all return home. If not, we ask for safe travel through your province so we may settle on the island of Baltia."

Osiris stood up. "You have been offered safe return home with the Immortals. The Duati have accepted you, and you are all welcome back, but may I make a different offer?" Toth nodded at him to continue.

"There is plenty of untouched land in Saggilmut. Especially to the southeast. Take the Sinai Peninsula and begin something new. Create your seal and become your own sect, completely equal to the rest of us. Not as Immortal or Duati, but as Sh'losh."

"Yes!" Toth immediately agreed. Ra buried his face in his hands and lowered his head to his knees, overcome.

Aaron looked at Dagon, who now had the largest grin he had seen. They all stood and shared embraces.

Jove beamed at Osiris and whispered to him, "Great idea."

Toth extended his arm to Osiris. "State it in an oath to me before these witnesses."

Osiris grabbed Toth's arm. "I, King Osiris of the Duati, give you a portion of Duat. The southeastern region once called the Sinai Peninsula. It is now under your full control and will be yours to own, care for, and rename as you all see fit. We will request a Crossing be placed there at the next assembly in the Hall."

Toth turned to Jove. "Will you acknowledge us as our own entity?"

Jove smiled joyfully, reaching out his arm. "Happily so."

"Then it is settled," Toth announced, clearly overjoyed.

"Congratulations," Aaron said, reaching out his arm to Dagon. Dagon wiped his eyes, then waved Aaron in for a hug. Aaron wrapped his arms as far as he could around him.

Chapter 79 *A king's request*

Jove shook Osiris' arm. "Not a bad first meeting." Osiris agreed, and the two clutched, enjoying the happiness in the room. Aphrodite waited for Toth to let Ra go, then opened her arms to celebrate with them with a hug.

Jove announced, "I have one more matter at hand I need your help with."

Osiris gestured for him to continue.

"You stated you would release Modi so he may return to claim the throne in Asgard?"

"Yes, we already released him," Osiris said. "When Tyr sounded the horn to withdraw the Asgard forces, we sent word by a hoopoe shortly after. Assuming Modi left the following morning, he would arrive sometime tomorrow."

"And did you tell him about everything that happened?" Jove asked.

"He knows his father and brother Magni have died in battle. He knows Baldr is sitting on the throne in Asgard. He also knows he is going home with *our* desire that he becomes king, with a hope for peace."

Jove rubbed his beard, staring at the ceiling in thought. "Then I will ask you if you would accompany me and a few others to Asgard as a mediator so we may be there by the morning? I am sorry to ask. I know you all are tired after everything you have done."

"Mediate for what?" Pangu asked.

"For peace," he answered.

"For a chance of peace, I am willing to miss some rest," Osiris said.

Pangu stepped to Jove and Osiris and placed a hand on each of their shoulders. "If tomorrow ends well, then we could see peace within this land."

"Then this place would actually *be* heaven," Aaron said, grinning.

He looked at Dagon. "You up for one more trip, *fishhead*?"

"I sure am, you *nether,* although at this rate you will never start your writing."

"Then let's hope those doctors don't pull the plug on me yet." He shrugged.

Near midnight they all set off toward Asgard. Jove, Ares, and Aphrodite rode along with the Duati on one side, as Aaron and Dagon rode on their other. Toth and other Sh'losh rode behind them, shepherding the caravan of the fallen.

They rode through the night, talking and sharing views on creating the perfect kingdom and what that would be like. Aaron watched the new King of Olympus interacting with the others, especially Osiris.

"You two seem to have a lot in common," he said.

"We do," Jove said. "And if we can achieve half the things we have spoken about, then Saggilmut is going to be a wonderful place. The people deserve it, Aaron. I know your life on Earth is complicated and unfair. Saggilmut is supposed to be a haven for you. A place that makes you want to stay. We plan to work together with the Sh'losh, and hopefully Asgard, to make major reforms for Saggilmut."

"Like what?" he prodded.

"Well, since you asked, one major change we hope to teach is that the gods should not be worshipped with sacrifices, burning incense, and lying prostrate in the streets. It serves no purpose. That type of worship was a creation of the ego from some of the old gods. Instead, we will teach the most important lesson either world could ever learn."

"Well?" Aaron urged. "You gonna tell me the secret to life, or keep me in suspense?" Jove looked over and winked, clearly enjoying Aaron's discomfort.

"Aaron," he said, "it is no grand secret at all. It is that kindness, a true and humble kindness, is the greatest offering anyone can make to another, god or human.

"Sounds awesome."

Osiris enthusiastically added, "It is *awesome*, Aaron. The era of mindless worship is over, but it all first begins with peace among the gods. For us to truly coexist, we need Asgard."

"And you think Modi will accept this version of peace?" Aaron asked.

"I hope so," Osiris said. "If he can become King. Baldr is not simply going to hand Modi the throne."

"Indeed," Jove replied.

"Did Modi say how he planned to handle him?" Aaron asked.

Osiris massaged his goatee, then hesitantly said, "He said he was going to kill him after what happened in Nekhen."

"That doesn't sound too harmonious," Aaron said flippantly, but none of the gods responded. With a sigh, he realized he shouldn't have said that. His shoulders slumped. *What type of jerk jokes about death like that*? Deciding to shut up, Aaron let his horse fall a little behind.

Osiris glanced back at him, then slowed down as well, drawing even with Aaron's horse.

"You know," Osiris said, still messaging his goatee, "I was thinking about when we were at the Hall not too long ago. Do you remember when Tyr interrupted the tension between Zeus and Odin? He said we all want true peace."

"I remember everyone laughing at him."

"No," Osiris corrected. "Not everyone. Truth is, I had never heard an Asgardian speak like that. To hear Tyr speak up in the Hall may have seemed insignificant to some, but it was enlightening for me. So when I joined the first trip taking their dead home I spoke to him about Modi. I put my faith in Tyr, believing he was someone deserving of that trust. He told me he would do everything in his power to ensure Modi takes *Gungnir* as king. He said he believes in Modi the way I believe in him. We shall see."

Aaron rode silently, now understanding just how important Modi was to everything they were aiming for. How nothing they wanted would be achievable if Modi was anything like his father and grandfather. They needed Modi if they were to fully realize their dream, but Baldr stood in the way first.

As dawn approached, they neared the northern gates of the Village walls. Tyr and other gods, along with thousands of Vikings, were already waiting near the wall to accept the dead. "You appear to have brought friends this trip," Tyr said to Osiris. He glanced at everyone there, settling on Ares. "How is the hand?"

Ares held his bludgeoned, discolored hand. "Better."

Tyr laughed and held up his wrist. "Just get rid of it, like I did. I will do it for you if you want." Ares declined with an offhand gesture.

Osiris nodded toward Jove, then said to Tyr, "He asked to come and speak to your king. I agreed to escort him. He has nothing but peaceful intentions. Has Modi arrived yet?"

"No, but he is close. We sent a few Vikings eastward late last night with a hoopoe. They met him near the western side of Mount Hor near the Meggido plains. He should be here shortly if they did not stop."

Osiris pointed toward a few nearby trees, "Is it all right if we set up camp here as we wait for him?"

Tyr stared hard at Osiris. "I know my nephew to be a fair god, level-headed, but to have Immortals here on behalf of their king after they just killed his father and brother may be--"

"Zeus is dead," Osiris said. "He was killed two nights ago. Jove is their king now. I ask you to look around." Osiris raised his arms, "He is alone. Both the kings of the Duati and Immortals are at your gate with fewer than a few thousand carrying your fallen warriors. We are putting a great amount of trust in you, just being here. We are here because we believe in the words you said in the Hall: 'true peace.' Remember?"

"Damn," Tyr said, unable to hold back his grin. "Good point. Did you practice that on the way here?"

"A little bit," he admitted.

"Wait here then by the trees. I swear by my name that you are all safe."

Chapter 80 *A son returns home*

The gods rode closer to the trees and dismounted. Aaron, exhausted from the night's ride, watched the dead being unloaded from the wagons, then fell asleep as Dagon watched over him. Tyr galloped off toward the rising sun on the road to Mount Hor. He hoped to find Modi and convince him to speak with Osiris and Jove.

"Nephew!" Tyr exclaimed when he saw Modi riding slowly along the road. Tyr kicked his heels against the horse's sides, waving his arm energetically while snapping the reins to go faster. Modi waved once, but continued at his sluggish pace. Tyr reached Modi and leapt off, brought Modi's horse to a halt, pulled his nephew down, and hugged him. "Damn, it is good to see you.".

"And you as well," Modi replied, still holding tightly.

"Are you all right?" Tyr asked.

"I failed, Tyr," he said, not letting go.

Tyr pushed him back, still gripping his arm with his single hand. "No, no. You did not fail, nephew." Modi buried his face into his shoulder.

Tyr held him, letting him weep. He whispered, "*Heil og sæl*, Modi."

His face still tight against Tyr's shoulder, Modi said, "My father and brother are dead, and it is my fault."

"What? No!" Tyr insisted sternly. "Do not for a moment believe that. Listen to me." He again pulled Modi away to look at him. "Fate, dear nephew. Fate does not care to ask us what we want, rather she guides us wherever she sees fit. We have no say on where it will take us, no matter how badly we want to. She chose them to die. I am just thankful she spared you."

"Then what am I supposed to do?" Modi cried. "*Everyone* is dead."

"Oh, my boy, only you can know," he answered. "Listen to her. She will tell you softly where she is taking you."

Modi scoffed. "I can tell you that if I *could* hear my father in Sheol, he would command me to avenge him and fulfill Asgard's fate to rule."

"Modi..." Tyr held tighter. "Thor is not here, and that is not his voice. I was just in Guangdong searching for the Sanguan Dadi and overheard a conversation between Sjofn, and well, that is a long story, but he said that our thoughts pass by as if they were in a river, or something like that. I pondered that thought, Modi, and it is true. With enough time, these thoughts will flow past if you let them. But if you stop at each thought, especially the negative ones, then you will block your river and no other thoughts can pass."

Tyr rested his hand on Modi's shoulder. "If you do not let that voice in your mind pass, you will build a dam blocking any future thoughts. Thoughts that may bring growth, maturity, and change. That is where Asgard has failed. For too long we all have blocked our thoughts, never changing, stuck in the sayings of the old gods and their old laws. Listen to Fate. She speaks softly in an otherwise much louder stream of thoughts. If you listen carefully, you can redefine what it means to be Asgardian as king."

"That does not sound like *Asgardian* fate at all," he decided.

"Define your own fate with your choices," Tyr explained. "When you enter those gates, it is to take claim of what is rightfully yours. Or do not enter and go do whatever it is you see fit. The freedom of not being tied up in another's idea of fate gives you freedom. A freedom I know I plan to enjoy. Before you do anything, though, I ask that you come with me. I want you to walk the outskirts of the northern region with me. Osiris and King Jove await there to speak with you. I also believe it is important that you see the dead."

"King Jove?" he asked, confused.

"Yes, Zeus is dead." Tyr said, "And both kings are here basically alone, Modi. No army, not even personal guards. Jove is here putting himself into your hands simply to talk, king to king."

Modi looked at Tyr and nodded, "I will listen." The two rode on to find Osiris and Jove.

Sitting against a large oak tree, Osiris and Pangu talked quietly. Jove paced near them,

451

nervously twirling his beard. Aphrodite and Ares leaned against their horses nearby.

Tyr and Modi trotted up together. Tyr pulled up to greet them, but Modi remained silent, continuing past the group of gods, disregarding their greetings. He stared across the rows of the dead. The bodies had been laid side by side, row after row, far back to the tree line where the wagons waited, still carrying more. There wasn't enough space on the field to offload them.

Modi looked down at the closest bodies. A young man, eyes open, with an arrow still burrowed in his chest. An older man, silver-haired, with a sword's gash in his large belly. A woman with soft blonde hair braided tightly along her head, no wound he could see at first glance. He just stared, imagining how she could have died.

"Are you all right?" Tyr asked, calling out to him.

"No," he said. "They trusted us, and we let them die. A god should be there for his people, not using them for their own glorification. I never knew *any* of these people."

Tyr rode closer to him. "You can change that. You can show Asgard a better path."

"You are right," Modi concluded, albeit with a pit in his stomach. "I am now ready to meet with Osiris and Jove."

He turned his horse gently and rode back to Jove and Osiris.

"King Modi," Jove said with respect.

"Not a king yet," Modi stated. "But I am told you are King of the Immortals."

"Yes, I am," he said. "More importantly, I am here to talk with you about ending this war between us, for good."

"So I hear," Modi said to Jove.

He looked at Osiris, studying him. "And you, my captor. Now, *you* I do find to be very interesting."

"Why is that?" Osiris wondered.

"Did you hold me, knowing that it would result in us being here today? Knowing that after I heard my uncle Baldr's plan then learned of my father's death, that I would simply accept my people's defeat and agree to your terms?"

"King Modi, I am a god no different than you. I make plans and whatever happens, happens. I just wanted you to know, whatever took place, that we were not going to harm you, and that Baldr was not to be trusted. I am not celebrating Thor's death. The battle was terrible, as you can see. Gods died, people died, and it is my hope to never let that happen again."

Modi glanced at Tyr, who was stroking his horse's mane, listening. "If Tyr trusts you, then I will listen to what you both have to say. We will speak more soon." Turning to Tyr, he said, "Let us go visit my uncle."

"What do you want to do with everyone here for now?" Tyr asked, giving one last stroke along his horse's mane, then lifting himself.

"They will be our guests, bring them," Modi replied.

"Is that safe?" Aaron blurted.

Tyr replied, "Asgardian law teaches that one's guests are under our protection and safeguarded during their visit. As long as you are with us, then you are safe. I swear on that."

Osiris nodded in agreement and leapt back on his horse. He winked at Jove, who after a sigh, joined him and saddled up.

"Coming?" Jove asked Ares and Aphrodite. They agreed and with Aaron and Dagon following, they all rode to the gates.

"I respect that you are open to talk," Jove said to Modi. "I know it cannot be easy for you."

"You know, I had never really spoken to anyone outside of Asgard on friendly terms until Osiris visited me when he had me locked me up. He would bring food and talk about the challenges of ruling. He spoke about his vision for Saggilmut. I never said a word. He would just sit there with me for hours, sometimes in silence. Honestly, all I could think about was how I wanted to kill him. I could not hear anything he said over my anger. Seeing Baldr in Nekhen changed all that. It changed *everything*."

"How so?" Jove asked.

"He wa...I mean, Baldr *is* everything we are taught not to be," he said. "If you lie, that would not surprise me, since you are *just* an Immortal. You are not one of us. Asgardians never lie, or so I believed. If a Duati is two-faced, not only would I not be surprised, but I would expect it. But not so for one of us. Not an Asgardian. Listening to Osiris, I believed he was lying, saying those things to fool me. But seeing Baldr talk about killing Thor, my father, I snapped. I realized, if Baldr can be a liar, then maybe, just maybe, Osiris could be honest."

"So you have changed your thoughts?" Jove prodded.

"While you all were engaged in war, killing each other, I sat quietly with a war going on inside my head. So many questions. Who was my enemy? Was it Zeus? Maybe my father, for leading so many to war? Baldr for his deceit? Osiris? I decided that my enemy was not a sect, or person, but I am against anyone lacking principles. My enemies are those that would dare treat others like pieces of a game. Each person, god or nether, has to decide for themselves. And my uncle Baldr has chosen the wrong side."

Reaching the gate, Modi dismounted and tied off his horse. Jove did the same and hesitated, looking through the gate as he prepared to enter Asgard for the first time.

"What is your plan with Baldr?" he asked.

"In a single moment, a person can change forever. Do you agree?" Modi asked.

"Yes," he said.

"Then I have had my moment. I hope to see him have his."

As the two entered the gate, a small crowd noticed Modi and loud cheers erupted. They called out to him in joy and shouted their battle cries as they gathered around him. A few of the men glanced at Jove standing off to the side, but they did not recognize him.

"How does it feel to be unknown?" Tyr asked Jove, as they walked through the gates with Osiris.

"I welcome it," he answered with a smile.

"Good answer."

Chapter 81 *Asgard Castle*

Modi spoke to Jove, Ares, Aphrodite, and Osiris. "Because you are my guests, I ask you two things: stay near me, and do not insult or challenge anyone." They quickly agreed and followed Modi, as Aaron and Dagon walked closely behind.

"What do you think?" Aaron asked Dagon.

"I am hopeful," he said. "But we will see."

"Has anyone ever told you you're a glass-half-empty kinda guy?" Aaron said.

"A realist is always seen as a negative person to a naive optimist," he retorted, as they entered the gates.

"I'm not sure if I'm insulted or not by that," Aaron said.

Along the way to the sanctuary the crowd grew larger. They surrounded Modi, howling and chanting his name. He kept his attention on the gods behind him, waving them on. Reaching the castle entrance, he gestured for the group to encircle him.

"Tyr, you will take our guests to stand in the sanctuary near the steps of *Hlidskjalf*. Then command Loki to ring the bells calling for an immediate assembly. I will walk with the Writer to the Dining hall and find Queen Frigg, and meet with you." Tyr agreed, and they entered the sanctuary, separating in the foyer.

Jove whispered to Osiris, "Is this a good idea?"

"If he wanted us dead, we already would be," he said. Jove reluctantly agreed and they entered the castle, looking around in amazement.

Osiris, admiring the uncut stone walls covered in fungi and mushrooms, said, "This place is--"

"Amazing," Jove offered.

"Yes, amazing." Osiris leaned in closely, examining the shrooms.

"I forgot, this is your first time here," Tyr said, leading them to the sanctuary. He picked a mushroom off the doorway and popped it into his mouth. "The shrooms are euphoric if you were wondering, Osiris."

Osiris' eyes brightened, "Really?"

Modi, Aaron, and Dagon headed to the kitchen area, looking for Frigg. "She is always here," Modi said.

"Wow," was all Aaron could say as he walked into the empty dining hall. "Last time we were here this place was a madhouse. Sekhmet was over there," Aaron said, pointing at the corner, "wearing war paint."

"Sekhmet?" Modi asked. "*Here*?"

"Yeah, don't worry. It'll be in my book whenever I get to write it. So you'll read about her dancing on the table, eating shrooms, and singing

Viking songs. Speaking of my book, I'd like to hear the story of you in Duat whenever you can."

"Yes, we can sit down together and talk." Leading them through the dining hall, Modi pushed open a set of doors, entering the large kitchen.

Before anyone there noticed them, Modi leaned into Aaron and said, "Watch her face. She is going to cry, tears of joy, I know it. It is going to be great."

"And you call that *great*?" he asked.

"I was never fully accepted by my grandfather, or father for that matter. Frigg makes me feel loved more than anyone I have ever known." They stopped at the kitchen doorway and spotted her giving instructions to the women near a table full of spices.

Modi raised his hands to his mouth to carry his voice. "You are going to put too much coriander seed in the stew, you always do!" She squinted back, hot-tempered and ready to argue. When she saw who it was, her eyes lit. She dropped a spoon and ran toward him. By the time she had reached him tears ran down her face. She hugged him tightly, not saying anything.

"Grandmother," he said, holding her just as tightly. Aaron held out his arms to Dagon, grinning, inviting him in for a hug. Dagon rolled his eyes.

"Where is Baldr?" Modi inquired softly.

Slowly releasing him, she looked up into his eyes. "You know then, about your father and brother?"

"I do, my sweet Frigg," He said, hugging her closer. He brought his hands to her cheeks and kissed her on the forehead.

"I adore you, and I promise we will speak about everything, but for now let them cook whatever it is without you. I need to go and take hold of *Gungnir* as King, in sight of all of Asgard, and I want you there."

"But Modi," Frigg began nervously, placing her shaking hands over his hands on her face. "Baldr was pronounced King after we learned your father died. We believed you dead, and with Magni also gone..."

"Join me," he said, grasping her hand. He led them all toward the sanctuary. As they walked, the bells began to sound.

"What is that?" she asked.

"It is a call for my coronation," Modi told her. They continued toward the sanctuary, greeted by many gods who followed the ringing bells as well. A large majestic god approached Modi and placed his hand on his shoulder. He was much taller than Modi. He had white hair and a beard to match. He wore a shimmering white robe and cloak, with a royal belt around his waist. They approached the door of the sanctuary.

"Who's that?" Aaron asked Dagon.

460

"Belobog," he answered. "He rules as lord over the Szczecin islands, part of Asgard Province."

"A group of Viking islands? I'd love to go there one day."

There in the throne room, Baldr was already sitting on *Hlidskjalf* holding *Gungnir*. He was shouting at Tyr, who shielded Osiris and Jove. Tyr was yelling back, equally enraged. The crowd of gods watched the debate, enjoying the heated exchange.

Modi raised his voice above both of them. "*Heil og sæl,*" he proclaimed, still holding his grandmother's hand.

Chapter 82 *A Hel*

The crowd of gods and Vikings broke into an uproar. Each trying to welcome him home, patting his shoulder and embracing his forearm. Tyr appeared relieved that the confrontation with Baldr had paused. He said to Jove and the other gods standing behind him, "Finally."

Baldr turned pale as he saw Modi mingle through the room, moving toward the throne.

Baldr stood and slammed *Gungnir* against the floor, then pointed the blade at Osiris. "You lied to me! You told me Modi was dead!" Osiris remained silent. Baldr added, "I want him killed right now!"

Tyr stepped directly in front of Osiris, and unsheathed half of his dagger as he glared at the closest Viking. "They are my guests," Tyr said. "And they will be respected as such."

"No, Tyr," Modi said, reaching the steps to the throne. "They are *our* guests. You do know the laws regarding guests, right, Uncle? You have no authority over them." Modi faced the crowd. "Speaking of authority, I will be taking my throne now, as well."

"*Your* throne?"

Modi explained, "Asgard law teaches that we are a monarchy, correct? With my father's death, I understand the throne is then passed to the first son. Seems quite simple to me."

"We believed you were dead, Modi," Baldr said. "Osiris led everyone to believe he killed you. In taking the throne, I only acted in the best interests of Asgard." Modi stepped up to Baldr, reaching out his hand for the spear.

"As you can see, I am alive. Released by my captor." Modi again faced the room. "Released so that I may take my rightful place as the King of the Asgard." The Asgardians clapped and stomped on the wooden floor, shouting Asgardian chants.

Baldr stepped closer to Modi, speaking in an undertone. "Let us go and speak in private." Modi held his hand out farther, placing the tips of his fingers on Baldr's chest.

"Spear."

Baldr turned from Modi and stepped back near the throne. Gripping *Gungnir* with both hands, he yelled, "With all my love for you, Nephew, I will not be relinquishing the throne. I was rightfully proclaimed King according to our laws. And you arrive here, coming with these--"

"Your king will not ask again," Modi said. Baldr's eyes widened.

"Modi, no," he insisted. "You do not understand. I have to--"

Modi lifted both hands skyward and announced, "Baldr, son of Odin, I challenge you to a *Hel*."

The crowd erupted, stifling any chance Baldr had to speak. Modi walked down the stairs, mobbed by the gods around him.

He went to Tyr and the others. "Join me." Modi strode past them and continued down a long hallway.

"Was this your plan all along?" Tyr asked.

He leaned close, as the crowd was now singing battle songs together behind them. "Not at all. I just thought of it."

"You are as wild as your father."

"I will take that as a compliment," Modi said.

"Be smart in there," Tyr said. Modi faced the two walls, inspecting the thousands of weapons lined up around them. There were weapons of every type. Aaron gazed at the impressive arsenal. They appeared decorative, like trophies, each hung up cleaned and shining.

"What is happening?" Aaron asked Tyr.

"A *Hel*," Tyr said. Seeing Aaron's puzzled face, he glanced at Osiris and the other gods, who seemed equally bewildered. "A *Hel* is a ceremonial battle between two gods that have a viable claim to the throne. The last one was when my father fought and killed Borr, claiming *Hlidskjalf.* The two fighters will enter into the Pit. A fenced-in fighting arena out back. They both will enter with a single weapon. Whoever walks out alive is crowned."

"To the death?" Aaron asked.

"Yes," Tyr said. Aaron clamped his lip.

Jove leaned toward Osiris."If Modi dies, we die. Tyr will not be able to stop Baldr. We may need to leave now, so we are out of harm's way."

"You are safe," Tyr assured him. "I give you my word as your escort." Tyr glanced at Ares. "I cannot believe I nearly killed you, and now you are my guest."

"You really think that was how it was going to end?" Ares chuckled. Tyr glared at him, then burst into laughter, wrapping his arm around him.

"I think we are going to be good friends, you and I," Tyr said.

"Perfect" Modi announced, reaching for *Mjolnir*, where it hung on the wall. Taking hold of it, he studied the intricate designs on the hammer's head. He ran his fingers along the ancient lettering. "This will work," he said, more to himself than the others.

Modi walked calmly down the hallway, and Tyr led the others behind him. As they walked out of the door, Aaron raised his hand, blocking the blazing sun.

The rear courtyard of the castle was gorgeous. Filled with greenery, decorated with colorful flowers and foliage. In the center of the yard stood a short wooden fence that wrapped around four sides, enclosing a sandpit. Aaron went to the fence and leaned up on his toes to see Modi at the entrance.

Modi entered the Pit through the single gate. He tossed his hammer to the ground, then lifted his left foot, grabbing his boot and pulling it off, then did the same for the other. Taking off his fur cloak and shirt, he scooped up *Mjolnir* and walked to the far side, before facing back toward the gate.

Baldr stood at the gate. He looked at his nephew inside the ring, then at Frigg, who was holding her sister Freya tightly as they wept together.

"You have let those bastards in Duat fill your head with lies, Modi!" he yelled.

"Lies?" Modi replied, equally loud. "I was there, Uncle. I heard you in Nekhen at Horus' home, when you spoke about killing my father and making yourself king."

Baldr shook his head in disbelief, "What are you talking about? I went there to request your body because your father commanded me to. Nothing more, nothing less."

"And who tried to serve you wine in Horus' courtyard?" Modi asked, staring into his eyes. Baldr's face fell. Letting the facade go, Baldr wiped his eyes, then rubbed his palm down to grasp at his red beard.

"Damn it," Baldr smirked. "You and Osiris got me there. All right then, let us have a *Hel*, Nephew." He leaned *Gungnir* against the fence and took off his shirt and boots. He picked back up the spear and stepped in.

"And here I was believing I would not get the chance to fight at all," Baldr said. Modi held *Mjolnir* close to his chest, holding out his left hand toward Baldr. Baldr stood upright, holding his spear in both hands.

"Ready to join your father and brother, boy?" Baldr said.

"Death does not scare me," Modi answered.

Baldr lunged, driving the spear toward him and slicing Modi's hand. The two slowly circled, the sand burying their feet with each step.

Baldr thrust again, slashing his hand. Baldr leaped forward, aiming for Modi's face, but Modi swung his hand, parrying the spear and gashing his hand a third time.

Baldr spat at his feet. "Maybe the hammer does not suit you. You should have taken a pan from the kitchen." Modi didn't respond. He gripped *Mjolnir* close, holding his bloody hand out in front of him as a shield.

Baldr jumped, piercing the spear through Modi's arm. Baldr yanked the spear back, tearing it loose. Blood spattered over Baldr's face as Modi grimaced, staggering back.

They continued circling, studying each other's movements. Baldr took jabs and prodded, as Modi moved his wounded hand around for protection.

Baldr quickly faked a jump. Modi flinched back, then Baldr leaped, thrusting *Gungnir*. Modi raised his hand, letting it impale through. Modi jerked his arm toward his chest, bringing the spear closer, then swung, smashing the wooden shaft in half. He then slammed the hammer down on Baldr's hand where it still held the staff. The crack of Baldr's bones seemed louder than the shouting crowd.

Baldr retreated, dropping his end of the spear. Modi held his impaled hand out and struck the tip of the spear, driving it back through, and it fell to the sand. Modi crouched, ready to charge the defenseless Baldr.

"Kneel before me, Baldr!" Modi commanded. "You do not have to die today."

"You would let me go?" Baldr asked, panting and holding his bare hands up in defense.

"I will not offer again," Modi stated.

Baldr took a moment. He looked at his shattered hand, fingers extending in all directions, and at his spear under Modi's foot. Baldr hesitantly dropped to both knees. He placed his hands on the heated sand and slid them forward, lying prostrate.

Chapter 83 *The aftermath of Asgard*

Six days afterward.

In Asgard Castle

"How is it coming along?" Modi asked, from *Hlidskjalf.* Tyr stood at the end of the Great Hall where he was peeking outside the door. Reginn, an Asgardian god and master craftsman, was outside putting on the final touches after fixing *Gungnir.*

Modi's leg shook nervously in front of the many Asgardian gods at his first assembly by their new King. Frigg took a step over, gently touching Modi's leg to calm him. Sif, his mother, stood to Frigg's side, admiring her son.

"You can continue the ceremony without the spear for the time being," Frigg whispered. "The food will get cold," she said, raising her brows. He grinned, submitting to his grandmother.

He stood from the throne and raised his two hands, quieting the room. "Asgardians, I called this assembly to share with you my vision of where we go from here. We suffered a great loss, and many of our loved ones are now in Sheol. I lost my father, our King, and my brother as well. We are all grief-stricken, in pain, and left questioning many things."

He continued, "This pain is all understandable, but hear me when I say that we will never again accept any fate we do not desire. I do not accept this great loss. I do not accept we are beaten. Why? Because in this suffering we now have the ability to forge a new fate. For too long we have been at war with ambitions of ruling Saggilmut our way. Caught up in someone else's version of fate. Now, I stand before you as King, to tell you that our fate is not tied to our history, the old gods' desires, or even our outdated laws. It will not be dictated by the dreams of the past kings, but by our own decisions, and it is my decision to announce that the war is over."

He sat back on his throne. The assembly dissolved into a commotion. Gods hurled questions at him, but as he began to answer, another question was asked louder, then another. The noise rose quickly to a roar.

Waving his hand, he pointed at Rod, an Asgardian who ruled a larger Asgardian village south of the castle.

Rod asked, "What do you mean, it is over?"

Modi said, "As King, I declare the war over. We will no longer be the aggressors against the other sects, and I demand that each of you adhere to this. Anyone who does not heed these words will stand before me to explain why they ignored my ruling. Tomorrow I will go to Shamayim and stand in the Hall and proclaim the same."

Camulos shouted, "And what would you have me do? Farm? I have spent the last two thousand years training our warriors in Valhalla."

"Your fate is your own," Modi replied. "If tomorrow ends the way I expect, we will have discussed opening our borders for the first time since the conflict between Odin and Zeus began. My hope is you will be free to roam, travel, and do as you see fit throughout all of Saggilmut. You can do *whatever* it is you like."

Camulos asked, "You would let the other sects all flood here, intruding on our land?"

Modi said, "I would let the other sects come and trade, eat with us as we do the same. We will always need a defense. Valhalla will remain, but only to serve as guards and defenders, no longer invaders." The room had steadily grown louder as he answered question after question. He could hear the rumblings of how this would fail. He could see he wasn't winning over the crowd. He noticed his grandmother smiling at him.

"You did not expect them to change in one speech, did you?" Frigg said, just loud enough to be heard over the noise.

Watching the gods argue among themselves and shouting questions at him, he sat back calmly on his throne, enjoying the view. "Obedience does not demand understanding, but I believe they can grow eventually to learn peace. Besides, they are talking, and that is a great sign. Part of me expected them to erupt into a civil war."

Tyr approached him, holding *Gungnir*. The spear's shaft glistened. Reginn had replaced the wooden shaft with saggilmut stone sent as a gift from the Duati. Tyr handed it to Modi, squinting at the brilliant reflections it cast. With everyone watching in awe, Modi stood up and took hold of the spear. He tapped the end of the shaft on the floor, signaling for quiet.

"I understand you all have questions," he announced. "But I demand you follow your King toward peace as you followed the last to war. I ask that you open your minds to the possibility of everything I have said. I do look forward to you joining me at the assembly tomorrow in the Hall, so that we may represent our sect and listen to what the other sects have to say. We will reconvene afterward and speak more on the matter. Until then, I invite you to the Dining Hall for a feast."

The crowd roared its approval, and they swarmed to the tables, jostling for seats on the benches. Each table offered pitchers of various wines and mead. There were heaping platters of fire-roasted goat and lamb legs, as well as lamb stew seasoned with potatoes and spices. Next to the meat and stew were numerous side dishes that filled the room with a heady fragrance that silenced the commotion.

"They are so quiet now," Modi laughed, speaking to Frigg and Sif seated beside him. He closed his eyes, taking in the enticing aroma. "I can understand why."

Frigg wrapped her hands around her grandson's arm and said, "Good food always shuts an open mouth." Laughing, they took their seats at the head table, facing everyone. He grabbed his horn and drank it down as mead spilled out from both sides of his mouth. He grabbed a lamb leg and took a bite, the juices soaking into his beard. He chewed with his eyes closed, letting the flavors, the smells, and his hopes for peace sweep him away.

Loki stood, holding up a horn. "To King Modi!"

The dining hall cheered, "*Skol!*"

Chapter 84 *The aftermath of Olympus*

In Olympus

Jove stood with Aaron and Dagon in the tower overlooking the city. The blue sky offered a small added incentive for the Immortals to be out repairing the city. Many of the Duati volunteered to remain in Olympus and assist. The three watched as people replaced the damaged roofs with newer wooden planks while others recemented walls. Some small groups were parading the city, cheerfully clapping and singing songs for their new king, proclaiming him Jove *the Wise*.

"Beautiful," Jove said, mesmerized by the activities below him.

"What? Them singing about you?" Aaron said jokingly. He rested his head onto his folded arms, leaning on the battlement. "You're *so* cocky."

"The unification of the peoples, you *nether*." Jove jabbed his elbow at him. "That we have Sh'losh in our city helping, even after what we did to them."

"You fought to keep us here," Dagon said.

"I failed," Jove said. "But you all are here now, and I am grateful for it."

"And you would like to have the Sh'losh around?" Aaron asked.

"I hope so," he answered. "I am glad they have their own identity now, but the invitation will always be open for them to return." Jove pointed proudly at a Duati man helping an Immortal carry wood. "For too long we Immortals held up this image to the rest of Saggilmut that we were the only *civilized* gods. That we were further evolved, more intelligent. And there were plenty of lengthy discussions on how to *help* them become more like us." He paused, lightly hitting the battlement, frustrated.

He continued, "I argued on behalf of the Sh'losh when they were exiled, but when I was outvoted, I stayed. I debated the equality of the other sects, arguing that difference does not mean any less equal, but when the gods swayed toward Zeus' perspective, I stayed. I have to believe my decision to stay was for a purpose. That my choice to remain, despite many of the other Immortal gods leaving, had to mean something."

"Sounds like maybe you should have been king all along," Aaron said.

Jove glanced at Dagon. "Sounds more like I was too weak. I should have done more. At least now I can try to lead us toward a more fruitful coexistence with our neighbors. Honestly, seeing another sect's people stay here to help us through all this is doing more than any speech I could give to my people."

"No matter what, you're here now, *oh great King*," Aaron said, playfully bowing. "Seriously, though. You can help make Saggilmut what it's supposed to be."

"And that is?"

"Inclusive," Aaron offered.

"Hmm, it does sound so simple. I wonder how we confused it so long ago," Jove said, twirling his fingers into his beard. "Would you care to join me? I am going to walk through the city and greet the people."

"For sure," Aaron replied. He glanced at Dagon. "You coming?"

"Do I ever have a choice?" Dagon said.

"Let's make a deal," Aaron said, reaching out. "When I finally do kick the bucket, after the doctors finally pull the plug on me, I'll come and visit you in Shamayim."

Embracing Aaron's arm, Dagon replied, "I am just happy you finally said *Shamayim* correctly. Next, we will work on you saying Saggilmut correctly as well."

"I did say it! Shamamiyim, Shamayay, Sham--" smacking his forehead. "I *had* it."

As they left the tower, Jove pointed out a group of Duati warriors assisting his residents in rebuilding a crumbled wall. Approaching the group, he stepped toward the one who appeared to be their leader. His headpiece was more decorative, and the belt he wore was much broader and colorful than the others.

"May I ask your name?" Jove asked.

"Alara of Nubia," he said, bowing his head slightly.

Jove responded by dipping his head in return."I am grateful for all of your efforts." Alara looked at Jove with a curious expression.

"Are you okay?" Jove asked. "You seem like you have something you want to say."

"No, but I do want to give you something," he said. He took off a small bracelet. It was two gold strands intertwined, with a small scarab beetle at its center. The scarab was black with opened wings. He extended his hand, holding it in his palm.

Jove accepted it and inspected it closely. "Thank you, Alara. May I ask its meaning?"

"The scarab represents life, death, and reincarnation. All of the living creatures roaming the four realms need sustenance to survive. The beetle lives in the desert where the conditions are brutal and there is little to survive on, yet he thrives. Here in Saggilmut, we have everything. We just need to learn to be satisfied and accepting." Jove admired his new amulet. He bent the band and placed it on his wrist.

"Now you are Duati," Alara proclaimed, clapping. Jove lifted his hand, displaying his gift. The group of Duati cheered and howled, adding their ancient celebratory yelps. Jove laughed from the depths of his chest. He joined them in their clapping. Aaron watched, taking note of Jove.

"Thank you," Jove said, bowing to Alara, who bowed in return. Jove looked up, noticing some of his people on a balcony of the next apartment and his face fell. Jove pointed them out to Aaron. "See that."

Aaron glanced at the group. They glared, gesturing and spitting onto the street near the Duati tribesmen with an air of contempt.

"One day at a time," Aaron advised.

They walked quietly, Aaron watched the Immortals cleaning their city. He felt the overall sense of peace coming from the people, a sense of hope, albeit a glare at the Duati now and then.

"Ohh, that reminds me, Jove. I don't think I told you, I have a thing later today at the southern plaza, so I won't be able to see you tonight before I go back."

Jove was slightly taken aback. "You are leaving *tonight*? I thought you would accompany me to the Hall tomorrow for the Assembly."

"I would, but I think it's best to get at least one more night in the Library before tomorrow."

He was lying. He wanted nothing more than to go to his room in the castle of the Most High, so he could be transported back to his recreated apartment. Even though he knew his mom and Sarah wouldn't be there, he wanted nothing more than to sit on his favorite couch, and at least pretend that they were there. His mom would be in her room typing away, she was the *real* writer. And he imagined his sister was in her room getting ready for him to take her out for a coffee. He loved seeing her face as she drank it, trying to be *mature*, even though she hated the taste.

"All right, I will see you tomorrow then?" Jove asked.

"For sure," Aaron replied.

A short time later, Aaron took a basket of fruit from the castle kitchen and carried it toward the plaza with Dagon.

"Do you want me to leave when Sophia arrives?" he asked.

"No way," Aaron replied. "It's not like an *official* first date or anything. We'll probably just talk about tomatoes."

In the southeastern peninsula

Many of the Sh'losh had gathered at the southernmost mountain overlooking their new lands.

"For just a moment, imagine it," Horus said, pointing at the desert. "With us tending to the land, it will be bountiful beyond belief."

"I am sure it will," Ganesha said, leaning against a rock. The elephant goddess let her trunk sway in the wind, happily absorbing the radiance of the day.

"And the islands?" Mafdet asked.

"Not ours," Toth answered. "It is better that way. This way we stay together."

Mafdet approached Sekhmet, her feline sister, and hugged her. "I am so glad you came with us. I know you are going through a rough time, sister."

Sekhmet gently patted Mafdet, "Stop worrying about me."

"But I *am* worried about you," Mafdet whispered. "You do not seem like yourself."

"I have an idea," Sekhmet said dismissively. "Trust me, I am going to be just fine."

Ra held his hand skyward. "I cannot believe it. Our land."

"And what shall we call our new home?" Horus asked the group.

"What do you think?" Ra asked of Toth, speaking softly between themselves.

"Maybe we should wait for the others to arrive, then discuss it all together at our first assembly." Ra shrugged, amenable to the idea.

Toth announced, "We will afford another week for other Sh'losh of our own to join us before we dedicate the land. Today we must discuss who will represent us at tomorrow's assembly in the Hall."

Toth looked at Sekhmet and asked, "You? Will you be our leader, Sekhmet? You are strong and courageous. Wise and--"

"No," she answered sternly. "I have something more important I must do."

Toth shrugged and scratched his beak. "If she is unwilling, then I think it best we all chose together."

Ra said, "Toth, you are more studied and wise than any of us here. I believe you can best represent and lead us to become a strong nation of gods. Do any disagree it should be him?"

"I agree," Mafdet exclaimed.

Anubis raised his hand and shouted, "Toth, King of the Sh'losh!" They all cheered.

Toth held his wife's Ma'at. "What do you think, my love?"

"I think you already showed your great leadership and wisdom by looking at me to ask what I thought." Toth gripped her hand tightly, bringing it to his beak for a peck. She added, "You work so hard at being benevolent. To be fair and balanced. You are the right leader for us."

"My queen," he grinned. He stood, rubbed his beak and said,"I accept."

"I ask that you all settle here for now," Toth announced. "The ride from here to the Duati Crossing is no less than a day, so I must leave soon to ensure I am at the Hall in time. Would anyone like to join me?"

Horus spoke up, "My King, with all the respect I can give, I have to decline. I plan to sit right here and gaze at my new home until you return."

"I will go," Mafdet said.

"And I," Ra said.

"Sekhmet?" Mafdet asked. "Will you at least come with us?"

Sekhmet lifted the hood of her cloak over her eyes. "No."

Chapter 86 *The aftermath of Nekhen*

In Nekhen, at the former home of Horus

Osiris, Shiva, and Pangu sat at the table eating from a bowl of dates. Osiris rested with his arms folded, happy to be back in Nekhen.

"Hear them?" Pangu asked, biting into another date. His face tightened from the bitter taste.

"I do," Osiris said.

Outside the home, thousands were gathered waiting to see their gods. They were singing songs and chanting. The sense of unity was vibrant in the air.

"Going to go and speak to them?" Pangu asked.

"Of course," Osiris laughed. "I cannot move back to Nekhen and be forced to listen to this every day. That is why I left and settled outside of the city in the first place. If I do not stop them, I will never get any sleep tonight."

"I am glad you are moving back to the city," Pangu said.

"Thank you," he replied. "It was not easy for me to convince my wife, but we both share the vision of a better tomorrow." Osiris sighed. "We must go speak to the Sanguan Dadi after the assembly tomorrow. We will send a hoopoe and arrange a meeting. We have to correct this before it gets any worse."

"Of course," Pangu said.

Osiris stood and raised his hand toward the door. "Would you both care to join me?"

Pangu bit into another date, quickly spitting it out and throwing the rest into the bowl. "Yes, I am coming, otherwise I will sit here eating these things, getting more disgusted with every bite."

They walked out together to the joyful greeting of the people. The crowd lined the road, filling the streets.

Seeing Osiris, they dropped to their knees, chanting prayers and exultations.

"We must work on this," he said, watching them.

"What do you mean?" Pangu asked.

"Look at him." Osiris pointed to a man on his knees, hands raised, crying out to the god. "Can you hear his prayer? They speak of me as if I hear all things. They talk about us as if every god in Saggilmut is benevolent and offers justice. Certainly, they know I am not omniscient. I have never understood why they chose to worship us, living in such ignorance."

"Brother, you know these people," Pangu said. "They worship other men no different than themselves. They burn incense to animals that they were intended to lord over. They *even* carve rocks and wood into their own personal gods." Pangu gently patted a woman on the shoulder. "They will make anything into a god, Osiris. You expect them to not worship us? The best we can do is be benevolent to them."

"No," Osiris said. "Not if we teach them. Show them that even the gods are not immune to failure. Our egos have gotten in the way of us having a real relationship with them. I watched as gods sacrificed their men. How they hid behind men, letting them die so that they might attempt to live. For all they give, we should be the ones worshipping *them*. We must lead by serving them."

"Do you hear yourself?" Pangu replied. "They will offer their children if you demand it. They cannot be reasoned with nor taught to view us as peers. The best we can do is teach them to be kind to each other."

"Brother," Osiris said. "We can do better than that."

Pangu looked at Shiva. "You are not going to say anything?"

Shiva shrugged. "Sounds like it could be fun. We can learn from them as much as they have learned from us."

"That sounds insane, Shiva."

"Earth is changing since we have not been there. During the time the Most High has forbidden us to go, we can see that they are on a better path than we are. Slowly becoming a more inclusive world. I like it. They do not need us anymore.

Maybe Osiris is right. Now we truly can have a relationship built on more than silly worship.

Osiris lowered his hand to a woman who was kneeling in worship.

"Stand up," he said. "Give me your hand." She raised her head cautiously, but could not bring herself to look past his feet. "Please," he said, lowering his hand even closer to her.

"I can't, my lord," she cried. "I only came to praise you for coming to live among us."

"When was the last time you went back to Earth?"

"Not since your name was worshipped in all of Egypt," she replied. "Why would I go anywhere, when my god lives here?"

Osiris smiled. "I see there is so much work to be done."

Chapter 87 *The Writer and the throne*

The gods stood in the Hall of Shamayim, ready for the assembly to begin. Aaron sat in the same chair that he had nervously been led to by Asherah just weeks before. Now able to differentiate the gods, Aaron noticed the Duati, the Immortals, and some of the Sh'losh intermingling, as the Asgardians stood in one corner, reserved. He waved to Osiris and Jove, both deep in discussion with Toth.

Seeing Asherah standing with Idunn, he couldn't help himself. He waved with a cheesy smile, figuring she would be annoyed and wouldn't pay him any attention. He was right.

"Are you ready to start writing?" a familiar voice asked. It was Aphrodite.

"Almost, I plan to start after this meeting."

"And what have you concluded?" she inquired, taking a seat next to him.

"The truth?" he asked.

"Of course," she said.

He sighed and scratched his forehead, although he had no itch. "I have no idea."

"Remember what I told you in Olympus, Aaron," she said. "Just be honest. We need all Saggilmut to know what happened. With the borders possibly opening, your book can become a who's-who of the gods."

"True," Aaron said, unsure what else to say. She winked, and as she rose, trumpets blared.

The four angelic beings stood in their corners. "Holy, holy, holy," they proclaimed, lifting their heels off the floor with each word. The Most High entered the room.

Aaron's eyes brightened, seeing him again.

Everyone immediately ended their conversations and sought a chair. There weren't enough chairs with the hundreds of gods there to celebrate the end of the war.

The Most High approached his throne, but at the first step stopped, spun around, and gazed at the gods in the room, slowly, methodically. "I ask that everyone please sit, except the kings."

Jove, Osiris, and Toth stood next to each other, as Modi remained in front of the Asgardians who had joined him.

"Four kings?" The Most High asked.

"We have chosen to let the Sh'losh be their own sect," Jove answered.

"Really?" he said, looking at Toth. "And the Sh'losh selected you as their king?"

"Yes, my lord," he answered.

"Please," the Most High gestured to the middle of the room. The four kings made their way there. "Jove, you asked to speak first beforehand. It appears that a lot has happened in a very short time."

"That is true, a lot has happened," Jove said. "I asked to speak in hope that you three kings will agree with me on one final matter." He stepped forward and faced them. "I stand before you to ask that you confirm Osiris to be proclaimed King of the gods. We can rule directly under his authority, equal in a pantheon council."

Silence filled the room. Osiris was shocked.

Scratching his beard, Jove continued, "I saw him fight for gods that were not his own. He led an army across Duat to Olympus to help protect my people. I have listened to his philosophies and seen how his people helped mine. I believe he can make Saggilmut what it is supposed to be."

"And that is?" the Most High asked. "What do you believe it is supposed to be?"

"Peaceful," Jove stated. "And from the mouth of the Writer, inclusive." He peered at Aaron and gently bowed his head.

"I agree!" Toth proclaimed. "He opened his doors for us Sh'losh after we were exiled. I tell you all here today that to be considered a people, a sect, like you all are, you need three things." He rubbed his beak. "First is people! And because of Osiris, my people were able to remain together. We have been lost to the four corners of Saggilmut without him. Second is laws, and despite our differences with the Duati, Osiris let us be ourselves. He let us keep our customs and traditions in his province. Those would have been lost without his support.

The third thing a group needs to be a people, of course, is land. And thanks to him, we now own the Sinai region."

"You gave them Sinai?" The Most High asked.

"Yes," Osiris said, sounding dazed.

"I agree," Modi said. "You could have killed me in Nekhen. Had I been in your situation, I would have done so without question. Instead, you showed me that you were not my enemy. That there were far greater threats within my own sect." Modi glanced at Tyr, who pumped his fist toward him proudly.

Camulos, the trainer of Valhalla, stood and stomped out of the room mumbling angrily.

"Camulos!" Tyr called, but he didn't pay Tyr any attention as he disappeared through the whitewashed wall.

Modi continued after watching him go, "Our enemy was never the other sects. It has always been this false sense of fate looming over my sect. This idea, this single idea, that we needed to rule over others. It drove my grandfather crazy. It led my father to his own death, but I will not let it consume me or my people any longer. I followed blindly, believing this version of fate until Osiris unveiled my eyes. With the power to choose, I will accept him as my High King."

"Osiris, do you wish to speak on this matter?" the Most High said, leaning forward.

"I truly appreciate everything said," Osiris proclaimed, but he shook his head. "I understand how you see me, and I am grateful for that, but my views are..." He looked down as if searching the floor to find the words.

"Righteous," Aaron interjected.

"*Different*," Osiris corrected. "I am unsure you would truly want me as King."

"Let me tell you something," Jove said. "After returning from Asgard, I walked the city and spoke with some of your people who were helping us rebuild." He held up his arm, displaying the scarab amulet given to him by Alara. "I see it, Osiris. The nethers, I mean people, deserve to be our friends and not lorded over. You have three kings leading three sects, all believing in your vision of Saggilmut, Osiris. Ask yourself, when have we all ever agreed on anything?"

The Most High rose from his throne. Dagon stood at the bottom step waiting for a gesture. The Most High walked around the table, his robe trailing behind him. He stood before the four kings.

"Osiris, do you accept the role as King of the gods?" he asked.

Osiris paused in deliberation.

"Osiris?" The Most High said again.

"I am humbled, and I do accept, but only because each of you will assist me as a pantheon."

"Pangu," Osiris said. "Join these three, as the king of the Duati. A god as wise and discerning

491

as yourself will do well leading the Duati." Pangu stood, bowed to Shiva, and took his place with the other kings.

Osiris then turned to Modi. "Your trust in me reveals more about you than me. Only a truly humble god that desires truth, not their truth, or truth presented to them, but the harsh reality of truth, could change and accept that their cause was in error. I believe you have the strength to change the mindset of your entire culture from war to peace, from hatred to compassion, and yet remain completely Asgardian." Osiris stepped directly in front of him. "I was there when your father died in Olympus. Moments before, I spoke to him in a whisper and told him that you were alive. I told him that he should be proud of you, and that I would do everything in my power to ensure you became king of Asgard. His last thought was knowing that you would be king, and he thanked me for it."

Osiris faced the Most High. "With these four kings by my side, I accept the title as King of the gods and Ruler of Saggilmut, Sheol, and Earth."

The Most High faced the five kings, then gestured for the gods to stand. "Let it be known on this day, by my rule and countenance, that Osiris, the Duati, is raised to become the first King of the gods. He will be the sole authority on the laws that govern the lands. In his hands will rest the judgment over matters of life and death."

"Osiris," he commanded.

492

"Yes," he answered.

"Your real test begins now," the Most High advised.

Chapter 88 *The Visit*

"Okay okay, so that's it then?" Aaron asked, sitting deep into his cushion on the library chair a week after the assembly.

Yes," Dagon replied. He took a deep sigh, watching Aaron.

"Seems simple enough then." Aaron grabbed the book off the stand and opened it to the first page. "And so they'll just think it's a dream or vision or something like that?"

Dagon sat back. "Aaron relax," he said calmly. "As I said before, Sarah may decide it was her imagination, a dream, or a vision. Everyone is different, it all depends on them." Aaron stared at the book, his lower lip tucked into his mouth. Dagon continued, "She may be able to see and hear your manifestation. You will not know until you are there. Some people on Earth can only see or only hear a visit. In truth, many times, neither. I cannot tell you what will happen when you visit your sister."

Aaron glanced at Dagon. "I get it."

"But like I said," Dagon added. "Only you will be able to hear me. You are not traveling to the hospital, Aaron. It is just a manifestation, an image."

"Okay, it's better than nothing," Aaron concluded. Holding the book, he closed his eyes and took a deep breath, as if he was going underwater.

Everything stopped. Complete silence.

In thought, Aaron commanded, *Take me to my body.*

He tensed his entire body for as long as he could. His eyes locked shut in the blackness. Unable to hold his breath any longer, he gasped and opened his eyes.

He was standing in the hospital.

Disoriented, Aaron looked at the bed in front of him where his own body lay. Eyes closed, the typical hospital blue robe with a white sheet, neatly folded, covering him to his chest. Tubes ran from his arm to two machines. A clear mask draped over his mouth.

The bed next to him was empty, and a doctor and a pair of nurses were outside the doorway speaking to someone, but he couldn't see who.

In the chair nearest the bed, he saw Sarah, his Sarah, sitting quietly. She sat sideways with her feet on the armrest. She stared into the pages of a small book.

Her hair was held back into a ponytail, which he thought was odd. She never did that, but it was cute.

"Sarah," he whispered. Her eyes rose from the words in the book, but quickly went back to her spot.

"Sarah," he breathed out louder, trying not to scare her. She glanced at his body on the bed, but seeing him lying still, she began to tear up. Tossing her book onto her bag, she looked at the doorway and wiped her face.

"Sarah," he said louder, concentrating even harder. He wanted her to hear him, he *needed* her to.

She swung around, bringing her legs to the floor, and studied him there on the bed.

"A-Aaron?" she said, watching his face closely.

"I'm *here*, my little Sarah bee," he announced. "Can you hear me?"

"Yeah, you awake?" she asked. She stared at his mouth, partly hidden by the tubes.

"No, I'm *here*."

She stood at the foot of the bed, and leaned closer. "Aaron? Are you there?"

"I'm not t-there, I'm *here*," he said, choking up.

She turned around to face him. He swayed side to side, trying to get her to see him. Lifting her hand, Sarah brought it to his face and slowly reached, but it passed through him.

"I-I see you," she whispered.

"Hi there," he said. "I missed you so much, my little bee."

"I miss you, too, *JanitorMan*," she said. Her eyes flooded with tears. She was the only person in the world who called him a janitor in a loving way.

"I love you, Sarah." He brought his hand to her face. He couldn't touch it.

"Are you coming back? Your body's right here--just go back."

"I can't, my little bee. I just wanted to visit, and let you know I'm fine and you don't have to worry about me."

"Are you dead?" she asked, wiping the tears that streamed to her chin.

"Soon, but don't worry."

"I-I don't understand. Are you a ghost?"

"I don't have much time left." He stared into her soft eyes. "But just know everything is going to be fine, okay?"

She ran her sleeve across her face, then smiled. "Okay."

A voice from behind Sarah called out, "Aaron? Sarah?" It was Aaron's mother. Arms trembling, her bottom lip drawn into her mouth, she began crying. She rushed around the bed, grabbing Sarah.

"I-It's okay, Mom," Aaron said, trying to calm her.

"Mom, look," Sarah whispered, pointing. "He's a ghost, a nice one."

"Aaron, you only have a few moments left," Dagon told him.

"Mom, I have to go, but don't worry. I'm allowed to visit you every two weeks if you can believe it."

"What?" she said, shaking her head. "V-Visit?"

"I have to go now," he said. He could feel energy slowly dissipating from within. "But if you want me to, can I visit you?"

"Yes!" she shouted, holding Sarah a little too tight. His mother had a diamond ring on her left hand.

"Is that from Tyler?"

"Y-Yes," she answered. "I'm sorry, I don't want you thinking that--"

"I am so happy for you!" he said. "He's a great guy."

He glanced at Sarah and raised his hand. *Please work*, he thought. He lowered his hand, placing it on Sarah's hand. Her eyes widened brightly. She could feel his hand!

"I feel you!" she cried.

"Aaron, it is time," Dagon again. Aaron squeezed her hand. "I have to go now, but I'll see you soon."

Together, they said, "Bye, Aaron!" And they laughed. They had always had that sort of connection.

Aaron looked at himself on the bed. "Don't worry about what's about to happen. It doesn't matter. I am no longer in my body, so don't be scared. I love you, and I'll visit soon." He slowly faded and returned to his chair, staring at Dagon.

"Are you all right?" Dagon was kneeling in front of Aaron. Aaron burst from his chair, hugging Dagon. The two wept.

At the hospital, as Sarah held her mother tightly, an alarm on a machine near the bed sounded. The nurses ran into the room, scrambling to help as Aaron's body convulsed. Sarah held her mom, tightening her grip around her waist, smiling.

"It's okay. That's not him," she whispered. "He's with us."

~*--*--*~

"Ready to find out what sect you are in?" Dagon asked.

"Absolut I see him in the Duat sect ☺

THE END

Until Book II

A Letter from the King of gods

To the four sects, from the King of Gods, Osiris:

This first assembly taking place in seven days is to take our initial steps toward creating a truly peaceful society for all Saggilmut. I ask that you ensure to bring any topics not listed below that you may have. This assembly will be an open forum for all gods. I am looking forward to our first assembly in seven days time.

Topics to be discussed:

The opening of all borders. We hope to move to a free moving, trading society. I understand some of our people have never left their specific provinces and have never seen other gods. This will be a gradual process. Come ready to discuss timelines.

We will no longer accept any form of worship that does not serve a community building purpose. I expect to see your classes/lesson schedules with a brief overview on how you plan to instruct your people. Remember, it may take time to convince them that their sacrifice(s) will no longer be necessary,and we must be patient to retrain them, but it will be worth the investment.

The scheduled timeline to move the Library in Shamayim to the future library site just south of Mount Hor. Isis and I are excited to be able to provide such a resource, making it available to all.

The Unspoken. I ask that you keep vigilant. Most of the Unspoken are still unaccounted for and therefore a threat. I expect you to guard your people in their travels. Be aware that Odin, who remains in negative standing, will now be listed among them.

The travel ban to Earth. At this time we will continue to handle Earth as we have. It is off limits to all gods, and the people are free to worship as they see fit while there. We can and will visit this topic if they ever become a danger to their World or the freedom of those within.

The restrictions on alchemy. Be prepared to discuss the possible legalization of certain aspects of alchemy. Under no circumstances will the topic of life and death be negotiated. All souls lost in the battle will remain in Sheol.

Osiris the first
King of the Gods

I truly hope you enjoyed this book!

If so, it would mean a great deal to me if you would leave a review on Amazon! C.T.Ortega

Other books by C.T.Ortega:

The Warfare of the Gods Series:

The Writer and the Throne, 2021
Sekhmet and the Curse, 2021
Asgard and the Hunt, 2022
And more coming soon!

Standalones:
One Will Die, 2021
Jewels of Egypt, 2021
Assassin's Odyssey, 2022
The way of Dragons, 2022
And more coming soon!

Questions for the readers:

1. Which sect did you most identify with and why? Did the sect remain the same throughout the book, or did you find yourself changing?

2. Did any gods in particular resonate with you? Was it because you are similar in ideas or because they are the opposite of you, and that attracted you?

3. Which city would you like to visit the most, and why?

4. The concept of fate versus choice came into play a great deal in this book. What is your perspective on those two ideas? Are they opposite? Can fate and free will both be right?

5. Had you been in Aaron's shoes, and having seen all you had: Which gods would you have written to be the hero? The villain?

6. Which gods would you like to have seen more of, and why?

7. We all carry titles (father, mother, son, daughter, nurse, student, soldier), but how can these titles affect us and how we are perceived? How can having titles such as *God of war*, or *Goddess of love* have an impact, positive and negative?

8. Was there any character that you found did not "fit in" to the sect they were attributed to? Why?

9. We see how Aaron tries to use humor to persevere through his adversity. What tools do you use, when things are "piling up," to get through them?

10. Choose any one god and imagine them walking by you, embracing your forearm and sharing one bit of wisdom in passing. Who is it, and what would they have said?

The author, C.T. Ortega would love to hear from you and read your answers. Feel free to email him at OpenWorldPublishing@gmail.com ATTN: Author C.T.Ortega, or CTOrtega.com.

Glossary

Every god and place listed in this book can be found within our world's mythology. They were pulled from many different time periods, cultures, and folklores, both religious and secular. I took many liberties with their stories, and created them anew, reimagined.

This was done for creative purposes and is not intended to harm anyone's beliefs or theologies.

The list below is not exhaustive to the gods mentioned within the book, as I can only encourage you to have fun researching and learning more about them, the locations mentioned in the book, and the many wisdoms from the "writers" that followed them.

Gods (Broken down by the Sects within the series)

Asgardians

Baldr- (Norse) Son of Odin, he is considered the god of light, joy, and purity.
Belobog- (Slavic) Little is known of him, but is considered to have been a god of the sun, or light.
Bragi- (Norse) God of poetry and music.
Camulos-(Celtic) God of war, some scholars have seen him as a version of Mars.

Magni-(Norse) God of strength.

Modi- (Norse) God of courage.

Odin- (Germanic/Norse) Called the one-eyed All-Father. God of poetry, wisdom, death, and much more.

Thor- (Norse) God of thunder.

Tyr- (Norse) God of war.

Sjofn- (Norse) (pronounced *Seeofenn)* Goddess of love and affection.

Svetovid- (Slavic) (pronounced *S'veetoevid)* A god of many things to include fertility and produce. He was believed to have four heads facing in all directions to show his power of seeing all things.

Vali- (Norse) Believed to be the god of vengeance.

Idunn- (Norse) She is associated with apples and has knowledge over eternal youth.

Immortals

Aphrodite- (Greek) God of love, beauty, passion, and more.

Apollo- (Greek) Zeus' son, and god of the sun, music, healing and more.

Ares- (Greek) God of war.

Dadga- (Celtic) He is connected with agriculture, manliness, and wisdom. A kind, fatheresque god.

Hades- (Greek) God of the Underworld.

Jove- (Roman) Also known as Jupiter. He is considered the Roman equivalent to Zeus. God of the sky and thunder.

Neptune- (Roman) God of the sea.

Poseidon- (Greek) God of the sea.

Vulcan- (Roman) God of fire. A cripple who was also one of the rare gods to be considered ugly, although he married Venus, considered to be one of the more beautiful goddesses.

Zeus- (Greek) God of the sky and lighting. Known as a womanizer, also has a legend of having eaten his wife.

Duati

Ra- (Egyptian) God with a falcon's head. He was the creator of the universe.

Bastet- (Egyptian) She is depicted as having a black cat's head. God of cats, fertility, childbirth, and many other women's aspects.

Horus- (Egyptian) A falcon-headed god. He is attributed as being the god of the sky, and at times war. He lost his eye in a battle with Set.

Osiris- (Egyptian) God of the aspects of fertility within both agriculture and people. He watched over life, death, and resurrection as well as the cycle of vegetation.

Pangu- (Chinese) Using the Yin Yang and an axe, he created the universe.

Sanguan Dadi- (Chinese) According to Taoism these supreme three rule over Earth in all its aspects.

Sekhmet- (Egyptian) (pronounced *Sek-met)* Depicted as having the head of a lioness, she is known as a god of war.

Shiva- (Hinduism) One of three gods attributed with the creation of the world.

Toth- A god with the head of an Ibis (also sometimes depicted as a baboon). He is attributed to be very wise, and having been well studied in debating, sciences, arts, and magic.

Serving in Shamayim

The Most High- He is not attributed to any one religion or culture. He was written as being Omniscient and Omnipresent, although in the book he chooses to ignore those attributes. He is a conglomeration of many religions' ultimate take on god.

Asherah- (Ancient Canaan) Worshiped as a motherly goddess and often depicted with wooden idols and carved trees.

Idunn- (Norse) A goddess who was once responsible over magical apples that, if eaten, kept the eater young forever.

Dagon- (Ancient Middle East) Often depicted as wearing a fish-style hat. He is best known as the god to the Philistines, who led Goliath, the giant, against David and the Isrealites.

Locations

Asgard- Home to Asgardian gods.

Duat- (Egyptian)-Word for heaven. It is where the Egyptians believed the gods lived, and where the dead are gathered.

Guangdong- Modern Chinese city with a deep ancient history tied to many Chinese mythologies.

Lake Ronkonkoma- Located in New York state, USA. Considered by groups of Native Americans as a sacred lake, with healing energies.

Mount Hor- Also called Mount Sinai. It is the described location of the giving of the Ten Commandments to the Jewish people.

Mount Olympus- Located in Greece. It was once hailed as the home of the Immortals, led by Zeus.

Nekhen- Capital city of ancient Upper Egypt circa 3200 BCE.

Saggilmut- (Mesopotamia) Word for heaven.

Shamayim- (Hebrew) Word for heaven.

Sinai Peninsula- (Middle East) A large area that plays an important role in the Abrahamic faiths.

Szczecin- (Poland) Slavic location where paganism existed.

Valhalla- (Norse Mythology) Afterlife for Norse warriors.

Items/ Things

Norse Drinking Horns- These items made for drinking were common in Norse culture, and were made of various items. The wealthier would have fancier horns, made of gold and other metals.

Hieroglyphics- Means *sacred carvings,* alluding to the pictographic writing system found throughout Egypt. Some carvings are estimated as old as 3400 BCE.

Hoopoe- A historical bird found in various cultures' literature that later became known as messengers in Greek folklore.

Jankaea Heldreichi- is a purple flower indigenous only to Mount Olympus, Greece. The flower Sjofn grabbed on the Olympus battlefield.

Yggdrasil Ash tree- This ash tree is found in various Norse literature. Considered the center of the universe, the gods commonly met near the tree for assemblies and to discuss important matters.

Ekasha Gada- The Mace staff of Shiva, held in the story by his son Kaal. According to Hindu mythology, being hit by this mace is similar to being trampled by a million elephants.

Terms

Malaka- A derogatory Greek slang that is used in a variety of ways both positive and negative.

Fif'l- (Norse)- Fool, Idiot.

Em Hotep- (Ancient Egyptian)- Peace.

Heil og sæl (masculine) and Heil ok sæl (feminine) - (Norse) Be healthy and happy.

Bacrauf- (Norse)- A general term meaning an idiot, stupid, or fool.

Tandav-(Hindu) A tantric-style dancing special to the Hindu religion.

Special thanks

To the reader,

This book was obviously written for you. I hope you enjoyed the story, maybe had a thought-provoking moment or two, and would like to read more. I promise you this: This series has many more adventures coming your way! So many more gods and themes to share.

You haven't seen anything yet!

Whenever you see me, or reach out to me on social media (whichever platform you chose to), feel free to first tell me what sect you are! That is how I'll know you're a true fan!

To my family and friends; call me, I'll tell you personally.

To my editors; Jim Bessey and Emilie Knight: I had a ton of fun going through your insights and ideas on making the book a better read. You two have a large hand in making this a reality. I'm looking forward to seeing all your "red marks" on the future installments of the WOG series!

To my artists; Joshua Hoskins, thank you for visually sharing the world! To Black Widow Books: This cover is amazing, and I cannot wait to see what you do with the rest of them.

WARFARE OF THE GODS

Made in the USA
Las Vegas, NV
23 April 2022

47879668R20282